Uprising

Dean Urdahl

Taylor F

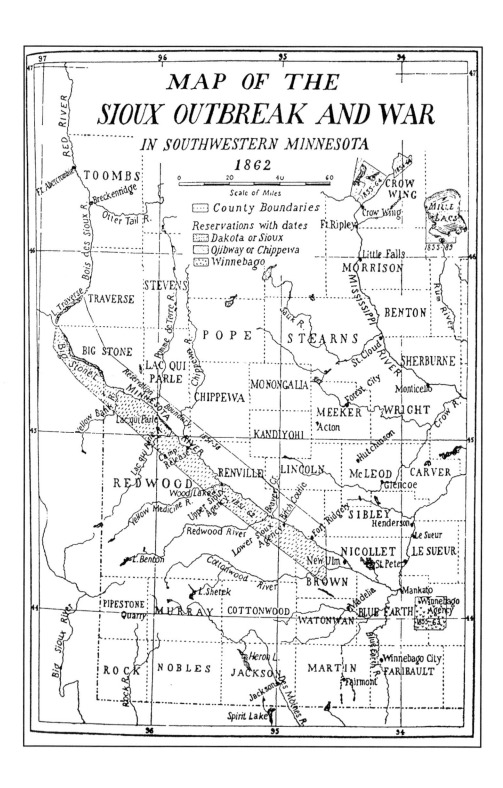

MAP OF THE
SIOUX OUTBREAK AND WAR
IN SOUTHWESTERN MINNESOTA
1862

Scale of Miles
0   20   40   60

County Boundaries
Reservations with dates
Dakota or Sioux
Ojibway or Chippewa
Winnebago

❧ Uprising ❧

A Novel

by

Dean Urdahl

NORTH STAR PRESS OF ST. CLOUD, INC.
St. Cloud, Minnnesota

Cover map: The David Rumsey Map Collection
www.davidrumsey.com

Frontis map from page 111, Vol. 2, Fallwell's *History of Minnesota*

First Edition: June 2007
Second Printing: January 2008

Printed in the United States of America

Published by
North Star Press of St. Cloud, Inc.
P.O. Box 451
St. Cloud, Minnesota 56302
northstarpress.com

Dedication

I dedicate this story to the memory of my dad and mom, Clarence and Violet Urdahl. By skipping a generation, I was able to include them as characters in *Uprising*. My dad is represented in the book as the painter, Slim Dahl. My mom, a Ness descendent, is Daisy Dahl. She never tired of regaling me with stories of family history, including the Dakota Conflict of 1862.

I also dedicate this book to my three grandchildren: Alicia Kraft, Violet Urdahl, and Lincoln Urdahl. My wife, Karen, was responsible for much of the editing and made countless suggestions. Her help was invaluable.

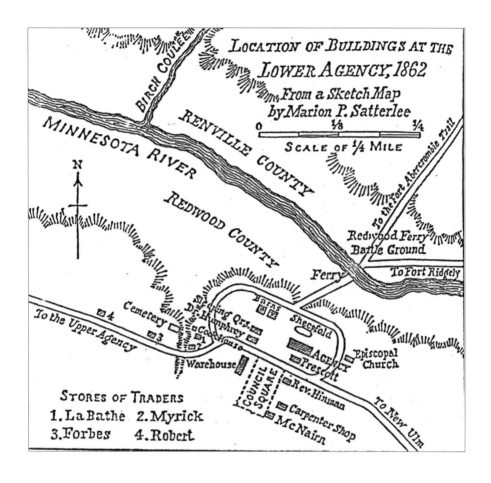

LOCATION OF BUILDINGS AT THE LOWER AGENCY, 1862
From a Sketch Map by Marion P. Satterlee

SCALE OF ¼ MILE

0   ⅛   ¼

BIRCH COULEE

MINNESOTA RIVER

RENVILLE COUNTY

REDWOOD COUNTY

N

To the Fort Abercrombie Trail

Redwood Ferry
Battle Ground

Ferry

To Fort Ridgely

Cemetery

To the Upper Agency

4

3

Dr. Humphrey

Boarding Qrs.

Court House

2

1

Barns

Sheepfold

AGENCY

Prescott

Episcopal Church

Warehouse

COUNCIL SQUARE

Rev. Hinman

Carpenter Shop

McNair

To New Ulm

STORES OF TRADERS
1. La Bathe   2. Myrick
3. Forbes   4. Robert

໑ Foreword ໨

A good historical novel is an enjoyable and enlightening way to learn about our past. By hanging a story on a canvas of authentic people, places, and events—then filling in the tale with additional characters, episodes, and conversations—heightens the experience of reliving an earlier time.

In *Uprising*, Dean Urdahl has crafted such a story about Minnesota's "war within a war" in the Minnesota River Valley during the autumn of 1862. His saga is enriched by unfolding his novel on an even broader background beginning with the bloody battle of Shiloh in the spring of 1862 and carrying his main character, Nathan Thomas, from there to Minnesota where he participates in an extraordinary number of adventures during the six-week ethnic earthquake variously known as the Sioux Uprising, the Dakota Conflict, and the Dakota War. In casting Nathan as his central figure and relating him to the two theaters of conflict during the great battles of Second Manassas, Antietam, Corinth, and others in the East, a low point in the fortunes of the North, with the causes, personalities, battles, and outcome behind the mayhem occurring on the Minnesota frontier, he adds meaning and depth to the power of his story.

Steeped in the history and lore of the area in which he lives and knows well, Urdahl has given us an absorbing story about human tragedy, heroism, and survival by ordinary folks on a grand scale during a clash of cultures whose legacy still lives with us today.

Russell Fridley
Past executive director of the Minnesota Historical Society

❧ Preface ☙

THE AMERICAN UNION had been strong, born from the blood of revolution and bound by its Constitution. Its people were forged on an anvil of diversity and hard work. They had come mostly from northern Europe, some seeking religious freedom, others economic opportunity; if they got lucky, maybe they'd get rich. But at the least, the immigrants hoped for a better life, free from distant kings, oppressive churches, the filth and disease of big cities, and the bottomless pit of poverty.

They came to North America to escape all that had troubled them in Europe. It was a paradise to many who were from places already overgrown, overused, worn out. The vibrant land teemed with fish and game. Azure skies embraced an emerald-green forest that stretched nearly uninterrupted from the eastern coast to the mighty river that wound like a great blue ribbon through the middle of the continent.

The people prospered in the new land. The Northeast flourished with small farms and industry, while the South developed a plantation economy based upon the labor of African slaves.

Since the first slaves had been brought to Virginia in 1619, the economy of the South had become more and more dependent upon what some termed its "peculiar institution." As the United States grew, it won wars, expanded west. Cities thrived, and industry boomed. But slavery was always lurking in the dark shadows of the nation's night.

It was there, eating away at the belly of America like a cancer, tearing at the very heart of the national conscience. Debates raged over economics, states' rights, and slavery. Compromises were pieced in futile attempts to heal the gaping wound.

But the South would not give up its perceived right to own slaves. The determination to protect its way of life and continue slavery led eleven states to rip the great Union in two, into Civil War.

Had the Northern-dominated government just let the Southern Confederacy leave, two countries could have developed in the center of North America. But the North determined there could be no secession and that the Union must be preserved. President Abraham Lincoln ordered troops into the South to bring the rebellious states back into the Union forcefully.

In 1862, one year after the war began, two great armies came together near Pittsburg Landing, Tennessee, just north of the Mississippi state line. Union General Ulysses S. Grant's 42,000 men camped on the Tennessee River awaiting reinforcements from General Carlos Buell.

In the nearby woods, 40,000 Confederate soldiers, commanded by Albert Sidney Johnston, prepared for a surprise attack, planning to crush Grant's forces before Buell arrived.

Battles and wars change lives, end lives, and alter the flow of history. Sometimes a small ripple, insignificant in its initial effect, widens and spreads until it washes over the hopes and dreams of those it touches, changing them forever.

Shiloh was one of the greatest battles of the Civil War, with tens of thousands of bullets fired in a maelstrom of death. One bullet struck a young officer and sent ripples to far off Minnesota, washing it in blood.

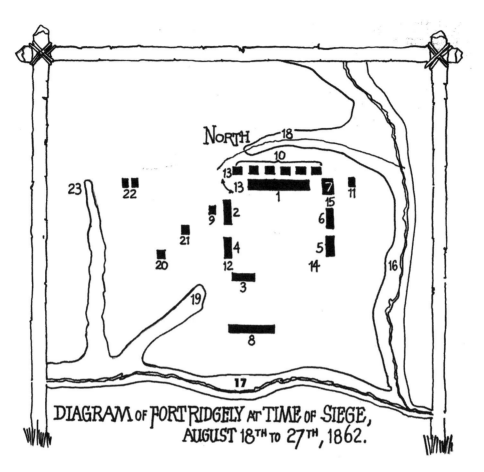

DIAGRAM OF FORT RIDGELY AT TIME OF SIEGE, AUGUST 18TH TO 27TH, 1862.

1. Barracks	13. Position of McGrew
2. Commissary	14. Position of Bishop and Nathan
3. Headquarters	15. Position of Gere and Whipple
4. Officers' Quarters	16. Fort Creek in Wooded Ravine
5. Officers' Quarters	17. Minnesota River
6. Officers' Quarters	18. St. Peter Road down Ravine
7. Laundry	19. Depressed Ground
8. Large Barn	20. Sutler Store
9. Blacksmith Shop	21. Guardhouse
10. Old Log Quarters	22. Powder Magazines
11. Building Wipple Fired	23. Timbered Ravine to West
12. Position of Jones and Renville Rangers	

Illustration by Bill Gabbert

❧ 1 ☙

I T WAS A STILL, BRIGHT SOUTHERN morning, April 6th, 1862. Birds chirped the fiery arrival of the sun as fragrant pink blossoms from lush green peach trees slowly wafted to the ground. A wide-open field lay between a wooded area and a lazy stretch of the Tennessee River. Sprawling in that grassy field was a city of tents, where tens of thousands were awakening. Like the low rumble of thunder, soldiers coughed, blew their noses and cleared their throats. Some had already risen for breakfast. The smell of smoke, coffee and frying bacon drifted temptingly to the woods beyond.

"Makes me hungry as a starvin' dog, Cap'n," a dusty, gray-clad soldier whispered to the tall young officer crouching nearby.

Nathan Thomas placed his index finger to his lips. "Quiet, Sam. We'll be eatin' their breakfast soon enough." He knew that the order would come soon, and they would go crashing out of the woods and into the camp. They would drive the Yanks into the river if it were a good day. He rubbed his long, muscular legs, cramped up from kneeling.

It was a long way from Virginia Military Institute to just inside the Tennessee border above Mississippi, not so much in time but in miles and experience. His thoughts floated back to VMI. There he had been trained.

Soldiering was the family business. His father and Uncle George had both fought in the Mexican War. George was now a general.

Nathan chuckled to himself as he thought of Professor Jackson, one of his instructors. "Old Tom Fool," the cadets had called him. He had been the butt of many a prank and joke. Now, "Tom Fool" was called "Stonewall" Jackson and was the right-hand man of Confederate General Robert E. Lee.

The twenty-four-year-old officer adjusted his position on the damp ground. Leaning back against a tree, he stretched out his legs. Then, removing his slouch hat, the young man smoothed back his straight dark hair and wiped his tanned, angular face. The morning was already hot.

Today, Nathan thought, the shoe would be on the other foot. Grant had moved down the Tennessee River in an effort to catch and destroy Albert Sidney Johnston's army. But as Grant's men camped, the hunted prepared to surprise the hunter.

In the distance a small white clapboard church was shrouded in a haze of campfire smoke and early morning mist. Someone had said it was a house of God called Shiloh. Nathan thought it ironic. Although it bore such a peaceful name, soon men would be lying cold and dead on top of the ground in the church cemetery and not just under the sod.

He reached to his shirt pocket and softly patted the small book there. It was a Bible, given to him by his two elderly aunts in Richmond. He should be bringing it to church this Sunday morning. In a way, he guessed, he would be, although not in a manner that his aunts would approve. But they were fine Southern ladies, devoted to the "Cause." Maybe they would understand that Sunday was sometimes a fighting day.

It was just about a year ago that Aunt Harriet had sternly handed him the New Testament as a farewell gift. "Read it," she admonished. "It'll help keep you out of Hell. Your Uncle George will be there. We don't need you down there, too."

Nathan smiled to himself as he remembered cajoling his aunts about being too hard on their brother. But Aunt Julia found little humor. "George is already dead," she said bluntly. "He died to us the moment he raised his sword against Virginia."

George was George Thomas, Virginian, graduate of West Point, veteran of the Mexican War, and currently a general in the Union army. Nathan had spent several summers with him in various posts where he had been commanding officer. Most of them were in the North.

When war came, his uncle did not try to pressure him, but simply wrote in a letter, "Do what you must, nephew. Lee says he cannot raise his sword against his native soil, against Virginia. I cannot raise mine against my country. I am an American first and a Virginian second. This country must not be divided. Whatever you choose to do, whichever side you choose to fight on, I know you will do it with honor."

There was never a question Nathan would fight. Uncle George had been away from Virginia many years, fighting across the country. To Nathan, Virginia was home. His neighbors were his friends. His family was all there. He could never fight against them, and he could never sit out the war. He chose Virginia.

Nathan's memories were thrust aside as it finally came, the order they had been awaiting, the order to attack. Musket and rifle fire exploded from the woods. A high-pitched cry ripped like strangled death from the massed soldiers. It was known as the rebel yell, and it burst as a chorus from Hell from thousands of throats. Waves of gray-and-butternut-uniformed men charged from the woods, swarming like angry ants into the clearing. The distant Union soldiers didn't panic but rallied into a defensive position.

Nathan Thomas led his men, a pistol in his right hand, a sword in his left. The blue soldiers in his front had retreated to low bluffs. Nathan's hat flew off, a bullet through the brim. His black hair glistened with sweat as he began an assault up the nearest bluff. Nearing the summit, Nathan felt a searing pain in his left arm and was driven back as if kicked by a mule. Numbed, lying flat on his back, he looked down at his mangled arm, still smoking from the wad of a minie ball. Then all went black.

When Nathan awoke, the rumble of gunfire echoed in his ears. Through blurry eyes, he saw a bloodstained, bearded man peering into his face.

"Welcome back, son, Ah, don't have much time to chat, but Ah'm glad to see that we didn't lose ya. We'll talk later." Then the man was gone.

Nathan's brain felt numb, but his eyes gradually struggled into focus, sharpening the scene around him. He was obviously in a hospital tent. Blood-covered tables held the bodies of bloody men. Their moans and screams filled his ears, drumming out the sounds of battle.

Suddenly two men in dirty, blood-and-pus-stained white coats snatched him up and roughly carried him out through the tent flap. Makeshift pallets lay on the ground beneath the shade of nearby trees. Nathan felt himself not too gently deposited on one. He looked back at the hospital tent and noticed small piles near the entrance.

One of the men who had hauled him out reappeared through the flap and tossed something onto a pile. Nathan, now more coherent, suddenly realized that the pile was a heap of arms and legs. With dread he looked down at his own arm. His worst fears were realized. Horror and nausea swept over him as Nathan Thomas looked at the stump where his left arm had been.

LATER THAT SPRING IN RICHMOND, Virginia, had it not been for the bustle of troops and government personnel, it would have looked like any other spring. Trees were lush green, some adorned by colorful blossoms mimicking the parasols of Southern belles. An early morning rain had left the air with a damp freshness.

Nathan Thomas had been summoned to Richmond, the capitol of the new Confederate nation. He knew the city well. At age ten, after his parents' death in a carriage accident, his two aunts had raised Nathan there.

He walked somewhat casually along the crushed rock walkway to the president's house. Nathan's boots crunched softly onto the pathway as he recalled his chat with the blood-stained doctor after the Battle of Shiloh.

"Get out of the war," the doctor had advised. "You're young, you'll heal. You just can't fight a war very well with but one arm. Go home, or if you must, find another way to serve the Confederacy."

Nathan had been asked to meet President Jefferson Davis this morning, and he hadn't the faintest idea why. What would the leader of the Confederacy want with a one-armed man?

The young captain walked more erectly as he approached two gray uniformed guards at a black wrought-iron gate in front of the marble-pillared house where President Davis lived and worked.

Nathan's dark hair was neatly combed. A freshly laundered gray uniform, the left sleeve pinned under the stub of his left arm, fit well over his broad shoulders. His aunts had sewn it for him.

"Best looking officer in the army!" they had exclaimed with bursting pride when he had modeled it for them. With piercing brown eyes, a dark complexion, and a muscular build, he looked every bit the heroic officer. That was over a year ago.

Today he didn't feel like the dashing "whole" man ready to take on the world, or even the American Union. Today he just felt curious. He approached the outer-office door, cleared his throat and spoke in his clear voice that carried but a slight Southern accent.

"Captain Nathan Thomas to see the president, sir." Nathan looked down at a small, bespectacled man behind a large mahogany desk in Davis's anteroom. Papers were piled on his desk and on the floor nearby.

The man peered up at Nathan from between two stacks of documents like a gopher emerging from his hole. He pushed his glasses up from the tip of his nose, ran a hand over his bald head and sighed.

"I'm Bisbee," he croaked in a dry, wispy voice. "President Davis said to show you right in. Follow me."

Nathan was ushered into a large office. Papers cluttered a desk that stood before two large windows overlooking the front gate. Light splashed through the windows and played with the dust on a worn carpet. A tall, thin man with nearly gray, medium-length hair and a goatee rose from his desk. His bearing was erect and military, like the soldier he had once been. His long arm extended to clasp Nathan's hand.

"Good to meet you, Captain," Jefferson Davis said warmly. "I'm glad you were able to get here so promptly. I'm sorry about your wound. I hope it's healing well."

"Well as can be expected, sir," Nathan answered, making a point of not looking down at his stump.

"Pittsburg Landing, Shiloh, whatever you call it, I know it was hell. The death of General Johnston in the battle will be difficult to overcome. He was a fine commander. Had he lived, we might have prevailed on the second day."

"I was shot early in the first attack. All I know is that we thought we had them beat. We had 'em about in the river. If Buell hadn't shown up with reinforcements, you might be able to visit General Grant in our local prison today."

"General Beauregard even sent me a dispatch claiming victory after the first day." Davis gestured for Thomas to be seated. "Then came Day Two." The president sighed and leaned back in his chair.

"They pushed us back. A lot of bloodshed." Davis's mind seemed to wander off. He mumbled, "If only Johnston had lived." Then he snapped back to the matter at hand.

"But you want to know why I asked you here today. I have in mind a special mission. One that at first blush you might find distasteful, but one that I think you are uniquely qualified for. I know your family. Your aunts are quite devoted to our cause. And I know your Uncle George. He is an honorable and brave man who unfortunately has misplaced his loyalties in this affair. You have spent some time with him, I'm told?"

"Yes, Mr. President, summers mostly and mostly at posts up north."

"You're from Virginia. But I don't detect much of an accent. Certainly not like I hear in my home state of Mississippi."

"My family, parents, and aunts stressed the King's English and proper pronunciation. Also, my time in the North has somewhat blunted my accent. But Ah kin talk down home win Ah feel the need ta."

"That's fine, Captain," Davis smiled thinly, "but it's actually your northern connections and lack of much accent that brought you to my attention. That and the fact that you might now be more useful in ways other than on the battlefield."

Thomas glanced at his empty sleeve this time and shifted uneasily on his feet.

"Nathan, have you ever heard of Stand Waite?"

"Cherokee in Oklahoma, isn't he? I heard he's fighting for the Confederacy."

"That's right. He's leading a detachment of Cherokee in the Confederate Army. He's providing a valuable service to us in the Southwest. We would like to duplicate his work in the North. Specifically, we believe that Minnesota is ripe for such a venture."

"And what does this have to do with me, Mr. President?"

"I would like you to go to Minnesota. Meet with Little Crow, a chief of the Santee Sioux, and encourage them to join us in war."

"You want them to enlist in the Confederacy?"

"Not necessarily, at least not for now. We need a diversion, we need for the Union to be forced to protect its frontier even as it fights with the South. I want them to be fighting two wars at once. They'll have to send some troops from the East away from us and to Minnesota. Troops from Minnesota will have to stay home to fight Indians.

"If we are successful, I envision tribes all over Union territory rising up like new grass in the spring. The Yankees will fear losing their western lands. It will cause Lincoln to throw a fit and could give us the advantage we need to be successful in the East."

"Why is Minnesota more ready for this than some other place?" Nathan wondered.

Davis sat down in the chair behind his desk. It creaked softly as he leaned backward. "Because it seems to be the spot where the federals are currently doing their best job of breaking the promises they made to the Indians. In 1851 and 1858 we . . ." A hint of a smile flashed over the former United States senator and secretary of war's face, then he continued. "They," Davis emphasized, "signed treaties with the Santee Sioux in Minnesota. The government was to pay the Sioux for most of the land they held there. The payments have not been made regularly. Hungry Indians are getting impatient.

"Little Crow is a leader, but not their only one. He was, however, one of the signers of the treaties. It'll be important to talk to him and get him on our side. But he may not be the most valuable ally you can find. Little Crow is making some efforts to accommodate the federal government's desires. Mainly, they

want the Sioux to give up their warrior-hunter way of life and become farmers.
I've heard that Little Crow even lives in a brick house.

"There are others more hostile to the North's plans, those who have
formed what my sources say is called a 'Soldiers' Lodge,' a secret society led
by those who opposed the treaties and wish to drive all whites off the prairie.
Those are the people I want you to find and enlist in our cause."

"Am I to go in uniform?" Nathan already knew the answer.

Something flitted across Davis's face. Then his expression firmed.
"That wouldn't be practical. You must not be detected. Once you've made
contact, offer the Sioux their land back in Minnesota. Treaties have been
eating away at it. Tell them when we win this war, we will protect them. But
make sure they know we'll leave them alone, that we have no desire to make
Minnesota a state of the Confederacy."

"Mr. President, a non-uniformed soldier in enemy territory is a spy."
Nathan said, his mouth tightening. "You're right, I find this distasteful. You
want me to incite an Indian uprising. Innocents will die. I remember a man
from my history, Simon Girty, who led Indians against whites in colonial
times. People in Ohio still spit when they say his name."

"Nathan," Davis soothed, "you're not really being asked to spy. We
know all we need to know about the military in Minnesota. Think of yourself as a conspirator, perhaps, one who is asked to foment an already
inevitable situation, as a watchmaker adjusting the clock of history. An
Indian war will come to Minnesota sooner or later. That is a certainty. We
just want you to help it along so it comes a little sooner . . . a little more
opportunely."

"Is there really a difference between a spy and a conspirator?"
Nathan was not convinced.

Davis shifted uneasily. "They're just words. Let's not get caught up
in them."

"Unfortunately, Mr. President," Nathan hoped he didn't sound im-
pudent, "they hang people, not words."

"Nathan," Davis reassured, "to me you are a captain in the Confederate States Army dispatched on an important mission. That's what's

important. Your new name will be Nathan Cates, of the First Indiana. It seems that such a man was wounded and captured by our army. He recently died in prison right here in Richmond. I'm told there are even similarities in appearance between you and him. It'll work as a cover for you in Minnesota.

"You must encourage the Sioux to attack only military outposts. I've heard that this Little Crow is somewhat civilized. Promise him his land, work with him and try to rein him in. Pose as a Yankee trader. We'll see that you are supplied with what you need.

"We do have a friend in Minneapolis, Samuel Meeds is his name. Contact him when you get there."

"Have I a choice, Mr. President?"

Davis smiled expansively. "Of course you do. But, Nathan, this is how you can best serve your country at this time. Let me emphasize that this can be extremely beneficial to our cause. Even more helpful than if you led an attack again. You should begin immediately. Timing is critical. This fall, in maybe September, Lee would like to take a trip north through Maryland. That is when we must have war in Minnesota."

"Give me the details, sir. I will do what I must."

"My secretary will brief you. Nathan, only you and I and two other men in my government know of this plan. They are sworn to secrecy. One is my secretary; the other is the secretary of war. If this plan somehow unravels, you understand that we cannot acknowledge that we sent you or that we have knowledge of your mission. Now, good luck to you. Communicate with us through Mr. Meeds."

Davis took Nathan into the anteroom and asked his secretary, Mr. Bisbee, to brief him in greater detail about their plan. Then Davis returned to his office. From a small side room, another man emerged. It was Secretary of War Judah Benjamin. He strode to Davis, who towered over him.

"You don't really think he can contain this to attacks on military posts, do you?"

"No. It might start that way, but it'll spread like wildfire. Our honorable young man will have done his part if he gets it started. He'll try to contain it, but he won't be able to. I want Indian wars to ignite all over the West. Every time our Union friends put one out, another will start up. If all works well, the Union army will be fighting us and Indians all up and down the frontier, and our Captain Thomas will have provided a great service to the nation."

"If he survives, I'm not sure he'll agree with you."

"Mr. Secretary, it's trite but true, sometimes the end justifies the means. We've got a war to win at any cost."

It didn't take Nathan long to tie up loose ends around Richmond. Bisbee really hadn't added much to what he had already learned from President Davis. The secretary did provide specifics on how to contact Meeds. Then he provided Nathan with some gifts for the Sioux, maps, false identification papers and transportation plans.

Meeds was a merchant in Minneapolis, a Mississippi River town. Nathan was to travel west through Virginia and West Virginia, board a river-boat steamer on the Ohio River, and stay on it until near Cairo, Illinois, where he would transfer to another paddleboat going north up the Mississippi to Minneapolis.

Nathan would pose as a cloth merchant dealing with Meeds' Mercantile in Minnesota. Nathan Cates, the man Nathan would become, was from southern Indiana. The residue of any drawl in his accent could be attributed to his home being in such close proximity to the South. The cloth he carried would double as his cover and later as gifts for the Sioux.

Bisbee told him that Davis wanted the mission to start immediately. On the morrow a guide would help Nathan begin his journey to the Ohio. In the meantime, he would have time to prepare at his aunts' home.

Nathan spent the day packing his meager possessions—obviously his uniform must stay behind—and studying the maps and other materials given him by Bisbee.

Dinner was served in the formal dining room of Harriet and Julia Thomas's modest but comfortable home. The room had a tired richness to it. Once elegant, through time it had become worn and practical. Now it reflected more the sacrifices its owners had made to the war.

The five-foot lead statue of George Washington that once stared out from a corner, searching for the far side of a distant Deleware River, was gone. It had been melted down for Confederate bullets. The drapes and tablecloth were a little faded, and the borders were tattered.

"We need to replace them," Julia had sighed to Nathan, "but until the war ends, well, we just can't."

Two old candelabra rested upon each end of a long, grand, oak table, casting a yellowish shimmer in the fading twilight.

Their only slave, a slender black woman named Jenny, served the three. The two elderly sisters wore hoop skirts under gray dresses that matched the color of their hair. They dressed for the meal not in their best finery but at least in clothing that was suitable for church. The two women insisted on protocol even in wartime.

As sometimes happens with people who spend a lifetime together, they were coming to resemble each other more and more as they aged, much more than they had in their youths. Harriet and Julia had never married. They were devoted to each other and their nephew, the only child of their dead brother.

Julia could barely contain herself. "Nathan, you certainly have kept to yourself today. What with your seeing President Davis and all this morning, Harriet and I are fairly bursting to find out what happened!"

Their nephew leaned back in his chair and slowly smiled at them. "I'll be leaving in the morning. The president has given me a special assignment. But I'm afraid that I'm not at liberty to talk much about the details."

"But where are you going?" Julia insisted.

"Mr. Davis can't expect you to fight, not with your . . . injury and all," Harriet added.

Young Thomas reddened slightly. He didn't like references to his arm, regardless of intent. "Honestly, Aunt Julia, there's not much I can say. I guess I won't be doing much actual fighting, but let me say that I expect to be where fighting is."

"How long will you be gone?" Julia wondered.

"A while, I guess. I have to travel a ways, I'll tell you that. It could be a pretty lengthy trip depending on how things go."

"But . . ." Julia began.

"Sister," Harriet interrupted firmly, "Nathan and President Davis have their reasons for how much they want known or not known. Whatever his mission is, I'm sure Nathan will serve the 'Cause' well, and we can be proud of him."

"I hope you're right, Aunt Harriet, and I may never be able to tell you what my mission is."

The rest of the meal was spent in idle talk about the early successes of the Confederacy in the war, changes in Richmond, and family matters. They didn't talk about George Thomas at all.

At dawn the next morning, Nathan Thomas stood in front of his aunts' house. He turned up the collar of his blue waist-length light coat and shivered in the chill of the early morning fog. His uniform had been placed in storage.

Good-byes had been said, and now Nathan awaited his traveling companion. He didn't have long to wait. Down the cobblestone street, dimly illuminated by gaslights, a lone figure approached on horseback. The slow trot clip-clopping of hooves from a bay horse echoed hollowly and was the only sound on the deserted street. The rider pulled to a halt in front of Nathan and gave a haphazard salute.

"I 'spect you're Cap'n Thomas. Name's Reese Jenkins, I've been a scout. Now they got me on somethin' called 'special assignment.' I'm the one that's 'sposed to get you to the Ohio River. Ready?"

Nathan was dressed in civilian clothing: a light, cotton shirt under his coat, woolen pants, and a wide-brimmed hat, similar to Jenkins'. Young Thomas returned the salute and reached up to shake the horseman's hand.

"Yes, I'm ready. Remember, I'm to be a merchant named Nathan Cates. No more 'Captain' or anything military."

"Understood, sir . . . er, Mr.Cates."

A mule and a horse were tethered nearby. Nathan picked up a large canvas suitcase and swung it clumsily onto the mule's back. With some difficulty the one-armed man strapped it onto the animal. Jenkins watched. If asked, he would help, but he had learned it was best not to help men such as the young captain unless they requested it.

Nathan walked to his black gelding, strapped a smaller satchel onto the horse, and swung up into the saddle. The animal blew and snorted, disturbed by the interruption from his munching of rich damp grass. Moments later, the two riders were disappearing down the street as they faded like phantoms into the haze. Only the echo of the shod hooves was left to the two women watching from their upstairs windows.

The men traveled west through that part of Virginia that had refused to leave the Union, using a road first blazed by young George Washington. Reese Jenkins was only about twenty-five himself, but he knew his way quite well. He was short and sinewy with reddish hair and a ruddy complexion. He sat well on his horse and moved with a sureness that left Nathan secure that Jenkins would get him to his destination.

The trip was uneventful, and they rode much of the way in silence, the less said, Nathan reasoned, the better for his mission. The fragrance of spring flowers filled the air as songbirds sang and nested. Nature didn't care about war, just about renewal.

The two men made good time passing through most of what was now called West Virginia. As they rode, Reese began to make frequent observations about landmarks and people living nearby.

Nathan wondered aloud, "Reese, you seem well-versed in this country. Are you from here?"

"I lived 'bout ten miles north from here. Small farm, prob'ly split up by my neighbors now." The bitterness in his voice was unmistakable.

"What happened?"

"You know 'bout most of these mountain people. Not many slaves, jealous of the rest of Virginia. Independent bunch. That's why it don't make sense for 'em to stay in the Union and get ordered about by a passel o' Yankees."

"Apparently you didn't see eye to eye with your neighbors."

"I just couldn't let the Yanks change everything. I believe in states' rights. I didn't have no slaves. Just wanted to work my land without bein' told what to do all the time."

"I guess they hate three-quarters of Virginia," Nathan added, "more than they hate the North. I understand not wanting to fight for slavery when most of them don't have slaves, but the war is about much more than that. What about your family?"

"My parents got the fever and died when I was fifteen. Got no other kin. I made my choice when the fightin' started and left. My land's gone by now. The vultures don't waste no time with a rebel."

Then Reese clucked at his bay horse and reached over to switch the pack mule lightly on its backside. "Old Maggie's slowin' down a bit. River's close. She'll be restin' soon and you'll be on a paddleboat."

The pair continued talking and riding through the low mountains, unaware that in a gully ahead, ragged men with guns hid in brush and behind trees. The only thing that kept the concealed men from firing right off was the uncertainty of the approaching riders' allegiance.

As they rode into the gully, Jenkins muttered in barely audible tones, "I don't like it, Mr. Cates. Somethin' here jest don't seem right to me. The short hairs on the back of my neck are standin' up."

Uneasily both men reassured themselves by touching the rifles held in scabbards alongside their horses. Trees lined both sides of the narrow trail, forming a green canopy as branches touched over their heads. It looked like a natural cathedral. The riders recognized it as a perfect place for an ambush.

Suddenly three men stepped onto the trail in front of them. They were dirty, unshaven and dressed in the homespun clothing common to farm folk in the mountains. Their rifles, held at waist level, were pointed at the horsemen.

The center one, who appeared to be the oldest, spat a long stream of tobacco juice onto the dusty trail. He flashed a broad smile that revealed yellow-and-brown-stained teeth between rotting stubs that left jack-o-lantern gaps. His short beard was mostly gray. It was hard to tell how much was still brown because of the tobacco spittle that soiled it. He studied the horsemen with mud-colored eyes. "Mornin', fellas. Where ya'll headin' on such a fine day?"

Nathan touched the brim of his hat. From behind came shuffles and sounds that indicated more men were on the road to his rear. He was sure others were lurking behind brush and trees on either side.

"Good morning to you," Nathan answered. "Just heading to the river, I've got some business up north."

Jenkins sat quietly on his fidgeting horse. He kept his head down so that the brim of his hat obscured his face.

"River's just 'bout three miles down the trail. What ya got in that case?"

"I'm a salesman, I just have some cloth and such."

"I'll take a look, Seth," a hawk-faced man to the right said eagerly.

Seth, the man in the center, was almost apologetic, "We gotta be sure ya ain't reb scouts or somethin'. Someday the whole reb army might march up here and try to force us back into Virginia or go through here on some sorta northern invasion.

"Don't mess his stuff up too much, Jed," he called to the man who was starting to reach for the case on the pack mule.

Just as Jed began to unstrap the case, Jenkins' horse took a startled little jump. Jed looked up into the face of the rider.

"I know you," he said. "You're that Jenkins boy from up the holla. Ain't he that Jenkins boy, Seth?"

Seth walked closer and gestured with his rifle. "Raise your head, boy."

Reese slowly looked up at men who had once been neighbors or friends of his family. He struggled to keep his expression impassive.

"Yep. It's Reese Jenkins all right. Thought ya was stayin' down South with your reb friends. What ya doin' here, boy?"

"Just fixin' to ride to the river with this here fella, Seth," Reese answered. "Thought I might even stop by and visit some of my folks on my way back. See my old place. Any of ya moved into my cabin yet?"

"Burnt the dang place down," Jed drawled. "Weren't worth nothin' annaway."

Another man showed a toothless smile through his wrinkled face. "We sent a message to any other traitors 'round here. This here's Union country. Traitors get out or we'll burn ya out and don't come back here neither. Ain't nothin' here for the likes o' you, Jenkins. You ain't trusted here no more."

"Eli," Reese countered, "I did what I thought was right, but I ain't never turned my back on no neighbor. I ain't got nothin' 'ginst any of you." He lied. It would be folly to let them know his true feelings.

"If'n he's here. I bet the both of 'em's up to no good." It was a voice from behind.

Seth looked them over. "Step down," he commanded in a firm voice. Gone was the lackadaisical demeanor. He cocked back the hammer on his rifle. It clicked ominously like the sharp snap of a breaking twig in the stillness of the morning. A cry from a distant crow sent a soft *caw, caw, caw* drifting to them down the tree-shrouded trail.

Reese Jenkin's mind whirled wildly. Surely they would be detained, probably brought to a Union patrol. Nathan's mission would be over before it began. Jenkin's face flushed a deeper red. Impulsively he whipped off his hat and slapped Nathan's horse on the rump. "Ride!" he screamed. "Get to the river!" As he spoke, Reese's right hand swiftly went to his rifle and slid it from the scabbard.

Nathan's horse bounded into the surprised men in front of him, knocking one to the ground as if he were a straw doll. In a flash, the horseman kicked out and struck Seth's rifle as he raised it. It burst a shot into the air. Galloping low in the saddle, Nathan sensed bullets whizzing like angry hornets past his head. He couldn't help Jenkins now. He rode hard.

Reese's rifle barked a quick shot, and Jed crumbled to the ground. Blood and tobacco juice ran together down the side of his face. The big bay reared, pawing the air and screaming at the men who now surrounded him. Reese fired wildly. Another of his shots found its mark, and someone rolled out of the brush. Then a volley brought him down. Reese dropped with a hard thud onto the densely packed earth. He was dead when he hit the ground.

Seth and his men were stunned. Like drunks pushed out of a bar at closing time, they stared blankly at one another. In a blink of an eternity, two of their friends were dead and another wounded. As the bloodied man was being tended to, Seth and most of his men scrambled through the brush to their horses, tethered some distance away. They cursed that they had tied the animals so far from the road. "Don't want no horse noises to let folks know we're waitin' for 'em," Seth had said. Now, as Nathan raced away from them, they wished they hadn't been so careful.

Surprise, quick wits and speed had saved Nathan. He didn't look back as he raced down the trail to the river. The landing was there as Reese had said it would be. Each day about noon a paddleboat stopped if passengers awaited it on the landing. Nathan prayed it was running close to schedule. It was near noon now, and Seth and his friends were likely in close pursuit.

He hurriedly purchased a ticket from an old gentleman at a boat-house, then sold his horse and tack cheap to a man who didn't ask questions about the winded, lathered-up condition of his gelding. Since the pack mule and case had been abandoned in the gully, the only luggage Nathan bore was the large satchel of clothes that he had strapped onto the black.

The old man, his face as weathered as the driftwood that floated near the riverbank, told him that the steamer *Union* was due anytime now. Nathan waited impatiently on the landing, his eyes narrowing as he intently peered up the river. Before long the cry, "Steamboat a comin'," rang out as the *Union* came into view.

As he gratefully watched it approach, Nathan stole a few moments to silently mourn Reese Jenkins. He had seen many die in the war, but Reese was different. For one thing, he had given his life to save Nathan.

Moments later Nathan strode aboard the boat and began his winding journey down the Ohio to the Mississippi River and eventually Minnesota. The dark plume from the smokestack of the *Union* trailed behind them, mixing with the humid haze of a hot southern day. In the distance Nathan saw horsemen galloping madly up to the landing. Seth and his men were too late to stop him.

❧ 2 ❧

SOLOMON FOOT ABSENTMINDEDLY patted his coat pocket as he watched the paddlewheel drive through the murky water of the Minnesota River on a gray Minnesota day. Yes, the money was still there. He knew it would be, but touching it somehow gave him reassurance.

It was spring on the frontier in 1862. Foot was glad to take the steamboat as far up the river as Shakopee. The walk from the Kandiyohi Lake region had been wet and muddy. Solomon would have preferred to wait, but crops had to be planted and a land payment made in Forest City.

The cash was for that payment. Since 1857, Foot had farmed and trapped furs with his family in west-central Minnesota. But that enabled them only to subsist. He had found it necessary to write to a friend back home in Ohio for money. The notice that cash awaited his identification and receipt at the express office in St. Paul was a godsend. Now Foot was headed home. The steady *thump, thump* of the paddles and the sound of rushing water had an almost hypnotic effect on Solomon. His mind traveled ahead to the lakes of Kandiyohi County, to his wife and the five little Foots.

Nearly one hundred miles to the north and west lay the green prairies and shimmering blue lakes rimmed with trees. In summer, from the high hills where the prairie rolled, they looked like rings of emerald bands

18

embracing an azure stone. On one of those pristine lakes the Foot family had settled five years earlier. As a small settlement had grown, people had come to depend upon Solomon Foot. His shooting and trapping prowess were well known throughout the lakes region, known by both red and white.

Occasionally Santee Dakota and sometimes Ojibway from the north visited his cabin. A few miles distant was Green Lake, which had become an unofficial dividing line between the two Indian nations. As a trapper, Foot found it wise to be on friendly terms with the native inhabitants. Many hours were spent alone in icy waters and woodlands. Spiteful Indians could find him an easy target.

Only once had Foot shown fear to the Dakota. He had been working on his farmstead when a distant "halloo" brought him hurrying to see if a new settler or land prospector needed help. His Colt revolver was tucked in his belt and his rifle slung over his shoulder.

Suddenly two Dakota braves appeared before him and Foot raised his rifle in involuntary defense.

The Dakotas extended their hands in friendship and shouted, "Hello, hello." Then they laughed upon realizing that they had scared a white man. That day Solomon resolved that he would never again show fear to an Indian.

He didn't regret bringing his family to Minnesota. Foot had spent his childhood on the banks of Lake Erie in Ohio. The son of Scot and English immigrants, his parents had seen to his education, and, at twenty-five, he began a lumber business in Ohio and later Indiana. But in his mid-thirties, Solomon got an "itch" he couldn't scratch. The lure of a new land and new opportunity nagged at him until the day he announced to his wife, Adaline, that they were moving to Minnesota.

Pamphlets advertising the state had spun tales of a rich, virgin land just waiting for the plow. From only 4,000 people in 1849, in a little over a decade, Minnesota's population had pushed over 170,000. Emigrants from New York State, New England, Norway, Sweden and Germany had flocked to the land of lakes, prairies and trees. They were lured by land that had been thrown open for settlement after being purchased from the Dakota in 1851. Solomon Foot had been among them.

It was midday when the steamer reached Shakopee. Under better conditions a traveler might continue on the steamer, even though the freight cost was prohibitive. But this spring an ice jam upriver made further boat travel temporarily impossible at any price. From here Foot planned to purchase a horse and make the rest of the journey west on horseback.

A drizzle had begun, driven by a cool breeze. Solomon shook the water from his wide-brimmed hat and buttoned up his mid-thigh black coat before he walked toward the gangplank. As he neared it, he noticed a young woman struggling with her baggage. Silently Solomon reached down and picked up her burden. The woman, slight of build, her long blonde hair drawn together in back, smiled up at him with even white teeth.

"Thank you, sir," she said. Her voice was bright and friendly. "There's a wagon waiting for me by the wharf."

"Glad to help," Foot said. "Where you headed?"

"The Lower Sioux Agency. I'm going to teach at the mission school."

The two walked side by side down the gangplank. Foot towered over the girl. He chuckled at her. "School marm, huh? We could use one like you out where I live in the Kandiyohi lakes. You take care of yourself around the reds. You never know how they'll be."

The teacher flashed a bright smile that lit up her pretty face. Her deep-blue eyes twinkled up at Foot. She had long eyelashes, high cheekbones, and a clean natural beauty.

"Maybe someday I'll take you up on that. But I'm told that the Indian children need help and that things are peaceful on the reservation."

"Things aren't always what they seem, ma'am," Foot replied as he hefted the bags into the waiting wagon. "You take care."

"I will, sir, and thank you. By the way, my name is Emily West." She held out her hand.

Foot's large palm swallowed the young woman's hand. "Name's Solomon Foot. Good luck to you." He nodded a tight-lipped smile, tipped his broad hat and walked to the livery.

A short time later Foot swung into the saddle of a serviceable bay horse. His six-foot frame settled onto the horse rather uneasily. He never really liked riding horseback but this would get him home sooner. The towns near the Henderson-Pembina Trail dotted the passage to the northwest. They were familiar stops to Foot: Young America, Hutchinson, Cedar City, Acton, Diamond Lake, Green Lake and then the shores of Foot Lake.

Foot's journey would take him away from the river, through the prairie, as he traveled northwest. As he neared his home, Solomon would encounter more and more lakes. Most of the lakes were still ice covered, but the ice was black, signifying that it would soon melt and break up.

The whiteness of the snow-covered prairie winter was losing its yearly battle with the sun and was broken by large patches of brown earth. Soon the snow would completely disappear, and the green of spring would signal Minnesota's annual renewal.

It would take several days of steady riding to reach his cabin. This trip necessitated a short detour off the trail to Forest City.

The trail was muddy but the day was warm, and Solomon removed his slouch hat to wipe the sweat from his brow and forehead. Ruefully he noted that there was a bit more skin than hair on his thirty-nine-year-old head as his hairline had begun its march to the rear of his scalp. "Oh, well," he mumbled to himself, "at least I won't be too much of a prize on some red's lodgepole."

But Solomon Foot's build was solid, powerful and dangerous. The Indian fortunate enough to take Foot's hair would prize the trophy no matter what Solomon thought. The man known as the "Daniel Boone of Kandiyohi County" fixed his dark, deep-set eyes on the road before him and set his mind on the long ride ahead.

It was twilight when he reached Cedar City. The chill of an early spring evening was beginning to sink into the frontiersman's bones like tiny icicles piercing his flesh. There was an inn in the village, a few rough cabins and not much else. Foot remembered it well. Just over four years ago, in midwinter, the Foot family had made their first pilgrimage through Minnesota to the west. They had gone through heavy snow and were grateful to reach sanctuary.

But Wilson, proprietor of the overcrowded inn, was not a gracious host. The word inn didn't accurately describe the near hovel that Wilson charged people to sleep in. It was smoky and dim inside the walls of the rough-cut hewn logs. Peering through the haze, Solomon felt like he was trying to see underwater in a swamp. The Foots had to provide their own bedding, sleep on the floor and cook their own food.

Wilson had grudgingly agreed to this arrangement. When another of the patrons was a few cents short on his bill and offered to drop it off on his next trip through, Wilson growled, "No, that won't do. I'm not keeping a stopping place for my health." The man had to leave a box of goods as security.

Foot had vowed never to patronize that inn again. Although he was cold and tired, Solomon camped on the outskirts of the village that night. He was grateful that it was early spring and not winter. Most snow was gone except for shrinking piles left behind by the prairie wind. It was still quite cool, but not frigid, probably above freezing.

Foot scraped down into the earth several inches. Where the frost still held tight, he smacked chunks of dirt with his hatchet. Then Solomon gathered hot ash and embers from his fire and spread them on the torn and scarred ground. After spreading the layer of dirt back over the embers he placed a blanket on it and lay down upon the warming earth.

It was something he had learned from the Sioux. Solomon considered that maybe the Indians had more to teach if he and his friends would pay attention.

Solomon gazed up at the night sky. The stars looked like smudges on a chalk slate as a light wind drove fleecy clouds past them toward the horizon. Gradually the campfire, bedding, and heated ground warmed him and he drifted into sound slumber.

Solomon was on the trail again just after dawn. The long, lonely ride left him with little to do but think. His mind drifted, seizing thoughts that randomly caught his fancy. He wondered how his parents were doing back in Indiana; his brother, Silas, had joined him in Minnesota. He thought about the war raging in the South and the East and hoped that the Union would be rejoined.

But mostly Solomon Foot thought about his new home. Sure, the winters were hard, and the mosquitoes sometimes felt like a few dozen sewing needles flung into one's skin, but to Solomon these inconveniences were minor. This was a Garden of Eden.

Foot had read the broadsides and pamphlets that land speculation companies had sent east to encourage settlement in Minnesota. Yes, they had exaggerated. The corn didn't grow ten feet high, and fish didn't leap out of the sky-tinted lakes into boats. But, Solomon thought, they weren't far wrong.

He had tried to study more reliable sources about the new state before making the move west. Foot read a book about the history and geography of Minnesota. It was the diversity that appealed to him. There were four distinct seasons and a wide variety of wildlife and vegetation.

Only in Minnesota, he had read, did coniferous forests to the far north and deciduous forests in the central and southeast adjoin prairie. In the center of the state they called the forest the Big Woods. It boasted a blend of leafy trees and, farther north, fragrant sharp-needled conebearers.

The prairie spread like a great ocean to the west and south. In the summer six-foot shafts of purplish grass undulated in the wind remindful of the waves of the great sea that had covered much of Minnesota in prehistoric times.

As Foot trekked to the northwest from the Minnesota River Valley, the prairie was mostly flat with occasional wrinkles. It reminded Solomon of a lumpy pancake. As he drew nearer his home in the Kandiyohi lakes area, the land would begin to roll with small hills covering the prairie.

Back before the Ice Age, a range of mountains had thrust peaks high above Lake Superior, far to the northeast. But those ancient monoliths had been worn down like the molars of an old man. Now they were only high hills, memories of past magnificence.

For about five months, from May into October, color abounded. Solomon relished the brilliance of his new home. No artist with a rainbow of hues could improve upon nature's work. An eagle high above could look down upon the green and purple of the prairie mixed with wild flowers and large splotches of blue, the thousands of crystal-clear lakes left behind by glaciers that had ripped into the earth during the past Ice Age.

When the glaciers melted and receded, the deep lakes remained. Trees were a scarcity on the prairie. Clumps of white oaks grew together in isolated spots as lonely sentinels overlooking the sea of grass. Along rivers and sometimes the northeast corners of lakes, willows, cottonwoods and others trees had taken root.

Solomon had wondered about the lack of trees. People from the East needed to live by trees. It was like the security provided a child by a mother's breast. Most Americans had grown up surrounded by trees. Many believed that, if a land didn't grow trees, it couldn't grow wheat.

Foot had looked at an old map by an explorer named Stephen Long. Across the northern and central plains of the continent was written "Great American Desert." Part of Minnesota was included. Long thought it was considered a desert because there were no trees.

Of course, Solomon discovered, it wasn't a desert. Just two years earlier, the reason for the dearth of trees became horrifyingly apparent. Fire! Fires, often the result of lightening bolts, raged across the grassland. Driven by powerful winds, the torrents of flame burned everything in their path.

All woody vegetation was destroyed, leaving only the stands of trees protected by water or missed by chance, or the corky-barked oaks that could withstand the ravages of fast-moving fire. The northeast corner of lakes often kept trees because the blazes, usually pushed by southwest winds, divided at the lakes, rejoining on the other side but leaving a pocket of earth untouched.

As fire raged near his homestead, Foot had watched from his cabin, on the northeast shore of a lake, as the skies blackened to the southwest. He and his family soaked down their cabin's roof with buckets of water from the lake and prayed that the fiery plague would pass them by.

Solomon's horse paused and rubbed its nose along the inside of its front leg. "Okay, boy, scratch and rest," the man mumbled softly as he recalled the horror of the fire. Thick smoke had nearly suffocated them. Solomon, his wife, and children had turned to the lake in hopes of survival. They waded into its waters, seeking refuge from the nightmare of flames, heat, and smoke.

The sky turned from pink to a boiling red that churned into the blackness of the smoke. Solomon and his family knelt in the lake and cupped their hands in the water as the heat threatened to sear their lungs like the blast from a furnace. Bending their heads, the Foots breathed through hands held just touching the water's surface, cooling the air just enough to breathe.

The firestorm had passed, leaving the Foots shaken but unharmed and their cabin unscathed. For Solomon, the blaze provided an unexpected benefit. The fire burned away the litter of dead grass from past years, purifying and cleansing the ground as it roared across the prairie. The ash would "sweeten" the soil for good crops.

With the fire-resistant grass roots safely below the ground, it simply grew back fast and tall without the choking clutter of litter. Crops grew better as well when planted after a fire.

But Solomon couldn't help smiling to himself as he remembered his wife's words, "One more time, Solomon Foot! If a fire comes that close one more time, we're going back home to Indiana!"

Maybe she meant it when she said it, Foot thought. But Adaline Foot loved this land as much as he did. In some ways she was stronger than he was. Solomon was smart enough to know that women were the background of the frontier, and his wife was tough, mentally as well as physically. She wouldn't bend in a strong prairie wind, and she wouldn't let a fire drive her out, either.

Indians were another matter. The pamphlets back east hadn't mentioned them much. They told of two treaties the Santee Sioux had signed in 1851 and 1858 that turned most of their land over to the whites for settlement.

The land companies assured settlers that the Indians were peacefully living on the reservations to the south and learning to become like white people. Hunting parties passed by now and again, however, appearing suddenly as ghosts from the mists of the nearby lake. Adaline could never quite get used to them.

By 1856 settlers were moving into the Kandiyohi Lakes region to stake out their claims. The Foots had arrived in 1857.

It was near noon when Foot reached the little settlement of Acton in Meeker County. Just a few buildings marked the spot, but they included a general store and a post office. Robinson Jones, who was newly married to Ann Baker, ran these.

Jones was well known to those who passed along the trail from Henderson on the Minnesota River to the Kandiyohi lakes region and beyond. His store was also something of a frontier tavern, and Jones was a hospitable host always willing to lend a hand to the weary and sometimes luckless travelers who came his way.

ROBINSON JONES POISED HIS SPLITTING MALL over a round of firewood and brought it smashing through the cold block in a single stroke. Jones was a big, muscular man whose dark, rugged exterior belied a gregarious nature. Solomon's horse sloshed on the soggy trail. Looking up at the approaching traveler, Jones wiped the sweat from his brow and ran his fingers back through his black hair.

"Afternoon, Foot. Bin awhile."

"Hello, Robinson," Solomon answered in his low rumbling voice, "Just heading home from St. Paul. Got any grub on the stove?"

"Come in and set yerself down. I'm sure the missus has somethin' cookin'."

"Mrs.? Last time I was here you were a bachelor."

"Been hitched just over a year. Got myself a ready-made family, too. Got my niece, Clara, her little brother, and just down the road there's my wife's son and his family."

"You're turning into a regular patriarch, Mr. Jones."

The two men entered the story-and-a-half log cabin. Even though three windows illuminated the interior, it was still dim compared to the brightness outside. But it was warm, and the smell of beef stew bubbling in a pot hanging over the rock fireplace drifted delightfully across the room. A trim middle-aged woman, with her dark-brown hair tucked into a bun, stood near the fire stirring the simmering stew.

"Ann, this is Solomon Foot from the Kandiyohi lakes. Best hunter and trapper around."

Ann Baker Jones turned her weathered face to Foot and extended her hand. "Nice to meet you, sir."

"Pleasure's mine, ma'am," Solomon nodded.

The woman ladled out generous helpings of stew, and the men settled into conversation.

"Kind of a long winter, wasn't it, Solomon. Have any trouble?"

Foot glanced up at the loft between spoonfuls. He noticed two forms there, likely Jones' niece and nephew.

"Not really trouble, not with reds anyway," Solomon said. "Had kind of an interesting hunting trip last December, though."

"What happened?"

"My brother Silas and me headed for the woods north of Green Lake to hunt deer. We trudged along the Crow River and the lake until we came to a partially finished cabin. The walls and roof were finished, but there were no windows or doors. The cellar was dug down three feet, so we ate cold corn cake and rolled up in our blankets and passed the night.

"Next morning we walked fast to keep warm and hunted through timber south of the lake. We passed through Irving and through more timber towards Diamond Lake. There we came upon the tracks of three deer. We followed to about a mile and a half from Diamond Lake, where the deer left the timber and went out onto the prairie and then into a grove of brush.

"My brother went into the brush, and I waited where I thought they would come out. Soon a large doe and two fawns appeared. I brought her down with one shot. 'Meat for the babies,' I yelled. We bled the deer and felt rewarded for our long cold hunt. But we wanted more."

"Ain't it always the way," Jones interrupted, "you head after the young ones?"

"Silas followed the trail of the fawns while I found a place to wait for the deer if they should come looking for their mother. I stood in the grove freezing. The wind and sleet seemed to penetrate right through my body.

"Meanwhile my brother was not doing any better. He had followed the trail until the fawns turned back like we thought they would. They crossed on the ice of a small lake, and he followed. The ice broke under him and he plunged into freezing water about six feet deep. Silas grabbed onto the edge of the ice and pulled himself to the surface. But when he tried to pull his body onto the ice, it broke under him again. By using his gun to distribute weight and again throwing himself upon the ice, he was able to slowly crawl ashore.

"He was exhausted and nearly frozen when he saw smoke from a nearby cabin. He made his way as fast as his frozen bones would let him to get to the heat of that fire. When he got to the cabin, occupied by a family named Delaney, he was unable to speak. Warm clothes, a roaring fire, and hot drinks soon brought him around.

"About that time, I saw the mile-distant smoke, too, and decided that I would forget about the fawns and try to warm my miserably chilled body. When I got to the cabin, Silas presented the most comical sight I had ever seen. My brother stood before the fire dressed in Dan Delaney's clothes. Now, Silas stands about six feet. Delaney's pretty short. Silas's pants were short on both ends, and the shirt only reached about halfway down his torso, leaving a rather large bare area between shirt and pants. He looked like one of those cartoon characters that fella Nast draws for *Harpers Weekly*.

"Well, we warmed up some, and then Delaney and I brought the deer in and dressed it. Mrs. D. hung a kettle over the fire and filled it to the brim with venison. We feasted on warm cakes, tea, generous cuts of venison. Then we rolled our blankets onto hay on the cabin floor and spent a warm, restful night. Quite a bit better than the night before in that unfinished cabin a few miles away. Next morning we shouldered our venison and headed for home where the little Foots were joyous at the prospect of fresh meat."

"Quite an adventure, Solomon. You tell a good story, too. Game's been plentiful here. We don't have to dive into lakes after deer."

"We generally try to avoid it. Any trouble with our Indian friends?"

"Not really," Jones answered, "Just the usual stuff. They drop by and beg for food and whiskey ever' now and then. They'll steal anything that's not nailed down."

"Robinson, you can't really blame them. From what I hear, it's tough on the reservation. They gave up a ton of land, and they're not gettin' paid for it. They think the white traders are the ones who'll steal anything."

"We paid for this land, Solomon, with cash, sweat and blood."

"Maybe we did. But we bought it cheap. We took millions of acres of some of the best farmland in the world, and we got it for a few cents an acre."

"Sure gave us a scare last summer, didn't they, Solomon?"

"Especially 'round Eagle Lake. John Pemberton and his Ridgely troops were there, you know, keeping Sioux and Chippewa bands away from each other and were camping right near my place. Then a messenger came from Ridgely, and they pulled up stakes in the middle of the night and went back to the fort.

"Word spread that the reds were upset because their annuity money hadn't come or that Dakota Sioux had come to the agency to punish the 'farmer' Sioux for taking up white ways and were warring on the whites, too. Neither was true, but with the Inkpaduta massacre at Spirit Lake in '57, we didn't take any chances. We all gathered at Sam Hole's place and were about ready to build a fort when we decided there wasn't any immediate danger and went back home."

Jones took a swig of cider. "False alarms are hard to track down out here. Telegraph would be nice, but that'll take awhile to get here."

"That's true, Jones, but sometimes word spreads like wildfire on its own. The trouble is trying to figure out what's true and what's not."

"Say, Solomon," Jones began, "isn't that Pemberton the same one who's now a Confederate general."

"The same. He's from Pennsylvania, but sympathized with the South. His brothers fight for the Union. Pemberton is kind of the reverse of our General Thomas."

Foot wiped his soup bowl clean with a biscuit and chomped it down. After some more casual conversation with the Jones family, he excused himself. He wanted to reach Forest City by late afternoon, make his land payment there, and then continue the final leg of the trip home.

ജ 3 ര

mily West was wide-eyed with anticipation as she caught her first glimpse of the Lower Sioux Agency, still a couple of miles distant. She was perched on a wagon seat next to her guide. In the back of the open box wagon, her meager possessions bumped along. Most everything she had was in three battered suitcases. Philander Prescott softly flicked the reins on his team of horses and looked over at his passenger.

"There it is, across the river, your new home." He gestured to the far-off buildings located on the opposite bank high on the bluffs overlooking the Minnesota River.

Emily straightened up. The buffalo robe provided by Prescott hung loosely from her shoulders and covered her shawl and blue woolen flannel dress. "How do we get across?" she asked.

"Ferry's just ahead," Prescott answered. "Charlie Martel, that crazy old Frenchman, will get us there."

Minneapolis, her home, was about 100 miles away to the east. Her father and mother were probably trying to sell off winter clothing at their dry goods store, Emily thought. "Work in the store, find a man and settle down," her father had advised. "After a while you can take over the store from us. Forget about this Indian business."

But that wasn't the life Emily wanted. She had taken training to teach. There were no marital prospects and besides, there was the lure of adventure in the West, even if it was just western Minnesota.

Emily and Prescott had journeyed several days over alternately frozen and thawing trails. The spring thaw was continuing. In early morning, the chill of a below-freezing night left the trail still somewhat frozen. But by afternoon, mud was sucking the wagon wheels, making for some hard going.

Emily had learned much to prepare for her post from her driver. Philander Prescott was nearly seventy. For almost forty-five years he had lived among the Sioux as a fur trader and now as an interpreter for the Lower Sioux Agency. His wife and three children were of Dakota blood. Prescott was still erect in stature and robust in health, his long white hair trailing behind a balding pate. His pants were wool and in need of washing. He wore a buckskin shirt and sat on a buffalo robe that he had removed as the day had warmed. The old man had been generous in his advice to the young girl as they rattled down the trail.

"This isn't like any other town, Missy," he had told her. "Got a hundred-some white folks living and working in our little village. Most of 'em have some connection with the government. But it's smack dab in the middle of an Indian reservation.

"To make matters worse, the Dakota can't even agree among themselves. You got your cut-hair farmer. They're the favorites of the agency. And then there's the so-called 'blanket' Indians. They try to hold onto the old ways. Most of our Indians are blankets. This leads to some pretty spirited activity between the two groups. Don't get in the middle of that stuff. Those that come to your school will be cut hairs and white agency kids. Don't be mixing with the blankets unless they come to you."

"How many students are there?" Emily asked.

"Oh, 'bout twenty, I'd say," he said, rubbing his stubbled chin. "Had over that once, but numbers dropped when the Dakota found out they weren't going to get a permanent school with clothes and meals. Remember, the term's 'bout up. You'll just be getting your feet wet before the school year shuts down for the summer."

"Yes, I'm to help in the mission over the summer. There's much to do, I'm told."

"More than you can do in a summer, Missy. They're tryin' to turn a whole civilization of Indians into whites. That's hard work even for those acceptin' of the change, even harder for those resistin'."

The wagon descended to the bottomland on the north side of the river across from the agency. The ferry landing, also known as Redwood Ferry, was actually a small community. There were a warehouse, a blacksmith's shop, a log house and barn, and also a steam-powered sawmill and mill employees' house. A system of ropes and pulleys was used to transport passengers by barge across the river.

Charlie Martel, short, stocky, of French descent, managed the ferry. He was dressed similarly to Prescott, except for a beret, owing to his heritage, that rested jauntily at an angle on his graying head. Charlie's ragged beard was likewise gray except where tobacco spittle had stained it in yellow-brown streaks.

"Bonjour, Philander. Good to see you again. Ma'mo'selle, I heard the agency was getting a new teacher. I expected someone older and statelier. You are a welcome sight to these old eyes, like a rainbow across a dismal gray sky." Martel bowed to Emily and winked as he gestured to the rustic barge.

"Step in. Your royal vessel awaits." His eyes twinkled with laughter as he helped Emily on board.

Emily blushed and smiled at the colorful riverman. "Thank you, sir. You are most kind."

"Don't these old bones get any help?" Prescott grinned at Martel.

"You get that old and decrepit in the last couple days?" Martel retorted.

"Guess not," the old man said as he easily stepped onto the barge.

In a few minutes the open wooden barge was grinding over rocks onto the bank on the other side of the river. As Prescott and Emily climbed out onto the riverbank, Charlie Martel touched the young woman's sleeve and looked soberly at her. "You take care. There could be bad times coming," he warned.

Emily smiled and replied, "Thank you, but I'll be all right. After all, I have Philander to look after me."

Martel laughed loudly, "Now you really have me worried!" He waved good-bye as he pulled the barge back to the ferry. "Watch your top knot, Philander, what's left of it."

Prescott waved at Martel, then helped Emily with her baggage as they ascended the well-worn path leading up the bluff to the agency.

Buildings were visible through a stand of trees between the village and the river. "Here it is, missy." Philander waved his arm when they reached the crest of the path. "We got about thirty buildings in our little village. Most of 'em have to do with the government, missionaries, or traders. But we've got just about everything ya need to live out here."

Their destination was Reverend Hinman's house, which lay on the southern edge of the village near Council Square. As Prescott and Emily walked the narrow dirt roadway through the agency, the old man played the role of tour guide. He pointed out the doctor's residence, the smithy, carpenter's shop, and boarding house.

Philander gestured toward the second story of a frame building. A ladder was leaning high on one side. A large man wearing paint-stained overalls was on the top rung, swinging a paintbrush. "That's Slim Dahl, the agency carpenter and painter. Big man, he is, almost six-four and nearly 300 pounds, but he'll move that ladder by bouncing it across the wall while he's still on it. Lots of our agency people are married to Indians. Slim married a Ness girl from Meeker County instead."

"Afternoon, Philander," a man called to Prescott from down the trail. The short, dark man waved and entered a stable.

"There's Joe Coursolle," Emily's elderly guide commented as he waved back. "He works for the agency as a teamster. Nice fella, half-French, half-Dakota. Raised by Sibley hisself after his parents died. Now he's got a wife who's mixed blood just like he is. She's a pretty girl with long, shiny black hair. Two little girls and a baby on the way, too. You'll meet others like him here. Lots of French trappers came through here, some married up with Dakota girls."

A road ran in an oblong circle around much of the village. At its east and west ends, the circle intersected with a main road. Prescott stopped at the east intersection.

"This is my house to the right. Across the road is Reverend Hinman's. That's where you'll be staying. At least for now. That's Council Square, across the road to the right. The warehouse is the stone building on the west side of the square. The school is by that."

"Where does the road go?" Emily asked.

"West it leads to the Upper Agency, other end of the reservation. East it goes to New Ulm. Other side of the river you noticed the two trails leaving the ferry. The one we took, that went by Fort Ridgely. The one goin' north would take you to Fort Abercrombie."

They crossed over the road to another stone house. The thawing mud of the dirt passage stuck to their shoes and made sucking sounds until they reached the brick walkway leading to the door. A dog barked, and the door was opened as they approached the front stoop.

Reverend Samual Hinman stood at his door. The young Episcopal missionary smiled broadly and greeted his visitors warmly. "Mr. Prescott, and Miss West, I presume, how good to see you! Come in."

Philander and Emily wiped the mud off their shoes as best they could before stepping onto the hardwood floor of the small, cozy parsonage.

"Welcome to our little village, Miss West." Greeting the new arrival as she entered the room was Elizabeth Hinman, the pastor's wife. Her face was plain, her body slender under her hoop skirt. She had her hair tied up in a bun and was attired in a tasteful, long gray dress. Although Elizabeth's manner appeared severe, she flashed a friendly smile at Emily.

The house was sparsely decorated. A rustic table and chairs centered the main room. Above the fireplace mantel, where most frontiersmen hung their rifles, the Hinmans had hung a painting of Jesus.

"I'm so glad to be here. Philander has already told me much about you and this place."

The pastor gestured to the fire and brought a couple of chairs near it. "Sit down, warm yourselves. Elizabeth, bring coffee, please."

After exchanging some pleasantries, inquiries about the trip, and recent news of the agency, Reverend Hinman leaned forward in his chair. Hinman was an earnest young pastor, of medium height. His dark hair, parted on the left, hung just over his ears. He dressed in black and wore the white collar of his calling.

"I think it's important to give you a little background before you get started, and now is as good a time as any. Philander, you've lived here for dozens of years and are more knowledgeable than I, so feel free to add whenever you wish. Miss West, if I'm going over ground that you've already been told, let me know."

"I'm anxious to learn whatever you feel I need to know." Emily sipped her coffee and nodded at Hinman.

The reverend wore no mustache and his cheeks were bare, but a short dark beard framed his lower face at the jaw line and chin. He rubbed his cheek with his right hand and began.

"I was ordained in 1860. John Williamson, the Presbyterian pastor, along with Stephen Riggs, and I are here to bring Christianity to the Dakota. It is not an easy task. We're part of this secular community. We work with the government and vice versa in our endeavor.

"Agent Galbraith's the man in charge here. This, and the Upper Agency at the other end of the reservation are the main bastions of civilization on the western frontier. Here the policies of the Unitied States government are carried out, here the Dakota come to be educated, to learn trades, and to be paid for the land we took from them. About 7,500 Indians live on the reservation.

"This is the beginning of a long chain, part of a bureaucracy that'll see six other levels deal with a request from the Dakota before a decision is reached. As of now we've got about fifty white families and roughly 200 people living here. Most are in some way connected with the government. For example, Wagner is our superintendent of Farming, Dr. Philander Humphrey, our physician. We even receive a small government subsidy because the government believes we're working to the same end they are, that of civilizing the savages."

"I'm an interpreter, salaried by the government," Prescott interjected.

"I have one question I'm somewhat confused about," Emily said. "I hear the terms 'Santee,' 'Dakota,' and 'Sioux.' All refer to these Indians. What do they mean?"

Prescott glanced at the pastor and answered. "The Santee are one of the three major divisions of the great Dakota Nation. The other two are now in Dakota Territory. The Santee are divided into four bands. I won't bother you with their names now. Sioux is the generally accepted term used by most whites, but it's a Chippewa word. Actually, it's an insult in their language, means 'snakelike.' 'Dakota' is what they call themselves; if you want to show respect, use that. Also, about names, Upper Agency is also known as Yellow Medicine. Redwood is what many call the Lower Agency, and the Chippewa and the Ojibway are the same people."

"Thank you, Mr. Prescott. There's so much to learn. I hope I'm up to it all."

"Our school is near the stone warehouse," the pastor continued. "It's not the only school on the reservation. Upriver there are several villages; Rice Creek, Little Crow's, others. John Reynolds has a school there.

"As you know, you're replacing Andrew Robertson, who recently died. Filling his shoes will be no easy task. He was much admired by both agency people and Dakota. Mrs. Robertson has been directing the school since Andrew's death. You'll work with her. The term'll be up shortly. However, there's more educating than that found in books. There'll be much to occupy you. I understand you also have some nursing training."

"I worked with a doctor in Minneapolis. His office was near my parents' store. He encouraged me to become a nurse. But education was always more to my liking."

"Whatever skills you possess will be useful here."

"I'm eager to begin. Where are my quarters?"

"Originally, I thought here; however, Mrs. Robertson has requested that you stay with her."

"I'd be glad to take her there," Prescott offered.

After a little more small talk and pleasantries, Emily and Philander left to take the short walk to the Robertson house.

Following an exchange of greetings with Mrs. Robertson, the old trapper left for his own home. "Remember, Emily, it's a small town. We'll help you anyway we can. You know where I live."

Alma Robertson was a gracious woman in her sixties. She still dressed in black out of respect for her dead husband. Former agent Joseph Brown called her husband's passing an irreparable loss for the education of the Lower Sioux. Her home was warm and neat. On one wall hung a wedding picture of Alma and Andrew. Mrs. Robertson noticed Emily's eyes focus on the photograph.

"We were a little younger then," she smiled as much to herself as to the young teacher. "I miss him terribly."

"I heard he was a fine man, Mrs. Robertson."

"Call me Alma," she replied. "And he was. I'm so glad they sent me someone young, someone with energy. We are, after all, trying to teach a whole new culture to these people."

"What about those who don't want to learn?"

"The blankets? They'll come around in time. Don't push them. I advise helping those who wish to be helped. You have much to learn about this place. Keep an open mind."

Emily sat on the offered chair and reviewed her background with the kindly widow. After a few cups of coffee and a cookie, Alma asked, "Any questions?"

"I'm sure I'll have many. How many speak English?"

"Surprisingly, quite a few speak passable English. At least those who come to school and to church. The 'farmer Indians,' those who are making an attempt to adopt our culture, are doing quite well. If you need help interpreting or learning some Dakota, talk to Philander."

"How are the Dakota adapting? Are they getting on well with all our agency people?"

"Mostly quite well, I think. Most Indians are still in the blanket category, of course, and they live on the reservation away from the agencies. Many seem to accept the teachers and missionaries. It is the traders that present a problem."

"Oh? How?" Emily inquired.

"They are both friend and enemy to the Dakota. It's true that they supply them with much of what they need. But they pay a price. The traders allow the Indians to buy on credit. When the annuity payments are made, the traders sit at the pay table. What is due the traders comes off the top. There is little left for the Dakota.

"I won't tell you that the Indians are being cheated. But they believe that they are. After all, they have no training in keeping books and ledgers. You'll discover much for yourself. Keep your eyes and ears open, but remember, you are here to help, not get mixed up in squabbles."

Alma took a sip of her tea. When she set her cup down, she said, "You'll meet the traders soon enough. We have four posts: LaBathe's, Forbes', Robert's, and the two Myrick brothers'. They are located just down the road to the Upper Agency.

"One other thing, Indian children are given white names at the school. If we're going to help them adapt to our way of life, they need to start thinking like whites. Indian names are counterproductive to our goals. Call them by the names printed on the cards on the desks. I'll be in the school office if you need me."

The sun was setting on the small but unique village as the two women lapsed into casual conversation about where they had been and where they were going.

∽ 4 ∾

A thunderstorm broke over the Mississippi River as the sternwheeler chugged by the bluffs overlooking the river near St. Paul. In the distance, high up on the bluff, Old Glory flew, outlined against a slate-gray sky. White limestone walls surrounded the flag. This was Fort Snelling, last Union outpost on the river. Constructed in the 1820s to protect the region from Indian attack and serve as a trading post, it now served as a port of debarkation for Union soldiers going east. Joining the river near this point was the Minnesota River, whose route led west past the Lower and Upper Sioux agencies.

To Nathan the river seemed in motion as rain-drops splatted across the wide ribbon of the Mississippi. Soon he would reach Minneapolis. Meed's store was there, and he would presently meet his Minnesota contact. The mission would then begin in earnest.

The *Union* pulled in to a landing on the west side of the Mississippi, the Minneapolis side. Merchants, salesmen in cheap suits, laborers, women holding umbrellas—all walked down the gangplank to the bustling grain town. The young city was fast becoming the mill city of the Mississippi as farmers settled to the west and sent their grain to Minneapolis. Founded in the early 1850s, it now had nearly 3,000 people.

The streets were muddy, and Nathan struggled to keep to the side as he walked to Meeds' store. With his one arm, he lugged his large suitcase. He stopped and asked an old gray-haired man standing on a corner for directions, but the man didn't answer. "Norsk, Norsk," was all he said.

Another elderly man nearby overheard. "Young man, you lookin' for Meeds' Mercantile? That fellow there can't help ya. Only speaks Norwegian. Just go to the end of the block and turn the corner. It's on the right." Noticing Nathan's empty sleeve he asked, "Where'd ya lose the arm?"

"Shiloh," he replied.

"Too bad, son. We need sturdy boys like you to keep fightin' them rebs. Damn 'em all, at least Grant stopped 'em. Bloody mess, though, wasn't it."

"Yes, it was," Nathan answered and continued down the street. He didn't want a long conversation about Shiloh. Memories were painful, especially from the side he'd fought for.

Meeds' Mercantile was just where the old man said it would be. It didn't look much like the headquarters of the Confederacy in Minnesota. Stuck in the middle of a growing, lively little town, it appeared to be a run-of-the-mill general store. It was built of rough-cut lumber and had a window on either side of the door.

The store seemed caught up in the patriotic fervor of the times. It was festooned with American flags like parade headquarters on the Fourth of July.

As Nathan entered, a gray-haired, balding, little man wearing glasses looked up from the newspaper spread out before him on a counter. "War's going bad for us, young man," the older man spoke in a breathless, wheezy voice. "But you look like you've already found that out for yourself. Can I help you?"

"You can if you're Samuel Meeds."

"I am he."

Nathan reached over the counter past the cracker barrels and extended his hand. As the old gentlemen matched the firm grip with one of his own, Nathan lowered his voice even though no one else appeared to be in the store. "My name is Nathan Cates. I believe you've been expecting me, sir."

Meeds' watery blue eyes lit up, "Indeed I have, young man. Come with me."

He led Nathan to the back of the store through rows of dry goods on shelves and past a curtain into a small dimly lit room. "No one in the store, but you can't be too safe. Yankees are everywhere in this town. Let's get right down to business. I've arranged passage for you by riverboat up the Minnesota to the Lower Sioux Agency."

"What do you know of my mission?" Nathan asked.

"Only that you're going to the agency, and I'm supposed to see you get there and give you what supplies you might need for yourself or to trade with the Sioux. I'm also to forward any messages you need to send south. Beyond that, I don't need or care to know anything. Even if I might be a tad curious, I've already got crates of goods ready, mostly pots, pans, cloth—that sort of thing. Course, if you remove the false bottoms, there are some fine rifles there, too."

"When am I to leave?"

"There's a steamer heading west tomorrow. You can be on it."

"I'm ready," Nathan replied.

"And I've registered you as an agent of Meeds' Mercantile with Fort Snelling. They want to know who's trading with the Sioux. They get pretty protective of their traders. Numbers are limited. You've only the summer to do your job."

"Time shouldn't be a problem," Nathan said.

The old storekeeper reached under his suspenders and took out a pipe. He silently filled it with loose-leaf tobacco and lit it. A soft glow from the pipe brightened his pale face, and a sweet aroma soon filled the little room. "You're welcome to stay here tonight if you wish. I got a spare room upstairs."

"I appreciate the offer. But I'm thinking that the less we're seen together the better. Besides, all these Yankee flags are getting me jumpy." Nathan's face opened into a small smile.

"Just putting on a front," Meeds said. "I gotta fly the flag, seem sorrowful at Union defeats when I'm bustin' with joy on the inside, and just appear to be a regular worshiper of Father Abraham. That way no one suspects the real business of this store."

"Where you from? You don't sound too southern."

"Nor do you, young man. I'm from Missouri. I've lived here since '55. Business was good so I stayed. I'm too old to fight, anyway. But I believe that states shouldn't be pushed all over by the Yankee politicians. My family owned slaves, but I don't care much about that. It's a matter of a way of life. I want to see my family and friends in the South live the way they want to. So, I wrote to President Davis, and his secretary, Mr. Bisbee, wrote back and said that they might have a use for me. And here you are."

Nathan spent the night in a nearby boarding house. Early the next morning he was back at Meeds', arranging to have the crates transported to a wharf on the Mississippi. The rain had stopped, and bright sunlight alternated with fluffy clouds across a severe blue sky. Workers loaded a dozen crates onto a wagon. The muddy street pulled at the wooden wheels as they rolled the cargo to the river. The *Franklin Steele*, another paddlewheeler, waited at the dock.

Steamboats had been crucial in bringing people to Minnesota. Regular service had been established between St. Louis and St. Paul in 1823. The *Franklin Steele* was typical. Its large paddle, at the rear of the boat, was driven by a steam engine that forced the paddles to churn through the water.

Midmorning found Nathan "Cates" on his way to the Lower Sioux Agency. Posing as a trader in mercantile goods, he was anxious for this last leg of his trip. He dressed in a cotton muslin shirt and woolen pants. Nathan started the day wearing a deerskin leather jacket but soon removed it as the day warmed.

He had made arrangements for messages to be sent via Meeds, and he'd also tied up whatever loose ends he could think of. Now it was time to get into the meat of the plan and enlist the Santee Dakota, unofficially, into the Confederacy.

The Minnesota River was still high after the spring thaw, so the steamboat made good time down the river. They paddled past little river towns on the brown stream. The burgs were splotches of activity in a vast expanse of water and greenery. The river cut through a prairie with wooded areas rimming its banks. It was beautiful land to Nathan. "No wonder the Sioux are so resentful. They lost a paradise to the whites," he thought to himself.

The valley of the Minnesota River dominated the scenery. A giant, ancient river formed the valley. It had stopped running thousands of years ago at the end of the Ice Age. The river was an outlet of the great lake that once covered much of Minnesota. The valley cut a wide and deep swath from Big Stone Lake on the western border, running southeastward to Mankato before taking a sharp turn to the northeast where it entered the Mississippi River at St. Paul.

Since ancient times the valley had been the winter home of Indians seeking protection from the howling winds that ripped over the open plain. Now it housed two reservations.

The muddy brown stream that Nathan watched twist through the valley was but a memory of the mighty river that once rushed through the prairie. But the river was still important to trade and travel. Deep and treacherous in places, it was generally about fifty yards wide with a flood plain that extended broadly on either side until the landscape climbed sharply to join the rolling prairie.

The paddlewheeler churned through the water upstream throughout the day and into a beautiful sunset as the western sky turned to a rose-colored fire. Early the next morning, they neared Fort Ridgely, mostly hidden by trees off the northern bank of the river.

Nathan stood on the boat deck near a railing and watched as the boat edged toward the shore. To his left stood a plump man in a cheap plaid suit; to his right, farther down the railing, leaned a young soldier in a new blue uniform.

"Just 'bout twelve miles to the agency," said the man in the suit. He spat a stream of tobacco into the water and looked over at Nathan. "You been through here before?"

"No," Nathan said. "I'm going to the agency to trade."

"You're lucky. Only a few traders at the agency now. You can make a killing if you play your cards right. Those reds don't know what end's up as far as money's concerned."

Nathan's questioner was unshaven with long sideburns. His checkered woolen suit was rumpled and obviously slept in. He was fat and flabby, and his round head looked like someone had rolled up a hunk of clay and plopped it onto his shoulders. Nathan didn't respond but just eyed him up and down.

"Me," the man said, "I'm on my way to the Upper Agency. Easy pickin's up there. I got the best pots and pans this side of the Mississippi."

"There's not much this side of the Mississippi, sir." Nathan couldn't resist the comeback. He turned and walked away. Soon they would land and he had crates to tend to.

As Nathan passed a young lieutenant, the soldier stuck out his hand. He gripped the offered hand as the soldier said, "I'm Tom Gere, Fifth Minnesota. I guess it's because of folks like that fellow that I get sent to Fort Ridgely and not east."

"Lieutenant Gere, my pleasure." Nathan answered. "He does appear a little slimy. If I were an Indian, I don't think I'd want to deal with him. I'm Nathan Cates, bound for the agency."

"Unfortunately, there are plenty like him. That's one reason why we have to keep soldiers at a frontier fort when we should all be fighting to save the Union."

"Lieutenant, I'm going to trade with the Dakota. I intend to do so fairly. I've done my part in the war. Maybe you'll get east. But the way the war's going, maybe not."

Gere shook his head. "McClellan got kicked off the peninsula, but he got close to Richmond first. Old Abe will find another general. We'll win. Just you wait and see. What outfit were you with?"

"First Indiana. Good luck, lieutenant, and I've been east. You're not missing much." Nathan casually saluted Gere and walked to the cargo hold.

In a few minutes they made a brief stop along shore to unload Gere and a few other passengers bound for Ridgely. Then the paddlewheeler pulled away from the warf and splashed through the twisting river again, going upriver to the nearby agency.

The *Franklin Steele* pulled up to the wharf on the south side of the river across from Redwood Landing. Before long Nathan and his twelve crates were in the little agency town. His first stop was at the livery, where he hired a wagon for his cargo. With the crates safely loaded, he turned his attention to the village. Soon he would have to meet Little Crow.

MILY WEST HAD PLUNGED WITH DEDICATION into her position as a teacher in the agency school. The day after her arrival, she faced her eighteen students for the first time.

She was to teach them the basics of a good education. But the unspoken goal, at least to the children, was to expose the Indian children to the white culture and, thereby, turn them "white."

Twelve of the students were Indian children, the other six white children of agency employees. It was April, one of the first warm days of spring, and only a few weeks remained in the term. The approaching end of the school year, coupled with a nice day, normally would have led to restlessness and inattention among the students. This day they were curious and focused. They had a new teacher, and she had their whole attention.

They ranged in age from six to fifteen, pretty evenly divided between boys and girls. The boys wore wool pants and homespun shirts made of linsey-woolsey, a homemade material, part linen-part wool. There was a wide variety of colors. The girls likewise wore homespun dresses with petticoats. White or red, there was little difference in how they dressed.

While the native children might have preferred to wear deerskin, it was discouraged. The agency bureaucrats had decreed that they would dress like whites. Some Indian children did wear their black hair longer and had beads around their necks, clinging to the ways of their ancestors.

The room smelled like elementary schools all over with a curious mixture of young sweat and assorted body odors.

While many buildings at the agency were of stone, the school was a wood frame building. Three rows of wooden tables, long side facing the front of the room, held six students per table. Mrs. Robertson had taken pains to make sure that white students were interspersed within the Dakota. In front of each student, on a tag, was a name. Names like "Billy," "Jimmy," "Jane," "Sarah," and "Fred" seemed incongruous in front of the bronze-complected faces.

Emily stood at a large wooden desk in front of the class. Behind her were two flags, those of the United States and the new state of Minnesota. "My name is Miss West," she announced, "I'm here to help Mrs. Robertson teach you for the rest of the school year. Let's begin by having each of you introduce yourself to me. Tell me anything you want about yourselves."

In turn each of the children spoke as they sat at their table. Most simply said their names. Several didn't look up. A couple of the white students added what position their fathers occupied in the agency. Little Elizabeth Coursolle, six-year-old mixed-blood, proudly announced that her father was in charge of the agency horses.

In back was the oldest of the Indian boys, Johnny, a fourteen-year-old. His black hair was parted in the middle and was greased back. When his turn came, Johnny was silent and stared at his desktop. Repeated prompting by Emily garnered no response.

Then Anne, a young white girl in the front, spoke up. "He's always like that, Miss West. He would hardly talk for Mr. Robertson."

"He thinks he should be out huntin' buff'lo or somethin'," Sam, another white boy, added. "Too good ta waste time learnin'."

Johnny looked up sullenly. "My father wills that I come here. My uncle is a warrior."

"He has what ya might call a mixed family." It was Fred, a boy in the second row. "Some blankets, some farmers. His dad's a farmer, that's why he's here."

47

"I'm told that your leader, Little Crow, has taken on many of the white man's ways," said Emily.

Johnny looked down again and mumbled almost inaudibly, "My uncle says that Little Crow has failed his people."

Realizing that it was time to change the subject, Emily started her first lesson. "Students, take out your slates and prepare for your lesson in arithmetic."

During the next few days she concentrated on teaching the three R's of readin', 'ritin', and 'rithmetic. She was surprised at how well the children did, especially the Dakota. They were polite and studious, and the Robertsons had obviously done well with them. But Johnny continued to be hard to reach.

"Mr. Robertson always felt that he had the most potential of the group," Alma Robertson told Emily. "But he's torn by his home life. His father follows Traveling Hail and those who are for change; his uncle, Lightning Blanket, listens to Shakopee and others who cling to the old ways. Farmers versus blankets, if you will. Do what you can for Johnny, but don't let him tax you too much. I'm sure he won't be back in school next year. It'll be time for him to help his family."

The next morning as Emily approached the school, Johnny, Billy, and Tom, the older Indian boys, were in earnest conversation with the scraggly looking Dakota she knew as White Dog. His hair was cut unevenly short, and his white man's clothes were dirty. She knew him to be a government employee hired to teach the Dakota to farm. When he saw Emily, White Dog abruptly left.

"What did he want?" Emily asked.

Johnny and Billy were already headed into the school. Tom stopped and answered, "He thinks we should quit school and start to farm. Says he will show us how to be men. Yet he is one who bows to the white man. My father says the old ways will not last, but even he does not trust White Dog."

White Dog walked back to Myrick's trading post. He was a man caught between two worlds. He longed for prestige and authority, but he was not a great warrior. Anyway, he reasoned, the white man's world is the future. Thus, hoping for a greater role among his people in the coming new world, he had become an employee of the government and a lackey to the Myricks.

White Dog hadn't gauged correctly the resistance of his people to change and the resentment assigned to those who did. Blankets held cut-hairs in very low esteem. Now White Dog felt like an outcast and longed for ways to be accepted again by his people, but he still couldn't quite let go of the little prestige the Myricks and the United States government had given him. He knew his people hated the traders, yet they paid him and treated him well. "I will find a way to help my people," he mumbled as he walked to Myrick's.

The last weeks passed quickly. As the weather warmed, green leaves sprouted from the buds on the cottonwood trees along the river. The prairie grass also began to green up and grow. Eventually it would reach full height and sway in the wind like the sea under a gentle sea breeze. The children in the agency school grew increasingly restless as the last day approached. Like youngsters everywhere, they longed to run and play and enjoy the freedom that came with the warm rays of summer.

On the last day of school, Emily announced that the class would go to Andrew Myrick's trading post, where she would buy a licorice for each of the students. The Indian children didn't greet this with the enthusiasm of the white children, but they dutifully rose from their desks and followed their teacher. They walked hesitantly as if they were going to the wood shed for a paddling and not to a store for a treat.

Rose, a ten-year-old Dakota girl, walked near Emily and confided in a soft voice, "Our people think that Myrick cheats us. He is a bad person."

"His post's the only one that sells candy. I'm sure he'll treat you fine."

Emily and her students made the short walk down the road to the trading posts. The four stores were clustered at the edge of the agency on the road leading to the Upper Agency. They were rough, log-cabin structures made for business and not for pleasure or comfort.

Andrew and his brother Nathan owned the post. Each of the four traders had several employees. When the school children entered Myrick's Post, James Lynd was clerking. The large room was dim owing to only two windows. In a dark corner sat Andrew with White Dog. A wide plank counter dominated the center of the room. The walls and shelves were filled with blankets, pots, pans, assorted dry goods, and hardware.

James Lynd, a man of medium height and build—a former state legislator—wore muttonchop sideburns and had a slight widow's peak in his dark hair. "What can I do ya for, Miss West?" he asked.

"One licorice for each child, please."

"I'll just count 'em out for you, Miss. Have 'em gather 'round."

As the students gathered near the counter, Johnny sidled off and began to explore the store for himself. A shiny new pocketknife caught his attention, and he picked it up off a shelf. He examined the blades and wondered how they would slice and skin a rabbit. Billy walked over to Johnny and handed him a piece of black licorice. As he took it with his left hand, his right hand closed over the pocketknife. Instantly, he felt himself snatched off the floor from behind.

"You thieving little savage! I'll teach you to steal from me!" It was Andrew Myrick, his round face flushed and quivering with rage. Flecks of spittle showed on his short black beard. Myrick grabbed Johnny by the back of the neck with an iron grip as he dragged him through the door into the sunlight outside.

"White Dog, get the cane!" the trader snapped.

The Dakota reached behind the door and brought a cane to Myrick. Johnny struggled, but the trader threw him to the ground as if he were a rag-doll. The children stood in shocked silence.

Emily screamed, "Leave him alone! He's done nothing!"

As she raced to Myrick, White Dog held out his arm and stopped her. Emily tried to wrench free and sharply kicked the Indian's shin. The cane slammed down on Johnny's back with a sharp whack like a beaver tail slapping the still water of a pond.

The Indian boy lay stunned face down in the dirt as Myrick brought his arm back to strike again. Suddenly Myrick felt a fist close on his wrist with a viselike grip. After a painful twist, the cane flew from his hand. He turned sputtering to face Nathan Thomas.

"Who in God's name are you and what do you think you're doing?"

"I'm a man who doesn't like to see grown men beat children."

Myrick noticed Nathan's empty sleeve and straightened his stocky body. His eyes narrowed. "I can beat cripples like you, too."

"You're welcome to try, mister." Nathan said it confidently, matter-of-factly, his right hand clenched and ready.

Something told Myrick that this tall young man was was not someone he wanted to test. There was more to him than he wanted to tangle with. He turned to Emily and snapped, "Get these brats out of here." Then he stomped into his trading post. White Dog, rubbing his leg as he limped behind, followed him.

Emily knelt at Johnny's side as the children gathered around. He was in obvious pain and grimaced as she touched him.

"Maybe we should get him to the doctor, Miss."

She looked up into Nathan's dark eyes as he spoke softly to her.

"I'll help you," he added. Johnny limped between Emily and Nathan as they walked to Dr. Humphrey's cabin.

Humphrey's cabin doubled as his home and office. It was equipped with the basics required for frontier medicine: morphine to kill pain, bandages, various probes, lancets, and of course, a hand saw. The doctor's bed was built into a corner of the small main room. In the center was an examination table. Johnny sat shirtless on the table, a stony expression chiseled on his face. Red welts raised on his back.

The doctor looked him over quickly but gently, then said to Emily, "He's just bruised across his back. He'll be a little sore, but I don't think anything's broken. Here, see that he gets this liniment." He handed her a container of goo with a strong smell that permeated its leather covering and asked, "What happened?"

Emily, still shaken, relayed the incident at the post. As she concluded, she seemed to really notice Nathan for the first time. She faced him and extended her hand.

"I haven't thanked you. What you did was very kind and maybe dangerous."

"Like I said, ma'am, I don't like to see children being beaten."

"I'm Emily West, teacher at the agency school."

"Name's Nathan Cates. I'm a new trader here."

"Well, you certainly didn't make a good first impression on the old traders."

"I'm not here to make impressions on the likes of them."

Johnny sat up and started to walk to the door. Emily reached out and touched his shoulder. "I'm so sorry this happened, Johnny," she said.

Johnny turned and looked her in the eye, his black eyes glistening. "My name is Traveling Star," he retorted and strode out the door.

∾ 6 ∾

A RICKETY, WOODEN OPEN WAGON picked up Tom Gere on the river-bank and brought him up the dirt road to the fort. Fort Ridgely sat on a plateau high above the Minnesota River, a lonely sentinel on the prairie. It had been finished in 1855. Its mission was to offer support to the Upper and Lower agencies and to assure settlers that it would be safe to homestead in the area.

Gere was nineteen years old. Five months earlier he had enlisted in the army hoping to fight rebels. Now he found himself approaching an out-of-the-way post on the edge of the Minnesota frontier.

There was no gate to ride through. Fort Ridgely didn't have walls. Gere traveled on a trail that led past assorted outbuildings directly into a large parade ground ninety yards square. Bordering the parade were the nine principal buildings of the fort. Two long fieldstone structures dominated the others. A barracks on the north end and the commissary on the west were the largest. The other seven main buildings were compact wood-frame struc-tures.

On a tall flagpole in the center of the green parade ground fluttered an American flag. All thirty-four stars waved from the blue field. Secession was not recognized by the Union in reality or in symbolism.

The wagon stopped in front of a white frame building marked "Headquarters." Lt. Gere stepped easily from the wagon seat and paused before mounting the steps leading to his new captain's office. He swatted a cloud of dust off his shoulders and smoothed his thigh-length dark-blue woolen frock coat. Then he checked to see if the darker-blue piping running the length of his light-blue pants was straight. Gere adjusted the French-style Kepi hat over his full head of hair. He liked the Kepi and thought it more stylish, with a flat, circular top angling forward to a narrow front visor.

Satisfied that he was presentable, the young lieutenant entered the white-painted structure to meet Captain John S. Marsh, commander of Fort Ridgely.

The room he walked into was spartan. Two wooden chairs and a desk were the only furniture. No pictures adorned the walls; no family likenesses rested upon Marsh's desk, only a kerosene lantern, some sheets of paper and the stub of a pencil.

Gere snapped to attention as Marsh rose from his desk. "Lt. Thomas Gere reporting for duty, sir." He spoke carefully and tried to lower his tones. He hoped that his youthful voice wouldn't crack, as it was wont to do from time to time.

"Welcome, Lieutenant." Marsh returned the salute. "I was just reviewing your papers. Stand at ease." The commanding officer strode across the room and offered his hand to his new lieutenant.

Marsh was somewhat disheveled in appearance. His blue uniform was wrinkled and had seen better days. A button just above his navel was held on by a thread, awaiting a needle and repair, and a slight paunch rounded his figure. But his eyes reflected sincerity and commitment. He was not a tall man, balding on top, clean-shaven and muscular. An aroma of tobacco followed him. Gere noticed a pipe in his captain's front pocket. Somehow, he felt that this was a man he could follow and trust.

Gere relaxed, hat in hand, a full head of dark hair neatly combed. Of medium height and build, he wore a mustache to try to age his baby face. The subtrafuge wasn't very convincing. He was fresh out of Hamline University in Red Wing.

A lawyer, Gere's father wanted his son to follow in his footsteps. Tom, however, was determined to fight in the war to save the Union. Without his knowledge, his father had pulled a few political strings to get his son an officer's commission. He needn't have. Tom Gere was a very capable young man.

"Lieutenant, we have about eighty men in the garrison. Most are young and green." Marsh paused, realizing that he was speaking to one of the youngest and greenest. He cleared his throat and added, "But we all have much to learn, Lieutenant, regardless of age or experience. Anyone with any experience is in the East. This was a regular army post. They were all transferred out, of course."

"I'm honored to serve here, Captain. I hope to fight the rebels myself. I know that you're a veteran of Bull Run. I want to learn from you."

"I was in the Second Wisconsin, Lieutenant. They allowed me a transfer to take command here."

A sudden crash of artillery from the courtyard outside startled Gere. His eyes widened, and he resisted the urge to rush out the door to see what was happening.

Marsh chuckled. "We do have one regular-army soldier left here. That was Sergeant Jones, our ordnance man. When the regular army withdrew, they left behind six cannons. He has a gun crew that he drills regularly. We'll probably never use them, but they're good for show, and it relieves the boredom around here somewhat."

Gere grinned sheepishly. "I didn't expect it. Hopefully, if we ever need it, the reds will do a little jumping, too."

"Things are quiet as far as the Sioux are concerned. It's been a rough summer for them. Most of their land is gone, but the agency seems to have things under control. We're here to support them, but they seldom ask for anything.

"We here at Ridgely, along with Company C at Ripley in the north central, and Company D at Abercrombie on the western border, are the defense of the frontier. They tell us to maintain a presence. I guess that's what we are. Corporal Sturgis is the guard you passed on the way in. He'll take you to your quarters and show you around. I'll have orders for you later."

Gere saluted. "Yes, sir. If I might ask one question."

"Certainly."

"Why aren't there walls around this fort?"

"Because the committee that picked this spot had some strange ideas of defense. We're on a plateau 150 feet above the valley floor with deep ravines on three sides, and we've got no walls. The site committee decided that having no walls would keep us less complacent and enable us to go on the offensive more easily. Lord protect us from the wisdom of committees. The ravines provide natural cover for any force that decides to attack us. It's kind of like being on a gigantic table top and not being able to see what's coming up over the edge at ya."

"Yessir. I guess I understand." Gere understood and yearned for the protection walls would offer. "I know a little about the treaties the Sioux signed with us," the young officer continued. "They'll just keep living up to them, won't they? There's been no trouble?"

Marsh ruefully shook his head and gestured to a chair near the front of his desk. "Sit down awhile, Lieutenant, you're not out of school yet. I've got some history to go over with you."

As Gere settled his frame into a creaking wooden chair, Marsh leaned back in his own chair, folded his fingers behind his head and began to speak while staring at the ceiling.

"As a Minnesotan, you likely know this, but I want to be sure you got it right." Marsh's eyes left the rafted ceiling and leveled at Gere. "Most of Minnesota was once Sioux land. They lost the north to the Chippewa and most of the south to us. The first treaty with the Sioux was in 1837. In that one they gave up their land east of the Mississippi. In 1851, July 23, I think, a treaty was signed at Traverse des Sioux, not far downriver from here, near St. Peter.

"Oh, it was a magnificent day." A hint of sarcasm touched the captain's voice. "Politicians came from all over. Thirty-five Upper Sioux chiefs showed up, Sisseton and Wahpeton. There weren't any buildings around big enough to hold everyone, so they built a big canopy of tree boughs. I bet it looked more like some wedding celebration than a land deal.

"The deal was simple. The two bands of Upper Sioux sold almost all of southwestern Minnesota, some of Iowa and Dakota for $1,665,000 in cash, plus goods and food, called annuities. We were also to give them schools, teachers, farms, and knowledge of farming.

"It was quite the impressive ceremony. Each of the thirty-five chiefs, dressed in colorful finery, beads, and eagle feathers, stepped forward and touched the pen used to sign the treaty papers. Little Crow, a Mdewakanton, was there as an observer.

"In August, the Lower Sioux bands met at Mendota. There Little Crow and other chiefs signed away the southeast quarter of Minnesota for $1,410,000 in cash and annuities over a fifty-year period."

"How many acres did we get?" Gere wondered.

"Twenty-four million acres of the finest farmland God ever created. They left the Sioux with two adjoining reservations about 150 miles long and ten miles wide on either side of the Minnesota River roughly from Redwood to the Dakota boarder. But, even with so many millions of acres, it wasn't enough. After the land was opened to white settlement in 1854, the government wanted more. In 1858 another treaty was signed. This time the Sioux only lost a million acres on the north side of the river. It took two years for Congress to figure out a price for them, thirty cents an acre."

"Why did the Sioux give up more land so easily?" The lieutenant posed the question as if he were still in class at Hamline University.

"Greed. Some of the Sioux chiefs liked the idea of increased annuity payments. Officials took them out to Washington to sign this time. Funny thing is, the Indians don't get much of the money anyway. Agency traders put in claims from their dealings with the Sioux and most of the money goes to them. This year nobody's got any yet. As far as I know, the money hasn't been sent.

"Another thing, the Santee hate the German settlers. It seems that at the eastern end of the reservation where there's some question about the boundary, Little Crow believes that the Germans—Dutchmen, they call 'em around here—built New Ulm on his land. It's a real point of contention. But when the Sioux protested, the government produced treaty language that backed the Germans."

Gere shifted in his chair and commented, "I'm still surprised they gave up the land so easily. Wasn't there dissent among the Sioux?"

"The government made it sound good. The Upper Sioux bands actually are pretty close to where they were living anyway. The Lower Sioux bands were a bit put out that they had to leave the Big Woods and prairies and stay in the river valley, but with the promises of cash and goods dancing in their heads, they signed.

"Probably a little dose of reality also entered in. There was a veiled threat that the State of Minnesota would just take the land if the Dakota didn't sell it. Little Crow's a realist.

"But you're close to the mark in your question about dissent." Marsh rose from his chair and walked across the dusty wooden floor to a window facing the parade ground. He gazed briefly at the troops drilling. They wore mismatched uniforms consisting of faded dark-blue wool tops called blouses and, like Gere, sky-blue woolen pants, some with patches and stitching.

The new, good uniforms had gone with the troops to the South. Company B was wearing hand-me-downs, with the exception of the new arrival from Hamline. Marsh turned back to Gere and resumed his discourse.

"Yes, there are those among the Sioux who opposed the treaty signing. They stay in the shadows, and we don't hear much from them, but it's not hard to pin them down. Red Middle Voice is one of the leaders of dissent, along with his nephew Young Shakopee, or Little Six as they call him. Little Crow lost a leadership position in part because of his support for the treaty, even though a farmer Indian replaced him."

"Isn't that good?" Gere was determined to learn what he could from his willing captain.

"Yes and no. Traveling Hail, the new speaker of the Lower Sioux, backs our policies, but, aside from that, he commands little respect from the younger braves. They'll still turn to Little Crow when they need him. His is the village closest to Redwood Agency. There are three others going upriver, Big Eagles, Little Six, and then the Rice Creekers. That's where Red Middle Voice and Cut Nose are, along with most of the troublemakers.

"I've even heard rumors of something called a Soldier's Lodge. It's supposedly made up of Indian rebels, those who oppose the treaty signings. Word has it that someday they'll rise up against us and kill whoever gets in their way, red or white." Marsh paused for effect and then continued. "And that's why we're here. To make sure that groups like the Soldier's Lodge don't get out of hand and to support the programs of the agencies. End of history lesson, Mr. Gere. Now it's time for you to get acquainted with our little bastion of civilization on the frontier. Willie Sturgis is outside waiting, he'll show you around."

Tom Gere stood and snapped a well-practiced but, thus far, little-used salute.

MARSH BROUGHT A TIRED HAND above his right eye in return and dismissed the young officer. He returned to his desk and sat his stocky body heavily into the chair. As he ran his fingers through his thinning hair, Marsh pondered again if he had made the right decision in leaving the Second Wisconsin. He had been a man of action in the center of the biggest war the world had known. He had traded that for a backwater fort on the edge of the frontier. The captain yearned for action, yet he knew that quiet was best for everyone. Now he had a young shavetail officer to break in.

"God help me," he sighed. "We're not ready for any war."

CORPORAL WILLIAM J. STURGIS, barely twenty, had sandy-colored hair and a clean-shaven face—if he shaved at all. He was waiting for the lieutenant just outside the captain's door. He wore sky-blue soldier pants with a darker blue stripe running down each pantleg, but his faded dark-blue coat had been discarded somewhere. He wore a red cotton undershirt with white suspenders. He had been leaning against the wall but snapped his lanky body to his version of attention when Gere stepped out.

Gere addressed him formally. "Corporal Sturgis, I'm Lieutenant Gere, the captain would like you to show me around my new home."

"Glad to, Lieutenant. Might as well start with that fella over there." He gestured to the bearded, rather large man standing by a door down the porch from the headquarters. "Hiya, Doc. Lieutenant, this here's our post surgeon, Dr. Alfred Muller. Came here almost direct from Switzerland."

Gere walked down to the thirtyish, full-bearded man in the rumpled white coat and extended his hand. "Glad to meet you, sir."

"Welcome to our little community. We heard you were coming, Thomas, isn't it?"

"Tom is fine, Doctor."

A woman appeared in the doorway behind Dr. Muller. The doctor looked over his shoulder and smiled. "This is my wife, Eliza, a woman of many talents."

"Welcome, Lieutenant." Also in her thirties, Eliza was attractive. Her dark hair was parted down the middle and tied in back. She was dressed in a simple gray cotton day dress, worn over a bone hoop, that went nearly to her ankles. Her broad face and brown eyes lit up in a genuine smile as she greeted Gere.

The lieutenant glanced sidelong at Sturgis and noticed that from seemingly out of nowhere the corporal had produced a blue jacket and was hastily fastening the four buttons up the front.

Gere knew that it was improper not to wear the uniform top in the presence of a woman, just as a proper woman always wore a skirt or dress over a hoop when she was out in public. Even on the frontier, social conventions were obeyed whenever possible.

"This is our office and home sweet home, Tom," Dr. Muller explained. "Our hospital is in one of the log buildings behind the stone barracks, directly across the parade ground from where we stand. We tend to the sick, fevers, dysentry and such. Fortunately, battle wounds are a rarity."

"Doc don't lose no patients," Sturgis interjected.

"We've been fortunate, Lieutenant. The conditions under which we work here on the frontier are a far cry from a city hospital. Fifty-two drugs the Army sends us. I can only think of five that are good for anything."

"Which ones are they?" Gere wondered.

"Quinine, chloroform, ether, morphine, and whiskey." The doctor's eyes twinkled above his beard. "The whiskey being the most popular remedy here at Fort Ridgely, it's frequently in short supply."

"We have rounds to make, Alfred," Eliza interjected. "Visit us, Lieutenant. We're a small community. New residents are a real occasion."

Tom Gere smiled and touched his hat. "I'd love to, ma'am. Well, Corporal," he looked at Sturgis, "let's continue our tour of the post."

"Call him Willie," Eliza said. "We all do."

"Well, Willie," Gere looked at the young corporal, "take me to my quarters, please."

They walked down onto the sun-washed parade ground. It was hot, unusually so for Minnesota in May. Gere wiped the back of his neck with an already stained white kerchief and guessed that it must be nearly ninety degrees in the sun.

In the distance, the booming cannon of the blue-clad gun crews disturbed the serenity of an otherwise beautiful late spring day.

"You were out of uniform, Corporal," Gere stated matter-of-factly.

"Well, sir," Willie responded, "Once you start workin' in the hot sun in these wool uniforms, you'll find that the prison camps the rebs got are lake resorts by comparison. Ya sweat, ya itch, and then ya itch and sweat some more. Long as no sergeant or officer don't say nothin', we all take off the tops. We'd take the pants off, too, if we could, but that might be pushin' things a mite, 'specially since some of these boys ain't used ta wearin' underwear yet."

"But, your shirt, Corporal . . ."

Willie looked down at his red shirt and grinned. "The wool blue jackets, blouses, shirts—whatever ya wanna call 'em—that's standard issue. Shirts are pretty much whatever we brought from home. Red, white, calico, whatever, mostly cotton muslin. Ya can't just wear the blue wool. A fella would sweat 'em up, and they don't wash good. 'Sides, sweatin's good in the cotton. It helps keep us cool, when the sweat 'vaprates. If officers don't care, the wool blouses come off when we're workin'."

"They don't all wear underwear?" Gere asked incredulously.

"Some of these farm boys never had none back home. The sergeants is tryin' to get 'em to wear drawers. Most do, it helps with the chafin' from the wool, and it cools, same as shirts under the tops."

Somewhat horrified, Gere followed the corporal across the parade ground.

"Here's your new palace, sir." Willie Sturgis made a wide gesture with his right arm. "On the right, various officers' houses and the bakery. At the north end over there, that's the barracks. Can hold up to 400 men easy, but we ain't got a quarter that many here now. On the left, the other stone building's the commissary. Next to that's more officers' quarters. Since you, Lieutenant Norm Culver, and Cap'n Marsh are the only officers we got, you pretty much got your choice of which cabin you take. Got some sergeants staying in some houses but you rank 'em. You can move 'em out if ya want to."

"Is the one next to the bakery taken?" Gere asked.

"Nope, she's yours if ya want it."

"Let's head over there, Corporal. I'll drop off my gear. What are all the buildings outside the parade ground?"

"All the comforts we need," the young corporal said expansively. "To the west's the sutler's store, warehouse, and home. Ben Randell's the sutler. He'll sell ya stuff the Army ain't got. Just south of his house are ice-houses and a root house. Granary is back of Doc Muller's. Back of the commissary is the guard house"

The two men were nearing the northeast corner of the parade where two small houses sat at the end of the square next to a bakery.

"Always liked the smell of baking bread." Gere smiled. "I'll drop my case off, and we can continue."

Sturgis stood in the doorway as Tom entered the sparsely furnished, dusty, little wood-clapboard building. The floor was hard-packed dirt. A table and a couple of chairs graced the center of the room. A single bed, with a nightstand, occupied a corner. There were no curtains over the windows. Only a layer of dust and a kerosene lantern occupied the table.

A tattered Bible rested on the nightstand. Gere placed his luggage on the bed and picked up the "Good Book." He blew a puff of dust off the top and flipped through the pages quickly. He turned to Sturgis, who waited in the doorway, leaning against a doorjamb.

"It's a well-read book," Gere noted. "Whoever left it must have felt the next occupant could use some help." He thoughtfully balanced the book in his hand for a moment, then placed it back upon the stand. "It shouldn't take long to get settled into this place. I'll tend to it later."

"Even if ya had a wife, she couldn't keep ya movin' furniture too long. Not hitched, are ya?"

"No, Willie, not even close." As they stepped back outside, the lieutenant gestured behind the barracks. "I know the hospital is back there. What are the other buildings?"

"Stables mostly. Couple of the cabins stand empty."

"So, that's it, Willie?"

"'Cept the buildings way over there to the northwest. Those are the powder magazines. Don't want them too close. Accidents happen."

As Gere and Sturgis strode back across the parade ground, the lieutenant paused to examine the activities of his new troops.

Some men marched in formation. They wheeled, turned and obliqued in files of four. Occasionally someone would get out of step or turn the wrong way. Gere smiled and shook his head at Sturgis.

Willie grinned at the officer, "They're gittin' a lot better. You shudda seen 'em before. Sergeant McGrew, he drew a "L" on top of some of the fellas left shoes and an "R" on the other. You know, so's they'ed know their right from their left. Problem is, they couldn't read neither. But, like I said, it's gittin' better."

Tom watched other soldiers who stood at attention near the edge of the post compound and went through the manual of arms as their sergeants barked orders, "Shoulder arms! Port arms! Inspect arms!" The men were all dressed in complete blue uniforms, including equipment.

A variety of hats was evident. Frontier posts were lax on headgear, especially since the most preferred, Bummers, also called forage hats, were in short supply. Many men simply brought a wide-brimmed hat from home. Most found these more practical in high sun or rain.

Bummers were similar to Kepis except that the top was taller and flopped down toward the visor. This allowed for storage space while foraging for nuts, berries or whatever food the wearer wished to gather in his hat.

Each soldier wore a leather belt holding a pouch with percussion caps and a scabbard for a bayonet. A leather strap over the left shoulder held a small satchel containing powder and bullets. Over the right shoulder were two straps, one, a haversack for food, while the other held a canteen. The latter was considered essential equipment.

Gere's attention perked up when he heard the sergeant order, "Load in nine times." Seeing them shoot might be interesting, the lieutenant thought. The sergeant would follow the procedures of the infantryman's bible, *Hardee's Infantry Tactics*. There would be nine steps in loading the rifles. He could either call out each one, or more likely would give abbreviated orders that contained several steps.

"That there's Sergeant Trescott," Willie offered proudly. "He's real good at gittin' the fellas to march and shoot straight."

The bearded sergeant cried "Prime!" His squad of eight men, in two files of four, moved their right feet back and formed a "T" between their right insteps and left heels. Holding their Springfield muskets at a forty-five-degree angle in the air, the men reached into the little leather pouches near their belt buckles and produced percussion caps that they slipped beneath the striking hammers of their weapons.

"Load!" Trescott commanded. Each man reached his right hand inside the powder satchel riding just above his right hip. Then all grabbed one little paper bag of gunpowder, ripped off the twisted top with their teeth, poured the gunpowder down the rifle bore, pushed the paper bag into the barrel and then seated a fifty-eight-caliber lead bullet. Immediately, the men slid ramrods from beneath the rifle barrel and forced the bullet, paper, and powder to the base of the barrel by ramming them down the long cylinder.

The command, "Ready!" followed. Each of the soldiers brought his rifle to full cock. "Aim!" The Springfields were all pointed at targets beyond the fort's perimeter, near a ravine. The soldiers in the second row leveled their weapons over the right shoulders of the man in their front. "Fire!" The eight rifles roared almost simultaneously, enveloping the men in a cloud of smoke. Little chunks of wood spit into the air from the distant targets.

The sergeant peered through a pair of pocket binoculars and shouted, "Huzzah! Boys, that was some hot shooting!"

Gere looked at Willie Sturgis, who was grinning widely, his chest puffed up with pride. "Mebbe some of 'em can't march too good, sir. But them farm boys can sure shoot."

"I'm impressed, Corporal," Gere replied. "It looks like they can."

"Three shots a minute they can git off, Lieutenant."

"That's good, Willie. But practice is one thing. I hope they can do it with thousands of rebs screaming, cannons roaring, and bullets whizzing all around them. I hope they can still stand and shoot when the fellow next to them gets hit and blood from him smatters into their faces."

Willie sobered up some and stammered defensively, "I . . . I betcha they can."

Gere nodded grimly and continued his tour with Sturgis around the parade ground. Activity was evident everywhere. Those soldiers not drilling in marching or riflery were working on the cannon gun crews, in the stables or the bakery.

"Everyone seems occupied," Tom Gere remarked.

"Now they do, but after mornin' chores and drill, it can be pretty borin' here. That's our main complaint. Lots of the time there's just nothin' to do. So, they make up stuff for us. Like Sergeant Jones havin' them fellas shoot those big guns. We'll never use 'em here for real, but it keeps the guys busy. The fellas that wind up in the guardhouse, they get there because of stuff that happens when they git bored. We all hope that pretty soon we'll git east."

"I do too, Willie. I want to go into the barracks."

Rows of cramped beds, with lumpy straw mattresses and rope springs, were the fieldstone barracks' only real features. In the center of the room stood a large round potbelly woodstove. A few soldiers were at work mopping and otherwise cleaning. One was sitting on a bed scribbling in a notebook. None wore the blue blouses, as Willie had; they opted to wear variously colored cotton undershirts. Their light-blue pants were plain. Only corporals and sergeants had dark-blue leg stripes, for officers were marked by navy blue piping down their pant legs.

Trying to sound soldierly, Willie barked, "Attention!"

The young soldiers, seeing an officer on the floor, dropped their mops, brushes, and, in one case, a pencil, and stood straight, arms at their sides.

"At ease," Tom said, "I'm Lieutenant Gere, just assigned to this post."

Gere walked to a gangly-looking redhead who had just been mopping. "What's your name, Private?"

"Bill Blodgett, Lieutenant. You don't know if we're gonna fight rebs soon, do you?"

"No, I don't, Private. We all have to wait."

"Just thought maybe when you was at Fort Snelling you mighta heard something."

"Second lieutenants are often the last to know," Tom replied.

"This here's our writer, Private Oscar Wall." Sturgis introduced a rather small young man to Gere. "He writes in that book of his every day. Ain't that right, Oscar?"

"I try to," he answered.

"What are you writing, Private Wall?" Tom looked at the book lying open on the bed, its pages filled with neat, cramped handwriting.

"Just a diary, sir." Wall seemed sheepish in his reply.

"Keep it up. Somebody may want to know what happens in a place like this some day."

"And this fella that was cleaning the windows is Private Eddie Cole," Willie said, moving towards the young man in question.

Cole gave an impromptu salute. Forgetting that he had a washcloth in his right hand, he smacked himself in the eye with the wet rag. He grew red with embarrassment as he sputtered, "Sorry, sir. Glad to meet cha."

Gere stifled a smile and saluted the three. "Carry on, men. I'm sure we'll get on well."

In moments Sturgis and Gere were back on the parade square. "I'm thirsty, Corporal. Where's the well?"

Willie scratched the back of his blonde head. "That's a little problem we got here, Lieutenant. Ya see, they never dug no well here. We got to go to the creek over there when we need water." He waved past the log buildings to the south.

Just then another young lieutenant walked over from where he had been watching drill. He smiled broadly at Tom and held out his hand. "You, I take it, are Tom Gere. I'm Norm Culver, First Lieutenant of the Fighting Company B, Fifth Minnesota Volunteer Infantry. Quite a mouthful when you say it all together, isn't it?"

"Glad to meet you," Gere answered the smile and the shake.

"Willie's told you everything you need to know, I suppose."

"Just about done, sir," Willie spoke up.

"Well, finish up, I won't detain you. Tom, I saw you enter the house next to the bakery. If that's where you're staying, I'm your next door neighbor."

"I hear it's customary for neighbors to honor new arrivals with a housewarming," Gere lightheartedly replied.

Culver laughed and turned back to his men on the parade ground.

"He's a decent fella." Willie offered his unsolicited opinion.

The cannons had ceased their roar, and the crews were cleaning the weapons. Sergeant James McGrew supervised a small group of soldiers as they rubbed and swabbed. Also disregarding regulations, McGrew and his crew had removed their blue coats and worked in the sweat-stained red or white long-sleeved undershirts.

The sergeant was a large, gregarious man. His belly protruded like a small watermelon between his suspenders and plopped gently over his belt. His full, reddish beard was bushy, but on top his hairline was receding.

"Take care ya clean well, me babies. You can't be knowin' when we might need those darlin's for real." McGrew watched with pride as his men worked. They had been fast learners and were doing well. They had never fired cannons in warfare, only in training on a shooting range. McGrew was confident they would be up to the challenge if it presented itself. At least he hoped he had them judged correctly. The sergeant himself had never been in combat. Only Ordnance Sergeant John Jones had had that privilege

Both Jones and McGrew were in their thirties, more than ten years older than anyone else in the company save Captain Marsh. With sergeants John Bishop, Arlington Ellis, Sol Trescott, and Russ Findley, they were the rocks that the youthful command looked to. Even though Bishop was only nineteen, he had an air of authority that the young company respected. Marsh, Culver, and Gere might be the officers, but the real backbone of Fort Ridgely was the sergeants.

Gere introduced himself to McGrew as he crossed the square toward the commissary.

"I'll help ya anyway I can, sir," the sergeant said. He had to bite his tongue so he didn't say "young sir" or "boy-o" to an officer fifteen years his junior.

As they approached the commissary, Gere noticed an unkempt old Indian woman alongside a window. She appeared more ancient than old. She was dressed in a muslin blouse and skirt, the colors of which were impossible to discern owing to dirt and stains. The woman was bending over and digging into the swill barrel in front of the window.

"That's Old Betz," Sturgis commented helpfully, "Some people say she's nigh on to 120 years old. Least wise nobody around here has ever known her when she wasn't old. She comes here from time to time and digs in the garbage for food."

Gere couldn't help but stare. Old Betz was short and fleshy. Skin hung from beneath her upper arms and jowls. Her long, scraggly gray hair looked like it hadn't been washed or combed in months.

Old Betz opened her squinty eyes as wide as she could and glared at Tom and Willie. She was holding her skirt like a basket into which she dropped choice objects from the swill barrel. The woman shouted hoarsely, "Se-chee!" From her skirt basket she grabbed a cold, half-rotten potato and flung it with amazing accuracy at Gere's head.

The lieutenant ducked as the vegetable missile flew by.

"Forgot to tell ya," Willie added laconically, "she's also the most orneriest person this si'da St. Paul, don't like to be looked at. By the way, 'sechee' means 'bad.'" The lieutenant and his corporal beat a hasty retreat, steering wide of the old woman.

Next to the commissary were more officer's quarters. Owing to the small number of officers on the post, non-commissioned ones like John Jones were able to live in a house with his wife.

Jones was just reaching his door when Sturgis and Gere approached.

"This is Sergeant John Jones, Lieutenant Gere."

Jones saluted the new officer. "Welcome to Ridgely, Lieutenant."

Willie continued, "The sergeant's our only regular army man, 'sides the Cap'n. He served in the Mexican War and let those Mex'es have it with a twelve pounder, didn't ya, Sergeant?" Willie didn't wait for Jones to answer but breathlessly added, "He's the one keeps us organized shootin' them big guns."

Jones was burly and muscular. A full, black beard hid much of his face. His blue eyes, thoughtful and serious, peered from beneath thick dark brows. The sergeant was the only man in the fort to have a red stripe running down his pants leg, the sign of an artilleryman.

"I've heard good things about your work here, Sergeant," Tom nodded his head toward Sturgis. "Willie, for one, is a big booster."

"I do what I can, Lieutenant. Training the boys is important. Someday they'll be fighting. If not here, then against the rebs."

The door to the house opened and a petite, obviously pregnant blonde woman shyly stepped out. She wore a blue-checkered apron over a long calico dress. "Lunch is ready, John," she said.

"One of the benefits of having a wife on the post is living and eating away from the barracks," added Jones.

"Martha, I'd like you to meet our new Lieutenant, Mr. Gere."

Mrs. Jones gave a timid smile and spoke softly. "My pleasure, sir. You're welcome here."

"The pleasure is all mine, Mrs. Jones. It's a small post. I'm sure we'll be bumping into each other from time to time. I'll be conferring with your husband. I've much to learn."

"We'll be moving to a cabin by the hospital behind the barracks soon," Martha Jones informed Gere. "We need more room."

As the corporal and lieutenant left for a lunch of saltpork, beans, and coffee with the enlisted men, Jones and Martha sat at their kitchen table.

"He's really wet behind the ears, Martha. They send us babies to lead other babies. At least this one seems wise enough to know he doesn't know everything." Jones removed his bummer cap and scratched his thick beard. A lock of heavy damp hair hung down over his right eye, and the sergeant brushed it away.

"Martha, they all seem so complacent. I was at the agency just two weeks ago. The reds are restless. You know their annuity payment's still not arrived. Farming isn't working out for many of them. It won't take much to stir 'em up. I fear bad times coming, Martha, and this is the greenest bunch of troops on the frontier."

"But they're good boys, John." Martha looked directly into her husband's blue eyes. "And you've done wonders training them."

"What with the baby due in a couple of months, I think you should go to St. Paul."

"My place is here with you, John." She looked down at her belly. "I'm sure we'll be fine. I won't leave you."

John Jones smiled at his wife and knew he couldn't change her mind. He placed his hands on the table over hers and silently blessed the day they had met. The lot of a soldier's wife on a frontier post was a difficult one, but Martha was one of a rare breed who could make it work.

After noon mess, Tom Gere returned to the headquarters building to meet with Captain Marsh. Marsh had his orders ready.

"Lieutenant Gere, I want you to familiarize yourself with our little part of the world. Tomorrow morning take half the company and march to Redwood Ferry. Learn what you can from the folks along the way about our Indian brothers. Your main purpose, however, is simply to show the reds, the agency, and the people along the river bottom that Fort Ridgely is ready to do whatever needs to be done to maintain security in the region. Take Sergeant Bishop with you and, if you want, Willie Sturgis."

After a moment's thought, he added, "It might also be a good idea to take Charlie Culver with you. He's our drummer boy, Norm Culver's brother. Since the idea is to draw attention to yourself, a little noise won't hurt. You should be back around nightfall."

That evening the company sergeants, along with Culver, Marsh, Alfred and Eliza Muller, and Martha Jones gave Gere the housewarming that he had joked about. The women put red plaid curtains in his windows and did some quick housecleaning and decorating. A vase of purple wildflowers brightened the center of Tom's table. After a snack of cold venison, the men walked onto the porch with a keg of whiskey.

They had made a haphazard effort to spruce themselves up. All buttons were fastened, and the top layer of dust brushed off their dull-blue clothing. Gere, with his bright-blue new uniform, looked somewhat out of place.

As the sun turned into an orange ball to the west, they drank and discussed the war in the East. The women talked of children, husbands, and the threat to their peace that lay just twelve miles up the river in Little Crow's camp.

"So McClellan's off the Virginia peninsula and high tailing it to Washington." Culver seemed agitated. "I'm starting to think the worst. We might lose this war, and we'll never get a chance to do anything about it."

"Don't worry, boy-o." The whiskey and informality of the moment caused a lapse in McGrew's propriety. "Old Abe won't throw in the towel yet. There's other generals to use up. There'll be plenty of war left."

"I tend to agree with the sergeant." Marsh drummed his fingers on a porch railing as he spoke. "The North has too many resources for it to end this soon."

"But we've got to start winning somewhere," Tom interjected. "What about Grant? He won at forts Henry and Donelson."

"And he almost lost his whole army at Shiloh," Culver answered. "Besides, they say he's a drunk."

"Grant likes to drink, but he's no drunk." Marsh looked directly at his first lieutenant. "People say he has no fear, that he'll hold on to an enemy in his front like a mad dog."

From the shadows, John Jones' voice cut into the night. "Since we're here and they're all in the East, maybe we should be more concerned about what's happening here. The reds have me worried. They feel cheated by the government and the agents, not to mention the traders. Their crops have failed, and game's scarce. We could have big problems in our river valley."

"Let them try!" Culver snapped. "Organized troops, even inexperienced ones can hold off and defeat any number of wild savages."

"Probably, Lieutenant," Marsh said, "but Jones is right, we must be vigilant and prepared. That's one reason why Lieutenant Gere and Sergeant Bishop are traveling to the ferry tomorrow."

The sun was now fully set. The officers of Company B, a little tipsy, headed back to their quarters. Martha Jones and Eliza Muller gently supported their husbands as they wobbled across the parade grounds.

❧ 7 ❧

THE NEXT MORNING, FORTY MEN of Company B marched along the trail to Redwood Ferry. It was late May, and the sun blazed brightly in the sky, the heavy early morning dew quickly burning away. It was hot by midmorning. The soldiers kicked up a small cloud of dust that clung to their sweat. Charlie Culver kept a steady beat on his drum, and from time to time the men broke out in song. "John Brown's Body" and the new "Battle Hymn of the Republic" were favorites. Bishop, the youngest of the company sergeants, marched alongside and barked out an occasional, "Left, right, left, right," in an attempt to keep the men in step.

The trail ran almost parallel to the Minnesota River. Save for the dusty road and the deep brown water, their surroundings were remarkably green. Trees and brush lined either side of the river. A wide flood plain rose to a rolling prairie that spread like an ocean to the north and south from the tree line. Late spring wildflowers gave purple and yellow hues that undulated as the grass moved in waves with the wind. Their sweet aroma mixed with the dusty sweat of the men as they marched and sang.

Tom Gere had the only horse on the march, a large brown beast that plodded along as if bored. Gere rode some but mostly walked at the head of the column of twos.

"A good officer sets an example," Marsh had told him. "Walk most of the way. Your men will think better of you for it."

On fertile bottomland near the river, farmers, mostly Germans, working the soil waved at the passing troops. At those cabins located near the road, Gere ordered brief stops to rest his men as he conferred with the occupants.

"Goot to see you are here. Keep da reds on der side of da river," a German immigrant said as he dipped cool water from a wooden-stave barrel for Tom. The hand that offered the drinking gourd was strong, calloused and hard. Dirt had seamed into every crack and clung under the German's fingernails.

"Let the fort know if you see anything unusual out here," Gere replied.

And so it was as they marched the twelve miles to the ferry. Swedish, Norwegian and German cabins were scattered along the way, inhabited by people who had come from the Old Country to seek a better life, people eager for the security that the United States Army could give them.

Near Redwood Ferry, Gere ordered a halt. "Sergeant, have the men break out their hardtack and canteens. Tell them to fill from the river if they need to." The sun was now almost directly overhead in the cloudless sky. "Have them wipe some of the dust off themselves and clean up some. I want a good impression made when we march into the ferry."

Wishing he'd shaved his scraggly red beard, Bishop mopped his brow as he strode to the company to deliver Gere's order. But McGrew and Jones wore full beards. It was a marked contrast to the younger men they oversaw. The company was all either clean shaven or were making rather poor attempts to duplicate their sergeants' full growth. In a way, the beards of the sergeants were badges of honor setting them apart.

Bishop moved smoothly and confidently, checking each of the men. They liked their sergeant. He was closer to them in age than the other sergeants. Still, John Bishop knew that a barrier needed to remain. He was their sergeant, not their friend. He was determined to be fair and to lead when called upon.

Charlie Martel, the ferryman, looked up from the pulley he was lubricating. From far off he heard the steady drumbeat. He finished his task and looked in the distance. A small cloud of dust signaled the approach of the infantry.

"Another show courtesy of Captain Marsh," he thought.

But the officer riding on horseback at the head of the approaching column wasn't Marsh. It was a much younger man, from the look of him, a youngster trying to look older and more important than his years.

Soon they marched down into the ferry. The young officer dismounted, "Lieutenant Thomas Gere, at your service, sir."

The Frenchman straightened and snapped a mock salute.

"Charlie Martel, ferryman, reporting for duty." Then he laughed and stuck out his hand to Gere. "Nice of you to visit us. Ees Marsh too occupied to make the trip?"

"No, Mr. Martel. I'm new to the post, and the captain thought I should acquaint myself with the area."

"Then, Lieutenant, step onto the barge, and I'll take you to the agency. You need the full tour."

"I hadn't planned to cross the river. We were to march right back."

"If you want to learn, you must cross," Martel insisted as he spat a stream of tobacco toward the river.

Tom made up his mind. "Sergeant Bishop, rest the men. I'm going to take Mr. Martel's advice and pay a short visit across the river."

It didn't take long for Gere and Martel to cross the fifty yards to the other side. He couldn't see the bottom through the murky swirl of water, but Tom knew it was well over his head. After Charlie assured Gere he would wait for him, the young officer climbed the twisting trail up the bluff to the agency.

Agent Galbraith was at the Upper Agency. Tom walked in his most military manner through the village, aware that eyes were on him. He wished that his uniform sparkled like it had when he reached Ridgely, but a day of trail dust had him looking like the rest of the command. "Dust, the great equalizer," he thought to himself.

The little town was bustling under the bright sun. People busied themselves at various tasks. The clang of the smithy's hammer rang clearly down the street, occasionally drowned out by the whinnying of horses in the livery or the thump of crates being unloaded.

In the absence of the agent, he determined to visit the home of the spiritual leader of the community. As he passed the stable, he asked a tall man with a neatly trimmed beard where the pastor lived.

"Pastor Hinman? Right over there, across from the square." The man straightened up from looking over a horse and pointed at Hinman's house. "Lieutenant, it's good to see you here. I'm Wagner, superintendent of Farming."

"Tom Gere from Fort Ridgely, Mr. Wagner. I'm just acquainting myself with the valley. How are the Sioux adapting to farming?"

"As my predecessor Cullen put it, it would be much better if every Indian that changes his dress and habits could be supplied with one yoke of oxen, one wagon, one plow, one milk cow, and some hogs, and poultry."

"We saw some Sioux plowing from across the river."

"Some are adapting," Wagner agreed, "but it's slow work." He paused to bend and raise the horse's right front hoof to inspect its shoe. Wagner grunted as he forced the hoof from the ground, then continued his comments, as he checked the bottom of the hoof.

"We do have an Indian helping us, White Dog. Unfortunately, he doesn't command the respect that we need in order to gain converts. But I'm off for an inspection upriver." Satisfied with his examination he released the horse's leg and patted its rump. "Care to come with me, Lieutenant?"

"Thank you, some other time. I'm due back at Ridgely tonight."

"Greet the pastor for me, then. Good day, Mr. Gere."

Wagner mounted his horse and rode down the trail as Tom took the short walk to Reverend Hinman's house. A pretty young blonde woman answered his knock at the door.

Tom introduced himself and asked if the pastor were at home.

"He left a while ago to minister in the Dakota camp. I'll be sure to tell him you were here."

"And what's your duty here, Miss?"

"I'm Emily West. I taught in the agency school. The spring term just ended. Now I do odd jobs for the Hinmans. Sometimes I'll go to the Indian camp. Today, I guess, I'm a housekeeper. Are you going to be quartered here?"

"No, Miss, I just arrived at Ridgely. It's been a pleasure meeting you, and please do extend my greetings to Pastor Hinman."

Gere left Emily and walked back through the agency toward the path leading back down to the ferry. A man on a horse rode the agency trail toward him. The man had one arm, and Tom recognized him at once as the man from the steamboat.

"Mr. Cates, I believe," Gere called. "How's the trading going?"

Nathan looked down and smiled. "Just getting settled in, Lieutenant. You didn't waste anytime getting over here."

"Orders," Tom replied.

"I'd like to talk more with you, but I have an appointment. I'm sure I'll see you here again."

"Come by the fort sometime," Tom called as Nathan trotted by.

Lieutenant Gere, after a brief walk around the village and short chats with a few residents, headed back down to the ferry, where Charlie Martel was patiently awaiting him. Most folks had expressed gratitude for the army's prescence but saw little impending threat from the Sioux. Once back on the north side of the river, Bishop assembled the company, and they began the march back to Ridgely.

Gradually the sun made its move to the west, and the air began to cool slightly. On the south side of the river, a band of Dakota galloped along the riverbank and hooted at the soldiers, teasing them as if they were small boys on a playground. Although none of Company B could speak Dakota, the tone left no doubt that they were being insulted.

"Just let me squeeze off one shot, Sergeant," Billy Sutherland pleaded.

"Don't even think about it." Bishop's voice was firm, his manner stern.

"Eyes front, ignore them!" the sergeant shouted down the ranks.

In time the Indians tired of their game, and the rest of the march to Fort Ridgely was uneventful. Before nightfall, as Marsh had predicted, Gere led his men back into the open parade ground.

๛ 8 ๙

ATHAN THOMAS HADN'T HAD TIME TO TALK to Tom Gere because he wanted to post a letter to Meeds for Jefferson Davis before the mailbag was sent downriver. Nathan had determined that the success of his mission depended on his learning more about the Dakota and the factions at work within the tribe.

Time was still of the essence. But Lee had beaten McClellan in Virginia, and the pressure was lessened. Nathan quickly discovered that he needed to know more about Little Crow and the other Dakota leaders before he revealed his message from the Confederacy to them. He was eager to visit the Rice Creek Village, where the Soldier's Lodge was centered. However, patience must balance with timing if his mission was to succeed.

And so Nathan decided to live in the agency and work as a trader. He was able to use a vacant cabin down the trail from the other traders. There he set up a store. For a few days he slept in the agency boarding house. The house was filled with the snoring and assorted smells of the agency laborers, and Nathan was glad to be able finally to set up sleeping quarters in the loft of his cabin.

His inventory was limited compared to the other traders, but he did much better than he expected. Word of Nathan's intervention when Myrick tried to beat Johnny had spread among the Dakota. They hoped that just maybe this trader was somehow different. Certainly, they reasoned, he couldn't be any worse than those who were already cheating them.

Nathan planned to work among the Dakota through June. In July, he would make his move. As long as no one discovered that the crates had false bottoms hiding rifles, he was safe.

From time to time, he met Emily West. Her warm greeting and bright smile were a welcome relief to the business he was set upon. She worked with the Dakota—teaching women how to sew "white people's" clothes, helping young and old learn English, and doing some nursing. The young Confederate would talk to her as their paths crossed in the small town. He found her open and easy to converse with. He learned of her childhood in Minneapolis and the dreams that brought her to the agency. Nathan asked her to visit his trading post, but she politely declined. She simply was not comfortable being in such close proximity to Andrew Myrick's place.

Early June was hot and muggy in the river valley. An inch of rain from a thunderstorm the night before led to a steamy day when a shimmering stickiness hung on everything that moved. It was becoming the type of day when a person could feel himself sweat. In spite of the heat, Nathan made the two-mile horseback ride up the river to Little Crow's village.

There were other villages dotting the 150-mile-long reservation. Various chiefs and subchiefs had their own cluster of followers. Red Middle Voice's and Little Six's bands contained many of the discontented angry young braves. Whites, Nathan among them, often had the idea of a supreme Indian leader that all followed. That was a misconception.

The Santee Dakota, in particular, were very fractious in their leadership. Most decisions were made by consensus in council meetings. In times of crisis, councils were frequent.

Nathan had made a point to visit with Prescott, the old interpreter, and had learned much about the tribal structure. They were divided into four bands. At the Lower Sioux were the Mdewakantons and Wahpekutes. Thirty miles upriver from the agency was the Upper Agency, which was responsible for the Wahpeton and Sisseton bands.

Nathan discovered from Philander that the Dakota were a very communal people. The strong cared for the weak and old. Upon returning from a hunt, choicest cuts were first given to those too feeble, sick, or old to hunt for themselves. Kinship was also a mighty bond that tied the Dakota familes as surely as a great knot. Little Crow had many relatives among the Upper Dakota, including Little Paul.

Wabasha was ostensibly the overall leader of the tribe. But each of the other pair of bands elected a speaker, and therein lay the real authority. Lower Agency had long chosen Little Crow but had recently replaced him with a "cut hair," Traveling Hail. To the west, the Upper Dakota had elected Little Paul, who, along with Chief Akepa, led a peace faction. Other leaders had their own camps and followers.

Philander had warned Nathan about the fourth village in line from the Lower Agency, the Rice Creek Village. "Stay clear of those troublemakers, son," the old man had advised. "Especially Red Middle Voice. He's their leader. Watch out for another fella a lot of whites haven't heard much about. His name is Mah-ka-tah. He's nasty, nothing but hate for whites in him and a lot of the young braves up river are starting to pay attention to him. If we ever have a war, God forbid, it'll come from those damn Rice Creekers."

Nathan also learned from Prescott that in spite of losing the speakership, Little Crow was still recognized as a war leader and a powerful influence among the Lower and Upper Dakota. For this reason, Nathan chose Little Crow's village for his first visit off the agency.

A strange mixture of dwellings greeted him as he rode into the home of Little Crow's people. A few of the Indians had permanent wood frame or brick houses built by the government. Some still lived in buffalo hide tepees. There were even bark lodges from the old days. Most, however, lived in tepees made of government-issue canvas.

As he slowly rode into the camp, he saw women preparing meals by cook fires. Others were working in gardens or sewing clothing. Someone had killed a deer, rare this summer, and its hide was being stretched and excess flesh scraped off. A woman and her young daughter labored with sharp fleshing tools.

The loud laughter of children at play caused Nathan to gaze at an open area where young, lightly clad boys were playing a hoop and pole game.

Here and there a Dakota brave was sleeping under the shade of a tree or tepee. A few were helping in the gardens. The Santee were suffering from a role crisis. Women had always been responsible for domestic chores. Most everything in the village affecting day-to-day life was up to them.

Men hunted and defended the village. In times past, this was critical to the function of the tribe. Now, wars against the Chippewa, and of course the whites, were forbidden. Hunting was limited and, if the agency food was delivered promptly, it was also unnecessary. The Dakota man was caught between the hunter-warrior way of life, which was becoming obsolete, and the life of a farmer. The latter life, for generations consigned to women, was now being pushed onto the men by the agency. Many continued to resist.

A majority of the Dakota dressed as Nathan expected. They wore their hair long and used breechclouts, leggings, and blankets. Some, however, adopting white ways, had cut their hair and wore pants, coats, and leather boots. A few others, caught in a culture warp, wore elements of both cultures. It was into this outwardly confused amalgam that Nathan Thomas rode.

Little Crow lived in a story-and-a-half brick house with his four wives. Nathan reined in his horse and pack mule and dismounted. He would pay the Dakota chief the courtesy of announcing his presence.

As Nathan tied the animals to a rail, the door of the house opened, and a slender Indian man walked out. Older, this man's face was deeply lined. He was dressed in soft-leather trousers and a long-sleeved, dirty, white, cotton shirt. His black hair, shoulder length, was streaked with gray. Nathan knew it was Little Crow.

Curious children and some adults had followed him as he rode into the village. Now they gathered around as Nathan met the Dakota chief.

"I'm Nathan Cates, new trader at the agency. I have come to pay my respects to the great Dakota leader Little Crow and to trade."

"I am Little Crow. Welcome. Come to my house. I wish to speak with you." His English was quite good and, despite his nearly sixty years, he moved easily and gracefully. He led the way into his home.

It was a simple house, solid brick. Due to help from the government, it was a little larger and better furnished than those of most white people in the West.

Somewhat expansively, Little Crow said, "Do you like my house? The agency has promised to build me a bigger and better one."

Nathan smiled. "It is a fine dwelling."

The rooms inside were simply furnished with the essentials. A cook-stove stood in a small kitchen. The largest room was a combination dining room-living room. It had a large rectangular oak table and straight back chairs.

The Indian sat on a chair at the end of the table and gestured for Nathan to sit at the first chair to his right. "I have heard of you, One Arm. You came to the aid of one of our children and are trading fairly."

Indians were named because of deeds done, natural occurrences at birth, or physical features. Knowing that, Nathan knew that a name like One Arm was inevitable.

Nathan looked down at his stump. "I was hurt in battle, a bullet passed through both arms."

Little Crow stretched out his limbs and exposed two withered wrists. "Was your arm lost fighting the rebels?"

Natha nodded. "It happened at the Battle of Shiloh." Not wanting to dwell upon his injury, Nathan quickly continued. "I helped the child because he was being mistreated. May I visit with your people and trade today?"

"Yes. But you know most cannot pay you. Our annuity money is not here, yet. But you traders," the chief spat on his wooden floor, "will get it all at the pay tables."

"They get all of it?" Nathan asked.

"Three times the Santee Dakota have signed treaties with the white man. Each time, nearly all the money we were to get was turned over to traders for claims against us. Now that they have most of our land and need not take more in treaty, the traders let us buy on credit. When the annuity comes, they show up at the pay tables and take the money. We get food and things for our houses and farming. No money. We do not want you traders at the table this time."

"I cannot change what other men do. Your debt to me is slight. I will not be at the pay table. But I know that the other traders are becoming concerned. They think your debt is becoming too large. They are talking of stopping your credit until the annuity comes."

Little Crow spat on the floor more vehemently, splatting a big fly that was crawling across a sun patch on the floor. "Let them. We will take what is ours. Why is the annuity not here? It is ours. Some of our chiefs fear that the money was spent fighting the South or that the gold is gone, and we will be paid in worthless paper. The traders would not accept that either."

"I know nothing of that," Nathan replied. "I am just here to trade."

"Why should we believe that you are different from Myrick and the others?"

"You know that I helped Johnny. All I can do is ask for your trust unless I am proven unworthy."

Little Crow rose to his feet. "We will watch you, One Arm. Trade here today if you want. The White Collar and the teacher are here as well."

"I have one more question, Little Crow. I hear of something called a Soldier's Lodge. What do you know of it?"

The Indian leader stared intently at Nathan. "It's best you know little about them. They are hot heads, fools who stand against their chiefs because they don't understand the way that things are. It makes them dangerous, not just to whites, but to other Dakota, as well. Stay clear of Rice Creek, One Arm."

An ironic smile played across Nathan's lips. Twice he had been warned about Rice Creek, once by a white man, and now by an Indian. But he knew that his mission depended on a rendezvous there in the near future.

Nathan stood and walked toward the door. Pausing, he said to the Dakota, "Thank you, Little Crow. I heard your words, and I will help your people if I can. Here is a gift." He handed a carved reddish stone pipe to his host. The Indian nodded his thanks, and Nathan walked into the steamy bright sunlight of a Minnesota summer.

He hadn't brought much with him; some cloth, beads, and small metal tools. The Dakota crowded around him. He marked down their names and what they were purchasing in a little book because they expected him to. Nathan knew he would never collect.

An Indian woman, still young and smooth-faced, handed him a leather shirt. Beaded designs were sewn on it in the shape of stars. "Ogle . . . shirt," she said. "Take it. I am Traveling Star's . . . Johnny's mother. Thank you."

Nathan called his thanks to her as she turned and walked swiftly away.

"Looks like you have a friend in camp." It was Reverend Hinman. The young pastor had abandoned his black coat, and his white shirt was stained with sweat.

Emily stood beside him. She smiled at the new trader. "Good morning, Mr.Cates. Looks like trading has gone well." She looked at the mule that now held empty packs on its back.

"Things are going fine. What brings you and the pastor here today?"

"Today we are teaching English. The more they learn now, the easier it will be for them to learn in the fall," Hinman responded.

A small Indian girl was standing between them. Emily looked down at her. "This is Wacapi Mani Wi, the Dakota call her Star Walks."

"Her name in school will be Susan," the pastor added.

"It's too bad," Emily mused. "Wacapi Mani Wi is such a pretty name."

Nathan reached into his pocket and removed a small piece of rock candy. "Here, Wacapi Mani Wi," he said and placed it in the girl's small hand. She smiled and ran off into a canvas-covered tepee.

Hinman excused himself to talk to an old Indian man standing nearby holding a Bible. Soon he was pointing at words and trying to explain them to the elder. Emily looked up at Nathan. Her long blonde hair was damp above her forehead and streaked from exposure to the sun. Small spots of perspiration marked her pale yellow dress.

"Word here is that you've made a good impression among the Dakota."

"I've not been here long, Emily, but in that time, I've at least learned this. A decent living could be made trading fairly with these people. It isn't necessary to cheat them."

"Are the others so bad, Nathan?"

"Some more so than others. Myrick is the worst. He leads the other traders. I'm sure you've heard the rumors that his clerk, Lynd, is the father of many of the half-breeds."

Emily blushed. "Yes, I've heard."

"Now they threaten to cut off trade if the annuity doesn't come soon, or if they are barred from the trading tables."

"Can't you help, Nathan?"

"Unfortunately, my inventory is far too limited. I was just sent by Meeds' Mercantile for the summer. I'm not sure he plans to send much more."

"Major Galbraith will help them."

All Indian agents had the honorary title of major, Nathan knew. "I hope so, Emily, but from what I've heard he's first and last a bureaucrat. He knows where his salary comes from. It's people like Pastor Hinman and your Bishop Whipple that can get the ear of the politicians."

"You talk like you could run for office someday." A small smile hinted at the corners of Emily's mouth as she spoke.

"I was a soldier, not a politician. Were it not for the ball that smashed my arm, I'd still be fighting. After the war's over, my future will take care of itself. One thing, I'll not work as a merchant or trader past this summer."

Soon Reverend Hinman finished his lesson, and the three rode the short trip back to the agency together. Since the day was still hot, he was grateful the ride wasn't any longer. He led the way along the dusty trail, occasionally smiling to himself as he listened to the small talk between Emily and Nathan as they rode side by side.

Just maybe, he thought, *my services might be required in this budding relationship.*

ജ 9 ൫

J UNE STRETCHED INTO JULY. Emily continued to work with the Hinmans in her various tasks. Tom Gere drilled his men at Fort Ridgely and listened to the cannons boom. Nathan traded with the Dakota and came to sympathize more with their lot.

Late on a rainy early July night, Nathan was asked to a meeting of the traders at Myrick's store. He'd had little to do with the other traders since his arrival. He was tolerated, but his run-in with Andrew Myrick had tainted his relationship with all of them. Myrick had not spoken with Nathan since that first day. Now he was asked to meet with them out of necessity and a desire for solidarity.

When Nathan entered, the five traders, William Forbes, Francois LaBathe, Louis Robert, and the Myrick brothers, Nate and Andrew, were already seated around a large round oak table. The clerk, James Lynd, was leaning on the counter. In the center of the table burned a kerosene lamp. It left the men in shadows and cast quivering yellowish reflections on the log walls.

"Come on in, Cates," Forbes called to Nathan. Andrew Myrick somberly looked up and glared.

"I guess this here little get together was my idea." Forbes continued, "We all need to reach some conclusions. We know that our red friends aren't

87

doing so well. Last year's crop wasn't good, and there aren't many of 'em farming anyway. For whatever reason the annuity money is late. Galbraith won't give 'em food 'til the money gets here. We've stretched our credit to them beyond what we can collect, and they want us kept from the pay table."

"That summed it up real nice, Billy," Robert concurred. "Now what do we do about it?"

"That's why you were asked here." LaBathe looked to Nathan, who was still standing in the background. "We've all got to be together on this."

"Cut their credit now," Myrick growled. "I'm not running a charitable service for them. I ain't gonna lose a cent of my own money on them."

Lynd, the former politician, spoke up. "Send a delegation to the fort. You should all go. Ask Marsh to make the Sioux pay."

"Let's do it!" Myrick snapped. "You with us, Cates? We go tomorrow."

Nathan bit his tongue before replying. He wanted nothing to do with these men. He wanted to point out that it was hard to lose money when the traders' books were altered to fit their needs. He wanted to lash out at Lynd for abusing Dakota women and at the Myricks for their pettiness and insults. But such would not aid his greater cause. If war came to such as these, it made his task easier. He merely nodded and said, "I'll go to the fort with you, and I'll do what has to be done to see that all get what they deserve."

"I hope that means you're with us?" Robert asked.

Nathan just looked at the men and made a noncommittal nod of his head.

"I don't trust him, Andrew," Nate Myrick spoke for the first time. "He's a dirty Indian-lovin' Son of Satan."

Nathan stared levelly at the younger Myrick. The room was deathly quiet. Only the steady plop, plop of heavy raindrops on the cedar roof dispelled the silence. He wanted to take his good hand and wrench Nate by the neck from his chair. Instead he smiled and said, "Don't worry about me, gentlemen. I said I'd go with you to Ridgely."

Then he walked into the rain.

❧ 10 ☙

HE PARADE GROUND AT FORT RIDGELY was no longer green and lush. The tramping of drilling feet had left many spots bare and brown. Now it was muddy from the rain. Each day was punctuated by the booming thunder of Sergeant Jones' cannons as the gun crews fired.

Occasionally Culver or Gere, or both, would make a show by marching around the reservation. Once Culver led the company to the Upper Agency to meet with "Major" Galbraith. On July 3rd, Captain Marsh called an officers' meeting in the Headquarters Building.

Gere and Culver buttoned up their blue blouses as they ambled up the steps to Marsh's office. As much as Gere had tried to stick to strict regulations in his decorum and dress, it had been easy to succumb to lapses. The hot sun had caused him to unbutton his uniform top. However, both officers understood that a summons to their commander's office required closer adherence to military code.

Marsh wasn't a stickler on discipline, and he understood the need for comfort while working in the hot sun. But he expected certain protocols when his officers were called. Being in uniform, properly dressed, was one of them.

"Gentlemen," Marsh addressed his two young officers, "you've been to the reservation as have I. What is your consensus of the feelings out there?"

"Well, sir," said Culver, "the Sioux are gettin' hungry. I wish the money would get here. That'd solve a lot."

"The Sioux are delaying their buffalo hunt to the west," Gere added. "They won't go until they get the money thing settled. By the time it comes, it might be too late to find any buffalo."

"And people, our people, are getting scared," Marsh sighed. "There's tension out there, and they can feel it. Although most still don't believe anything bad can happen. When the annuity comes, it's going to be more than we can handle. Food must be distributed, and we've got to oversee the payment to the traders. Therefore, I've sent for Company C from Fort Ripley. They'll be here any day now."

"Isn't that Tim Sheehan's company?" Culver asked.

"Yes, it is, Lieutenant. He's a good officer. We can use him if things get dicey. Another thing—seems we're getting some visitors this afternoon. The traders from the Lower Agency are coming. Should be interesting. I'll have you in here when we meet."

As they left Marsh, Culver asked Gere, "Well, what do you suppose the traders want?"

"I wouldn't know, but I bet they aren't coming to celebrate the Fourth of July with us."

"That's tomorrow, anyway," Culver answered, "I hear Jones has some big plans for his guns. Marsh even invited some people from the agency for the performance."

"What's this Sheehan like?"

"'Bout twenty-five, twenty-six, son of a farmer. He tried to farm himself, but it didn't set well with him. Then the army bug bit him bad. Sheehan's a little older than us. Tough as nails. Type of man you'd want coverin' your backside in a fight."

"Let's hope we won't need any backsides covered, Norm."

"Frankly, Tom, I'm itchin' for a little action. But it's rebs I wanna fight, not Indians. First chance I'm gone. I hear Major Galbraith's tryin' to organize some half-breeds in Renville County to go south. I hope to go with 'em."

"I guess that's why we all joined up, Norm. Do you think half-breeds can be trusted to fight?"

"They'll fight just fine, Tom. 'Slong as it's white rebels they're fightin' and not Indians, I feel just fine about them. I think some of them feel like they're gettin' ta kill whites on a free pass."

Both officers left for their morning inspections, looking forward to meeting the traders in the afternoon because of the change in routine that their arrival promised. Boredom was the greatest enemy of the army, particularly on the frontier. For every moment of danger and intense excitement, there were endless hours of drudgery. For this they were paid barely thirteen dollars a month.

Desertions were a big problem as a result, but not in Minnesota in 1862. The young men had enlisted, some even falsifying their ages to qualify, because they wanted to fight in the big war to save the Union. They were guarding the frontier while they waited for their chance.

Shortly after noon mess, the traders from the Lower Agency arrived: the Myricks, Forbes, Robert, LaBathe, and Nathan Cates. The five traders, trying to look official, were dressed in cheap plaid suits. Nathan wore a light cotton shirt and gray muslin pants. They were ushered into Marsh's office with Culver and Gere. After introductions and handshaking, Marsh walked behind his desk in his small office and sat down while everyone else remained standing. It was a subtle reminder of who was in charge of the situation.

"What may I do for you, gentlemen?" the captain inquired.

Forbes cleared his throat and somewhat nervously began. He was a small man, and his voice was a little high pitched. But he was even tempered and made his points well. For that reason, Forbes had been selected their spokesman.

"Captain, you know the trouble we're having. We've extended credit to the reds beyond our limits. Now they want to cut us out of the pay table. That's our only sure way of getting our money."

"And how does the Fifth Minnesota Infantry fit into that picture?" Marsh asked.

"We'd like you to help us get our money . . . from the Sioux." Forbes replied.

Marsh leaned back in his chair and clasped his hands behind his head. "I'm sorry, sirs, but the United States Army is not in the collection business. You'll have to find another way."

"You mean you won't help us!" Andrew Myrick exclaimed.

"I mean it's not our place to do what you ask." Marsh rose to his feet.

"Why, you worthless . . ." Myrick bristled, his face flushed scarlet.

"Now, Andrew," Robert soothed, "I'm sure there are other ways the army can help us. Let's not antagonize anyone here."

"We will protect your lives and your property, but," Marsh repeated, "we will not act as your collection agents."

"Let's get out of here," Myrick snorted, and the others followed him out of the office.

Nathan stopped in the doorway and shook Tom Gere's hand. Turning toward Marsh, he said, "I apologize for my colleagues. The dollar sign is dancing before their eyes. They fear their fortune this year might be less than last."

"I understand them, Mr.? I'm sorry, I've forgotten your name."

"Cates, Captain," Gere answered, "He's Nathan Cates. I met him on the *Franklin Steele* and at the agency."

"Mr. Cates, I've invited some from the agency for a visit to celebrate the Fourth tomorrow. Come if you wish. See Pastor Hinman about it. Oh, and leave your trader friends behind."

"No problem, Captain. I might just take you up on your offer. Now I better find my 'friends' before they head up the river without me."

The Confederate officer in the Union fort walked from Marsh's office and hurried to join the departing traders. Tomorrow he would return.

↪ 11 ↩

A T THE LOWER AGENCY THE NEXT MORNING, the residents of the little village gathered for a ceremonial flag raising. They stood on the green grass in the square across from the church as the American flag slowly ascended the flagpole. Musket and rifle shots cracked in the air after "Old Glory" reached the top of the mast.

Major Galbraith mounted a platform in Council Square and made a brief patriotic speech to an assemblage that included a smattering of curious Dakota. A black beaver top hat that hid his bald pate topped his gangly form. Galbraith spoke of the war in the East and about the men he was recruiting to send into the fray. He ended by urging whites and the Dakota to work together for a better life.

Nathan stood near Emily. She, the Hinmans, Agent Galbraith, A. H. Wagner, Philander Prescott, and Alma Robertson, along with Nathan, would board a paddle-wheeler headed downriver shortly after noon. They were fortunate that another boat would be headed upriver the morning of the fifth, so they would spend the night. They could have traveled the twelve miles by wagon, but the timeliness of the steamboats made it unnecessary.

The little group from the agency stood together on the deck of the boat and peered over the railing as they chugged by the tree-lined riverbank.

The river level had gone down since spring, but near the center it was still over most men's heads, with a strong, tricky current. The men wore dark suits and white shirts, but most would soon remove their coats as the day heated up. Nathan, wearing an off-white cotton muslin shirt and dark wool pants, also had a light, soft leather jacket that he had traded for in Little Crow's village.

For the women the special day gave them an occasion to wear their best dresses. All wore colorful cotton day dresses over the usual assortment of pantaloons, camisoles, and hoops that custom required of them.

It was a bright, sunny day, the kind ideal for picnics and holiday celebrations.

"Well, Mr. Wagner, how do the crops look?" Philander Prescott asked the superintendent of Farming.

"Better than last year, Philander, but we'll need timely rain. By the way, White Dog is not employed to work with the Sioux farmers anymore. They hope that Ta-opi, Wounded Man, will do a better job. There's politics involved. Wounded Man apparently has some friends in the right places."

"The way I see it, White Dog is about out of friends. He hangs around Myrick more than his own kind."

"To me, Philander, it looks like those two are one of a kind. I wouldn't trust either of them. In a larger sense, I wish the annuity would arrive. If the harvest isn't going to be as good as we hoped, they'll need money. Food is running short, and there's not much game on the reservation."

"I'm sure it'll be here soon," Galbraith interjected, "but we can't give the food until the money comes. It sets a bad precedent."

"Sometimes doing what's right is more important than precedent." Nathan couldn't resist the comment.

"You're new to Minnesota, Mr. Cates. The Indians in Indiana were tamed long before you were born. I have the responsibility to administer over seven thousand Sioux, and I must show no weakness to them."

"Mr. Galbraith," Nathan slowly shook his head, "we just don't agree on what's right, and I don't expect we ever will."

The men continued their conversation while Nathan and Emily walked along the rail away from the group.

"Nathan, you should watch how you talk to Major Galbraith. He's got a lot of power out here and friends in St. Paul. He could have you removed as a trader."

"He's a government company man, Emily. He does what he thinks best, but he lacks imagination. People like him can be dangerous, not always intentionally, but dangerous nevertheless. And don't worry, Emily, he can't hurt me."

"Do you miss the war, Nathan?"

He looked down into her eyes and, as if thinking aloud, said, "It's what I was trained to do. The military is part of my family. Yes, I guess I miss it."

"I hope you don't find it here."

The irony of her comment struck him. "I promise you this. If it does, I won't let it harm you."

Emily was taken somewhat aback by his sudden solemnity, but warmed by his promise. The twelve miles to Fort Ridgely passed quickly. Through much of it, Emily thought about the handsome new trader. There were many questions she wanted to ask him about his life and his plans. In many ways, he was a man of mystery, and she yearned to know more about him. But he offered little, and she thought it unseemly to pry. Soon the steamboat docked, and the little group from the agency was being transported by wagon to the fort.

Captain Marsh was a gracious host. The sun was high in the sky swept with thin clouds when they rolled into Fort Ridgely. A long table filled with a bounty of food awaited them in the parade ground. The post bakery had worked overtime, and the aroma of fresh bread lured the hungry visitors. Blackberries and raspberries had been gathered, and two of the few hogs remaining at the fort were now the roasted centerpieces of the table.

At Marsh's order, Charlie Culver beat a drum roll, and the company assembled. The shabby blue suits they wore had been cleaned and mended as well as possible. The brass buttons were polished and their black boots rubbed free of dust and dirt.

As they stood at parade rest, McGrew whispered out of the side of his mouth to John Jones, "The boy-os look real pretty today, don't they? Nice shiny buttons and buckles make fine targets."

"They can scuff 'em up tomorrow, Sam," Jones whispered. "They want to look nice for their audience." Captain Marsh moved into position and stood before his company.

"Men, welcome our friends from the agency. After eating, we'll reassemble for our Independence Day observance. Follow our guests on either side of the table. Enjoy the day."

Four privates—Charlie Beecher, Levi Carr, Jimmy Dunn, and Sam Stewart—did the serving as the civilians and then the soldiers filed through the line.

"Hey, Charlie," Willie Sturgis called out, "this here looks pretty good. You musta been off duty when it got fixed."

"It's too good for the likes of you. I got salt pork set aside for you."

More good-natured joshing followed as the men eagerly dug into the feast. It was a welcome respite from their usual boring fare of coffee, beans, salt pork, and bread. On campaign they ate hardtack. Fresh meat was a rarity and much appreciated.

The corporals and other enlisted men sprawled on the ground in the shade of buildings. A long plank table had been arranged for everyone else. Emily, Elizabeth Hinman, and Alma Robertson from Redwood joined Eliza Muller and Martha Jones from the fort as the only women present.

The women's dresses weren't elegant by Eastern standards, but they were colorful, long and better than most seen on the frontier. For the first time since her husband's death, Alma Robertson wore a color other than black in public. Her dress wasn't fancy, but it had shiny buttons and was a pale green. Women were interspersed among the men as they sat on planks supported by wood blocks. Tom Gere sat across from Nathan and Emily. Next to him were Norm Culver and Eliza Muller.

"Well, Nathan," Tom asked, "how did the other traders react to their session with the captain?"

"They cut off credit, Tom. Things could heat up."

"Bull," Culver caught himself. "Excuse me, ladies. They know they'll get their money."

"Unless the government sends paper money," Tom replied. "That's what really has them scared. Paper doesn't pay like gold."

"Mr. Cates," Eliza paused over her plate of berries and pork, "you're a trader, yet you don't sound like one of them. Aren't you concerned about your money?"

"Nathan isn't at all like them," Emily blurted out. Several smiled at Emily's reaction.

Nathan spoke. "Mrs. Muller, maybe I am different. I'm not trying to make a killing as it was once suggested I do. If I can be fair and make a little profit for my employer, I'm happy. That's the American way, isn't it?"

"And those rebs are trying to end our way of life," Culver mumbled as he bit into a pork sandwich.

Nathan had made a habit of ignoring comments about the war and making only noncommittal replies when prompted. However, he couldn't let the lieutenant's remarks go unchallenged.

"Lieutenant, in southern Indiana my business brought me into Kentucky on occasion. The view from them is that it's the North trying to change a way of life and not them. The fact is that if Lincoln hadn't ordered troops into the South, there'd be no war. They just want to be left alone."

"Ya sound like you could be one of Jeff Davis's boys, yerself."

Nathan smiled. "I'm just passing on opinions I've heard in my travels. Would a rebel really be in Minnesota?" The group laughed at his joke.

Captain Marsh stood at the head of the table where the older members of the contingent had mostly congregated. "Ladies, officers, sergeants, agency friends, we have a brief program of drill and artillery display arranged for you. After the demonstration, you're free to roam our grounds at will.

"Our visiting ladies will be housed in one of our vacant officer's quarters tonight. The rest of you will be quartered in the main barracks. We have plenty of room there. At dusk, Sergeant Jones has cooked up a little fireworks display for us with his cannons. I hope you'll enjoy your day and have a good trip back upriver in the morning."

Another drum roll by Charlie brought the company to attention. The officers and sergeants ran the men through the manual of arms and several marching formations. Their shiny brass buttons glinted in the afternoon sun.

They were eager to show off what they had learned. The young soldiers were like little boys showing off new Christmas presents. Most of them were less than a year from farms, homes, and parents. Captain Marsh and the agency visitors watched from a makeshift wooden viewing stand.

Philander Prescott leaned close to Alma Robertson. "Ain't they pretty, Alma? Nice soldier suits and scrubbed faces."

"They're good at playing soldier, Philander. If need be, let's hope they look just as good in practice."

"Could you lead them?" Emily asked Nathan.

"They're just boys, but they have spirit. Who's to say what will happen if bullets start flying, though."

Marsh strode into the ranks. Sergeant McGrew bellowed, "Present arms!" Eighty men snapped their Springfield rifles parallel before them, barrels skyward, all eyes front on the middle of the barrel. The captain paced between the files of soldiers, occasionally taking a rifle from a soldier and examining it.

Most of the company then marched in formation on two sides of the parade ground. Two gun crews of five men each, under the direction of Sergeant Jones, wheeled out two cannons.

Sergeant Jones faced the viewing stand and addressed the visitors in a loud voice. "Ladies and gentlemen, we are going to demonstrate our proficiency in firing the six- and twelve-pound cannons. Our gun crews are from five to six men; the manual calls for nine. However, the small size of our garrison led to a corresponding reduction in our crew.

"There are several positions involved in the firing of a cannon. Each of our men knows all the positions and maneuvers. Therefore, it is possible for us to operate with as few as two or three on a crew.

"Each of the gun positions is numbered as follows, according to specific duties; number one stands to the right of the gun. He will tamp the powder and shot down the barrel. Number two, at left front, will place the round of shot down the barrel. Number three places a needle-like object into a small hole at the rear of the cannon and pricks the woolen bag that contains the powder that is attached to the shot. Number four places a brass primer into the hole and, with a heavy string, pulls a friction pin from the primer. Hence the order 'Prick and Prime.' The resulting spark ignites the powder and fires the shot.

"Number five then delivers another round of shot from the rear to number two, while number one swabs out the barrel with water to kill any embers that might ignite the next round prematurely."

Jones' artillery lesson impressed Nathan. He whispered to Emily, "He should teach at some military academy. Not only can he shoot, he can explain it to others."

Jones' lesson continued. "The number on a cannon indicates the weight of solid shot it can fire. A twelve-pound Napoleon can fire twelve pounds of shot. A six fires six pounds of shot. Canister or explosive shot fires shrapnel that spreads over a wide area. It takes thirty to forty seconds to load and fire each shot.

"A solid shot ball, fired correctly at a massed enemy, will go at a low trajectory and richocet off the ground into them. It can take out forty to fifty men. A hollow ball is called a 'shell' or 'explosive shot.' Gunpowder is inserted through the fuse hole into the shell. A fuse is inserted into the hole.

"When the shell is fired from a cannon, the blast will ignite the fuse. The shell will explode and burst into pieces. The length of the fuse obviously determines when the shell goes off.

"Please note that, for ease of movement, two large wheels support each weapon," Jones continued. "They will roll back with the concussion of the shot. Anchoring them would break the caisson.

"Sergeant Bishop's crew will demonstrate the firing of a twelve-pound Napoleon. It has a range of 1,600 yards and can fire solid or explosive shot. Large wooden targets have been set up to the northwest between the corners of the commissary and barracks."

At Bishop's command, the Napoleon roared. Red flame and black smoke streamed from the front of the cannon as the shot smashed a target into splinters. The company roared "Huzzah, huzzah," and the viewing stand occupants joined in the applause.

"Sergeant McGrew, the six-pounder, if you please!" shouted Jones.

The crew rolled their piece into position and hurled a three-and-a-half-inch ball 1,500 yards. Another target was obliterated. With surprising accuracy, considering the greenness of the crews, the soldiers of Fort Ridgely demonstrated their skill with solid, explosive, and canister shot several more times.

An afternoon of games followed. A new sport called baseball was becoming popular. The soldiers laid out a playing field in the middle of the parade ground. They had to dodge around a couple of cannons, but that didn't seem to bother anyone.

The troopers used sticks and hit a cowhide ball before running bases. Willie Sturgis took three mighty swings at the offerings of little Oscar Wall. He connected with nothing but air and grumbled to Billy Sutherland, "This here sport'll never catch on. Who ever heard of hittin' a ball with a little stick. Now runnin' and jumpin', those are real sports."

"If'n ya hit the ball, Willie, then you could run and jump," Levi Carr teased Sturgis.

The men, soldiers and agency alike, gathered around the ball diamond. Nathan, for the first time in months, let his guard down and relaxed. From the viewing stand where she sat with the ladies, Emily noticed how natural a smile looked on Nathan's usually serious face.

Eliza Muller noticed her gaze and whispered, "He seems to be a fine man, Emily."

The young teacher blushed. "Does it show so awfully much?" she asked.

"Only to trained eyes," Eliza laughed.

"He's so serious and in some ways mysterious. Yet I know that he's the kind of man people can count on."

"You mean someone *you* could count on, don't you, Emily?"

"Yes, Mrs. Muller," she lowered her eyes, "someone *I* could count on."

"Give it time, Emily. I'm sure he's not blind to your feelings."

"Martha!" Eliza changed the subject when she looked at Martha Jones. "You're flushed and overheating, and you have a baby due next month. Let's get you into the shade."

With that the other four women, doting over Martha Jones, moved to the relative coolness of shade next to the stone walls of the commissary.

In late afternoon, they dined on cold pork, bread, and coffee.

"I, for one, am impressed with the garrison," Wagner said to the group of civilians around him.

"They sure can shoot them big guns," Philander responded.

"It might have been wise to have invited the Sioux here today," Galbraith said, adding, "They need to be impressed by the cannon."

"If they were impressed by the cross, we wouldn't need to fire cannons." Pastor Hinman, quiet much of the day, offered his opinion.

Philander smiled and said, "Keep workin' at it, Parson. You'll get 'em all converted someday."

"The fact is," Nathan said, and the group looked to him, "you wouldn't want Indians here today no matter how many cannon you have to fire. This garrison's undermanned. There are no walls and ravines on three sides. God help anyone in this place if they face a massed assault."

"Oh, I wouldn't be such an alarmist, Nathan," the pastor replied. "I'm confident things will work out peacefully."

"Remember, you're a trader now," Superintendent Wagner chided Nathan, "you're thinking like a soldier."

"I was a soldier first, sir, and I firmly believe that these people should be alarmed."

As the shadows of late afternoon lengthened toward dusk, conversations ranged from the Civil War to Indians to baseball to personal relationships. Little Charlie, cap off, tousled red hair showing above his freckles, beat a slow cadence on his drums. Johnny Taylor began to play the fiddle and Allan Smith started to sing.

Other soldiers joined in. Thousands of songs were written during the Civil War. They sang the favorites of the day: "John Brown's Body," "The

Battle Hymn of the Republic," "Lincoln and Liberty Too," and others. For the last, as the sun disappeared slowly in the west, they sang their favorite, a melancholy tune called "Lorena."

It seemed ironic that as the last strains of the tender love song faded into the twilight, all six of the post's guns crashed simultaneously. The flash of powder and smoke lit up the newly darkened sky, and the explosives burst fire and flame when they smashed into the earth. As a finale, a keg of gunpowder from the magazine was set off hurling orange and red streamers etching into the sky.

Once again cries of "Huzzah, huzzah," and applause echoed into the night. Then, just as incongruously as it had ended, the melody of "Lorena" softly began again. Soon all was quiet. The soldiers were ordered to their quarters for the night, and most from the agency also retired.

Sturgis and Sutherland had built a bonfire behind the barracks, and the dry timber had produced a crackling, roaring fire. Now occasional flames danced from dying embers as Nathan, Emily, Tom Gere, and Norm Culver spoke in low tones and occasionally poked with a stick into the fire.

"My compliments to your Captain Marsh, lieutenants, it was a nice day." Nathan placed a small log onto the fire as he spoke.

Culver looked up. "The Fourth needs to be remembered. Lots of fine men died freein' this country and now lots of 'em are dyin' makin' sure it stays a country."

"And we're here making sure Indians don't try to take it back," Gere added.

"It really eats you two that you're here and not fighting in the East, doesn't it?" Nathan said.

"A soldier should be where the action is." Culver looked into the fire as he spoke.

Softly Emily began to hum the strains of "Lorena."

Tom Gere looked at her and smiled softly, "Pretty, isn't it. Every time I hear that song, it takes days to get it out of my head."

Nathan looked pensive, then said slowly, "I hear that some southern regiments have forbidden their men to sing that song."

"For heaven's sakes why, Nathan?" Emily asked.

"Because they get so homesick after hearing it that they want to go home to their mothers, wives, or sweethearts. They desert."

"So much for the 'Cause.'" Culver's sarcastic comment seemed out of place.

"There are many causes to be fought for, Norm. Even in the South, I'm told, the 'Cause' means different things to different people."

"You seem to know an awful lot about the South," Tom Gere stated it as a fact, not a question.

"I'm from just north of the Indiana-Kentucky border, and like I said, I've traveled the South."

"Doing what?" Tom asked.

"Business, just business, until the war."

"Well, business around here starts about five o' clock in the morning," Norm stifled a yawn. "Lieutenant Gere, it's time for us to toddle off to our quarters. Good night, ma'am, good night, Nathan." Tom gave a sleepy salute and followed Culver.

Emily and Nathan sat next to each other staring into the embers of the fire. A log fell and kicked up sparks that floated into the black night. The young man from Virginia was lost in thought and confusion. The worst possible thing had happened. He liked the people against whom he had been sent to incite war.

He knew he must see Little Crow soon and present himself as a Confederate officer. But the plan was no longer as clear as it had been in Richmond. The enemy now had a face, a past, and a future.

He wrestled with the specifics of the order, an order never written down. One thing was certain. The war must be against the military only. Gere, Culver, and the others were at least soldiers. They were trained and prepared for war. God help them, they wanted to fight. From his military history at VMI, he knew that soldiers suffered few casualties in war against Indians. Nathan rationalized that for Tom and Norm the risk was low.

Perhaps the main goals, tying up Union troops and creating confusion and diversion, could be obtained without great loss of life, especially if the guns in Meeds' crates were not delivered. There was nothing in Davis's order to him about guns. Just maybe . . .

"Nathan, Nathan," Emily's voice shook him out of the near trance into which his thoughts had taken him while staring into the fire.

"Nathan, you seemed so distant, I didn't want to bother you. Are you all right?"

He looked at her with relief on his face. "I'm fine as long as you're safe."

"What do you mean, Nathan? I'm here with you. Of course I'm safe."

"Emily, there are things about me that you don't know. Maybe even things you wouldn't like. Understand this," he turned to look into her eyes, his somber face tinted red by the glowing coals of the fire, "I mean to do what is right, and I'll never let you be hurt."

"I don't understand, Nathan. What . . . ?"

His strong right arm brought her closer to him, and he gently kissed her full lips. She responded by wrapping both arms around him and holding him close. They held each other silently for a long moment as dying embers turned to ash.

❦ 12 ❧

JT WAS THE FOURTH OF JULY in the village of the Mdewakanton Dakota as well. There were no speeches, no picnics, and no fireworks. However, there was a gathering. As the agency personnel were plying down the river to Fort Ridgely, the chiefs and sub-chiefs of the Lower Sioux rode or walked into the village of Little Crow.

They all lived in villages within twenty miles of the Redwood Agency, strung out to the northwest along the Minnesota River. Little Crow's community was the closest to the agency, just a few miles upriver.

Political turmoil roiled among them. There was a deep division between what the whites referred to as the Indian party and the white man's party, the Santee who held to the past and those who were adopting white culture. The influence of the Soldier's Lodge, led by Mah-ka-tah of the young men, was growing. The lodge would make war, not just on whites but also on those Santee who stood with them. They believed that they stood beyond the authority of their chiefs.

The factions gathered in a circle on the green grass, shaded by a big old cottonwood tree. A soft breeze rustled the leaves as the sun beat down. The Santee clothing reflected the divisions they faced. Some of the leaders dressed in traditional Indian dress, wearing skins and breechclouts. Others wore the shirts and pants common to the white agency personnel. Still others, perhaps symbolic of inner turmoil, wore clothing of both cultures. Little Crow, with a black frock coat and beaded leather pants, fell into the latter category.

First they passed a ceremonial pipe and offered the smoke of the tobacco to the spirit that watched over his Indian children. On the fringes of the circle, other Santee stood or sat as they watched and listened. Among them were younger braves like Mah-ka-tah of Red Middle Voices's band. Next to him was White Dog.

Wabasha, their leader, looked around the circle. Little Shakopee was there. He was named for his father, now dead. The older Shakopee had been a great man and wise in his dealings with the whites. His son was not a match, but now that his father was dead, he had changed his name; most called him Little Six.

Cut Nose, who hated the whites, was there, swatting flies with an old buffalo tail. Red Middle Voice, chief of the Rice Creek Village and thus a leader of many disgruntled young men, sat next to Mankato. Strong, solid Mankato. Wabasha hoped that Red Middle Voice could learn something from him.

The old chief, Wabasha, was tired. Lines seamed his weathered face. His white hair was in need of washing. His profile looked like it had been chiseled from worn granite. Wacouta stretched his long legs in front of him. The tall one would speak for peace; he always did. Wamditanka, the Big Eagle, was there. Wabasha knew he was a man of reason.

Traveling Hail, the new speaker, a farmer, smiled broadly and greeted those who had recently elected him despite his friendly leanings to the whites in the agency. White Dog, skinny, his cut hair hanging shaggy over his ears, wore ragged woolen pants and a grimy leather shirt. He grinned stupidly, belying his cunning nature. No one was sure of his allegiance from one day to the next.

Chaska sat with them. He was known to have many white friends at the Yellow Medicine Agency. A farmer, he didn't want to fight the whites, but he still clung to some of the old ways.

And, there was Little Crow, another Santee who bore the name of his father.

Early in his life he had been a wastrel and disappointment to his family. He had signed the treaties that had surrendered almost all Dakota land to the whites. For this many distrusted him. But no one questioned his bravery or ability to lead the young men to war.

Little Crow had fought the Ojibway and within the Mdewakanton Santee had fought his own brother in a civil war for leadership. It was then that a bullet had smashed his wrists. He had won, and his brother was killed. He then told the Santee warriors they could kill him or follow him. They had followed.

Leadership changed Little Crow. He gave up whiskey and womanizing, married, and became a respected leader. White and red men alike admired Little Crow as an eloquent speaker and a shrewd politician. All his talents were needed as he continued the tricky course of combining the best of both white and red cultures.

The signing of the treaty at Mendota in 1851 had set Little Crow upon a road of accommodation with the whites. There were rumors that some Santee opposed to selling the land would kill the first signer of the treaty. Little Crow defiantly stepped to the signing table before any one else. He took the quill in his hand and cried to those who stood beyond the circle of chiefs, "I am not afraid that you will kill me. I believe that this treaty will be best for the Dakota."

Little Crow had tried to cling to the old ways while adopting from the whites what he thought was good for his people. The realist in him knew that the whites would eventually force whatever they wanted upon his people, and it would be better to try to have a say in what was happening.

Some opposed his attempts and now Traveling Hail was speaker to lead the Lower Dakota. Little Crow's heart was filled with resentment toward those who defeated him. Many of them sat in the circle.

Wabasha spoke, his low voice rumbling over the splashes and gurgles of the nearby river. "Today the whites celebrate their country's birthday. They gather together to eat and play. It is good for us to talk today."

"We must do more than talk," Little Six barked, "the people are starving."

Cut Nose was so named because his left nostril had been sliced off by the knife of another Santee, John Otherday. He implored Wabasha, "We must leave to hunt buffalo to the west. We have delayed the hunt to wait for the money. We can wait no longer, there is no game on the reservation."

"Little Paul says that the buffalo have already gone to the land of the Yankton," Mankato grumbled.

His words brought cries of anger and disgust from the circle of Santee.

"Where are Little Paul and the Wahpetons and Sissetons? Why are they not here to council with us?"

Wabasha answered, "Little Paul said they will council by themselves."

"They are women who fear the white man. They are afraid to hear voices that they do not agree with!" Red Middle Voice's words spit out in anger.

"Already bands are gathering at the Yellow Medicine Agency." Wacouta turned to Red Middle Voice as he spoke. "Little Paul says that some Yanktons have arrived, and they are not even supposed to receive annuities.

"Our people are hungry. There is little game here, the buffalo are gone, and the traders threaten to stop our credit. The agency warehouses are full of food, but Galbraith will not let us have any without the money. And the money is not here. What do we do?"

"We go to the agency and take the food. The young men are ready." Red Middle Voice was vehement. "A Soldier's Lodge has been formed. They will keep the traders from the pay table."

"Washta, good, Red Middle Voice speaks true," Little Six echoed.

"We must wait longer. Galbraith says the money will be here soon." Traveling Hail spoke for the first time.

"We have waited long enough," Cut Nose countered. "How do we know that they are not using our money in the war against the Graycoats, or that they will send us worthless paper money? Paper money will not satisfy the traders either."

"Maybe the Bluecoats will lose the war," Red Middle Voice offered hopefully.

Big Eagle slowly looked around the circle. "The whites must be desperate for men to fight the South, or they would not come so far west and take half-breeds to help them." He spoke of Agent Galbraith's plan to recruit mixed-blood agency employees for the Union Army.

"One side is as bad as the other." Little Crow spread his arms wide as he spoke. "Cut Nose, we don't know why they hold the money in Washington. But here we sit in a circle. There is power in a circle. None of you must do anything without the circle of chiefs. The white man has great power, but we should go to Galbraith and ask him to give us what is ours. We will wait until the middle of the month to ask. If there is no money, if there is no food for us, we will have to take it."

He spoke with authority, as if he were the speaker of the Lower Santee. The sun had risen higher in the sky, and the shade had disappeared. Silence, like the stillness of a night, greeted Little Crow as the perspiring chiefs considered his words.

Then Wabasha stood. "Little Crow speaks true. In two weeks we go to the Upper Agency at Yellow Medicine. We must have food."

"The young men are ready now," Mah-ka-tah shouted from behind the chiefs.

"I, too, am ready," White Dog echoed.

Little Six looked up with disgust. "What are you ready for, White Man's Dog? Does the white man's spit bucket need cleaning? You are angry only because you no longer work for the agency."

"You will see, Little Six. I will perform a great service to our people."

Cut Nose snorted, "If you can decide who your people are."

Red Middle Voice stirred uneasily and then spoke a final time. "I am troubled. We speak of money and annuities. Yes, we have been cheated. The whites have never paid what is owed us from any treaty. But brothers," his voice rose beyond the chiefs to the warriors behind, "an even greater wrong is being done. We prize our kinship; it is the basis of our bands, yet the whites try to split families apart into separate small farms.

"The Great Spirit has long cared for his people in the valley. Now the black coats tell us that it is the white god's son, not the Great Spirit who watches over the Santee. They want to take the Spirit of our fathers from us. This must not be. We must be able to live like Santee or die like the warriors we are!"

Cheers and cries of assent erupted from the young braves. Several of the chiefs fervently nodded approval of Red Middle Voice's words.

Then the demonstration subsided as Wabasha stood with the sacred pipe in his hands. "Much truth has been said here today," he cried. "There is no wrong in the words of Red Middle Voice. We know that the whites have not lived up to their words. They even refuse to move the Germans who built New Ulm on land given us by treaty. But, chiefs, we must move with caution. Little Crow has said that soon he will act to get food from the agency. We will give him the two weeks."

After smoking again, the Santee leaders stood and departed, talking in low voices with one another. White Dog and Mah-ka-tah walked away together. Little Crow went into the coolness of his house knowing that he had gained one more chance to reestablish his power in the tribe.

≈ 13 ≈

THE SPRING OF 1862 WAS A TIME of promise for the settlers on the Minnesota frontier. Solomon Foot felt that he was finally getting over the hump. He was now entering his fifth year in the Kandiyohi lakes region. Money had been scarce, the work hard. He had had to resort to trapping in the winter to get the cash he needed to support his family and his farming enterprise.

In 1860 and 1861, Foot had grown two crops of wheat from the few acres he had carved into the prairie. He had settled on the banks of a lake. Water and game were plentiful. Timber, while not scarce, was concentrated along rivers and lakeshores and in clumps here and there on the prairie.

It was into this tough prairie sod that Solomon Foot and his neighbors broke their backs and plows trying to rip scars into the earth that would eventually reap a harvest of wheat and other grains. In 1861, Foot sold one hundred bushels of wheat at thirty cents a bushel. He still depended on trapping for supplies and some groceries.

The Foot cabin was a little more substantial and larger than the typical frontier house. It was built of whole, hewed logs laid lengthwise on top of one another. Fitted grooves were cut in the logs that formed the connecting sidewalls. Soloman and his family had filled the cracks in between the logs with a mixture of clay and dried grass.

While many cabins had dirt floors, the Foots had split logs and laid the round side on the ground to form a servicable wooden surface.

The roof was of more thinly split logs covered with bark. Foot was proud of his sturdy door, complete with iron hinges. He also took pride in the fact that his windows were not covered with oiled paper or cloth, like many of his neighbors. Solomon had obtained real glass. He had also constructed an addition and had two full stories, with windows.

The cabin sat amidst the green grass of the prairie, with a stand of spreading oak trees and a greenish-blue lake only about twenty-five yards from the front door. His wife, Adaline, and their five children had every reason to look to a bright future in 1862.

The residents of Meeker, Kandiyohi, and Monongalia counties gathered at Solomon's cabin to celebrate the Fourth of July 1862. The small acres of crops were planted; herds of animals grazed peacefully on the prairie. The guns of the Civil War were thundering unheard far away to the east.

Foot had invited all those in the vicinity to celebrate their nation's birthday at his homestead. Early in the morning, they began arriving. The guests were borne by wagons, some covered but most with open beds, and pulled by oxen and horses. They came with families and loads of food and drink. Wagons came from as far as Forest City and Manannah, nearly thirty miles to the east on the Crow River.

The visitors were dressed mostly in homespun clothing of linen or wool, rough but clean. A few of the men had donned buckskin shirts and pants. Some of the Norwegian women wore long, colorful dresses or aprons from their former homeland. The children had been freshly scrubbed, like so much laundry. It was hard to tell with the little ones if their rosy-red cheeks reflected good health, or how hard their mothers had rubbed to get the dirt off.

The day brought out many of the younger and some of the older Norwegians and Swedes in the area. The Scandinavians tended to settle together and keep to themselves. Foot thought it was good to see them getting involved in the community.

By 1854, after the treaties in 1851, German and Scandinavian immigrants, looking to escape autocratic authority and worn-out land in Europe, had begun to move in large numbers onto the Minnesota frontier.

First came the Germans along the Minnesota River. Then Swedes and Norwegians settled to the north and west, reminded of the farmland and climate of their homeland, without the backdrop of mountains.

It took until 1857 before permanent homesteads were established in the Kandiyohi lakes region. Meeker County, just to the east, had settlers in 1855. Most of the immigrants to these regions were Scandinavian.

A long table, placed under the shade trees, was loaded with the bounties of frontier life. The centerpiece was a roast pig with an ear of corn in its mouth. A procession was formed and everyone marched to their places at the table to the beat of a drum.

It was amazing how quickly the pig and other victuals were devoured. Eating was serious business. There was little talk, mostly just the sounds of knives and forks clattering on plates and dozens of mouths smacking happily on good food.

Then, as the men lit up their pipes, conversation turned to events of the day. They talked about things that farmers always speak of: crops and weather. Next, talk turned to news of the great war to the south and east. The bloody battle of Shiloh had been fought that April. Although the North had won a marginal victory, both sides had suffered terrible casualties.

The pioneers of western Minnesota were concerned that the North just might lose the war, and they'd see their country divided. But then conversation turned to more immediate concerns. Almost everyone had a story to tell about recent encounters with the Dakota.

Mrs. Delaney of the Diamond Lake region, a large woman with a large voice, spoke up. "You've got to show that you're not afraid of 'em. Two big braves came to our cabin and demanded bread. Being neighborly, I gave them a little. Then they asked for flour, which I wasn't about to hand over to 'em. One of 'em grabbed my arms from behind and held me while the other scooped flour into a blanket. Well, that raised my dander some, and I twisted around and smacked that Indian in the nose; bloodied it, too. He grabbed his nose and exclaimed, 'Ugh, big squawl!'"

Mrs. Delaney laughed in spite of herself. "Then I grabbed the guns and threw them outside into a pile of wood. Those redskins ran out the door with their tails between their legs and headed for the timber."

Solomon looked down both lengths of the table and then spoke in a loud, clear voice. "You new people especially, listen to me. When the reds show up at your door, and they will, be firm. If you resist their begging and demands in a resolute way, they'll be civil and leave. But if you show the least fear, they'll take every morsel of food you have in your cabin.

"One night I was returning from the Kingston mill. My daughter met me in my yard and told me that six Indians were in the house, and they were ugly and mad because our dog had bitten one of them as they came in at the front door. The Indian raised his gun to shoot the dog, but my daughter stepped between him and the animal. She led the dog inside, where she tied him in another room. The reds then entered the house.

"When I came in, I was confronted with ugly, scowling faces. I tried to put on my most hostile expression to match theirs. I told them that they should let us know if they were coming to visit us. That the dog was the children's guard, and we would have tied him in the house.

"I asked the injured buck to show me the bite. He showed me his upper thigh where the dog's teeth marks were plainly visible. I said to him, 'I got some medicine, cure that, good medicine, cure quick.' I doped the wound quite liberally with liniment. I might add that I took a little pleasure in his reaction, which indicated that the cure might have been more painful than the injury. Then I gave them a supply of home-grown tobacco, and they left in good humor. They respect strength. Show it to them, and you'll be all right."

One of the young Norwegians called out, "How much do dey come by here?"

"Hard to say," Foot answered, "at least several times a year. They come from the Minnesota River Valley, pass through to the Crow River and northern timber to hunt deer and bear. Some autumns there might be twenty tepees in camps just south of here. Most times they mean no harm. They come to my place to trade furs, feathers, and moccasins for potatoes, turnips, pork, and flour. Treat them fair. Lots of times they have their women and children with them. Be a little more careful if they're just bucks, especially if they just had a fight with the Chippewas. Green Lake is kind of an old boundary between the two tribes. Sometimes they have run-ins there. If the Sioux have had a tough time of it, they'll be in a sour mood."

Then Foot rose to his feet. "We can talk later about the reds. Let's get on with the celebration."

The settlers formed another procession and marched over to the speaker's "platform." This was a stump with the top flattened. Mr. Gates stood upon the tree remnant and read the Declaration of Independence. Then A.C. Smith, a lawyer from Forest City, mounted the stump to speak. After some greetings, thank yous, and casual remarks, Smith warmed to his main topic.

"Let's let the words of the Declaration of Independence burn into our minds," he said. "Just as we had to fight to become free from the British, just as we are fighting now to keep our country united and free from the slaveocracy, let us be resolved not to surrender our freedom here on the frontier. We bought this land fair and square from the Sioux. Now the Indians say they were cheated. They want their land back. They even have white allies in the East who agree with them."

Smith rose to the occasion as if passionately pleading his case to a jury in a tight case. He wiped the sweat from his brow and began again. "What would they have us do? Give the land back? Civilization has advanced. The strong, the civilized always conquers the savage. It's the nature of history since the beginning of time.

"These are people barely removed from the Stone Age. Read your history. We're in the Industrial Age. Rifles have replaced bows and arrows; railroads will replace the horse. The Sioux must adapt to survive. Those who sympathize with them here in Minnesota or in the East must understand that.

"As for us, we must stand for what is now ours, and we must be prepared to fight for it if it comes to that." He stepped down from the stump to warm applause from the small crowd of neighbors.

Loretta Woodcock, the young wife of E.T. Woodcock, an early settler on Green Lake, was then helped upon the "platform" to lead the crowd in patriotic hymns. Her pretty, youthful face was framed in dark curls. In a clear, sweet voice she began with the "Battle Hymn of the Republic," newly written for the Union soldiers by Julia Ward Howe. They sang "Yankee Doodle," "Sweet Betsey from Pike," and "The Battle Cry of Freedom."

Foot stood by his wife, Adaline, and rumbled out the songs in the low, gravelly tones that passed for his singing voice. Mrs. Foot happily looked up at her husband. She was slender, of medium height, with strength that belied her physique. Her face was still pretty, although lines around her eyes betrayed the hardships of living on the edge of civilization. Deep-brown eyes complemented her long, dark hair. The sun highlighted just a few strands of gray. She was the kind of woman a man in the frontier could count on, and Solomon knew it.

Adaline, or Ady as her husband called her, smiled at Solomon. "It's great to see so many different people here today," she said. "There are some I've never met before and, even though they're our neighbors, we really don't see the Endresons much." She nodded and smiled at the broad-faced Guri Endreson, who shyly smiled back.

"Ady, the Endresons and their son-in-law, Oscar Erickson, are new and Norwegian; remember, they barely speak English. But they're good, solid people. Even old Harris Holvay from across the lake." He gestured to the slender, big-eared old gent drinking from a jug as he leaned against a tree trunk.

"Did you notice that the West Lake people are here, the Lundborgs and the Brobergs?" Solomon continued, "They came from way over on the northwest boundary of Monongalia County. More of our good Scandanavian friends."

"It's just nice to have more people move nearby, Solomon. With your hunting and trapping, it gets lonely for the children and me. I don't exactly treasure the visits from the Sioux, either. It's nice that Charley Carlson has a cabin close by. He's been a big help when you're gone." The strains of the last song were dying away as her husband squeezed Ady's hand.

Then Solomon Foot got up on the stump. "I'd like to thank all of you for coming today. I hope you had a good time. We have a fiddle player, and you're all welcome to stay and dance, talk, sing or whatever. But I'd like to finish off our little celebration with a salute to the flag. One problem, we don't have a flag. But look yonder at the tall oak tree. We've got two eagles, symbols of our country, nesting there. Let's salute them."

The men raised their guns and shot into the air in the direction of the tree. Then a rousing cheer went up all around. The eagles, startled into flight at the sound of the guns, began to soar high in the air above the big oak, screaming their defiance to all below.

A loud *ker-boom* suddenly disrupted the moment. It echoed and reverberated across the lake as a geyser of water spewed into the air. A small rowboat next to the cascading water rocked violently, and its sole passenger nearly tumbled overboard.

"What in thunder was that?" exclaimed E.T. Woodcock.

"If I'm not mistaken, Woodcock, that would be my neighbor down the lake, Harris Holvay. He likes to dip into the barley corn a little and then celebrate the Fourth of July by setting off a keg of gunpowder in the lake. Fool's gonna kill himself someday. Last summer we were having a get-together at my cabin. Harris was invited, but it was near dark, and he hadn't come by.

"Just as most folks were leaving, he comes walking up here soaking wet. Seems that after a hard afternoon of pulling the jug, he rowed over here, hit some weeds and thought he had reached shore. He stepped out of the boat into five feet of water."

"Lucky he didn't drown." Woodcock chuckled at the image Holvay's swim conjured.

"Did yoose hear my report? It vass a loud one, eh!" Harris shouted as he stumbled up the bank. The old, skinny Swede was again drenched by water. Beads of it rolled down his large red nose, washing over a single big blackhead that proudly anchored two big blue veins.

In spite of themselves, the people laughed and applauded. "Great job, Harris!" they yelled.

"Thomas Jefferson himself couldn't have expressed it better," A.C. Smith cried.

Harris smiled, a big, gap-toothed grin reaching from one big floppy ear to the other. "Now doss anaone have anating to drink. I tink I dropped my yug in da lake."

"Over here!" one of the Lundborg boys shouted as he hefted a jug high above his head. Harris's eyes lit up as he ambled unsteadily toward the proferred refreshment.

Lars Endreson smiled at his wife, "See, Guri, like I always say, a Swede is just a Norwegian with his brains knocked out."

Anders Peter Broberg, middle-aged, broad-shouldered farmer from West Lake, walked up to Solomon and extended his big hand.

"Thank you, Solomon, for having us here. There are few of us to the west. It's good to see others."

"That might be, Anders, but your own family makes a small town. How many are with you, anyway?"

"Eighteen came wit us today. My wife and four children. My brother Daniel, his wife and three children. Den we have our neighbors. Der claim is next to us. Andreas Larson Lundborg with Lena and der five children. Three of dem are grown men."

"Well, Anders, more will be coming out soon. The counties hereabout are growing, and people will be moving farther and farther to the west."

"My family thanks you. Come by if you're in our neck of the woods."

"I will, Anders. I hear the trapping's pretty good out there."

After another handshake, Broberg joined his family and the Lundborgs, who were already loaded into wagons. It was midafternoon and a journey of several hours lay ahead of them.

Harris Holvay left. He waved at the Foots and shouted, "Remember, Solomon, I'm yust up da lake. If ders anating ya need, ya yust come on by."

Within an hour or two most left the Foot homestead. They were filled with hope, patriotism, and optimism. Within a few weeks all would change. Many of the celebrants on the shores of Foot Lake would never meet each other again this side of heaven.

❧ 14 ❧

THE DAKOTA HAD LONG HAD AN INSTITUTION called the Soldier's Lodge. There were several such lodges, or societies, and they were primarily organized for hunts. However, perceived transgressions at the hands of the whites had given the lodges another, darker purpose. They would stand to right the wrongs of the white government. Specifically, they would keep traders from the pay tables and kill any man who stood against them.

The lodges stayed in the shadows of Santee life. They were mostly mentioned, if at all, in council, and their goals and actions were to be secret. They were called by various names: The Bear Dance Society, The Elk Lodge, Dog Liver Eaters Society and the Sacred Dance. Perhaps with a forboding feeling of finality, Mah-ka-tah called his simply the Soldier's Lodge.

The societies also served as vehicles of protest when it became apparent to many that the council of chiefs could not or would not act to solve problems with the agent and other government officials.

Through the lodges, the young men could defy their chiefs and councils. Indeed they threatened anyone who stood in their way. Rebel chiefs were involved with the secret society. Little Six, Cut Nose, and Red Middle Voice sympathized with the Soldier's Lodge formed at Rice Creek by

Mah-ka-tah. Some whites even considered Cut Nose to be the head of the lodge, but in the end the young men would follow Mah-ka-tah.

Mah-ka-tah and White Dog left Little Crow's village just as the meeting concluded on July 4th. It was nearly ten miles back up river to the camp of Red Middle Voice, where Mah-ka-tah lived.

They rode side by side on spotted ponies; a half dozen younger braves rode a respectful distance behind. The followers were Mah-ka-tah's young lieutenants, sworn by the code of the Soldier's Lodge to guard the life of their leader.

While others riding to their various camps laughed and joked, this small group was marked by intensity and watchfulness. As they rode, their eyes were continually moving, lest some unforeseen danger should overcome them.

White Dog seemed out of place from his fellow riders, with his hair cut unevenly short and wearing his agency-issued white-man's clothing. The Soldier's Lodge were devoted traditionalists, clinging desperately to the ways of their forefathers.

Mah-ka-tah wore an open leather beaded shirt. A necklace of bear claws clicked together on his bare chest. He was not a chief but a chosen leader of a select group of young men from the bands of the Redwood Santee.

Just over thirty years, Mah-ka-tah had followers who were mostly in their early twenties or younger. Mah-ka-tah wore his jet-black hair long. His face was a rich copper tone. A small white, jagged scar, shaped like a lightning bolt, was etched on his right cheekbone, the result of a knife fight with a Ojibway warrior. Mah-ka-tah was not a big man, but his compact body was muscular. He had sworn an oath that he would not take a wife until the whites had been driven from the Minnesota River Valley.

The little party of riders rode on a trail through the prairie, to the north of the Minnesota River, bordered by willow trees, water gurgling over the rocky bottom.

The Santee leader looked to White Dog with thinly masked disdain. "You asked to ride and talk, you have been in my shadow all day. What is it you want?"

"I am trusted at the agency. I can help you when the time comes."

Anger flashed through Mah-ka-tah's dark eyes. "You are a white man's Indian. You've even lost your job with the whites."

"Wounded Man is Galbraith's pet," White Dog snarled. "I still have friends among the whites, but no one owns me. That is why I can help if you need me, I see and hear things."

Mah-ka-tah snorted disgustedly, "If Wabasha, Little Crow, and the other old tired ones who signed the treaties have their way, the whites will continue to do what they will to us. They will make us wait for what is owed us, and let the traders steal from us at the pay table. This must stop.

"If it falls to me and the young men to stop it, we will. All who stand in our way, Santee or white, will die."

"When war comes, I will be by your side," White Dog declared.

"I do not trust you, White Dog," Mah-ka-tah said matter-of-factly. "You are a cut hair. You are friends with the traders and worked for the white government. I do not know your heart. But I have heard your words. Maybe your friendship with the whites can be of help to us at the proper time. We will talk more, White Dog. But if I find that your words are not true, I will think you an enemy of the Soldier's Lodge and you will die."

White Dog reined his pony to a stop, a glint of fear deep in his black eyes. "I must return to the agency, Mah-ka-tah. Trust me. I will learn things there, things that can help you."

The Santee leader didn't respond. He stared intently at him for an instant and then dug his heels into his horse's side and trotted upriver. White Dog wheeled his mount to the Redwood Agency, hoping that he had dispelled doubts and won a measure of trust.

As the horseman rode back to Redwood, Brown Wing, one of Mah-ka-tah's followers, rode alongside his leader. "I don't trust him." The younger man pointed an outstretched finger at the departing rider. "He would sell you out just as easy as the whites he works for. We fear for you."

Mah-ka-tah simply nodded and grunted, then continued in silence.

After several more miles of riding, Mah-ka-tah and his party reached the Rice Creek Village. Red Middle Voice was already there. There was no particular order to the village. Hundreds of buffalo-hide tepees were strung out along the banks of the murky, brown river.

Naked children played in the stream like sleek young otters. Their mothers and grandmothers rubbed clothing clean on the riverbank rocks.

As he neared his chief's lodge, Mah-ka-tah watched as Red Middle Voice, still dressed in leather-beaded finery from his meeting, stepped though a hide-covered opening and gestured for him to stop.

Mah-ka-tah rode to the chief and gracefully slid off his pony. He strode to the taller Indian and stood expectantly.

Red Middle Voice motioned him into his tepee. It was dark inside, and it took Mah-ka-tah a moment before his eyes adjusted and he could see that they were alone. A cook-fire smoldered in the center of the lodge, its smoky tendrils winding slowly upward, in no particular hurry to escape the musty dwelling. Fur pelts, for sleeping, lay around the campfire in a circle.

Red Middle Voice sat cross-legged near the fire, and Mah-ka-tah did likewise. The chief puffed from his pipe and brushed gray-streaked long black hair from his creased face. He passed the pipe to the head of the Soldier's Lodge. "You heard the words at Little Crow's camp," Red Middle Voice began. "What will you and the young men do?"

"We will wait," Mah-ka-tah answered, "but not for long. The people will soon be starving. Food fills the warehouses of the agencies, and we will take it whether the money comes from Washington or not."

Red Middle Voice snorted, "When it comes, this time, the traders must not get the money."

"We will stop them," Mah-ka-tah said confidently. "It would be easier if Little Crow and the other chiefs stood with us."

The older chief poked a stick into the dying fire and stirred up the ashes. Red sparks floated upward, like a swarm of fireflies, toward an opening in the top of the tepee.

Red Middle Voice spoke slowly, "I have known Little Crow since we were both boys. For a long time, he didn't care about the people. He drank the white man's whiskey, took many women and fought a war against his brother.

"Then he changed. He decided to reach within himself to find the leader hidden there. But he led the people and other chiefs wrong. He brought them to the treaty signings, where our land was taken from us."

Rage grew in Mah-ka-tah as he thought of what had happened at Traverse des Sioux. Through clenched teeth he snarled, "How could they sell the land of our fathers? No one owns the land, only the use of it."

Red Middle Voice shook his head sadly, "Many thought it was only use of the land they were selling to the whites. They didn't understand that when whites own something they try to possess it completely."

"To own the land," Mah-ka-tah replied, "is like telling a Santee that you own this chunk of air." He drew a box in the air before him with the index finger of his right hand. "Tell a white man this is my air, you cannot breathe it, and he will kill you for it," he concluded.

"Air cannot be owned and neither can land," Red Middle Voice agreed. "The time is coming when we must make the whites understand that. I think that when the day is here, Little Crow will lead in war. I hope he does because many wish to follow him. But if he stands against us . . ."

"We will kill him," Mah-ka-tah finished.

"Wait for now," Red Middle Voice commanded, "but you are right. Soon we must act." The chief tapped his pipe sharply several times on the rocks ringing the campfire, a sign for Mah-ka-tah to leave.

The younger man nimbly rose to his feet. "Yes, Red Middle Voice, we will wait for a time. But remember, no chief is over the Soldier's Lodge. If we decide to act, we will, and anyone, chief or not, who stands in our way will die."

Those words hung in the air, like a blast of frigid air from the month of the tree-popping moon, as Mah-ka-tah disappeared into the bright daylight.

ℬ 15 ℛ

T HE SUN SPARKLED LIKE DIAMONDS on the surface of Lake Ripley. Its rays danced over the cool, pure water of the nearly round glacier-carved lake, creating a shimmering effect.

Jenny Olson found the coolness of the water a welcome relief from the scorching heat of the day. It had been a hot summer. Today there wasn't even a breeze. Her father, Olav, worried that the crops might suffer for it.

She waded into the water, pulling her blue cotton dress above her knees, then mid-thigh as she went deeper. Recently arrived from Rock County, Wisconsin, she came from solid Norwegian farm stock. Many of the new immigrants didn't speak English. Jenny had lived near a country school in Wisconsin. The teacher there had taken great pride in teaching proper English to the young Norwegians. Jenny had been one of her prize pupils.

She cupped her hands and splashed water into her well-tanned face. Relishing its soothing coolness, the seventeen-year-old turned her bright-blue eyes around the green lakeshore. Lake Ripley was a round pearl on the prairie, rimmed by trees, and named for a doctor who had perished on shore during a winter storm. Settlers' cabins at irregularly spaced intervals dotted the lakeshore. It was a new settlement started just six years before when three families had arrived, also from Rock County.

It really wasn't much of a settlement at all; just a few cabins here and there. Church services were held infrequently in Ole Halverson Ness's granary. The Ness farm was a few miles to the southwest.

It was July 5th in south-central Minnesota. While older men farmed, many young men had marched off to war to save the union and free the slaves. Jenny's and the other families of Meeker County were left behind to scrape together a new beginning on the prairie.

The frontier was protected by three companies of the Fifth Minnesota Infantry: Company B at Fort Ridgely on the Minnesota River, Company C to the north at Fort Ripley on the Mississippi, and Company D at Fort Abercrombie on the Red River of the North. Ridgely was the closest to Meeker County, about forty miles to the south.

Jenny was so lost in thought and the sublime coolness of the water that she didn't notice the approaching rider until he had dismounted and led his horse to drink at the water's edge. The young girl quickly turned to shore, her blond hair flashing in the sunlight. A young officer dressed in dusty blue stood smiling at her.

"Hello, miss," he nodded. "You found a nice spot on such a warm day."

Jenny, embarrassed and flustered, shot back, "It was peaceful, too, until you came along." She splashed ashore to where the soldier stood.

He smiled again. "I'm sorry for startling you. I'm Lieutenant Timothy Sheehan of the Fifth Minnesota. My men are just down the road. We're going to rest a bit by the lake."

"And why are you marching on a such a hot afternoon?" she wondered.

Sheehan took off his cap and wiped the sweat from his long face and short beard. His sandy colored hair, a little shaggy on the sides, hung limply on his forehead. His uniform fit well over his broad shoulders. The young girl thought to herself, "This man looks like a soldier. If he wore civilian clothing, he'd still look like a soldier. Something about how he carries himself."

"We're from Fort Ripley," the lieutenant replied. "Just got ordered to Fort Ridgely to help out when the payment comes for the Sioux. Or, God forbid, to deal with any situation that might come up if it takes much longer for the annuity to get there."

"You think there's gonna be trouble?" Jenny inquired, now more interested. She stood on shore, her dress soaked with water from above her knees to her hem.

"No, miss, I don't want to alarm you. We're just here to let the Sioux know that the government is serious about keepin' things peaceful. Things have been quiet in the valley, and we expect it to stay that way."

"We see Indians every once in a while. They hunt and beg for food."

In the near distance, Jenny could see the dust cloud raised from the trampling feet of dozens of men. Through the still air she heard a muted collective thump as the hard-soled marching shoes thudded onto the hard packed roadway.

Sheehan's horse snorted and shook his head. Jenny stroked its nose, then turned her gaze once more to the young lieutenant. "I thought all the soldiers had gone south."

"Most have," Sheehan answered. "But this is a frontier. There are Sioux about and some of us have been quartered here. I hope to fight rebs soon."

"I certainly hope there's no fighting here," Jenny replied.

"Don't worry, Little Crow and other chiefs have been to Washington. They won't start a fight. They know they could never beat us, even with the Civil War going on."

The soldiers were quite close now, and in the distance Jenny could hear her father calling.

"I've got to go, Lieutenant. Good luck."

"I'll be back through here, miss. What's your name?"

She smiled over her shoulder at him and answered, "Jenny, Jenny Olson."

"Remember, don't worry about Indians," Sheehan reassured. "If there's trouble, we'll take care of it."

The young girl ran along the sandy beach, her long hair streaming behind her, yellow in the sunlight, her bare feet kicking up behind her. Her distant father waited for her where he had been tending his corn in a field by the side of the lake.

Company C fell in behind Sheehan. "Like the scenery, Lieutenant?" Sergeant John Hicks gestured at the lake as he watched the girl disappear from sight.

"The scenery's fine, Sergeant," Sheehan looked out at the lake to hide a smile. He was twenty-six. Most men his age were fighting the Confederacy. At Fort Snelling they'd told him, "Bide your time. We can't send every experienced officer east. Some have got to stay and command the volunteers and, for now, you're one of them that have that job." The commandant at Snelling went on to praise Sheehan for his levelheadedness and ability to make good decisions under pressure. He appealed to his vanity by telling him that the frontier needed more officers like him.

Tim Sheehan took it all in stride. *Praise is easy to come by when someone's trying to get you to do something you'd rather not do*, he thought.

"Sergeant," he turned to Hicks, "see the men get rested. We'll keep marching until about six. I want to make it to Ridgely tomorrow."

"Yessir," Hicks saluted his lieutenant and shouted to the dusty, sweaty company. "Clean yerselves up abit and rest some, boys. We march again today."

Amid groans about continuing in the heat, Company C washed and stretched out on the lakeshore. Tired and grimy, the next day, they knew, they would be on the banks of the Minnesota.

ഌ 16 ൈ

EMILY PAUSED OVER THE SCRAPE SHE was cleaning on a Santee boy's knee. Nathan waved to her as he rode on the road toward Little Crow's village. Her heart fluttered when she saw him smile and continue down the trail. It had been two days since the night at the fort.

After kissing, little had been said. They had walked hand in hand to her quarters for the night. Nathan had embraced her again and then left for the long barracks. On the return trip to the Redwood Lower Agency he had behaved as always toward her, friendly but not overly affectionate.

But as they walked down the gangplank on the agency side of the river, he had leaned over and whispered in her ear. "Remember, Emily, whatever might come our way, I won't allow you to be hurt. You are . . ." At that moment Philander Prescott had slapped Nathan on the back.

"Great Fourth, eh, Nathan, but one day of vacation is enough for me." He laughed when he realized he had interrupted a moment between two sweethearts. "Sorry for botherin' you two. Guess my eyesight's a bit dimmer lately. Not blind, though." He laughed again.

"You were saying, Nathan?"

"Oh, nothing more, I guess. We'll talk later."

That had been yesterday.

When Nathan got back to his cabin he had sent a note to Meeds asking for more crates of goods, no "special material" needed. He was sure the old man would understand the reference to guns. He also included a dispatch to Davis informing him that he would meet with Little Crow on the morrow.

Then he thought about Emily and the unexpected turn of events. Nathan hadn't expected to fall in love, but he was on the verge of doing just that. He didn't want to consider the implications to his life or his mission. He only knew that, because of his actions, she might be in danger, and he must be sure that she was protected.

In the morning he would go to Little Crow and outline his mission. He surveyed his cabin/store. The inventory was running low. He hoped Meeds would respond quickly. Along the back wall the crates, empty except for rifles in the false bottoms, were stacked. The remaining goods were displayed on counters and shelves.

A few Santee came in before midday. They were hungry, but he didn't stock foodstuffs. They bought drygoods and hardware, and Nathan dutifully marked it into a ledger.

Shortly after noon the door crashed open, and the Myrick brothers burst inside the cabin. "You son of Satan!" Andrew Myrick's face was beet red. "We agreed to cut off credit to the red devils 'til we get our money. You're still tradin' with 'em."

"Let's just say that I'm not into them for as much as you are, Myrick." Nathan spoke calmly as he stood tall behind his counter.

Nate Myrick glared ominously and sneered, "You're going to mess up everything, our whole way of doin' business here."

"Maybe it needs to be messed up and put back together." Nathan met his glare with a steely gaze.

"Maybe things should get messed up *here*." Nate reached for an axe handle and took it from a barrel. He smashed it onto a shelf, sending its contents onto the floor. He raised his club for another blow. The loud click from a Colt service revolver stopped him. Nathan brought the pistol up from under the counter and leveled it at Nate Myrick.

"That's about enough, gentlemen." He coolly looked both men in the eyes. "Now you two worthless pieces of trash get out of here, or I'll see if it takes more than two shots to kill both of you."

Hatred steamed from every pore as the Myricks stared at Nathan. "You ain't heard the last of this, Cates. There's somethin' about you that ain't right, and we'll find out what it is. We'll go to Galbraith, Fort Snelling even. We'll see you get out of here."

"Do what you want," Nathan cooly replied. "Just remember what waits for you here." He fired a shot above them into the thick log wall. As the room filled with blue gunsmoke, the Myricks hastily retreated out the door, like two scared but defiant dogs. They tried to look brave but betrayed their fear through their eyes.

More Santee came to trade in the afternoon as Nathan tried to plan exactly how he would approach the Indian chief come morning. He knew he should see Emily, but it would have to wait. Big things were starting to happen. He could feel it. Nathan just hoped that he could somehow guide the course of the stream he was set upon.

That afternoon Emily heard about the confrontation between Nathan and the Myricks. Even on the frontier, a gunshot in the middle of the day drew attention. She wanted to talk with Nathan about what had happened. However, she thought it best to stay away from the traders' cabins. He would tell her soon. But she didn't hear from him the rest of the day.

Then it was morning, and Nathan was riding on the road going northwest, to Little Crow's most likely. Alma Robertson paused as she walked by Emily on her way to the church office. "He certainly has created attention around here. Traders hate him. The Santee seem to like him though."

"You hear how they talk. They think he's fair in his dealings with them."

"One word of caution, Emily. You're young and you're doing a fine job here. But be careful of Mr. Cates. Don't fall too hard too soon."

"What do you mean, Mrs. Robertson?" Emily seemed perplexed and turned innocent blue eyes toward her companion.

"Just a feeling, Emily. I don't doubt that he's a good man but . . . oh, maybe it's just the imagination of an old woman. There's just something about him."

"Yes. He is different," Emily defended, "and I'm glad he is." She began dabbing at the Indian boy's scrape a little too hard, and he winced.

"Take it easy on Billy, Emily. He'll need that knee." Alma smiled to herself as she walked on to the church.

ᔍ *17* ᔭ

A SMILE LIT UP GURI ENDRESON'S BROAD, tanned face as she looked out an open window over her spinning wheel, across the green grass to the trees and lake beyond. "Yes," she sighed to herself, "it's a good land. A fine place to raise children."

Her eyes scanned the small, simple one-room log cabin. She was thankful for the loft where five of her children slept. But Guri wished silently to herself that Lars would soon get around to the addition he had promised to build.

Guri shifted uneasily in her chair. She was a big woman, not fat, just big in places that most women prefer to be small. Her hips and shoulders were wide, and her upper arms strong and muscular. She had worked alongside her husband, Lars, for years in the fields, and it showed in her strength and physique.

Life as a frontier woman could be lonely, but Guri felt fortunate. She had her family and in the Kandiyohi lakes region there were many Norwegian homesteaders, scattered around the lakes. Guri, herself, was surprised at how many had gathered at neighbor Foot's cabin on the Fourth of July.

Her daughter Gjertrude, married to Oscar Erickson, lived just a few miles away on another lake. Solomon Foot lived between the Ericksons and the Endreson homestead. It was good to have such a man nearby, Guri thought; he knows how to deal with the reds.

She didn't really fear Indians. They appeared at her door from time to time wanting food and offering items to trade. But Guri was never really at ease when they were around. Knowing that Solomon Foot was but miles away was a comfort to her.

It was July now. Lars was out cutting early wheat. The next month they would begin harvesting in earnest. Guri wondered about another event coming up in August. Sometime in the middle of the month, Reverend Jackson was due. A real pastor in the Norwegian Lutheran Church, he traveled from settlement to settlement, holding church services and offering holy sacraments to church-starved Norwegians. It had been nearly a year since Guri had Holy Communion. She felt dirty inside, like the grime in an old coffee cup. She eagerly longed for the inner cleansing that the pastor would bring in the form of blessed wine and bread.

The cabin had little in the way of furniture: a rectangular plank table, eight spindly wooden chairs, and a trunk brought from the homeland were about it, besides the bed in one corner where she and Lars slept upon a mattress stuffed with cornhusks. Similar bedding for the children was in the loft.

There was a makeshift bed, more like a large box, in another corner. A small figure snored softly upon it. Little round-faced, blue-eyed Anna, nearly three years old, was napping as her older siblings fished in the nearby lake.

They had two daughters who lived elsewhere: Helga had remained in Norway, and Gjertrude.

Guri's nimble fingers returned to the wheel, and soon the spokes were a blur, and the machine whirred softly as she spun woolen yarn to make into a shirt for Lars. They had been on the Minnesota frontier since 1857 and the clothing brought from Norway, except for the one dress she kept for special occasions, such as the Fourth of July, was long worn out.

Guri and other frontier women faced the arduous task of making clothing for their families. She spun linen from flax and wool from sheep, often combining them into linsey-woolsey for shirts, pants, dresses, and shawls.

In fact, most of everyday needs of the family were satisfied by women, from making soap to candles to quilts, food, and innumerable other tasks. Guri was wearing a brown muslin dress, covered by an apron. She had made both of them. In the trunk was her one luxury item, a hoop for her good skirt.

The hoop was rarely worn because it wasn't practical on the frontier. One of the most common causes of death for women was burns from fires caused when clothing ignited over campfires or cookstoves. It was better not to tempt fate wearing a hoop unless it was a special occasion.

Sometimes with Lars' help, Guri would tan hides and make deerskin clothing as well. But the cloth was needed now, and she turned her attention back to her spinning when the cabin door opened.

A shaft of sunlight splatted onto the wooden planked floor as Lars Endreson stepped into the dim cabin. "I should have put in more than three windows, old woman. It's too dark in here."

Lars, at fifty-nine was ten years older than his wife. A farmer since boyhood in Norway, his hands were big and gnarled. He rubbed his graying brown hair and scratched the backside of his woolen pants. "Uff da may, hot as Hades it is," he mumbled more to himself than his wife.

"The light is fine enough," Guri soothed, "it's more room we need."

"Maybe after harvest," Lars answered as he pulled a wooden chair to the table in the center of the room. The slender, sinewy farmer reached for a hunk of dark bread that rested on a plate and sliced off a piece.

He chomped a few bites like a hungry wolf and then, his mouth full, teased, "While Endre and I have been working our fingers to the bone and breaking our backs stacking wheat into bundles. What have you been doing?"

Guri smiled at her husband's propensity for exaggeration. "Making you a shirt and thinking about how good we have it, in spite of living in a little cabin with five children."

"I'll agree that it's better than Norway. The land, what there was of it, was worn out there. Here there's more than we can work with. Two feet of top soil."

"Is that what you really like the best, Lars, the land?"

"That and the fact that there's no one standing over me telling me what to do and when to do it all the time. No king, no army, not even a parson to stand over me and tell me how to live my life."

Guri paused from her spinning wheel, "Yes we had it bad, but it was even worse for the Swedes what with seven layers of authority over each of them."

"It's better here, wife, in every way. I could never go back to Norway. We have opportunity here to live better than we ever could have back there. We already do. And our children will do even better than us."

"I never want to cross the ocean again, that's for sure," Guri agreed. "One trip is enough for my lifetime. So little room on the ship, filth, and people getting seasick and vomiting all over—I want none of that again."

Lars smiled and shook his head. "You never have to worry about making that trip again."

Guri gazed out the window and watched as four forms emerged from the tall grass by the lake. "Lars, it looks like fish for dinner. Young Guri has a stringer full."

In moments the door burst open as little nine-year-old Britta rushed to her mother's side. "Wait 'til you see the fish we caught, Mommy," she said breathlessly, "Ole got a big one."

On cue Ole Endreson, fourteen, marched through the doorway lugging a big northern pike across his outstretched arms. A smile lit up his freckled face, and his blue eyes danced beneath blonde bangs.

The other two Endreson children, Endre, nearly twenty, and sixteen-year-old Guri, followed close behind. The boys wore linen shirts and woolen pants, and the girls long cotton muslin dresses. All were bare-footed, blonde, and blue-eyed. Darkly tanned faces and arms were the result of hours of working with their parents outside in the fields and gardens.

Laughing, Guri took the fish from her son. It wiggled in her hands, and the slimy creature almost eluded her grasp. Guri, her namesake daughter, held up a heavy stringer of pan fish. She flashed a smile of brilliant white teeth, looking like ivory in contrast with her tanned face.

Endre hefted the northern pike from his wife. "Must weigh at least six pounds. Who caught it?"

"Ole hooked him, and I waded into the water and helped drag him in," the younger Endre explained. "And he put up quite a fight, let me tell you."

"Good job." A big smile lit up elder Endre's face revealing slightly crooked, tobacco-stained teeth. "But you know only half the job is done if we want fish for supper."

"Yes, Father, we know," Endre replied. "We'll take them out back and clean them. Get the stove ready."

As the older children left the cabin to tend to the fish, little Anna began to stir in her bed. She started to whimper, and Lars walked softly to her. The big man reached down and enfolded the small child in his arms. "There, there, it's all right," he cooed. "There are no ugly, wart-faced trolls in America to bother you."

Lars sat on a rickety chair by the table and crossed his legs. He placed Anna astride the crook made by his foot and ankle and slowly rocked his leg up and down like a ready made teeter-tooter. Then the tough old farmer begin to gently sing an old Norwegian nursery rhyme about a child riding a horse: "*Rida, rida ranka. Hasten heter Blanka!*"

Anna grinned up at her father as Guri gazed at the scene. Yes, life was good here and she knew it could only get better. She was wrong.

ᴐ 18 ᴄᴑ

NATHAN THOMAS RODE DIRECTLY TO THE HOUSE of Little Crow. Since the Fourth of July, two days earlier, he had wrestled with his conscience. Words like "duty," "honor," "loyalty," "friendship," and even the "Cause" had coursed through his mind. Now he felt he was ready. He would explain what he wanted Little Crow and the Santee to do. Perhaps this wasn't exactly what Jefferson Davis wanted, but Davis was in Richmond. Honor was important to Nathan, and he wouldn't compromise it for any man. However, he knew that one man's honor was another man's treason.

He knocked twice on the wooden door and was admitted by a wrinkled, gray-haired woman wearing a red dress. She was one of Little Crow's wives. The Santee leader was in a sitting room off the kitchen. The woman silently led him there and gestured for Nathan to enter. A few chairs and a small table were the only furniture. Little Crow appeared contented and sleepy. He remained slouched in his chair and motioned for Nathan to sit across the table from him. The chair creaked beneath him. "Welcome, One Arm. Do you want to eat?"

"No, thank you. I just had breakfast at the agency."

The morning sun streamed through a window, warming the Santee leader, as if he were an old cat curled up in a window box. "When the gov-

137

ernment built the house, I told them I must have a window facing the morning sun. In the old days, the entrances of our tepees always faced east. Why do you come here today?"

"Ta-oya-te-duta," Nathan used the Santee pronunciation of Little Crow, "I come here today with words from the Graycoat Father, Jefferson Davis. I am not the man people think I am."

"We knew you were different, One Arm. Tell me."

"Do you know of Stand Waite?"

"The Commanche who fights for the Graycoats in the Southwest. Yes, I have heard of him."

"President Davis knows of your trouble here. He knows that the Bluecoats have broken their word to you and taken your land. He knows that they have not paid what they promised to you."

"Yes," Little Crow narrowed his eyes as he looked at Nathan, "and what does this have to do with the Commanche?"

"The Great Father in Richmond thinks that this is the time for the Santee to rise up and take back their land. Most of the Bluecoats are fighting in the East. The soldiers left here are young, and the forts are open to attack. The war in the East goes well for the Graycoats. Lincoln may not be able to send more soldiers here to help."

"One Arm, I am a Santee, an Indian. I am also a leader in war. The Bluecoats will notice a war at their backdoor."

"I, too, am a war leader, Little Crow. I am a captain in the Confederate Army. This fall, northern territory will be invaded. Wait until September. Then attack the forts and military outposts. The Bluecoats will be afraid of you and the Graycoats. You must only attack soldiers."

"Tao-oya-te-duta does not make war on women and children. When we fight, it will be on the soldiers only."

Although he tried to conceal it, Nathan was relieved by Little Crow's words. He continued, "When the war in the East is over, President Davis wants you to keep this land. Do not fear that the Graycoats will try to take it. The Graycoats will protect you. They will help you stop the Bluecoats if they try to take this land back."

"I understand how your people will be helped if we attack. It will help your raid into Bluecoat land. How are we helped? Will you send us men?"

"We have created the time for you. There will never be a better time to regain your land. We have caused most soldiers to leave Minnesota. Yes, it will help the Graycoats if you cause the Bluecoats' attention to be divided. But the Union will not be able to send many, if any, soldiers to fight you as long as we are winning in the East. We hope it will cause them to end the war over fear of losing the West. We can't send soldiers here yet. Perhaps later, when our position is more secure in the East. But we will protect you when the war is over."

"Do you have guns for us?"

"Not now, maybe later." It was the first lie Nathan used.

"Why should we believe the Graycoats? How are they different from the Bluecoats who lie?"

"The Bluecoats are trying to change both our ways of life. The Santee and the Graycoats only want to be left to themselves."

"You have told me much to think about, One Arm. If the money owed us doesn't come soon, there may be war anyway. Already the bands are gathering at the Upper Agency on the Yellow Medicine. We will talk again before September."

"Little Crow, you must tell no one about me." Nathan looked earnestly across the table into the Indian's dark eyes. "My mission to you must remain unknown. And, remember, only soldiers can be attacked."

"Do I become a soldier like Stand Waite? Will my men be soldiers of the Confederacy?"

"Unofficially, yes, but it would not help either of us if the Bluecoats knew that the Confederacy had any place in this. Later, President Davis may make you an officer himself." Truth? Perhaps. Nathan didn't know what Davis intended for Little Crow personally in the event of success.

"Go now, One Arm. I will talk with you again of this. For now I must think about what you have told to me. You have my word that your words will stay with me. I told you once before, and I tell you again, do not talk of this to the Rice Creek people."

"Thank you for listening to me, Little Crow, I have heard your words, and I will trade with your people until the day of war comes."

Nathan Thomas left Little Crow's village knowing that he had presented Davis's message properly. He had meant to be totally honest with the Chief, but until he was sure that it would be a war of army against army, he could not give the guns in his crates to the Santee.

Nathan also knew that the time had come to go to Rice Creek, despite Little Crow's warning. He had learned that it was in the village of Red Middle Voice where discontent fermented. It was there, on that fertile ground, that the bounty of his mission could sprout seeds.

Nathan was a soldier. He could understand soldiers fighting soldiers. But a war against civilians, against friends he had made, against Emily, would be intolerable. He had done his duty; yet as Nathan rode back to the agency, he felt like the three-and-one-half-inch ball from a six-pounder rested in the pit of his stomach.

๑ 19 ๛

ON JULY 6, LIEUTENANT SHEEHAN and fifty men of Company C marched into Fort Ridgely. Sheehan removed his dusty hat and slapped miles of trail from his uniform. He looked at his youthful command. They were tired and dirty but eager. The north-central frontier was quiet. The threat from the Chippewa was much less than that presented by the Sioux. They had been sent here because of the possibility of danger, and the men of Company C welcomed the change. They were too inexperienced to recognize the peril. The lure of adventure danced before them like the glimmering northern lights that lit up the northern sky at Fort Ripley.

"Sergeants," he looked at his veteran non-commissioned officers, "Hicks, Blackmeer, and Ross see to the men. Get them fed and quartered. I must report to Captain Marsh."

As he mounted the steps to the headquarters building, two other young officers joined him. One, Culver, he knew. The other, who looked like he still belonged in grammar school, was a stranger.

"Tim, glad to see you here," Culver turned to Tom Gere as he shook Sheehan's hand. "This here is Tom Gere, fresh out of Hamline University and ready to fight Indians, rebs, or anything else Father Abraham desires."

Tom smiled sheepishly and clasped the new lieutenant's offered hand. "Welcome to Ridgely," he said.

"Norm, Lieutenant Gere. It was a nice 200-mile trip." He smiled at the two younger officers and poked a finger into Culver's ribs. "We heard you fellas needed some help managing your Indians. We're pleased to be of service. Let's go in and see what your captain has to say."

After exchanging greetings, Marsh sat behind his desk and gazed at the three officers standing before him. Culver, impetuous but a fighter; Gere, green and untried, yet he seemed solid; and Tim Sheehan, perhaps the best lieutenant left in Minnesota. He had a reputation of being cool and decisive when action was called for. Marsh was glad that he was the man sent from Fort Ripley.

"Gentlemen, word has come from Agent Galbraith that large numbers of Sioux are beginning to assemble on the Yellow Medicine River. They are waiting for the annuity payment. Food is scarce, and demands may be made for the food in the warehouses at the agency."

"Three questions, sir," Sheehan asked pointedly. "First, how far to the Upper Agency? Second, why is the annuity delayed? And third, why not just issue some food?"

"In order of question, Tim: about fifty miles; Congress is debating whether to pay in gold or paper; and Galbraith won't issue food without money. The traders must be paid, you know."

"I hope foot dragging, ignorance, and greed don't start a war." Sheehan was concise in his analysis of the situation.

"We don't want things to reach a flash point. That's why we asked for reinforcements. Tim, I want you and your men and fifty men of Company B with Lieutenant Gere to proceed immediately to the Yellow Medicine Agency. Defuse any trouble and keep the peace. Stay there until the annuity arrives and is dispersed, or until some agreement is made with the Sioux and they break up and go to their villages."

"If it's all right with you, sir, my men need a few hours to rest. It's been a tough, hot march."

"Of course, Lieutenant. We have room in the long barracks for all your men. You, of course, as the ranking lieutenant, are my second in command as long as you are attached to Fort Ridgely. Oh, one more thing, take a twelve-pound howitzer with you. The Sioux don't like the big guns. Any other questions?" He waited the barest of moments, then said, "If not, you're dismissed."

"Permission to speak privately, sir," Culver asked.

"Certainly, Norm."

Sheehan and Gere left the office. Norm began somewhat hesitantly, "Sir . . . I . . . uh . . . I . . . was just wonderin' why Gere gets to go with Sheehan and not me."

Marsh smiled reassuringly at his young officer. "Nothing to do with your capabilities, Norm. We need one of you here. Gere's inexperienced. He can learn from an officer like Sheehan. It's time he gets his feet wet. I tell you what. Galbraith's trying to organize a company of halfbreeds, mostly half-French, half-Sioux, to send into the big war. I'll send you to Fort Snelling with them. Once there, if they can send me a replacement, I'll agree to let you accompany the new recruits east."

A huge smile brightened Culver's face. "Yes, sir! I don't know how to thank you, sir!"

"Now get out of here," Marsh said brusquely, "even out here, captains have paperwork to attend to."

Norm Culver stepped into bright sunlight and rushed to Tom Gere to inform him of Marsh's promise.

"Good for you, Norm," Tom was genuinely happy for him. "I hope to be joining you soon."

"Learn what you can from Tim Sheehan. If anyone can help you get out of here, it's him."

"Why's he here and not fighting rebs?"

"Because he's just too good for his own good. Now you better see to your men and get ready to go. When Sheehan's ready, he won't wait for you."

In three hours' time, one hundred men of Company B and C marched from Fort Ridgely. A caisson pulled a twelve-pound howitzer cannon in the rear of the column. At the head rode the two lieutenants. By late the next day, they planned to be at the confluence of the Yellow Medicine and Minnesota rivers, site of the burgeoning gathering of Sioux.

ℬ 20 ℛ

A S SHEEHAN LED HIS MEN to Yellow Medicine, Nathan Thomas, on a frisky black horse, traveled a much shorter distance on the opposite side of the river. Despite warnings from white and red alike, the time had come to visit the Rice Creek Village.

Nathan skirted the string of villages between the agency and Rice Creek. This day he didn't want to be bothered with trade concerns; his mission was of a much different sort. He wore the beaded leather shirt given to him by Traveling Star's mother in Little Crow's village.

Rice Creek looked much more like Nathan had expected from an Indian village. Vestiges of the white civilization, save iron cooking pots and rifles, were almost totally lacking.

Hoops, sacred circles signifying the interconnectedness of all life, hung from lodgepoles. There were no Christian crosses evident. Buffalo hide tepees were in abundance but no frame or brick houses as were interspersed in Little Crow's village.

These were people determined to live life as their fathers had. This is where the Soldier's Lodge had sworn to value the traditions of family and kinship, to maintain faith in the spirits of their ancestors, and to make the whites live up to their treaty promises.

The people, young and old, were engaged in many of the same domestic practices common to the other villages. But here he saw no confusion in dress or lifestyle. Only leather clothing and traditional breechclouts were worn. Many children, noisily at play, ran naked, and no missionaries admonished them of the sin of such freedom.

Whites were not welcome here, and as Nathan rode into the village he felt hateful black eyes burning into him like dozens of red-hot poker irons. He briefly wondered how he would find Mah-ka-tah. Then he dismissed the thought. He knew that Mah-ka-tah would find him.

He hadn't long to wait. As Nathan neared the center of the village a short, well-built man strode to meet him. Contempt lit the Indian's eyes above a jagged scar.

"White man, we do not want you here," Mah-ka-tah snapped. "Leave before a bad thing happens to you. Traders are fools to come to this place."

"Are you Mah-ka-tah of the Soldier's Lodge?" Nathan inquired boldly, ignoring the Santee's tone.

"I am Mah-ka-tah," he replied. "But I know nothing of a Soldier's Lodge."

"Mah-ka-tah," Nathan slid down from his animal, "I am not what I seem to you. I have heard great things about you, and I must speak with you. I think my words will be of interest."

Curious, but not convinced, Mah-ka-tah considered the white's words. "They call you One Arm. Some say that you are different from the other traders. I will listen to you. But only for a little time."

The young leader gestured to an opening in a tepee, and Nathan bent low to enter, followed by Mah-ka-tah. The Indian sat cross-legged upon a buffalo robe near the open pit of a smoldering fire. He motioned for Nathan to sit on bare ground across from him.

"Speak," he commanded, hatred still unveiled in his hooded dark eyes.

Nathan determined it was best to get straight to the point. He looked directly into Mah-ka-tah's black eyes. "I am Captain Nathan

Thomas, Confederate States of America. I've been sent here by the Great White Father from the South, Jefferson Davis. He knows that the Bluecoats and the government in Washington have cheated the Santee and stolen their land. He sent me here because he thinks we can help each other."

"I said people feel you are different." Try as he might to remain impassive, Mah-ka-tah's face revealed a flicker of surprise. "What do you want of us, One Arm?"

"In the Southwest, Indians have been recruited to fight for the Graycoats. Stand Waite is an officer in the army. Even here in Minnesota, mixed bloods are signing up to fight for Bluecoats."

Mah-ka-tah spat disgustedly into the fire. The spittle sizzled as it struck a hot coal. "The bloods are traitors. They don't know who their people are. They think that by helping the Bluecoats they will become important to the white man. Don't they know that when the war is over and the whites have used them up, it will be just as before. We will kill any mixed blood who joins Galbraith's army."

"Mah-ka-tah," Nathan said directly, "a war is coming here in the valley. You can help your people by helping the Confederacy. Attack soldiers here while the Graycoat army attacks into the North."

"All whites should die. Bluecoat or gray, it makes no difference. All cheat the red man. Why should we kill one side over the other?"

"Mah-ka-tah," Nathan continued earnestly, "your war here will keep Bluecoats from going to fight the Graycoats. It will scare other northern states into keeping soldiers in their states in case other Indians attack them."

"So the Graycoats are helped by us if we attack. Why is it good for the Santee?"

"There will never be a better time for you," Nathan persuaded, as he had Little Crow. "You know that many soldiers have left Minnesota. The Bluecoats still here are mostly young and untrained or old and weak.

"When the Graycoats move into the North to attack, then you attack. The Bluecoats will not have men to spare to send against you. When we win the war, President Davis will protect you from the whites here or give land elsewhere if you wish."

146

A scowl covered Mah-ka-tah's face like clouds passing over the sun. "Why should I believe that one white man's word is better than another's?"

"Because we share a common enemy. The Bluecoats try to change our way of life just as they try to change yours. Anyway, can you be worse off? At least if white soldiers are cleared from the river valley, you have a chance to start again. The Graycoats live far to the south. They don't want Santee land."

"Your words interest me, One Arm," the Indian leader responded. "Can you give us guns?"

"Maybe later, not yet." Nathan, as with Little Crow, was still not ready to turn the contents of his crates over. "And the war must be made against soldiers. The great soldiers of the Santee must not make war on women and children."

"You talk like Little Crow. Does he know of this?"

"No," Nathan lied in order to appeal to Mah-ka-tah's vanity, "I was told to find the head of the Soldier's Lodge and enlist his help."

Mah-ka-tah sat up like a banty rooster among hens. "One Arm, I know it is the soldiers who must die first. If the white farmers leave the valley when war starts, we will let them go." This time it was the Indian who spoke words he didn't know he could fulfill.

"In the fall, the Graycoats will move into the land of the Bluecoats," Nathan concluded. "That is when you must attack."

"If the Great Spirit wishes, that is how it will be," Mah-ka-tah began. For the first time he gazed upon Nathan as a person and not vile pond scum. "But, One Arm, you and I don't control events, things happen.

"Already hungry Sisseton and Wahpeton gather at the Yellow Medicine Agency. We must have food soon. If the Great Spirit means for a war to start in the valley at the same time as the Graycoats attack, that will be good. If it is to happen before or after, then it will. We cannot stop the buffalo once they start to stampede. Leave now. We will talk again."

As Nathan rose to his feet, Mah-ka-tah poked the ashes of his fire with a wooden stick, then slowly stood to face the white man. "Just one thing," Nathan requested. "I don't think it would be wise to tell anyone the purpose of my visit here."

"I make no promises to white men," the Indian said directly, "but if it serves the Santee to say nothing of your mission, I will remain silent. For now I will be silent."

Nathan squinted in the bright sunlight as he left the tepee, followed by Mah-ka-tah. He swung back onto his waiting horse, nodded at the silent Santee leader and wheeled the animal at a brisk trot out of the village.

For the second time after meeting with a Dakota leader, Nathan felt dirty. But the filth wasn't on his clothes or skin. Nathan felt dirty inside. He was a soldier on a mission from his president, and he was fulfilling his assignment in the best way he knew. But Nathan liked it less and less. He felt as if he had a wildcat by the tail and couldn't let it go. "Please," he whispered to the wind as he rode away from Rice Creek, "please help me let it go."

ഇ 21 ର

MAH-KA-TAH THOUGHTFULLY WATCHED as Nathan rode across the prairie. If the white man's words were true, the time for war might come sooner rather than later. The Santee leader was anxious. *If the time to fight and die like a warrior is near*, he thought, *let it come. I am ready to join my ancestors.*

Talk of the mixed-bloods, those of white and Indian heritage, joining the blue coat army troubled Mah-ka-tah. Louis Bordeau, a part French, part Mdewakanton from Little Crow's village was visiting relatives at Rice Creek.

Mah-ka-tah knew that he had sympathies with the Soldier's Lodge and called to him. "Bordeau, come here. I wish to speak with you."

The French-Indian was sitting cross-legged in front of his cousin's lodge. He stood and ambled on bow legs to Mah-ka-tah. Bordeau wore buckskin leggings and a dirty, white cotton shirt over a solid frame. His scraggly black hair hung nearly to his shoulders. He was clean-shaven and stood nearly six feet tall.

Bordeau smiled through uneven teeth at Mah-ka-tah. "Yees, what does the great leader of the young men want?"

The Indian ignored the attempt at a compliment and motioned him into his lodge. "Bordeau, sit." Mah-ka-tah pointed to the spot recently vacated by Nathan. The Indian leader took his place on the robes, picked up his still smoldering pipe and puffed hard on it. Then he reached across the fire pit and handed it to Bordeau.

"I want to know what Galbraith is doing. What about this army of mixed-bloods he is forming?"

Bordeau returned the pipe to the Santee and stared a moment at a dying ember in the fire. "The agent, he thinks it will make him a bigger man if he helps the Union army with more men. Most come from Renville County. He calls them the Renville Rangers, and they are all mixed-bloods, most of them part French.

"They will go to Fort Snelling first, and then to the South. Galbraith is getting close to fifty of them. People say Galbraith will make money off them. White people can pay a bounty rather than serve in the army if they can find a replacement soldier. Some say that the agent is being paid for bringing replacements. He is building an army, but they have no guns. The army is unarmed."

"How can they fight for our enemies?" Mah-ka-tah demanded.

"Galbraith tells them that things will be better for them if they come back as Union war veterans. They will be paid each month for fighting in the war. These men don't expect to fight Santee. They will fight the Graycoats and be warriors. Most are cut hairs anyway, more white than red. Many work at the agency."

"As long as a drop of their blood is red, the white man will never treat them as brothers. They will always just be half-breeds."

"Your words are true, Mah-ka-tah. Is there anything else?"

"Yes." The Indian stared intently through the gloom of the lodge into his guest's blue eyes. "I want you to join the Renville Rangers."

The French-Santee was shocked. His face blanched as he responded, "My family is Santee. I don't even know my French father or his family. I live in a lodge like you, not a house. Why would I do such a thing?"

"To help your people," Mah-ka-tah rejoined. "I want someone among the whites I can trust. I want someone to tell me what they are doing and when. I want to know when things are bad for the Santee. Since the white people are putting Santee into their army, let one of them be a Santee warrior."

"But," Bordeau countered, "they are recruited to go south. I don't want to go south. How could I help the Santee there?"

"It will take time before they act. I know these white people. They must train and talk. You will be at Fort Ridgely for some time. You will see things there that can help us. Maybe there will be opportunity for you to serve us at the fort. If they send you to Fort Snelling, find a way to leave them before you get there and come back here."

"I believe in the Soldier's Lodge and I will do what their leader asks of me. Tomorrow I will become a Renville Ranger," Bordeau concluded. They smoked once more before both men stood and walked into the freshness of the early evening.

As Bordeau walked back to his relatives, Mah-ka-tah considered his day. A white spy had come to him, and he would send a red spy to the whites. The results would be interesting. *No*, he thought, *the results will be deadly.*

ॐ 22 ☙

FTER A HARD MARCH up the Minnesota River, Companies B and C reached the Yellow Medicine Agency late on July 7th. The Upper Agency, or Yellow Medicine, stood on high ground on the west side of the Yellow Medicine River just a mile from where it joined the Minnesota.

The tributary was a much smaller river. It sluggishly emptied its murky flow into the larger river. Both waterways had much lower levels than in the spring. This was usually the case in late summer, but even more so this year owing to scarce rainfall. But, near its center, the Minnesota was still deep and treacherous.

Agent Galbraith, who oversaw both agencies, lived most of the time at Upper Sioux. Like Redwood in the lower valley, the Upper Agency saw to the needs of Santee, in this case, the Sisseton and Wahpeton bands of the northwest portion of the reservation. It was another small settlement.

A few miles upriver from the agency were two missions: Pajutazee, where Stephen Riggs ministered, and Thomas Williamson's Hazelwood. Beyond the missions was the village of Red Iron, a Santee chief who tried to maintain cordial relations with the whites. Standing Buffalo, also a "friendly," located his village at the north end of Big Stone Lake on the Dakota border.

A much larger encampment was located a few hundred yards upriver from the agency. Santee and even Yankton from the Dakotas were gathering. Each day their numbers grew. Like flocks of geese readying for fall migration, more and more came to await the annuity or a dispersal of food.

Yellow Medicine had less people and fewer buildings than the Lower Agency. Eight structures interspersed on either side of a dirt road made up the agency. Five of them were located between the road and the Yellow Medicine River behind them. The main buildings were large, two story, brick buildings. One of them doubled as a warehouse and residence of the agent. The trader's stores were a short distance away in the river valley.

Sheehan called a halt between the first two big buildings as he entered the village.

"Sergeant Trescott, Sergeant Bishop, the men look like they've been to war. It's been a hard, hot march, and I'm not going to keep these people sweating in formation while Lieutenant Gere and I report to Galbraith. March them to the river, dismiss them and let them relax. Then bivouac and set up camp. There are no buildings capable of housing us all."

Thomas Galbraith approached from the far end of the agency. The agent was tall and lean. His bald head was fringed by reddish-blonde hair. Sideburns curved down to the middle of his cheeks. He was a political appointee, a by-the-book bureaucrat new to his job.

"Thank God, you finally got here!" Galbraith sputtered, his face sagging with relief. The agent's prominent Adam's apple bobbed as he talked. "Do you see them all up the river? Each day more and more. I was afraid they'd become violent before you got here."

"We have a hundred men, Major," Sheehan replied. "From the looks of the camps, there are already hundreds of braves there. You're not secure yet."

They walked past the Manual Labor School and two duplexes that housed employees of the agency as they approached the Annuity Center. The center, one of the biggest buildings, was located at the opposite end of the community. It housed Galbraith's office and quarters and doubled as a warehouse. Here the food awaited the arrival of gold before it could be given to the Santee.

Galbraith's office was dusty and hot. The smell of grain permeated the floor from the storage bins below. "Gentlemen, order must be maintained at all costs."

Sheehan looked out an open window at the distant Indian camp. "One thing I'll do is send for another twelve-pounder from Ridgely. A show of force may be necessary. But, Major, isn't there a better way to keep peace? Those people are hungry. The land's been stripped bare of anything they can eat. They'll be eating dogs and ponies soon. Issue some food. That'll defuse the situation."

"You don't understand, Lieutenant. It just isn't done that way. The gold must come first. The traders have debts owed them, and the gold is used to pay them and to be exchanged for food."

"Is it more important that the traders get their money or that people not starve?"

"Lieutenant," the agent was exasperated, "if we give them the food now, when the gold comes and the traders are paid, the Sioux will get little or nothing. Then it'll really get hot around here."

Sheehan was equally frustrated. "Major, we'll do what we can to keep order here. However, in order to do that, I insist that at least a portion of the food you have here be issued."

Galbraith glared at him, his fists tight. Then he let out a long breath and said, "Oh, all right. But first I'll do a reconnoiter of the camp. We're not going to feed Sioux from the Dakotas, too."

"When will you do that?" Gere demanded.

"Soon, gentlemen, soon."

The two officers left Galbraith to join their men. Their sergeants had directed a camp to be pitched on prairie between the agency and the tree-lined riverbank. Tim Sheehan shook his head and looked at Tom. "People like that cause wars, Mr. Gere. We're going to have our hands full here."

ဆ 23 ca

THE DAYS LENGTHENED INTO A WEEK. Galbraith continued to drag his feet and tried to ignore the swelling camp. Thomas Williamson and Stephen Riggs, the two missionairies from just upriver, journeyed into the Santee village and reported back to the soldier camp.

As it had been since the first Spanish conquistadors came to North America in the 1500s, the Christianization of the Native Americans was professed as a major goal. Some recognized it for what it was, a justification for conquest.

Minnesota was no exception. French missionaries had been among the first to trample through the virgin wilderness to visit the camps of the Ojibway and Dakota.

Williamson and Riggs were men of good hearts who tried to do what they felt was best for the Dakota among whom they lived. Each ministered to the Dakota who lived near the Yellow Medicine Agency and Red Iron's village farther upriver.

Williamson was also a doctor of medicine, and he implored Sheehan, "Conditions are becoming desperate, Lieutenant. They're eating dogs and digging roots for food. Children are becoming sick. Some are starving. They say they'll wait no more. They want you and Lieutenant Gere to meet with them." The doctor's hairline was past the middle of his head, his lower face framed by a short, reddish beard. He wiped his ample brow with a handkerchief. "You've got to find a way to help them."

"It's critical, just critical, that something be done now," Riggs echoed.

"We'll go to the village," Sheehan answered. "Lieutenant Gere, we'll travel with an escort of only Sergeant Trescott and Corporal Sturgis. See to it, please." He turned back to the missionaries. "I'm not sure what going to them'll do. But talk sometimes leads to understanding. At least it's not shooting."

The four soldiers from Fort Ridgely rode slowly into the sprawling Indian village. Dogs, many with cut or fly-bitten ears, yapped and barked at them. The camp was a mess. Butchered carcasses of dogs and ponies lay scattered in front of tepees. Skinny children sat listlessly in front of smokey campfires. Flies buzzed everywhere in the hot sun. The unmistakable odor of decaying flesh stuck in the nostrils of the white men.

"Well," drawled Trescott, "I've been to where they throw their garbage. Now where do they live?"

Standing Buffalo, a Sisseton chief, strode to meet them. His face was creased with wrinkles, like a piece of crumbled brown paper. He appeared older than his years. The Indian wore a leather shirt stained with oil and sweat. "Come, bluecoats," he said, "we wish to council."

He led the two lieutenants into a large tepee. Inside it was hazy. Men sat in a circle around a small, dying fire. Wisps of smoke lazily floated to the opening above.

Once again a smell hit them. This time it was a curious mixture of sweat, smoke, tobacco, and a stronger sweet smell that the soldiers couldn't identify. Gere whispered in Sheehan's ear, "This is like trying to breathe with your head in a basket of goosedown feathers."

The older lieutenant put his finger to his lips. Many, but not all, of the Santee leaders had gathered. Both agencies were represented this time, with Standing Buffalo, Little Paul, Red Iron, and Akepa of Yellow Medicine joining Little Six, Big Eagle, Mankato, Red Middle Voice, and Little Crow of Redwood.

Sheehan and Gere, sitting side by side, joined the Santee in the circle. Little Paul, a smallish man with slightly stooped shoulders and an oval face, spoke first. "Welcome to our council fire. We asked you to come because our need is great."

"When will the gold be here?" Red Middle Voice asked impatiently.

"We don't know any more than you do," Sheehan replied, his eyes still adjusting to the dimness of the enclosure.

Little Six rose to his feet. "These are a great people. Never were we beaten in war until the white men gave guns to our enemies, the Ojibway. Once we were given guns, they could push us no longer. We sold our land because it was better than war with whites. The earth is our mother, it cannot be owned anyway. Only the use of land is owned.

"Last harvest was bad. Cutworms ate our crops. The winter was hard and people died. Now we come to be paid, but there is no gold. Agent Galbraith says we must wait for our food until the gold comes. The people are starting to starve."

"He wants us to wait until the gold comes so that the traders get it all first." The words twisted out of Red Middle Voice's mouth like a bit on a hand drill.

As Little Six sat down, Little Crow began to speak. He looked at the soldiers. "I have been to Washington and met with President Buchanan. I know the power that you have. It is greater than ours. The president said that you are a fair people. Then why do you let the traders sit at the pay tables and call off their accounts against every Santee? They take all the gold before we even touch it. We ask to see their accounts, but we do not understand them. We ask you, the bluecoat officers, to keep the traders from the pay table.

Gere asked, "Have you spoken with your agent about this?"

"Yes," Mankato answered, "but his ears do not hear us."

"I'm sorry." Sheehan looked around the circle at the chiefs. "There is nothing that Lieutenant Gere and I can do. We have no power to restrain the traders without the consent of the agent."

Amid angry cries and protestations, Sheehan's voice rose, "But one thing we can do is insist that you be given some provisions from the agency stores while you wait here. When we return to camp, we'll go to the agent about this. I know it's hard," Sheehan concluded, "but wait a little longer."

The two lieutenants stood, saluted the Santee, and rejoined Trescott and Sturgis, who were holding their horses outside.

"Sounded like they were a mite unhappy in there." Sturgis worked the words out around a wad of tobacco.

"They don't have much to be happy about." Sheehan swung easily into his saddle, and the four rode back to the agency encampment.

Once at the agency, Sheehan and Gere immediately paid a visit to Galbraith. After a heated discussion regarding the situation at the Indian camp and the demands of the Santee, the agent was convinced to release a small quantity of foodstuffs from the warehouse.

On July 14, agency personnel made an inspection of the camp. Before a small amount of food was issued, an attempt was made to exclude several hundred Yankton Dakota. Both efforts, the food dispersal and excluding Yanktons, were ineffective.

Tim Sheehan once again confronted Galbraith in his office. "Major, this accomplished nothing. The amount of food issued to the Santee had about as much effect as raising the temperature of the river by peeing in it. Sure, a few Indians left; most didn't. Tempers are getting awful hot in the village. I've sent for that extra twelve-pounder I was talking about."

"Good, Lieutenant, good. That's what we need, more show of force."

"No, what we need is more food given to the Santee."

"Lieutenant Sheehan, at your request I issued food. The situation has not improved and, as you say, it is even more threatening. I will give no more food. We must have some on hand when the annuity comes."

Sheehan shook his head in disgust and left the agent to his ledgers.

A few days later on the eighteenth of July, Williamson and Riggs, accompanied by Standing Buffalo and Little Paul, came to the soldier camp. Little Paul straightened to his full height. This still left him about chest high to Sheehan. The Santee's eyes were sunken, highlighting dark circles below. "The people are dying. We have searched everywhere for food. There is no game and nothing to gather, not even roots. We must have more food."

Riggs earnestly nodded his head toward the camp. "Lieutenant, Dr. Williamson and I just watched two small boys die of hunger. You must do something. We talked to Galbraith earlier today, and he still refuses to act."

Standing Buffalo looked tired and gaunt as he spoke in a hoarse voice. "Bluecoats, we cannot control the young men much longer. I fear they will take what they feel is theirs unless they are fed."

"Well, Gere, let's try again," Sheehan sighed. He looked at the missionaries. "Wait here, we'll see what we can do."

Major Galbraith looked up from his desk as the two lieutenants entered his office. Seated across from him was his assistant, Nelson Givens. Wearily the agent asked, "And what do you want today, as if we can't guess, huh, Nelson?"

"Major," Sheehan's voice conveyed no nonsense, "we said before that the food given on the fourteenth was not enough. Dr. Williamson and Mr. Riggs have just been to the camp. They report that a crisis point is being reached. More food must be issued if, for no other reason, than to save lives. We can't just sit back and let them die."

"I talked to the missionaries this morning, Lieutenant." Galbraith paced to the window and looked out as he spoke. "I'm aware of their concerns. You still don't understand my position here. However, I will authorize a dispersal of more food. But, first, I'll conduct a count of the village and lodges. Before we invite people to supper, I want to know how many places to set."

"It better be a big table, Major. How soon 'til you start the count and issue the food?"

"We'll get on it soon. But it will take a little time. Tell your friends that they can expect the issue shortly."

Sheehan and Gere left the office hopeful that Galbraith would soon open the stores, yet not convinced he could be trusted. Their suspicions were justified.

The door had barely closed when Givens asked Galbraith, "Gave in pretty easily, didn't you, Major Galbraith? Do you really plan on issuin' food now?"

"Mr. Givens, don't worry. A delay here, the count takes longer than we thought there. A little more foot dragging and, before you know it, either the Indians leave or the annuity shows up. Either way we hold onto the food stores."

"What about the village? Should we be scared of what they might do?"

"Nelson, I think it's exaggerated. It'll all blow over soon. Today's the eighteenth. We'll take some time planning the count. Then, after a few days our soldier friends will come back all puffed up and demanding to know why the count hasn't been taken. I'll hem and haw and give 'em another excuse or two. Eventually I want you to take some agency employees to the camp and do a count. Get George Gleason to go with you. He's staying here awhile before he goes back to Redwood. Make a big show of it. Then come back here, and we'll take a few more days to digest the figures."

"What about the soldier boys?"

"Sheehan and that young twit Gere? They're do-gooders who are supposed to be fighters. Next time they come in here they'll probably suggest giving the land back to the savages. Don't worry, Nelson, it'll all work out just fine."

Galbraith's ruse had the desired effect of buying time for the agent. The Santee, after talking with Sheehan, left for their village hopeful but far from convinced that something would be done soon to help them.

ᴔ 24 ᴄᴈ

MILY AND NATHAN STOOD HIGH on the bluff overlooking the river and the ferry below. It was early evening. The sun half hid behind a cloud near the western horizon turned the sky into a crimson twilight. Across the stream dust was kicked up from a few horses and the wheels of a cart.

Nathan peered intently. "Looks like soldiers from the fort and a twelve-pounder. Likely they're on the way to Yellow Medicine. That's not a good sign. It means the soldiers at Ridgely feel they need more support." He didn't add that Meeds had informed him that Lee was moving into Maryland in September. A July Indian war in Minnesota was too soon.

"Do you really think there'll be trouble, Nathan?"

"It's getting tense, Emily. Have you been to the villages lately?"

"Yesterday, with the Hinmans, but there's hardly anyone there. Many are going to Yellow Medicine Agency. They're desperate for food."

"Things are slow at the trading post, too. I don't have food to trade and that's all they want now."

"I heard the Myricks went to St. Paul," Emily said as she gazed at the distant brown water.

Nathan nodded. "They returned this afternoon. I've been told they went to Fort Snelling to complain about me and have my credentials as a

161

trader revoked. I'm not worried. My employer, Mr. Meeds, has some friends at Snelling himself. He supplies the soldiers there with some of their hardware needs. Besides, what grounds would they have? Accusations of being too fair?"

They began to walk down the well-worn trail. A boulder rested at the top of the path. For ages it had stood as a lonely sentinel above the valley. Time, rain, and erosion had loosened its base.

Emily noticed Nathan glance at it as they passed. "Have you heard the story of the rock?" she asked.

"No," Nathan replied, "what is it?"

"Philander told me about it. A Dakota legend says that a great chief, wounded in battle, climbed atop the stone for a last view of his beloved river valley. He spread his arms and prayed to the Great Spirit to guard his people. Then he was turned into an eagle and flew away. Whenever an eagle lands on the boulder the old ones say their chief has returned to look after his people and his valley. They say that as long as the stone is there, the people of the valley will be safe."

"From the looks of the loose soil around it, that might not be very long."

As they approached ruts in the path, the result of summer rains, Nathan reached for Emily's hand and clasped it until they reached the flatlands at the bottom of the bluff. They waved at Charlie Martel, who toiled across the river. Nathan picked up a flat stone and skipped it into the brown water of the slowly moving current. It plopped a half dozen times before disappearing below the surface.

"Nathan," Emily placed her hand on his arm and looked into his eyes, "when we returned from Fort Ridgely after the Fourth, you started to say something to me. Then Philander interrupted. I had hoped that we could resume that moment, but . . . well, I guess maybe the time hasn't been right. What were you going to say?"

For a long moment Nathan Thomas stared over the water. In the west the sun had escaped the clouds and made a last attempt to flash its brilliance before its inevitable descent. Golden rays shone behind Emily and radiated through her hair as he turned to look into her eyes. The beauty of the moment didn't make anything easier.

"Emily, I remember exactly what I was saying. I said that I wouldn't let any harm come to you and . . ."

"And what, Nathan? That's where you stopped."

Nathan took a small step closer to her. "Emily . . . I love you. But there's so much that I can't tell you. There's danger here, Emily."

She stepped toward him and gently placed her arms around his neck. Then Emily pulled Nathan's head down and kissed him. "And I love you. I have since the moment you grabbed Myrick and threw him down. Whatever's bothering you, I know you'll tell me when it's time."

"I wish it were that simple, Emily. Time may make things right, but I've got hold of something that I can't let go of." With his strong arm he drew her close, and they kissed again. Then, hand in hand, they walked up the path in the gathering twilight.

About two-thirds of the way up they heard a loud rolling crash. Nathan's brain raced through possibilities: Thunder? Guns? Then it was almost on top of them. The boulder from the top of the path! Nathan pushed Emily hard to the side and dived after her as the huge rock careened by.

In the shadows at the crest of the hill, three figures raced unseen back to the agency.

Emily was still shaken after Nathan left her at the Robertson home. As he lay on his cot, he worried about her. Had the rock fall been an accident? When it was light, he would search for signs of sabotage.

Nathan couldn't bear the thought that Emily could be in danger because of him. A soft rap on the door brought him quickly to his feet. He strode to the door and flung it open. Emily stood in the doorway. Moonlight behind her silhouetted her slender figure. She wore a light cotton dress that opened down the front. The top buttons were loosened.

She smiled shyly at Nathan and looked up at him through soft tears. "I need so much for you to hold me."

The door closed behind her as Emily pressed against Nathan's chest.

❧ 25 ❧

N July 21, true to Galbraith's expectations, Sheehan and Gere once again beseeched the agent to do the count. "The camp's so big, gentlemen, just the planning takes time," Galbraith explained to the frustrated officers as he gazed at them from a chair behind his desk.

Tom Gere slapped his hat in his hand and exclaimed, "We'll do the blasted count. I'll send my men in this afternoon."

"No, you won't, Mr. Gere." Galbraith met Tom's gaze levelly, his Adam's apple bobbing in agitation. "This agency's administered by civil authority, not military. You have no power over me or anyone else at Yellow Medicine. I will count the Indians and provisions, and see that the Sioux return to their homes, with or without the annuity. And I will do it as I see fit."

"As people die of starvation less than a mile away, you sit here with a warehouse full of food." Sheehan spit his words through clenched teeth.

"I am doing what the regulations require. I've told you that we will count and issue food: that's stretching the regulations. However, I'm willing to do that to help the needy."

"Why, you sanctimonious . . ." Sheehan's face turned beet red as he clenched his fists and moved toward the agent. Gere grabbed his arm.

"Easy, Tim," the young man told his superior.

Galbraith slid back his chair. In a shaky voice he summoned words to his dry mouth. "Don't . . . threaten me. Unless . . . if you don't have an order from the president, get out of here and let me do my job in my own time."

"Your own time is going to kill people, and not just Indians!" barked Sheehan as Gere ushered him out the door. As he walked away from the warehouse/office, Tim Sheehan directed a stream of profanity at Galbraith that would have done his Irish forefathers proud and caused the women in his family to cover their ears in horror.

"Careful, Tim, he can have you thrown in the guardhouse," Tom whispered as they walked the path back to camp.

"If putting a bullet between his ugly eyes saved lives and ended this travesty, I'd do it and not worry about the consequences."

"Think about what you're saying, Tim. You're needed here, by the company and even by the Sioux. And I've got a feeling we'll need you even more later. Don't say or do anything stupid. Eventually Galbraith'll come to his senses."

"Hopefully before it's too late, Tom."

In his office Galbraith summoned Givens. "Nelson, you were right, our young officers are getting excited." He dabbed at perspiration on his cheeks with a white handkerchief. "Within the next week, go to the village and count the Sioux and their lodges. I can't hold against these boys very much longer. I wish the damn gold would get here so we could pay the traders, give the reds their food and get everybody out of here."

"Any word?" Givens wondered.

"None. Infernal Congress is still trying to decide if it's gonna be gold or paper. How do they expect me to maintain order if they won't do their job. It's just not fair, Nelson. I've been here just a year. If everything blows up, I'll lose my job because of their inaction. But they won't care or understand that."

On the 26th of July, Givens, Gleason, and their crew of agency employees did a count in the Santee camp. Sheehan and Gere acted as observers. Here and there, on the fringes of the dwellings, burial scaffolds dotted the landscape as monuments to bureaucracy.

"Gleason," Gere chided sarcastically, "don't bother to count the ones up there." He gestured at the wrapped bodies atop the frameworks. "They can't eat anyway."

It took twelve hours to count the people and lodges in the miserable hovel that the village had become. Galbraith's jaw dropped in amazement when he read Givens' report. "Over five thousand Indians! Seven hundred and seventy-nine lodges! There must be a mistake. There can't be that many."

"Major," Givens replied, "if anything, we're low. It would take almost all our food stores to feed 'em."

"It can't be done, Nelson."

"So, what are you gonna do, Major?"

"Wait some more, wait some more."

ഇ 26 ര

LIFE IN THE CAMP WAS AN INTERMINABLE BORE. The sergeants drilled their men in march just to give them something to do. And they dug. They piled up dirt and stones on the riverbank to slow erosion. Of course, they dug latrines. In the heat they took off their blue blouses and worked bare-topped.

Willie Sturgis leaned on his shovel as he watched his squad dig a latrine trench. "Put a little more back into it, Private Foster!" he cried. "My daddy told me to alwa's try to be the best at whatever I did. You fellas are gonna dig the best crap trench this side of the Mississippi."

Jimmy Foster grinned a toothy smile at Willie. "Why don't you jump down in here, and we'll have a start on the crap?"

Sturgis feigned anger by waving his shovel at the private. "You just dig, boy, or I'll drop ya like a dead fly."

Will Blodgett and Jim McClain joined in, and the dirt flew as if a kennel of dogs dug for bones for a minute or so. Then they all started leaning on their shovels again. "Looky there," Blodgett pointed, "the missionairies are comin' back from the Sioux camp again. Wonder how many died today?"

"The lieutenants was talkin'," McClain said. "Sheehan said he can't figgur how the Sioux have taken it this long. Somethin's gonna happen soon."

"They take it," Willie Sturgis said, "because they ain't got nothin' else. What they gonna do? There's nothin' for 'em on the reservation. No game, buff'lo gone, no crop last year, and nothin' yet this year. Only thing they can do is wait. Wait for gold, food, or both."

"Sheehan's right." Ole Svendson flipped a shovel full of dirt as he spoke. "If the agent don't do somethin' soon, ders gonna be trouble, you betcha."

"Then I heard Gere ask Lieutenant Sheehan if'n he was gonna talk to Galbraith about the food anymore." McClain continued, "Sheehan, he said that he ain't gonna beg Galbraith no more. The agent's just gonna hafta figgur out for hisself what's right, and the lieutenant can't make him do nothin'."

Private Blodgett shook sweat from his blonde bangs. "Well, we joined up to fight. Maybe it's time."

"We joined to fight rebs, not reds, Will," Jimmy Foster said between shovelfuls.

"Either way, boys," Willie Sturgis drawled laconically, "I think the time's a comin'."

OVER A WEEK PASSED AFTER THE COUNT and still no provisions were issued. Word from Thomas Galbraith was always, "Soon," or "maybe tomorrow." Sheehan sensed trouble and moved his men into the agency compound. Finally the deplorable conditions in the Santee village reached rock bottom. On August 4th the crisis erupted.

Two Dakota braves rode briskly into the soldier camp. The lieutenants hurried to meet them. The Indians were painted with lightening bolt designs on their faces and chests. They held rifles in their hands. The older of the warriors looked down from his spotted horse. He pulled the reins tight as the animal skittered. Then he spoke in a solemn, earnest tone.

"Bluecoats, warriors are coming to make a show for the agency. They carry guns, but there is no plan to fight. First, Ta-oya-te-duta wishes to speak with Agent Galbraith. He comes now."

In the near distance Little Crow rode at the head of a band of about two dozen braves. Sheehan turned to Trescott. "Sergeant, go to the Annuity Center and tell the major he has company. See that he comes here. Sergeant Bishop, assemble the men behind me."

"What do you suppose they want, Tim?" Gere asked in low tones.

"I think our little crisis is reaching what they call a climax, Tom. They're coming for the warehouse."

Just as Little Crow reined his horse in front of the lieutenants, Agent Galbraith hurried across the courtyard. "What's going on, Sheehan? I've got work to do. Now what do your friends want?"

"Whatever it is, I think you better listen to them."

The Dakota leader wore a headdress of eagle feathers. His hair hung long and black, and he had abandoned the white man's clothing he occasionally wore in favor of traditional Indian garb. The long, leather shirt was out of place in the heat of August. But he was determined to keep his withered arms covered.

They were near the warehouse and Galbraith's quarters at the west end of the road that ran through the agrency. The ground was interspersed with sparse grass. The Yellow Medicine River slogged and gurgled nearby. As the two peoples looked at each other, the couple dozen of Dakota on one side and the hundred or so whites on the other, all was quiet, save the sound of the river.

Little Crow came quickly to the point. "My people are starving. The agency warehouses are full of food. Give it to us."

Galbraith cleared his throat, removed his hat, and wiped his bald head. He fretfully kicked at the dirt. Then he cleared his throat again and replied, "Now, Little Crow, you know I can't do that. The money hasn't arrived yet."

"My people are starving," Little Crow repeated. "They cannot eat money. They must have food."

"Your people owe money to the traders at the agency. The debts with them must be settled before we give you provisions."

"You give us nothing," Little Crow shot back. "The provisions are ours, owed us for our land. The traders mark their account books however they wish because they know that they will get first share of the money, and we will get what they say is left."

Galbraith furtively glanced over his shoulder at the one hundred soldiers standing at shoulder arms in the hot sun. He hoped they were ready for trouble.

"Be patient a little longer," he advised. "I'm sure the gold will be here soon."

"I have been patient long enough," Little Crow replied. Then he raised his crippled right arm and swiftly brought it down. Instantly, from seemingly out of nowhere, hundreds of Indians on horseback appeared on all sides of Galbraith and the soldiers. Their screams and rifle shots echoed like a chorus from Hell in the soldiers' ears as they struggled to maintain their position.

"Tarnation, Sarge, how many do you suppose there are?" Willie Sturgis wondered, looking around with white-rimmed eyes.

"Hard tellin', Willie," John Bishop answered tensely. "Five hundred, maybe a thousand."

Glaring at Galbraith, Little Crow raised his voice until it echoed through the valley. "We come not for war but to take what is ours, the food that you have long promised us."

The soldiers, now encircled by the Santee, still stood in formation. They cocked their weapons and tensely eyed the Indians as they awaited orders. The hot sweat from the sun was replaced by the cold sweat of chilled fear. Gere and Sheehan kept telling them, "Stand easy and don't do anything foolish."

Mah-ka-tah dashed to the warehouse and sent wood splinters shattering into the air as his tomahawk crashed into the door. His warriors burst into the building and began to carry out sacks of flour.

Gere coolly, with an even voice, now ordered his men. "Gun crew, march over to the howitzers, remove the tarpaulins, and train the guns on the warehouse door. Await my order to fire."

When the cannons were leveled at the Santee, those removing the sacks of flour dropped them and moved away to the right. This left an open-

Dean Urdahl

ing through which Sheehan and a squad of sixteen men raced into the warehouse. The Sioux now faced a disciplined, trained unit of soldiers, with bayonets fixed and rifles pointed at them.

Sheehan commanded them, " I want every Indian out of this building now, or we will open fire with rifles and the cannon."

Mah-ka-tah replied, "We will leave, but what will you do then? You will not see another sunrise."

The Santee left the building, and the soldiers followed them out the door. Then they stood resolute and defiant in front of the doorway.

"Sergeant Trescott, hold this position. I'm going to meet with Galbraith." With that order, Sheehan marched to Galbraith's office. The agent had hurried there for cover at the first sight of the massed Indians.

Tension remained thick at the warehouse. Soldiers stationed at either side of the doorway crossed their guns to bar access to the building. But the Indians, buoyed by their advantage in numbers, hurled themselves back at the entrance. Private Jimmy Foster's gun was covered from lock to muzzle with red hands as they tried to wrest it from him. A shot rang out into the afternoon sky. Gere immediately jumped into the fracas, his men forming a battle line behind him.

"Hold," he shouted. Then he appealed to the Santee, "Stop this before it's too late. Sheehan has gone to talk with Galbraith. Wait until he speaks with you before you carry this any farther."

Mah-ka-teh raised his arms. "We will wait, but not long."

Two armies, at close quarters, stood facing each other. The one sullen, desperate, betrayed and hungry. The other tense, scared, outnumbered, but, although young, trained and ready. They would do nothing rash as they awaited orders. Still, they knew a massed attack would crush them.

For moments there was no sound other that the hoarse deep breathing of men under great pressure. The tension seemed so thick that it could be sliced through with a Santee tomahawk.

The scene in the agent's office was also tense.

Sheehan kicked a wooden chair careening into a wall as he stomped through Galbraith's office and slammed his fist on the agent's desk. "Don't

171

be a fool, Galbraith. You've put off doing what's right for weeks. Gere and me have about begged you to open the warehouse. If any blood is spilled here today, it will be on your hands. Give them food now, or we're all going to wind up with our skulls split."

"Lieutenant, I must maintain discipline here. How can I manage this agency if the savages can march in and take anything they want whenever they want it?"

"First of all, give it when it's due them. Secondly, if you don't issue the food, we won't be marching anywhere, ever. I'm not going to let that happen."

"And just what does that mean."

"That means I'll protect my men. If that means someone must be sacrificed to that end, I will do it."

Galbraith's eyes narrowed, and he stared intently at Sheehan. "Again, what do you mean by that."

"I have orders to return to Ridgely when I think proper. We just may decide to leave soon."

"You wouldn't leave us here? Defenseless?"

"What are you going to do, Galbraith?" Sheehan's words were ominous, his bright eyes burning holes in the shaken man.

The agent slumped in his chair. "Have your men distribute the provisions of Warehouse One to the reds. No more. Just the one warehouse."

Without a word Sheehan left the room and returned to the Santee.

"Lieutenant," he spoke to Gere, "allow the Dakota to enter the warehouse and remove its contents." He turned to the Santee, "You may take what is in this building and this building only. I will arrange another meeting with your agent regarding more food and the Lower Agency."

In a short time one warehouse of the Annuity Center was stripped bare of all provisions. As many warriors carried the stores back to the village, others stayed with Mah-kah-tah in the agency. All one hundred soldiers formed a battle line in front of the center buoyed by the two howitzers.

"Bluecoats," the leader of the young men cried contemptuously, the black and red paint on his face glowing ominously in the dying sunset, "this is not enough. The people need more, and we want it now. Tell the agent."

Sheehan stepped forward. "Today this is all you will get. If any brave comes close to the warehouse, the big guns will fire, and many will die."

Mah-kah-tah glared at the soldiers with hot hatred in his black eyes. Then in a fluid motion he leaped onto his pony's back, wrenched the reins around and led his men galloping back to the village.

"Sergeant Trescott!" Sheehan called out as he watched the Indians disappear, "Take a squad and go building to building. Gather all agency personnel and civilians and bring them to the Annuity Center. If we have to make a stand, it's going to be right here."

❧ *27* ☙

THE SUN WAS BEGINNING TO SET. It cast a dimming glow as the Dakota chiefs gathered for council. A fire danced and snapped in the center as they took their places around it. Mah-ka-tah, although not a chief, sat with them as a leader of the Soldier's Lodge.

Many were still hot with anger because of their treatment at the agency and failure to secure more than one warehouse. Standing Buffalo of the Sisseton Santee spoke first in an attempt to defuse the explosive moment.

"Mah-ka-tah, you did well in leading the young braves. Ta-oya-te-duta," he nodded toward Little Crow, "your words were true and helped us to get the food. Now it is time to wait to see if they will give us more soon."

"No, Standing Buffalo, we wait enough." Cut Nose stared through the fire at the Sisseton. The shadows played over his ruined nose, giving him a sinister appearance. "The young men are ready. If war must come, let it be now."

Asssenting cries of "Ho, ho . . . ho, ho," met Cut Nose's words.

Mah-ka-tah, encouraged by the sounds of approval, cried out, "A handful of soldiers and a couple big guns cannot stop us. Yes, some may die, but we are warriors. We know it may happen. They must reload the guns, even the big ones, and when they do we will overrun them. If they hide in the houses, we will burn them."

Again, enthusiastic cries sprang from the throats of the Santee leaders. One by one they spoke for war: Little Six, Medicine Bottle, Cut Nose, Red Middle Voice. Then Red Iron of the Wahpetons spoke. He raised his voice that those standing beyond the circle could hear.

"Yes, Mah-ka-tah, maybe today you can overrun them. But what of tomorrow? We will get food today, and for as many tomorrows as you can count we will be running from the white man. How will you feed the young ones then? The time is not right for war. I don't think it ever will be again."

Little Paul tried to support Standing Buffalo. "I believe the annuity will soon come. Yet, even if it does not, the crops are looking better now. Soon we can harvest."

Little Crow was torn. He knew that winning a war against the whites was impossible. Still, he remembered the talk with One Arm. If they waited until September when the big fight would be carried into the North, maybe there would be hope. He also knew that if he completely defied the will of the council, he would forever be finished as a leader of his people. For now, still a politician, he chose a middle ground.

"Standing Buffalo and Red Iron say some true words. Today is not the day to fight. But that day will still come. Agent Galbraith has put out the word for mixed-bloods to join the Bluecoat army to fight the Graycoats. See how desperate they are. We will demand more food and see what happens. There should be no war now."

The council grumbled and then voted. A majority of the chiefs needed to vote for war before the tribes could be bound to fight. They took their stand by filing past Little Crow and throwing colored sticks into one of two piles. Black were for peace and red for war. Soon the pile of red sticks was much larger. War looked certain.

Standing Buffalo rode alone to the soldier camp. His pony plodded softly over the hard, prairie earth. It was dark and drizzling. A flash of lightning scratched across the sky as a picket called for the lone Indian to halt. Almost immediately, Tim Sheehan, wearing a blue cape over his uniform, stepped out from the center to confer with Standing Buffalo.

The chief, bare headed with a leather robe draped over his shoulders, sat upon his mount. Raindrops were running down his cheeks like tears.

"Bluecoat," he began, "I know that you have tried to help us. I come to warn you. The council voted to fight. Maybe tomorrow, maybe later, I don't know when. Prepare yourselves and try to find a way so this doesn't happen. You know what the people want?"

"Yes, Standing Buffalo, I know. I hope we can convince others before it's too late. Thank you for coming here tonight."

"If war comes, though I spoke against it, I must fight with my people. I am sorry for this, bluecoat." The Sisseton chief slowly rode back into the mist. To Sheehan, hopes of peace were disappearing as surely as the Indian had evaporated into the gloomy night.

∞ 28 ∞

ARLY THE NEXT MORNING PREPARATIONS were made in the event of an attack. Barricades of crates, earth, and wagons were piled in front of the Annuity Center. The howitzers were uncovered again and prominently displayed in the wall of defense. All able-bodied non-military men were issued rifles. Sheehan talked with Galbraith about Standing Buffalo's warning. The agent, however, was adamant. There would be no more issues of food. Since he knew he wouldn't use it, Sheehan didn't issue another veiled threat to leave.

Through the morning and early afternoon, the soldiers waited. Occasionally gunshots and loud cries streamed from the nearby Indian camp. The sun rose hot like a molten lead ball in the August sky, and the misty rain from the night before added to the humidity. The men sweated and waited. And nothing happened.

In mid-afternoon the lieutenant sent for Tom Gere, who was over-seeing construction of breastworks at one end of the line.

"What do you need, Tim?" Gere inquired.

"I want you to take a few men—we can't spare many—and ride to Fort Ridgely. Tell Captain Marsh what's happened here and that we are in great peril."

"I'll leave right away, Tim."

"Get through or . . ."

"I'll get to Ridgely. You just be here when I get back."

Within minutes, Gere and Willie Sturgis, Jim McClain and Ole Svendson were galloping down the trial to the fort. No effort was made by the Santee to stop them.

Even though the Santee council had voted to fight, through the efforts of Little Paul and Standing Buffalo, action was delayed. Once again both sides were waiting for something to happen.

Through the afternoon and night the four men thundered over the trail down the river to Fort Ridgely. Only brief stops were made to rest and water the horses before the men pushed on. The fort was dark and quiet when they reached the garrison. They galloped past a sentry and into the compound. At three o' clock the morning of August 6, Tom Gere pounded loudly on the headquarters door of Captain Marsh.

Marsh peered at Tom with sleepy eyes. He had pulled on his breeches and slipped suspenders over his bare chest.

"Is something wrong, Lieutenant?" Alarm showed in the captain's voice.

"Captain," Gere breathlessly panted, "the Sioux have moved large numbers into Yellow Medicine. It's bad, sir. They demanded food, and Galbraith wouldn't issue any. Then they, well at least over five hundred of them, stormed the warehouse and tried to take some."

"Casualties? What's the present situation?"

"No casualties. Not yet anyway. The men did their jobs very well. We stopped them from taking food until Galbraith agreed to issue some. The Sioux wanted more. The agent said no. Now the Indians are threatening to attack, and Lieutenant Sheehan has taken a position of defense in front of the Annuity Center."

"Dang fool Galbraith. Remember, Tom, politicians start wars, not soldiers. We just clean up the mess. Get fresh horses for you, your men, and myself. Roust Culver and tell him he's in charge. I can't reduce the garrison force any more. We leave for Yellow Medicine within the half hour."

Another hard ride brought the small group of solders back to the Upper Agency by one-thirty the next afternoon. Marsh rode past the Dakota village and directly to the Annuity Center. After a brief conversation with Sheehan, he burst through the agent's door.

"Galbraith, are you trying to start a war intentionally or are you just that stupid?" the captain growled.

"Don't use that tone with me!" Galbraith reddened and stood up from behind his desk. "I am handling this crisis according to proper procedures and regulations, and I want to protest the actions of your officers. Sheehan threatened me!"

"Your procedures are going to lead to war up and down this valley. I back Sheehan totally. He likely saved your life."

"Don't talk to me about starting a war," Galbraith sputtered. "If war comes, it's because the Sioux refuse to become civilized. If they continue to want to live like savages they have to expect to be treated like savages. Change is sweeping down the valley, and many Sioux stand in its way."

The agent was exasperated. "I've done my best. I've continued the policies of my predecessor." He stopped looking at Marsh and began to pace the small room. "Remember, the theory was to break up the community system of the Sioux, weaken and destroy their tribal relations, individualize them by giving each a separate house and have them subsist by industry, the sweat of their brows . . ." His voice trailed off, and Marsh brought him back to the moment at hand.

"Major, you must issue more food now."

"No . . . I can't."

"You can and you will. My men and this agency will not be sacrificed over regulations. You will now come with me to council with the Sioux. I've already told Lieutenant Sheehan to let them know we're coming."

"Must I?" Galbraith asked weakly.

"You must," was Marsh's firm reply.

A dozen soldiers marched to the Santee camp with Marsh, Galbraith, and Sheehan. Gere remained behind in charge of the defense line. The same Indians who had voted to fight the day before met the whites around the same council fire. They looked fierce in their native clothes and war paint.

"Leaders of the Santee Dakota Nation," Marsh addressed the Dakota first. "We understand your impatience over the delay in the annuity payment. We know that your people face great hunger, and I personally thank you for your wisdom in avoiding violence. Agent Galbraith has something to tell you."

The Indians waited expectantly as the agent cleared his throat and looked around the circle. His eyes began to blink rapidly as he spoke, "People of the Dakota nation, if you come to the Annuity Center in an orderly fashion we will issue some—"

"*All*," Marsh commanded.

"Er, all of the stores of the agency warehouses," Gabraith looked at the ground as he finished.

"Ho, ho, ho, ho," the Santee cried in unison.

Then Little Crow rose to his feet. "This is fine and good today. But what of those still at the Redwood Agency. They too must have food."

At this, Galbraith puffed himself up again and looked at Little Crow. "Go back to Redwood Agency. In a few days we will administer supplies to you there as well."

Sheehan intoned to Marsh. "Captain, I sure hope he keeps his word this time. They aren't going to take well to being lied to again."

The captain merely nodded, then said, "Tim, when we get back to the agency, organize the dispersal of all food from the stores. Don't let Galbraith hold anything back."

Over the next three days, all food in the Yellow Medicine Agency was turned over to the Santee Dakota. The issue was done in an orderly manner, and by the time the last of the supplies were gone, the great Indian camp had disappeared like some mirage city. On August 11 the company of soldiers with its officers returned to Fort Ridgely. Galbraith asked them to be at Redwood Agency on the fifteenth when he would meet with the Lower Sioux band to issue food.

✤ 29 ✤

WHILE THE CRISIS WAS BEING AVERTED at Yellow Medicine, pressure was building at the Redwood Agency. Many Santee, primarily those of the farmer faction, or white party, did not go to the Upper Agency. Although they hated the traders, they still depended upon them.

Nathan had received a small shipment of the goods he had requested from Meeds. He received only a fraction of the flour and grain he had asked Meeds to send. A message read, "I'm sorry I couldn't send a bigger shipment; however, I didn't anticipate the quantity required or the length of your mission. This is all that's available. Our friend sends his best and urges you to continue your mission as planned."

At least Nathan knew that Davis was getting his dispatches. He wished he knew how Lee's invasion plans were progressing. But matters at hand were more pressing, and he felt himself thinking more of the plight of the Santee than of the Confederacy.

Nathan kept trading and extending payment with his limited inventory. His foodstuffs were soon gone. The other traders had cut off credit with the Indians until the annuity came. Knowing the other traders had more of what they needed, the Santee kept pressuring LaBathe, Foster, Robert, and the Myricks to give them goods.

181

Red Day, a middle-aged farmer, made one last attempt to get flour from Andrew Myrick. "Please," he begged, "when the annuity gets here, I will pay you double. My crops are good, but they are not ready."

As he spoke, Gray Hawk, a younger Santee, entered the store. The trader looked at him and gestured to both. "You people should have thought of that when you tried to get the traders barred from the pay tables," Myrick scowled.

"I am not a chief. I was not at council and took no part in such demands," Red Day pleaded.

Gray Hawk angrily retorted, "You say that you will give us no more credit, and that we may starve this winter, or eat dirt or hay. Now when you want wood or water, do not get it on our reservation."

Myrick's face turned stormy, his voice was icy. "All right. When you're cold this winter and want to warm yourselves by my stove, I'll put you out in the freezing night. Now leave my store until you come back with money."

Both Dakota left with frustration and anger in their hearts. These were supposedly "good" Indians, those of the white party. The traders and the agency officials were further alienating friends.

PASTOR HINMAN SAT IN HIS STUDY in the church and read his copy of the *St. Paul Pioneer Press* as Emily cleaned and dusted pews. The lead story concerned the *Trent* Affair. Confederate agents bound for England aboard the British ship *Trent* were removed from the vessel off the coast of Cuba by a Union warship. This created an international crisis and brought England to the brink of declaring war on the United States, or at least actively aiding the Confederacy.

Hinman, still holding his paper, walked into the church sanctuary. "Emily, I've been reading about the *Trent* Affair again. It seems it created quite a commotion across the Atlantic. Strangely, even our Indians are talking about it as well. Last Sunday after church some of the Santee warned me that if England went to war with us, there would be Indian wars all over the frontier. Several seemed to even look forward to such a possibility. In a few weeks, school starts up again, but if you want to go back to Minneapolis, we'll understand."

"I came here to teach, and I barely got started. I'm eager to have a full year. Don't worry. We'll be safe, I'm sure of it."

"I hope we will be, Emily." Hinman was solemn and earnest. " They talk of a Soldier's Lodge led by the young braves. It is a secret society pledged to clean out the white people. Those who told me of it were risking their lives by doing so. Don't underestimate the danger here."

"He's right, Emily, you should go home." Nathan had entered through the open door in the rear of the church and stood behind her in the aisle between the pews.

"Not yet," she smiled at Nathan. "If the government evacuates the agency, maybe then I'll go. If you accompany me."

Pastor Hinman smiled wanly, nodded at Nathan and returned to his study.

"Really, Emily, Minneapolis is safe. Go there for now and come back when the crisis blows over. I wasn't going to tell you this, but I'm not sure that boulder rolled down the path by accident."

"What do you mean?" Emily said with alarm in her voice..

"There were footprints around where the stone had been and a pole that could have been used as a lever."

"But you're not sure. It maybe wasn't." Emily tried not to be convinced.

"No, I can't be positive. But I want you to be safe," Nathan insisted.

"Remember, Nathan, you promised that you would keep me safe. I'm not worried as long as you're around."

Nathan leaned down and kissed her gently on top of her head. "And I will, Emily. I was just hoping you'd make it easier for me."

When he returned to his store, the trader from Virginia discovered his windows smashed and his supplies strewn about inside. Luckily the crates along the back wall hadn't been smashed. Nathan walked behind the counter and removed the Colt Navy revolver from its hiding place and stuffed it into his belt.

Then he took an axe handle and walked to Myrick's post up the road. The Myricks and White Dog were in the shadowy store sitting at a table playing cards. A pistol lay in front of Andrew. They knew Nathan would come.

"What's wrong, Cates?" Nate Myrick asked.

"Hot day, isn't it. We're thinking of opening our windows," Andrew sneered. "I see you already have." He picked his teeth with a wood sliver and looked through the open door at Nathan's store.

"How're those sunset walks, Cates?" Nate asked. "Do we need to put up a sign that says, 'Look out for falling rocks'?" He snickered.

"You are two of the most worthless creatures God ever placed on this earth, and I'm about to make up for his mistake." Nathan's voice was icy and calculated.

"At least we're not Indian lovers. You're ruining it for us all, you one-armed son of . . ."

At that instant Nathan swung the axe handle and sent pots, pans, and other hardware crashing from shelves to the floor. Nate Myrick bull-rushed him and slammed his shoulder into Nathan's stomach, shoving him back against the wall. Nathan straightened him up with a knee to the chin and flattened him with a swift blow to the head from the handle.

Andrew reached for his pistol and drew back the hammer. Before he could fire, the Confederate officer threw the axe handle, striking him across the face. Dazed, the elder Myrick looked up into the barrel of a Colt revolver pointed between his eyes. White Dog, a spectator up until now, reached for a knife in his belt, hatred gleaming in his eyes.

"Myrick, tell White Dog that if he makes one more move for that knife, the next thing he'll be doing is cleaning your brains off the back wall."

"Don't do nothin' stupid, Wh-Wh-White Dog," Myrick stammered.

"I swear to you now, Myrick. If you ever touch me, my store, or Emily West again, I will not hesitate to kill you."

He ripped the pistol from Myrick's hand and flung it through the window, shattering the glass. With a sidelong glance, he looked at White Dog and then smiled sardonically at Myrick. "There, Andrew, I opened your window for you." He turned his back to them and strode away.

ಬಿ 30 ೫

ON THE MORNING OF FRIDAY, AUGUST 15, the soldiers of companies B and C, Fifth Minnesota Volunteer Infantry, assembled at the Lower Agency. Once again Tim Sheehan, Tom Gere, and Captain John Marsh were to use their troops to keep order as Galbraith kept his now delayed appointment with the Dakota of Redwood.

Several hundred Mdewkantons led by Little Crow gathered on the flats below the bluffs, ready to move into the small town to receive food from the warehouses. About fifty yards away, 150 soldiers stood in ranks waiting for the agent to begin the proceedings. They stood at ease and impatiently swiped at horseflies that buzzed their ears and exposed skin.

Both Myricks, Robert, Forbes, and LaBathe walked between the soldiers and Indians, accompanied by Agent Galbraith. Nathan Thomas was already there waiting.

Sheehan looked sidelong at Marsh and harshly whispered, "What's Galbraith doing coming down here with the agents? He's gonna keep his word to Little Crow, isn't he?"

"I don't know, Tim, he looks a little cocky today."

Galbraith felt bolstered by the other traders and by the troops that he had requested to help keep order. He strutted like a banty rooster until he stopped before the Santee. The traders stood behind him with the soldiers behind them.

"Little Crow. I have had time to think more about the events at Yellow Medicine. We gave you food at the Upper Agency. I have decided not to issue any more until the annuity of money arrives."

Little Crow responded for his people. "We have waited a long time. The money is ours, but we cannot get it. We have no food, but here are these stores filled with food. We ask that you, our agent, make some arrangement so we can get food from the stores, or else we may take our own way to keep ourselves from starving. When men are hungry, they help themselves. We want the traders kept from the pay tables."

Galbraith did not respond directly to the Santee. He turned and asked the traders what they would do. Andrew Myrick glared at the Dakota chiefs who were with Little Crow. "So far as I am concerned, if they are hungry, let them eat grass or their own dung."

Myrick's words stunned the Santee leaders as if each had been slapped in the face. Their faces darkened like storm clouds on a June night. There was a moment of silence, then angry shouts as the Santee arose as one and left the council. Little Crow had tried to help his people. He had tried to regain the leadership position and reason with the white men. He had failed once again.

As Galbraith walked past Marsh, the captain stepped forward and grabbed the agent's arm. "You said you would feed them. What have you done?"

"I couldn't empty out everything here, too. We already did that at Yellow Medicine. It's my only hold on them and the only way to see to it that the traders get what's coming to them. They won't do anything violent as long as they still expect the annuity and more food."

"You forget, Galbraith, that you are the agent of the Indians, not the traders," Marsh admonished.

Sheehan stared at Myrick, who was waiting for Galbraith. "Myrick, that was about as stupid and insensitive a remark as I've ever heard. You make your living off these people."

"I'm not a charity, soldier boy. This is pay-as-you-go now."

The traders, excluding Nathan, smirked and laughed as they walked back to the agency with Galbraith.

Nathan walked over to Gere, still in line with his troops. "Tom, that agent is one of the most ignorant, stubborn men I've ever seen, and trust me, I've seen more than you would believe."

"It worries me, Nathan." Tom's eyes followed the departing "major" as he spoke. "You're lucky you weren't at the Upper Agency. That was one hellacious predicament. I thought for sure that they were coming for us."

"Keep your eyes open, Tom. You're lucky you've got good officers."

"Maybe Galbraith's right," Gere hoped, "maybe they'll just wait. I know they're hungry, but Little Crow's no fool. What choice do they really have?"

"Soon we may know, Tom. Real soon."

WHEN NATHAN REACHED HIS CABIN, Mike Jensen, a red-headed little boy from Emily's school, was standing outside his door waiting for him. He clutched a wrinkled envelope in his hand. "Mister Cates," Mike blurted breathlessy, "I bin waitin' for ya. The boat brought ya a letter. It was paid special for someone ta bring it to ya. So, here it is!"

With a crooked, proud smile lighting up his freckled face Mike handed the letter to Nathan. The man reached into his pocket for a coin and flipped to the boy. Mike snatched it out of the air and gripped it tightly in his right hand. "Thanks, sir!" he exclaimed as he jogged back up the worn path to the agency.

Nathan immediately recognized the handwriting. It was another missive from Meeds. He entered the dim interior of his cabin and tore open the letter. The words alarmed him. "Nathan," Meeds wrote, "It is becoming apparent that certain local personages are becoming aware of my sideline business. This could lead to some business difficulty for you as well. Some of your competitors have already come to St. Paul questioning your business methods. I plan to take an extended vacation. If your work permits it, perhaps a vacation should be in your future, too. Best Wishes, Meeds"

So, Nathan considered, *they're getting on to Meeds. He's right, if they can connect the two of us, my neck'll be in a noose. Nate Myrick must be at Fort Snelling, sent by his brother, no doubt.*

Nathan collapsed into a chair and ran his hand back through his hair. Questions and thoughts raced through his mind. What should he do? Galbraith's actions that day were pushing the Santee closer to war, but it wasn't time yet. Lee hadn't begun his invasion. But his time might be running out? What about Emily? Would the Sioux fight soldiers and not women and children?

Nathan felt as if he stood between two lengths of rope, each tied to a post. Try as he might, Nathan couldn't get enough slack to bring the ends he held close enough to tie together. There was no neat splicing to this situation. The Virginian resolved that soon he must travel to Rice Creek again. It was time to meet once more with Mah-ka-tah. Tomorrow might be too soon. Mah-ka-tah would be in an ugly mood after what Galbraith had done at Redwood.

But Sunday, Nathan considered, Sunday would be the day to see the leader of the Soldier's Lodge.

ೞ 31 ೞ

MEEDS HAD JUST DISPATCHED THE LETTER to Nathan. He scurried around his cluttered, dim store stuffing items of importance into a carpet-bag suitcase. Notes and other correspondence he stuffed in his burning cookstove.

He hadn't told the full story in his final message. Nathan wasn't his only project. It turned out that Jefferson Davis was interested in military goings on in Minnesota. Meeds had relayed troop movements and departures from Fort Snelling, in addition to Nathan's progress, via a courier to the South.

The day before, the courier had been stopped by Union soldiers near Red Wing. A search had revealed incriminating documents in the courier's boot. Meeds knew it was only a matter of time before this information was traced to him. Even though Nathan wasn't mentioned directly, Meeds also reasoned that with a little deduction by federal authorities, his one-armed associate would also be in danger.

Just as he tied down the strap on his suitcase the front door burst open. A bluecoated captain and two armed privates spilled into the room. The rifles leveled at the old storekeeper, who squinted through his glasses into the suddenly sun-soaked room. "You Samuel Meeds?" the officer demanded.

"I am, sir." Meeds answered shakily.

"Put the bag down and come with us."

"Does the army require mercantile goods?"

"No," the officer retorted sternly, "the army requires *you*. It seems that a Confederate messenger had on his person certain documents that indicate that you may be a Confederate agent yourself."

"Me?" Meeds replied with as much incredulity as he could muster. "Look around you. I got Union flags and pictures. Why, this is a virtual shrine to Abraham Lincoln."

"There's an old saying, Mr. Meeds, that a book can't be judged by its cover. You might be all stars and stripes on the outside, but we think you're stars and bars inside. Tell us what we want to know, and it'll be easier on you."

"I've got nothing to say to you."

"Maybe not now," the captain said, "we'll see if we can change that at Fort Snelling."

Under an escort of armed soldiers, Samuel Meeds made the short journey to the fort.

ɕ 32 ର

NATHAN WAS RIGHT. THE SANTEE were insulted and outraged by the actions and words of Galbraith and the traders. They didn't leave for their various villages right away. Many milled about on the river plain near the agency. The leaders gathered once again to council, sitting on the prairie grass near the river.

"You said we would have food, Little Crow," Red Middle Voice said accusingly. "Instead they tell us to eat grass. The young men will wait no longer!"

"They must wait." Little Crow insisted. But his voice was sullen, and he looked at the ground as he spoke. "Soon the annuity will come. I am sure of it." He said the words but his voice betrayed doubt.

"What are we to do?" Little Six asked. "Wait and watch children and old ones die? We took food from the agency before, let us take it again."

"This time they will be ready for us. More big guns and soldiers," Wabasha implored in support of Little Crow. "We cannot do it as we did at Yellow Medicine. People will die."

Mah-ka-tah, sitting within the circle, stirred to his feet. "People do die in war! Let us go to New Ulm then. They have much food. The Germans are rich. We will take from them as they took from us."

"No!" Little Crow rose and faced Mah-ka-tah. Anger flashed in his black eyes. "It is not time. Galbraith said we might leave the valley to hunt. First do that. Then we'll see what comes next. Maybe the annuity will be here."

"Yes, let us do that." Red Middle Voice agreed. Heads turned in shock at the Rice Creek chief's words. They had expected vehement opposition. Even Little Crow's eyes showed surprise.

Red Middle Voice, after pausing for effect, continued. "Little Six, you've spoken of a wagon you left near the Big Woods. Go get it and hunt. This would be a good time. My people will hunt downriver to the east. Maybe game will be there."

"My people also will hunt as Little Crow wishes," Cut Nose added.

Little Crow seemed relieved. He didn't want another confrontation that day. The council broke up, with many chiefs and young men considering where to hunt.

Mah-ka-tah sidled alongside Red Middle Voice and Cut Nose. "What are you doing?" he snarled angrily. "Are you going to become cut hairs too and farm for the agent?"

Red Middle Voice turned to face the younger man. "Cut Nose and I have talked. Yes, we will hunt. But then we will go to the prairie outside Fort Ridgely. There we will dance and demonstrate. We will strike fear in the hearts of the soldiers. They are young and know little of war. If they make a mistake, if the soldiers provoke the young men with us . . ."

"Blood may be shed," Cut Nose continued.

"War may start," Mah-ka-tah finished. "The Renville Rangers, I'm told, are coming to the fort. Soon they will leave for Fort Snelling."

"They are traitors to the people." Cut Nose spat the words like bullets.

"Some," Mah-ka-tah smiled thinly. "Maybe not all. Maybe some others will join us."

That afternoon and all the next day, Saturday, August 16, the Santee hunted in the vicinity of Fort Ridgely. Their efforts were meager, and many were in a foul mood as over 100 Indians camped about sixty yards to the west of the fort.

Early Saturday evening, Thomas Galbraith arrived at Ridgely with fifty men. These were his Renville Rangers, a company of mostly Santee-French heritage, ready to go fight rebels in the South.

The night was sticky and warm, as most of August had been. But the Dakota built a blazing fire and begin to chant and dance. Drums beat in a steady rhythm as the silhouetted forms danced around the fire.

Soldiers came out from Ridgely, among them Oscar Wall, Ole Svendson, and Andy Rufredge, who sat upon a pile of fence rails as they watched. They were unarmed.

"Look at 'em, dancin' like a bunch of wild Indians," Rufredge snickered at his attempt at humor.

"As long as they keep over there it's all right with me. Right, Ole?"

The tall, skinny Norwegian kept silent. His eyes were widely transfixed on the performance in front of him. He swung his long legs rythmically as he sat upon the pile of rails.

"Usually they dance to celebrate a hunt." Louis Bordeau had come from the fort and stood near the sitting soldiers. "But I only saw a couple of skinny deer, not much to dance about."

"Der gettin' closer!" Ole whispered loudly, his eyes widening.

The Dakota were dancing toward the soldiers, flames flashing behind them. Knives and clubs were flourished with defiance at the blue coats. Soon the Indians were passing the rail pile, encircling it. One brave reached out as if to grab a lock from Rufredge's full head of red hair. Andy jerked his head away, eyes wide with fear.

"Move back now!" The words were screamed in Dakota above the din, and punctuated by a pistol shot into the air by Peter Quinn, the post interpreter. Behind him, Jones and McGrew's gun crews had wheeled two cannon into position. Their barrels were leveled at the Santee.

"You will confine your hunting and dancing to the prairie. Go back at once!"

"I just came to see if the soldiers wanted to buy this pipe." Cut Nose held a pinkish colored stone pipe. "Others followed me. They mean no harm."

"Go back!" Quinn repeated.

Cut Nose smiled and turned away. This would not be the day to fight the whites. Mah-ka-tah moved near Bordeau. Louis spoke in a low voice. "Is it time for me to leave these men and come back to my people?"

"No, I don't think so," Mah-ka-tah replied. "Soon, but for now you might be able to help us from inside the fort. Wait and look for a way. As I told you, before you get to Fort Snelling, then you may leave. But when you leave this place with the Rangers, get word to me."

The soldiers retreated to the confines of Fort Ridgely. The Dakota returned to their fire and danced long into the night. But when the first rays of the bright morning sun hit the glistening dew of the long grass, they were gone. Only a smokey pile of ashes and trampled sod betrayed that the Dakota had been there at all.

ɷ 33 ଔ

SATURDAY MORNING, JOHN MARSH was faced with a decision. Fort Ripley had requested that Sheehan and his company return as soon as possible. Marsh weighed the threat and the mission Company C had been ordered to Ridgely to perform. Late in the afternoon, he called Sheehan into his office.

"Lieutenant, you have done a good job here. I'll commend you for your actions at Yellow Medicine. However, Captain Hall at Fort Ripley also values you and wants you back. I've decided that, despite the best efforts of our agent and the traders, the immediate threat to peace has been defused. You were sent here to help with the dispersal of the annuity. Frankly, as far as I know, the day of the payment may be in a couple of days or a couple of months. I can't hold you for that. Sunday morning you will depart with your men for Fort Ripley."

"Yes, sir." Sheehan seemed agitated.

"Is something bothering you, Lieutenant?"

"Just a feeling, sir. I'm not as confident as you that the Dakota will wait patiently for their annuity."

"Well, Tim, Galbraith loosened things up somewhat. More Dakota are being given permission to leave the reservation to hunt. That might ease the food shortage a little. I hope I'm right. You see that our compound is filled with Galbraith's halfbreed recruits for the Union Army. Renville Rangers, he calls them. Even though they just got here last night, they leave tomorrow. I'm sending Culver off with them."

"It might be wise to keep them here awhile. What about what happened outside the walls last night, Captain?"

"I can't keep them, Lieutenant. First of all, they're under the agent's direction. Secondly, Fort Snelling wants them as soon as possible. That demonstration last night was a harmless incident. Even if some had more malicious intent, you saw what happened. A show of force, and they broke up."

Sheehan wasn't as convinced as his superior. "I've enjoyed serving under you, Captain," he said resignedly. "If you need me . . ."

"I'll send for you immediately."

Culver and Gere were sitting on the far end of the porch with Dr. Muller when Sheehan stepped from Marsh's office. Culver creaked back on his chair and rested his boots on the porch railing. The officers had loosened the collars on their blue blouses.

It was early evening, and Muller had produced a bottle of wine and glasses. "Join us, Tim." He handed Sheehan a full glass. "Have a little bit of civilization here on the savage frontier."

Sheehan took the glass and nodded at Culver, "This is to you, Norm. I'm awfully envious of you. Marsh says you're going to Fort Snelling with some Rangers. I trust you're going all the way to the war with 'em."

"That's the plan, Tim," grinned Norm.

"Everyone says you'd be there, too, Tim, but you're just too valuable here. You showed it at Yellow Medicine," Gere added.

Sheehan shook his head ruefully. "Thanks, Tom, but you're stretching it a little."

"We're glad you're here," Dr. Muller added.

"But not for much longer. Captain Marsh just ordered me to return to Fort Ripley on Sunday."

"We can't spare you!" Tom's voice rose in alarm.

"Captain Hall wants me back. Marsh thinks things will settle down now with the Sioux, and who knows when the annuity'll be dispersed. Therefore, it's Company C to Ripley. Don't worry, they'll bring us back if there's a problem."

Muller spoke slowly and softly, just above a whisper, "If there's trouble, I only hope you can get back in time."

Louis Bordeau lay back on a thin blanket over the packed grass of the parade ground. Another recruit softly snored beside him. His small tent was near the flagpole, and the stars and stripes snapped in the wind above him.

Bordeau had managed to get a message through to Mah-ka-tah but really hadn't had much of consequence to relay except that they were leaving on Sunday. He didn't know Sheehan had been ordered back to Ripley. Soon Louis would be traveling down the river with the soldiers. He resolved to leave the Rangers before they got to New Ulm.

Culver and Sergeant Arlington Ellis joined the Renville contingent the next morning. The Rangers were much more rag-tag in appearance than Company B. They wore civilian clothing, linsey-woolsey, muslin, or leather mostly. If there was a uniform color, it was various shades of brown. No one had any part of an issued uniform. They didn't even have rifles or muskets. Hunting knives tucked into belts were the only weapons they carried.

Most of Galbraith's recruits had unevenly cut dark hair. They were darkly complected, some showing evidence of French heritage, others looking more Santee. Many had been agency employees. They hadn't spent much time drilling, but Ellis got them into files four across and hoped they could stay reasonably in step.

They marched out of the fort toward the river road led by Galbraith and Lieutenant Jim Gorman. To the rear a jangling, rickety wagon followed with supplies. One of the privates struck up a French tune, and, as they disappeared down the road, the strains of "Frere Jacque, Frere Jacque, Dormez vous, Dormez vous," echoed behind.

Later Sunday morning, Company C and Tim Sheehan left for Fort Ripley. The force at Ridgely now numbered fewer than one hundred men.

✂ 34 ✃

IT WAS A BEAUTIFUL SABBATH MORNING at the Redwood Agency. The stately stone Episcopal Church was bathed in sunlight as if God had sent a beam from heaven to guide people to this place of worship.

The bell in the steeple pealed a welcome to the people of the valley, red and white. Flying Owl, an elderly Santee from Little Crow's village, pulled the heavy rope that swung the bell.

Down the bluffs and over the river bottoms, the full, deep tolling of the bell called for unity and peace. They came to worship. Little Crow, dressed in a black suit, sat near the front with his wives and children. Philander Prescott and his Indian wife were seated behind them. Many of the agency personnel and Santee filled the little church. Nathan and Emily sat together to the right of the altar.

Soon hymns rang through open windows and entrance doors. As Pastor Hinman stood in the pulpit, he could look out onto the green grass of the circle where the agency buildings sat silently.

After the pulpit hymn, Samuel Hinman took the three steps up into the enclosed platform and looked out on his congregation. He smiled down at his wife, Elizabeth, in the front row. He had heard much in the past week, talk of violence, of war, of hatred. The pastor thought that this was the most important sermon of his fledgling ministry. He needed to appeal for peace for the sake of the Santee and the soldiers as well.

"Beloved in Christ," he began, "I'm going to depart from the gospel text today and speak of our Savior's commandment to you to love one another. We are different here on the reservation. Two cultures have clashed. One culture is being asked to change greatly. We have asked the Santee to give up their woodland way of life, move onto the prairie and abandon the ways of their ancestors. We say hunting is no longer the way. That they must become farmers and learn to live like the white man if they are to survive in the white man's world.

"The white culture has taken Santee land, and I am ashamed to say that payment has not always been complete or timely. There have been hot words lately between whites and Indians. I ask you all, white and red, to remember the words of Christ that we should forgive those who trespass against us. We are all His children—only our outer coverings are different. For those who come to Him, their souls are His."

Pastor Hinman went on to preach of the need for tolerance, compassion, and patience. Little Crow listened intently and occasionally nodded approval. Emily, at Nathan's right, placed her hand atop his and gently squeezed it.

"The Lord is watching over this agency. He knows what is happening in this valley," Hinman concluded. He had spoken in a simple, straightforward manner. Now his voice rose. "Have forbearance and have faith. In life we all have victories and defeats. The Santee have lost land and a way of life. But rejoice in the prospect of a new and better future. We enter a new age knowing that we have eternal life through our faith in Jesus Christ."

At the conclusion of the services, Hinman stood in the doorway and shook hands with the parishioners as they filed by. Little Crow warmly clasped his hand and said, "Fine sermon, pastor. Your words were good. I hope they are heeded."

Nathan followed the Santee chief and briefly left Emily talking with Alma Robertson and Elizabeth Hinman. When they were apart from the others, he spoke in low tones to Little Crow.

"September is almost here. Soon the invasion will begin. Then it is time for war on the frontier. Are your people ready to fight the soldiers?"

"Didn't you listen to the pastor? There should be no war," the chief chided Nathan, and then smiled grimly. "When the time comes," he said, "especially if the annuity does not come soon, there will be war whether we want it or not."

Nathan had waited to speak with Little Crow before going to Rice Creek. Time was running out for them all. This day he must talk to Mah-ka-tah once more.

The people of the agency went to their homes. The whites would enjoy a sleepy Sunday afternoon, chicken dinners, and bountiful picnics. The Santee went to their villages to eat their meager fare and watch with despair as their way of life continued to slip away.

ॐ 35 ॐ

FIFTY MILES NORTHEAST OF REDWOOD AGENCY, while people worshipped with Pastor Hinman, young Santee hunters were going home empty handed. Members of Little Six's band had taken advantage of Galbraith's policy allowing hunting off the reservation. They were near the edge of the Big Woods in Meeker County. The hunt had gone badly, and four members of the band had become separated from the others. They were young men, members of the Soldier's Lodge. Near the Acton home of Robinson Jones, they found some chicken eggs alongside a split-rail fence.

One of the Indians bent down to pick up the eggs. A companion warned, "Do not touch the eggs, they belong to the white man."

Angrily, the first Santee lashed out, "You are a coward. You are afraid of the white man. You are afraid to take even an egg from him, though you are half starved. Yes, you are a coward, and I will tell everyone so."

The two Dakota fiercely stared each other down, their two friends watching intently. At their feet, by a fence post, lay the nest of chicken eggs.

"Brown Wing, I am not a coward. I am not afraid of the white man, and to show you that I am not, I will go to the house and shoot him. Are you brave enough to go with me?"

Killing Ghost answered without hesitation. "Yes, I will go with you, and we will see who is the braver of us two."

Breaking Up and Runs Against Something When Crawling joined in, "We will go with you. We will be brave, too."

Robinson Jones was the postmaster of the tiny settlement of Acton. He was a powerful man, six-foot one-inch in height, ramrod straight, with a dark complexion, jet black hair and whiskers, and bright penetrating eyes. Captain George Whitcomb at Forest City described him as the beau ideal of a cavalry officer. Jones presided over a village that consisted of a few houses including that of his stepson, Howard Baker.

It was close to noon on Sunday, August 17th, 1862. The day was scorching hot as the four young braves padded from the fence line to the Jones house. All other members of their band headed back to the reservation.

Jones saw them approaching and walked from his house to meet them. His wife and his niece, fifteen-year-old Clara Wilson, remained inside with her two-year-old half brother. Jones had adopted the little boy.

"What do you want?" Jones asked the Indian youths.

"Whiskey," Brown Wing answered.

"We have none of that for such as you," Jones snapped. " And you," he stared intently at Breaking Up, "didn't you borrow that gun off me last winter?"

"No. It is my gun," Breaking Up replied.

"Then get out of here, you thieving savages!" Jones spun on his heel like a martinet soldier and slammed into his house.

Disgusted, the four young Dakota next went to Bakers. There they found Baker, his wife, and two immigrants newly arrived from Michigan, Viranus Webster and his wife. Baker was more hospitable than his stepfather. He gave them water and, when asked, tobacco. The Dakota filled their pipes, smoked, and engaged in friendly conversation with the Bakers and Websters. Then Robinson Jones, still bent on retrieving his rifle, came over along with his wife.

"You're going to give me back my gun!" he ordered.

"I told you that this is not your gun," Breaking Up answered.

Meredith Baker questioned her mother-in-law, Ann Baker Jones. "Did you give them any whiskey?"

Ann scoffed, "No, we don't keep whiskey for such black devils as they."

The Indians looked at each other with irritation. The expressions they gave said there was no turning back now. They would proceed with their deadly objective.

Brown Wing rose to his feet and eyed Jones. "White man, I can shoot better than you." He spat a brown stream of tobacco for emphasis.

Jones sneered and took up the challenge. "I'm not afraid to shoot against any damned redskin that ever lived. You want a contest?"

All four Dakota nodded assent and picked up their guns.

As Baker, Webster, and Jones prepared their weapons, the silent Mrs. Webster spoke up. "Viranus, I don't think this is a good idea. All these guns. The children are sleeping."

Webster looked into his wife's pleading eyes and felt her tug on his shirtsleeve. "Oh, all right, I'll stay here. Baker and Jones don't need my help anyway."

Killing Ghost smiled at Webster and said, "The lock on my gun does not work. Can I use yours?" Obligingly, Webster handed it over.

A V-shaped mark was placed on a tree a short distance away, and the six men all fired at it. Jones' shot was dead on the mark, cutting the V at its juncture, the bullseye of the frontier. "There, you red devils! Now you know what real shooting looks like."

After each shot, the young braves had carefully reloaded their guns. Jones and Baker had not.

Once again the Indians exchanged glances, murmured low in conversation before Brown Wing turned to answer Jones.

"White man, it is now time for us to show you what real shooting is."

The Dakota raised their guns and fired. Ann Baker Jones and Howard Baker crumbled to the ground, mortally wounded. Robinson Jones was hit but turned to run to the nearby woods. Another shot slammed him thumping like a rag doll to the ground. Viranas Webster was ambling toward his covered wagon—not a part of the shooting contest—to get a cooking pot from his wife when Brown Wing's rifle spit lead and Webster dropped.

Runs Against Something When Crawling and Breaking Up broke into Jones' cabin. Clara Wilson was dead before she could rise from her chair. Brown Wing and Killing Ghost approached Baker's cabin.

Meredith Baker, her baby cradled in her arms, had watched the murders through her window. Gripped with horror, she frantically searched for a place to hide from the oncoming killers. The trap door to the cellar was open and, baby and all, she slipped and fell down the stairs, stifling her cries of terror and pain. Meredith gripped her child tightly and tried to shield him from the fall as she rolled down the stairs and onto the packed earthen floor. Amazingly, the baby looked into his dazed mother's face and smiled.

The two Dakota opened the door to a cabin that looked empty to them. They also didn't bother to search the wagon where Mrs. Webster lay hidden. Their work done, the young men turned to the south and the distant reservation.

For some time, Meredith Baker and Florence Webster remained hidden, too scared to move. Then they timidly ventured onto the killing grounds. They placed pillows under the heads of the dead and dying. Robinson Jones had suffered fiercely. In his agony, he had stuffed handfuls of dirt into his mouth and dug great holes with his heels into the hard earth.

The two women sat in numbed silence as they endured the cries of anguish from Webster and Baker. There was little they could do except make them as comfortable as possible until they joined the Joneses and Clara Wilson in death. Mercifully, within the hour, death came to both men. Then the women took the baby and and began walking east. Word of the massacre must spread to Lake Ripley and Forest City. They had the sorrowful task of serving as the messengers of death. Nearby neighbors were the first to hear the news from the lips of the two women. Ole Ingeman rode to Forest City to spread the alarm. He arrived there about 6:00 p.m. By the time Meredith Baker got there several hours later, the small town was up at arms.

Meanwhile, around the Acton community, seven men journeyed to the Jones cabin to verify the tragic news. The corpses of the dead were still lying where they had fallen. The men cautiously approached the Jones cabin, fearful that the Sioux might have occupied it. They entered the home and immediately found Clara Wilson, dead in a pool of blood. But another surprise awaited them. Sleeping on a bed was Robinson Jones' young adopted son. Mrs. Baker and Mrs. Webster had supposed him dead. In the gloomy darkness of the horrible day, he smiled up innocently at the bearded faces of his rescuers.

ᔡ 36 ᔥ

IT WAS NEARLY SUNSET WHEN NATHAN arrived at the Rice Creek Village. He rode directly to Mah-ka-tah's lodge. A slender man he recognized as Lightning Blanket entered the tepee. In moments the leader of the Soldier's Lodge stepped out of the dwelling.

Mah-ka-tah's dark face and glaring eyes reflected an ugly mood. The words of Galbraith and Myrick kept replaying in his mind and wouldn't give him peace. "Do you have grass with you to help feed us?" he snapped. His voice was filled with sarcasm.

"Myrick is a fool," Nathan rejoined. "I must speak with you."

"Walk with me, One Arm," Mah-ka-tah commanded.

Nathan followed in silence as the Santee walked to a cluster of oak trees on the prairie near the village. A breeze rustled through the leaves and long grass. Mah-ka-tah sat upon a fallen mossy log and looked up impatiently at the white man. "Speak what you will," he ordered.

"I know that tempers are short. You feel betrayed again. I'm sure that many of your young men want to attack now. But wait. Wait a little longer. Lee will move in a few weeks. Another war in the West, while the Confederate forces battle near Washington, will strike a double terror in the hearts of the Bluecoats."

Mah-ka-tah appeared tired as he responded to Nathan. "I told you before that I won't determine when war starts. The Great Spirit will set in motion the events that lead to war. He will tell me if the time is right when your army attacks. Or maybe it will be another time, or maybe not at all."

Nathan paced a few steps, turned his back to Mah-ka-tah, and then faced the Santee again as the sun set behind him. "I don't know how long I'll be able to stay here. I've delivered the message to you that President Davis sent me here to give. Now it is up to you and Little Crow. Remember that the soldiers are your enemies. Fight them first."

Mah-ka-tah stood and faced the soldier from Virginia. "We always fight our enemies first, One Arm."

The Santee turned and walked determinedly back to his camp. Nathan followed, but no words were spoken. The interview was over. But a figure lingered behind an oak tree while the Indian and white man disappeared into the village. A smile curled the sullen lips of White Dog. Myrick would pay well for what he had to tell him.

ॐ 37 ◌

WHITE DOG RODE HIS PONY HARD down the river toward the Redwood Agency. The sun blazed like a crimson ball as it dropped over the horizon, but the Santee hardly noticed it. He had news for Myrick.

Owls hooted, crickets chirped, and dogs barked. White Dog heard only the hard, rapid thump of his horse's hooves as they thundered down the well-used trail. It was night when he reached Redwood.

Though many of the cabins were dark, an occasional glow of yellow light illuminated some windows. White Dog trotted past them until he reached the cabin of Andrew Myrick.

The light from a single lantern burned within, and the Indian rapped sharply on the cabin door. There was no answer, and White Dog rapped hard twice more. The door lurched open, and Myrick stood in the doorway, a wavering light cast shadows on the wall behind him.

The trader's face was flushed, and he held a jug in his hand. The smell of whiskey was strong. "Whadda ya want, ya red devil?" Myrick slurred.

"It's about One Arm, Nathan Cates. I know something."

A gleam wiped away the fog from Myrick's eyes. He stumbled to one side, and White Dog walked into the cabin. "Si'down and pour yerself a drink. What you got ta tell me?"

White Dog sat across the rough plank table from Myrick. Even though he licked his lips and his throat burned for it, his hand didn't touch the tin cup that the trader filled with whiskey.

"Will you pay for what I say?" the Santee asked. "You can destroy One Arm with it."

"Sure, sure," the trader mumbled. "I always pay you."

"One Arm was sent here by the Graycoats to cause the Santee to attack the Bluecoats and make a war in Minnesota. I heard him tell Mah-ka-tah at Rice Creek."

Myrick leaned forward, trying to draw his drunken brain into focus. "You sure? That sure explains a lot about that Indian-lovin' bastard. I wish my brother was here. But he's in St. Paul now bringin' up stuff about Cates."

He shuffled to the window and looked out. *This'll sure shake things up. We'll nail his hide to the wall with this,* Myrick thought silently, reaching for the door knob. "No," he considered, "it's too late tonight. Tomorrow'll be soon enough. First thing in the morning, White Dog, I want you here. We'll go to Galbraith and the other traders then."

"You pay me." White Dog demanded.

"Have some whiskey. I'll give you something tomorrow."

"No whiskey. Money now."

Myrick raised his heavy fist threateningly and held it before White Dog's face like a hammer. "Look, you red scum. You show up and do what I say, or I'll see that you're finished working around here. I already pay you more than you're worth anyway. I said I'd give you a little something for your trouble tonight, and mebbe I still will. But you get smart with me and you'll get nothing. Be here early, now get."

White Dog sullenly rose from the table. He didn't look back as he rose from the table. Although it was late, he decided to ride back to Rice Creek. Myrick would cheat him, he knew it now, and he had no desire to help him in the morning.

❧ 38 ❧

THE FOUR YOUNG BRAVES STOLE TWO HORSES from a nearby farmer and, riding double, hurried back to the river valley. They realized that the murders at Acton would have dire consequences for the Santee nation. The night was clear as they galloped across the prairie. Stars shone brightly in the blackness above. As they neared Rice Creek Village, four miles above Redwood, it was before midnight.

It was a sticky night, hot and muggy, the kind of night that made Little Six kick off his blankets and turn down the fur side of his bedding. The young killers from Acton glimmered with sweat when they were ushered into the Santee leader's lodge. Breaking Up looked down into a dead fire pit and began hesitantly, "Little Six . . . we . . . we . . . have done a . . . great wrong."

Brown Wing looked at the chief directly. "We have done nothing wrong. We have killed whites. They cheat us and steal from us, and we have killed some."

Red Middle Voice, summoned from his tepee, joined the small group and with his nephew, Little Six, listened to the account of what had happened on the edge of the Big Woods.

Around Rice Creek Village the story spread like the wildfire on the prairie. Half-clad braves rushed from their tepees to spread the word and await a decision regarding a course of action. Mah-ka-tah raced to Red Middle Voice's lodge.

It was still quite dark as White Dog arrived in the village on his tired, spotted pony. The commotion and assembled men signaled him that something big had happened. Just as he was about to grab a young brave to ask what was going on, Little Six, Mah-ka-tah, and Red Middle Voice emerged from the chief's lodge.

They were met by hundreds of noisily clamoring followers demanding to know what was going to happen. White Dog raised his voice with the others.

Little Six shot his rifle into the air and, after an instant, all was quiet. In the distance a mourning dove's call echoed a lonely cry over the hills and bluffs. The Santee spread his arms and loudly addressed his people.

"Hear me. We have listened to these young men." He gestured to the four. "They have killed five white people by the Big Woods. There are several roads we can take. Last night we met in council. It was decided to go to Fort Ridgely and demand the annuities and then, if we must, go to Fort Snelling to make demands. Now our course is different. If we do not turn these four over to the whites, the whole band of Rice Creek Santee will be held responsible."

"No! No!" the people shouted. "They are our brothers! We will not give them up!"

"Then," Red Middle Voice screamed above the din, "we go to Little Crow."

Little Crow's village was several miles downriver, closer to the agency. Messengers were sent to gather the other Santee leaders. As the Dakota rode or ran along the trail, others joined them. No one needed to explain to newcomers what was happening. The war cries were enough. Half naked, hair streaming, they screamed and fired shots into the air as they rushed the short distance to the home of their war leader.

Little Crow was still asleep when he heard shrieks and howls from outside his upstairs window. He looked out into the dim early morning twilight and saw horsemen thundering through clouds of dust. In moments the leaders were thumping up his stairs and into his bedroom. When they burst through his door, Little Crow was sitting up in bed, a blanket crumpled at his feet. Red Middle Voice blurted out the story of the murders.

The Santee war chief pushed down through the crowded stairway into his main downstairs room. His house was already packed to overflowing. Many crowded outside and waited for word from their leaders. As best they could, the people pressed away from the center of the room to give space to their chiefs.

Cries of "We must have war!" and "Death to all whites!" were ringing in Little Crow's ears. He raised his arms above his head and waited for quiet. Most Dakota tried to sit cross-legged on the floor. Along the walls they remained standing. The smell of body odor and smoke mixed with the muggy morning air, stifling the restless mass of Santee.

Big beads of moisture stood out on Little Crow's forehead as he began to admonish his people. "I have been told what happened. The four young men are fools. The time is not now to fight the white man." He thought of Nathan's admonition to wait until September. "Why do you come to me now? Is not Traveling Hail your speaker? Should you not go to him for advice?"

"You are still our war leader, the greatest of our chiefs. Where Little Crow leads, we will follow!" Red Middle Voice shouted.

"No Santee's life is safe now!" Little Six exclaimed. "It is the white man's way to punish all Indians, even if only one or two have committed a crime."

"Yes," shouted Red Middle Voice, "let us attack them now! We must kill all whites. Should we just sit here and wait for the soldiers to come and kill us?

"Many soldiers are in the South and East fighting Graycoats," he continued. "Galbraith has showed us how desperate they are by taking mixed-bloods to fight. Now is the time to fight them!"

"Other tribes will join us!" Medicine Bottle exclaimed. "They will come from the West, maybe even the Ojibway and the whites of Canada. Remember, they once promised to help."

"That was long ago," Little Crow replied. "Canada is ruled by a woman now and will not remember a promise made to my father's father."

Red Middle Voice then looked directly at those who he knew wanted peace: Wabasha, Big Eagle, Mankato, and Traveling Hail. He said simply, "It is too late to do anything but fight. Our hands are bloody."

Wabasha instantly shot back, "You speak like children. Blood will not wash off blood."

Others, including Wacouta and Big Eagle, spoke for peace. The new speaker, Traveling Hail, implored, "We have no cannon and little ammunition. We are few, and the Americans are as many as the leaves on the trees in the Big Woods."

Then an old man, Tamahay, was helped to his feet. With the aid of a cane, he stepped forward and slowly, haltingly, almost inaudibly advised, "You are about to commit an act like that of the porcupine who climbs a tree, balances himself upon a springy bough, and then gnaws off the very bough upon which he is sitting. When it gives way, he falls upon the sharp rocks below. I do not say you have no cause to complain, but to fight is the end of us all. I am done."

Sensing he was losing the fight, Red Middle Voice made his last effort to sway Little Crow. "It is not I who wants war. Little Six does not want to kill the whites. Medicine Bottle would continue to pay the traders more for pork and sugar than the white man pays in New Ulm. It is the young men who want war. Listen, Little Crow, to the voices of the young men."

From outside came a low ominous wailing from the gathered warriors. The sound built, until it became continuous, like distant rolling thunder. Red Middle Voice strode to his war chief and warned, "They want to kill. Do not stand in their way. Those who do may die."

"They are fools, too!" Little Crow's words swept through his house like a thunderclap. "Yes, there will be vengeance! Women were killed. It was a stupid thing to do. A Dakota warrior does not make war on women. The whites are much too powerful. The days may be past when we can beat them. Maybe there never was such a time."

From those seated on the stairway, a cry rang out: "Ta-oya-te-duta is a coward!"

The war chief straightened his body. His face grew haggard and somber. Sweat began to drip from his nose, and he wiped it off. Then he replied to the gathering, "Ta-oya-te-duta is not a coward, and he is not a fool! When did he run away from his enemies? When did he leave his braves behind him on the warpath and turn back to his tepee? When he ran away from your enemies, he walked behind on your trail with his face to the Ojibways and covered your backs as a she-bear covers her cubs!

"Is Ta-oya-te-duta without scalps? Look at his war feathers! Behold the scalp locks of your enemies hanging there on his lodgepoles! Do you call him a coward? Ta-oya-te-duta is not a coward, and he is not a fool. Braves, you are like little children. You know not what you are doing.

"You are full of the white man's devil water. You are like dogs in the Hot Moon when they run mad and snap at their own shadows. We are only little herds of buffalo left scattered; the great herds that once covered the prairies are no more. See! The whites are like the locusts when they fly so thick that the whole sky is a snowstorm. You may kill one-two-ten; yes, as many as the leaves in the forest yonder, and their brothers will not miss them. Kill one-two-ten, and ten times ten will come to kill you." Little Crow held out his hands with fingers spread apart. "Count your fingers all day long, and white men with guns in their hands will come faster than you can count.

"Yes; they fight among themselves—away off. Do you hear the thunder of their big guns? No. It would take you two moons to run down to where they are fighting, and all the way your path would be among whites as thick as tamaracks in the swamps of the Ojibways. Yes, they fight among themselves, but if you strike at them, they will all turn on you and devour you and your women and little children just as the locusts in their time fall on the trees and devour all the leaves in one day.

"You are fools. You cannot see the face of your chief—your eyes are full of smoke. You cannot hear his voice—your ears are full of roaring waters. Braves, you are little children—you are fools. You will die like the rabbits when the hungry wolves hunt them in the Hard Moon of January."

Little Crow stopped and slowly looked around the room. Sweat matted his hair and ran down his cheeks. Then, as if resigned to his fate, in a

214

deliberate voice he finished. "Ta-oya-te-duta is not a coward; he will die with you."

Wabasha, Wacouta, and finally Big Eagle raised their voices for peace, but they were shouted down. Little Crow called out, "Brothers! Wait outside. Your chiefs must plan. We will talk with you soon."

The house emptied quickly as the braves left. The Santee war chief, now in full control, began to feel the exhilaration of the moment. His eyes blazed like hot coals as he looked at the men who would lead his warriors.

"When it is lighter, before seven, we will attack the agency. Have the braves quietly go to the homes of the whites, surround the houses but make no demonstration of violence. They should wait quietly until I fire a signal shot. Then kill the white men and any cut hairs that get in the way. Leave women and children alone. We make war on the government and soldiers only. I will lead the attack on the traders. It is from their cabins that the signal will come."

"This is all a mistake. Stop this before it's too late!" Big Eagle made one last plea for peace.

"The decision is made." There was finality in Little Crow's voice. He turned to Cut Nose. "Send messengers to the Sisseton and Wahpeton. They must join us. We go now to the agency."

As Little Six filed past him, Little Crow reached out and held his arm. He spoke softly into his ear. "If Big Eagle doesn't lead his band, I want him killed."

Little Six nodded and joined the other chiefs outside as they instructed the braves. There was no turning back now.

White Dog, outside with hundreds of others, smiled to himself. The time had come to help his people. Andrew Myrick had ordered him to be early. He would be.

୬ 39 ଓ

AROUND SIX ON THE MORNING OF AUGUST 18, Joe Coursolle—or Hinhankaga, as the Dakota called him—was waking from a fitful sleep. His log cabin was small, and the bedroom was stuffy and hot. The humid air hung above him as if he were in a sweat lodge.

Distant drums from Little Crow's village made Joe's stomach turn over in apprehension. His wife, Marie, was quiet next to him on their bed, but he sensed she was awake. Joe rolled over onto his side, his back to the doorway. Their baby boy, nine-day-old Cistina Joe, whimpered from his near-by crib. Then he was quiet.

Joe felt a hand softly touch his shoulder. Before he could turn in alarm, a woman's voice whispered into his ear. "Hinhankaga, be still. I am a friend. But don't look at me. Big trouble is coming. Soon warriors will kill all whites. Go now, before it's too late. Tell no one you were warned or I, too, will die."

Then, as silently as she had arrived, the woman was gone. Joe didn't even try to see who she was. Swiftly, the Coursolle family dressed and left their cabin. Joe hurried them to his canoe on riverbank.

"Marie, the boat's so small," he explained to his wife, "there is just room for two grown people at a time. I'll take you and the baby across and then return for the girls."

216

He looked at Elizabeth, who was six, and little four-year-old Minnie. Kneeling, he looked them squarely in their wide black eyes, and said as slowly and as calmly as he could, "Girls, I must leave you here for a very little time. After your mother and little Cistina Joe are safe on the other side, I'll come back for you, and we'll go to the fort. Hide in the bushes near the bank."

The little girls, tears brimming, somberly nodded and hugged their father. Then they retreated to the brush.

In the half-hour before seven that morning, Santee braves began gathering at the Redwood Agency. They seemed to be aimless as they wandered around houses and squatted on porch steps. The sun had slowly risen in the east. Bright rays were shining into agency homes as people sat down for breakfast. Smoke from cookstoves slowly tendrilled from stone chimneys, and the aroma of frying eggs and bacon wafted through the air.

There was some activity outside. Superintendent Wagner was overseeing the cleaning of the stables. Samuel Hinman was outside his church loading a wagon for a trip he was making downriver.

Nathan Thomas had suffered through a hot, mostly sleepless night. He moved his pallet from the loft and tried to sleep on the floor behind his counter, where he hoped it would be cooler.

Suddenly a rifle shot shattered the early morning stillness. An instant later, Nathan's door crashed open, and Little Crow with two young braves burst through the doorway.

"Our war has begun, One Arm!" There was a thrill in the chief's voice as he told the startled Nathan the news.

"Little Crow, it's too soon," Nathan replied.

"Sometimes these things have a time of their own, One Arm."

More shots and now cries and screams rang from outside. Alarm spread over Nathan's face. "Emily!" he cried. He looked at Little Crow accusingly. "You said only soldiers would be attacked!"

"Your woman is safe. No women or children are to be harmed. We came for food, and the war will be against soldiers, but this agency must go. The white government is here. This war was meant to happen now, whether you had come here or not. Stay inside, One Arm, I have told my warriors not to harm you."

"I must find Emily."

"Stay here. You may be killed outside," the Santee ordered.

Nathan pushed aside one of the young men and tried for the open door. The second Santee brave brought the blunt end of his hatchet down with a glancing blow alongside his head. Nathan fell in a heap onto the floor, unconscious.

Little Crow looked at the crates along the back wall. He turned to his companions and said, "People have wondered about those crates. Smash them with your hatchets. Maybe there is something more than we know about them."

Several blows from each weapon sent splinters and wood chips flying into the air and revealed stacks of rifles in the bottoms of the crates.

The chief smiled down at Nathan and told the unhearing soldier, "You brought us more than you said, One Arm." Soon hoardes of Santee had taken the weapons to use in their bloody work.

The trading posts were hit first. Many of the post employees slept in stores or else had reported early for work. At the first sound of gunfire, James Lynd jerked open the door of Myrick's post. Three shots hit him point blank in the head and heart. George Divolle stepped out to see what had happened and met the same fate. Old Fitz was cooking breakfast by the stove. Before he could react, a tomahawk split open his head.

Andrew Myrick grabbed a rifle and raced upstairs. "Com'on up, ya red devils," he shouted down the stairs, "let's see how far ya get with lead in yer bellies!"

"No!" Mah-ka-teh cried back, "we won't come up! We'll burn the cabin! Come down or roast!" He took coals from Fitz's stove and piled them on the wooden floor at the base of the steps.

Soon the floor began to smoke and crackle as flames danced through it. Mah-ka-teh heard a thud outside. Through the doorway he saw Myrick, who had jumped from an upstairs window, racing toward some brush. The leader of the Soldier's Lodge stepped outside and calmly aimed his rifle. A single shot sent the trader tumbling to the earth with a bloody round hole in the back of his head. Other warriors gathered around and drilled a dozen arrows into his body. One grabbed a hay scythe and drove it into Myrick's chest.

Then Brown Wing stood over him and warbled a fierce cry to the heavens. He ripped a handful of grass from the ground and vehemently stuffed it into Myrick's dead mouth. The warrior shouted, "He told us to eat grass. Now he can eat it forever!"

The other posts were hit at the same time. Francois LaBathe was killed in his store. Two clerks, munching on bacon and eggs, were shot in Louis Robert's post. George Spencer was the head clerk in the Forbes cabin. Middle-aged and stocky, his body was lumpy, like an overgrown sack of potatoes. At the sound of shooting, Spencer and four others raced onto the porch to see what was happening. Bullets from a dozen rifles riddled them, leaving four dead and Spencer wounded. Three shots had pierced his body.

The head clerk stumbled back into the store and pulled himself up the stairs into the loft. One Indian fired at Spencer as he struggled to climb, but missed. Spencer threw himself onto a bed and waited. Would they burn the building? Would they rush up to kill him? He was too weak to do more than wonder. Whatever his fate, Spencer hoped it would be quick. He had no desire to roast slowly like a pig on a spit in a flaming cabin.

Patrick McClellan, a clerk in Louis Robert's store, stepped into the sunlight, pipe in hand, and ready to greet a still, sunny morning. Four rifle shots left him lying in a puddle of blood.

Joe Coursolle had left his wife and baby on the opposite side of the Minnesota. Hearing gunfire explode as he paddled back across, he frantically searched the brush near the riverbank for Elizabeth and Minnie. They were not too be found. Realizing that more delay meant certain death for the remainder of his family, Joe swallowed his dispair and returned to Marie and Cistina Joe for the race to Ridgely.

The shooting was concentrated below the village proper on the trail at the south end of the agency. At the first shots, Wagner, in the stable, shouted to his teamster, John Lamb, "Well, John, sounds like some of the boys are still celebrating the Fourth."

"That's gunshots, sir," said a worker pausing over his pitchfork of horse manure. Then a half dozen Santee braves burst into the stable.

"We take your horses!" they cried and began to grab the halters of several animals.

"Hold on now. Just what do you think you're doing?" Wagner used an authoritive voice as if he were speaking to children.

"The war against whites has started. If you stand in our way, you will die." The Santee who spoke was painted red and black over his face and chest. A lightening bolt scarred down one cheek.

Wagner, not grasping what was happening, was indignant. "What do you mean, war? Wait till Agent Galbraith hears of this. You're lucky he's at Ridgely." He looked up and saw Little Crow standing in the open wide doorway of the stable. "Little Crow, tell them to stop this nonsense," he commanded.

Ignoring Wagner as if he was an insect to be crushed, the war chief looked at his warriors. "What are you doing?" he asked. "Why don't you shoot these men? What are you waiting for?" Immediately the Santee braves raised their rifles and killed the three white men.

Little Crow walked to Wagner, who lay on his back with a bullet in his heart. His unseeing eyes were wide open, staring blankly. The Santee leader reached into a pouch and removed a skinned crow. He dropped the totem upon the white man's bloody chest. "Let them know whose work this is," he called to his braves.

White Dog ran past the church. Hinman yelled at him, "What's happening?"

The Indian paused and looked sadly at the pastor. "Awful work has begun," he blurted. Then he sped on his way.

Soon after, Little Crow himself came to the church. Again Hinman asked what all the shooting was. The Santee merely scowled at his minister and hurried past. Now the sound of firing guns was almost continuous, and the acrid smoke of burned gunpowder touched Hinman's nose. He raced into his house and grabbed Elizabeth. Together they climbed into the ready wagon and whipped the horses to a gallop out of the village.

Back in Forbes' post, George Spencer waited for the footsteps on the stairs that would signal his death. From below he heard a voice cry, "Where is Spencer?" Then came the pounding of feet on the steps. Big Eagle's form filled the doorway to the bedroom. "Are you dying?" he asked the wounded man.

Spencer peered up at the big Indian. The clerk's bushy beard on his chin quivered weakly as he mumbled, "No."

"Come with me, I'll help you down the stairs. You are safe with me." Big Eagle reached down and helped the trader to his feet.

When they reached the bottom of the stairway, the waiting Santee braves cried, "Kill him. Kill him! Spare no one!"

Big Eagle pulled his hatchet from his belt and looked menacingly at the young braves surrounding him. "I will cut down the first man who tries to harm Spencer. He has treated you fairly. If you had killed him before I saw him, it would have been different. But this man has been my friend for ten years, and I will protect him or die with him."

Once outside, Big Eagle found a wagon and turned Spencer over to a couple of Indian women. "Take him to my lodge," he ordered. Then he turned back to the slaughter. Big Eagle knew he must lead his band. But he would not see his friends and the innocent killed.

Emily West had been sipping coffee in Mrs. Robertson's sitting room when the killing began. Alma had left the day before for Faribault, and Emily was alone in the house. She ran to a window and watched in horror as Indians shot down her neighbors. The scene unfolded as if in slow motion to the young teacher. She saw the red splotches spread slowly on the bodies of her friends and watched hair being ripped from their scalps after a slice of a hunting knife.

Dr. Humphrey lurched from his office across the square. The man who had cared for the health of hundreds of Santee clutched his chest and dropped face first into the dirt.

Loud pounding on the door broke Emily from her trance. "Emily, Emily! It's me, Philander! Let me in!" She hurried to the door and threw it open. The old man was wild-eyed as he burst into the house.

221

"It's started, Emily. The dang fools are killin' people! Come with me. We've got to get out of here!"

"Where's your wife, Philander?"

"Visiting relatives upriver. Let's go!"

With eyes fixed straight ahead, they rushed down the path toward the ferry.

On the other side of the river, Charlie Martel heard the crescendo of gunfire popping all over the agency. Soon smoke and flames were visibly erupting from buildings. The old Frenchman knew what was happening. Quickly he spread the alarm throughout his little settlement.

"The agency ees under attack!" he screamed. "Leave now while you can!"

Within minutes a mounted George Reed cantered up, "Jump on, behind me, Charlie!" he shouted.

Martel glanced at the horse and then across the river where people were gathering on the riverbank. He looked up at the horseman.

"I cannot, George. Those people need me. They'll be massacred over there eef I don't help them."

"Charlie, they'll kill you, too!"

"Maybe, but I must try. Now ride, George. Ride!"

When George still hesitated, the Frenchman whipped off his hat and slapped his friend's horse on the rump, sending it galloping down the path.

Martel pushed and pulled his barge across the river and took his first load of refugees back to the ferry side. Back and forth, the Frenchman kept risking his life to save the lives of the agency people.

Many were dying. Yet, miraculously, just as Big Eagle had saved George Spencer, other whites were being rescued or warned by Santee friends. Then the warriors turned their attention to looting the warehouses, stores, and houses. For a time, their attention was diverted from killing and became focused on food, bright cloth, guns, and other objects that grabbed their interest.

The whites of the agency and Charlie Martel seized the opportunity to flee across the river. As they hurried through the village, Emily suddenly froze. "Philander, what about Nathan? I've got to find him!"

Prescott firmly took her by the shoulders and turned Emily to face him. "Listen, we've gotta keep going! Nathan's either got away or they killed him. There's nothing you can do for 'im but save yerself. Let's go!"

In minutes they were in Martel's barge. Charlie grabbed Philander's arm and exclaimed, "They finally did eet, didn't they? Galbraith and the fool traders! They should have seen this comin'."

"If they did, Charlie, they ignored it."

Once on the north side of the Minnesota, Emily and Philander stood momentarily and looked up the bluff at the agency. Black billows of smoke mixed with flashes of fire against a bright blue sky. Then they joined other refugees in flight to Fort Ridgely.

The attackers of Redwood Agency were not the only Santee sent on murderous missions that day. Cut Nose and Red Middle Voice had also sent braves up and down the river on either side of the agency. No cabin or farm was safe from them.

Word of the attack spread and many managed to escape. Many others didn't. Joseph Reynolds, the teacher who lived near Little Six's village, avoided the Dakota. But his niece and two hired girls who were riding in a wagon with a hired man were captured. The man was killed, and the girls carried off. Many other women met similiar fates.

Bands of Santee began to run down the fleeing whites on both sides of the river. One group overtook Philander Prescott and Emily West. The Indians' horses pranced nervously as the Santee surrounded the two whites. Hatred gleamed through warpaint that couldn't hide their emotions. The leader of the half dozen Indians looked down from his pony and said, "You must die, white man."

Prescott stood in their midst on the open prairie with Emily at his side. The wind blew his long white hair behind him. Now, without fear, he looked them in the eyes and answered, "I am an old man. I have lived with you forty-five years. My wife and children are of your blood. I have never done you any harm. Why should you wish to kill me?"

The leader was matter of fact. "We would save you if we could, but the white man must die. Such are our orders. You are a white man. We cannot save you."

Philander turned to Emily and brushed his lips on top of her head. "Good-bye," he murmured. "Tell my wife . . ."

Then he turned toward the Indians and opened the front of his shirt. A single shot pierced his chest. Emily, sobbing, fell at his side. One of the young braves jumped from his horse and grabbed a handful of her hair as his knife went to her throat.

"No!" shouted another Santee. "Leave her."

The brave holding Emily looked up briefly. She took advantage of the pause and began to struggle. The brave raised his knife and prepared to thrust it down.

The other Santee swiftly brought his war club across the first brave's head. It cracked sharply, sending him reeling to the ground. Then the brave leaped off his pony and stood by Emily's side. Glaring at the others, he said, "This woman is my friend. You will leave her alone."

He looked down at Emily, who was still sobbing and shaken. "Miss West, don't be afraid. It's me, Traveling Star . . . Johnny."

≈ 40 ≪

I T WAS NEARLY TEN O'CLOCK WHEN Nathan regained conciousness. His head throbbed as if Charlie Culver were beating time inside it. Blood matted his hair just above his left ear. Unsteadily he struggled to his feet and plunged his head into a wooden bucket full of water. As the world came back into focus, Nathan saw buildings either in flames or smoking. Dead and mutilated bodies were strewn everywhere, all of them white men. His thoughts flew to Emily, and he hurried along deserted streets to her home.

Flying Owl was sitting on the stone steps of the church, his head held in his hands. With tears in his eyes he looked at Nathan. "She's gone, One Arm. Last I saw of her, she was going to the ferry with Philander." Then he stared at the stone step between his feet and mumbled as if to himself, "Yes, she's gone. Soon everything will be gone."

Nathan knew the refugees would be heading to Fort Ridgely. Emily must be on that path. He bolted down to the river, once slipping hard onto his back when his feet hit loose gravel on a downslope.

The barge was on the other side, but a small, leaky skiff had been pulled onto the riverbank on the agency side. He rowed quickly, even though it was a struggle with just one arm, and reached the far side before the seeping water capsized the boat.

225

Nathan found Charlie Martel lying dead near the barge. The brave Frenchman had been scalped and mutilated. The sound of galloping hooves and dry grass being ripped apart made Nathan wheel around. A lone horseman stormed out from rushes near the riverbank. The Santee hadn't found Martel's pistol, and now it was in Nathan's hand.

Screaming, "Die, One Arm!" the warrior headed straight for Nathan.

The white soldier from Virginia calmly stood his ground in the face of the onrushing Dakota, holding his pistol behind his back. Then, as the horseman closed on him, Nathan raised his weapon and a shot spit from the barrel. The Santee flew backward and bounced on the ground, one neat bullet hole between his eyes. The pony, confused by the loss of his master, slowed and looked back. Nathan grabbed the bridle and firmly held the animal.

The Indians liked their horses small and fast. They traveled light and frequently used hit-and-run tactics in battle. The United States Army favored big, strong animals capable of hauling large men and equipment many miles.

Nathan was reminded of this as he swung onto the back of the Santee's pinto. His long legs stretched low on either side of the animal. Feeling like he was riding a big dog, he longed for an army horse. Yet, the pony was surprisingly tough and fast, and Nathan raced over the route he was sure Philander and Emily must have traveled.

About a mile from the ferry, he rode over a small rise on the prairie trail. A still form lay crumpled ahead. The unmistakable thatch of white hair identified him clearly, even from a distance. It was Philander Prescott.

The old man looked at peace. He lay on his back, his hands folded and eyes closed. Only the red stain on the front of his buttoned shirt indicated the violence of his death. There was no time to mourn. Nathan galloped on. The Dakota had Emily, or she was still on her way to the fort. Either way, he reasoned, Ridgely had the answer.

He passed others on the way. Many were from the agency, some from the ferry, and the rest lived near the river. They traveled on foot, by horseback and in wagons. One thing was common: the haunted look of fear in their eyes, the stark realism reflected in their faces that death could await them at the next bend of the trail.

226

❧ 41 ☙

ABOUT NOON, WORD OF THE ATTACK at Redwood reached the Sisseton and Wahpetons of Yellow Medicine Agency. The Upper Santee leaders gathered to plan a course of action and to act on Little Crow's request that they join in the war.

These Dakota had always had more peaceful relations with the whites than their cousins down the river. More of them farmed, and the Treaty of Traverse des Sioux had left them closer to their traditional territory. But there was still frustration with the deception of the white bureaucracy.

The chiefs met on the prairie upriver from the agency between Red Iron's village and the Hazelwood mission.

Speaking strongly for peace were the Upper Santee leaders: Little Paul, Red Iron, Chief Akepa, Standing Buffalo, and John Otherday, who was married to a white woman. However, many young braves, led by Sweet Corn, demanded that the bands join their brothers to the south in war. No consensus was reached, and the Upper Dakota were left to decide for themselves whether to join Little Crow or not.

Rumors began to spread into the agency itself. Most quickly dispelled the warnings as just talk. In the absence of Agent Galbraith, his assistant, Nelson Givens, didn't know what to think.

Dr. Wakefield, the agency physician, chose to believe the stories and sent his wife and children on the road to Fort Ridgely with George Gleason. Shortly after they left, John Otherday came to the Annuity Center and asked to speak with the agent. Givens received verification from Otherday that the rumors were, in fact, far worse than what they suspected.

"You must get your people together in a safe place," the Santee warned the assistant agent. "Soon our council will break up. Many speak for peace, but many of the young braves are determined to fight. We will not be able to stop them."

"Should we leave now?" Givens asked.

"No, it would not be safe. Put them here, in the center. Tomorrow I will lead them to safety."

Later that afternoon the people of Yellow Medicine filed into the brick Annuity Center. John Otherday stood on guard that night as the trading posts and stores in the valley below were attacked and burned.

಄ 42 ಇ

MID-MORNING OF AUGUST 18 was like most mornings at Fort Ridgely. Soldiers marched and drilled, the hot August sun already baking the parade ground. Jones and McGrew were preparing their gun crews for another round of artillery practice.

The pounding of hooves on the ferry road abruptly interrupted the routine. J.C. Dickinson, boarding-house manager from Redwood, galloped across the parade ground to the headquarters building. He slowed his lathered animal to a trot and leaped off, taking a running start into the captain's office.

John Marsh looked up from his desk. The man before him was scratched and streaked with blood. He was soaked with sweat, a look of desperation in his eyes.

"Captain, the agency, the Sioux attacked!" Dickinson blurted the words breathlessly, spitting them like bullets. Then he paused to compose himself before continuing. "People are dead all over. They hit us this morning . . . at breakfast. No warnin', nothin', they just started killin' everyone."

"Who are you?" the captain demanded. "How do you know this?"

"I'm Dickinson, I run the boarding house at the agency. I was there. Just barely got away. If it weren't for Charlie Martel, I wouldn't have."

A commotion from outside drew Marsh's attention as a wagon noisily rolled into the fort. The captain, followed by Dickinson, hurried onto the headquarters porch. Several refugees were in the wagon. One of them was badly wounded, and Dr. Muller rushed to his aid.

"See, Captain," Dickinson cried, "ya need any more proof?"

"No, Mr. Dickinson, I don't." He yelled for his drummer boy. "Charlie! Beat the long roll!"

The young soldier ran excitedly to the parade ground and beat a continuous loud roll on his drum. From all over the post, men raced to formation near the flag in the center of the grounds.

Tom Gere sprinted from the stables to Marsh's office. The captain was seated at his desk, hurriedly slipping balls and percussion caps into the cylinders of a Navy Colt revolver. Another full cylinder lay on the desktop before him.

"What's happened, Captain?"

"The Sioux attacked the agency, Tom. I've got to take part of the company to Redwood. Maybe a show of force can save some lives. Maybe I can talk some sense into those people. Sergeant," he said, turning to Findley. "Get me Quinn. We'll need an interpreter there. I want you and Trescott and Bishop with me."

With an excited "Yes, sir!" Findley was gone.

"Tom, I'm leaving thirty men here with you."

"Captain, let me go."

"Tom, Culver's gone. You're the only officer here besides me. Frankly, I'm older and more experienced than you. If it comes to negotiating with Sioux leaders, I'm the one to do it. Tom," Marsh's voice softened, "if something happens to me, you're in command of the company. This fort's all that stands between the river valley and St. Paul. This is the gate through which they can't pass. You've got to hold it closed."

"With thirty men, sir?"

"Send McClain after Sheehan. He can't have got too far."

"I'll do my best, Captain. But you'll be back to help."

Marsh scratched the back of his head and looked over Gere's head at the bright blue sky. "I hope so, Tom, but . . ."

"But what?" Gere asked.

"Nothin'. . . just a feeling. It's nothing." Then the captain riveted his attention on his assembled men. "Let's get to it."

In moments, Marsh stood before his command, and in a few words outlined that the agency had been attacked and that they were heading there to calm the crisis. Within minutes, forty-six men of Company B were marching in order down the road to Redwood Ferry. Captain Marsh and Peter Quinn rode on horseback. Four wagons, hastily being loaded with equipment and ammunition, would follow.

It was twelve miles on the road to the ferry. Almost at once the little force began to meet fugitives from the agency and the surrounding area. About halfway there, they encountered flaming buildings and dead bodies lying along the roadside and in farmsteads. Men, women, and children were mutilated and scalped. The supply wagons caught up with the column, and the young soldiers rode in them as they soberly considered their future.

Billy Blodgett sat next to Will Hutchinson in a rough bone-breaking wagon. "If we don't get kilt by the Sioux, this wagon might do the job, Will."

"Look out there, Billy. I never figgured it could be this bad." The horizon in every direction was dotted with pillars of smoke stretching into the heavens.

Eddie Cole fretted in a low voice, "We shouldn't be doin' this. We shouldn't be out here. There's prob'ly hundreds of 'em out here. We got under fifty men. How does the cap'n expect us to fight 'em?"

"That's just it, Eddie," Blodgett answered. "I don't think he plans on doin' no fightin'. We're for show. He wants to talk 'em out of this war."

"By the looks of what we're seein', it's gonna take some pretty fancy talkin', Billy." Eddie Cole's eyes grew wide as they passed another dead body, an old man, near the roadside.

Several refugee groups heading to the fort met the advancing column. They were pitiful little parties. After the initial hysteria, a look of blank shock reflected in many faces. Some were wounded, women sobbed softly and men brushed tears from their own weathered cheeks as the company from Ridgely approached. The soldiers' march slowed as Marsh briefly questioned each band. The message was the same. The agency had been destroyed and many killed. The words were different, but the message to Marsh was similar from all the fugitives. "Go back to Fort Ridgely; if you keep going you'll be killed."

After speaking with one such group, Marsh turned in his saddle and faced Quinn, the veteran white-haired interpreter. "Well, Mr. Quinn, they seem to be unanimous. But they're civilians and possibly don't read the situation like we do. In any event, it's a dilemma. We could pull back and defend Fort Ridgely and the people who seek safety there, or we can continue and maybe stop this thing before it gets any more out of hand. Which way do we save more lives? I just can't believe that cooler heads won't prevail."

Quinn turned Marsh's words over in his mind and replied slowly as if thinking out each word. "Little Crow should know better. He knows they'll lose in the end. If we can get the thing stopped now, the Sioux won't keep on rampaging in the valley while we're safe in the fort."

Marsh pressed on, but the closer they got to Redwood Ferry, the more he began to doubt his decison. They would enter the valley about three miles from the ferry. A couple miles from that point, Nathan Thomas rode into the column.

"Mr. Cates! Glad to see you made it out. I heard things went real bad for the traders." Marsh seemed genuinely glad to see Nathan.

"They did, sir. Myrick, LaBathe, several clerks are dead. I don't know who else. Have you seen Emily West?"

"No, we haven't, we've run into dozens heading toward Fort Ridgely but I can't say that I've seen Miss West. Maybe she's on the other side of the river."

Nathan looked over the river and then back at Marsh. "I don't think so, Captain. She crossed at the ferry with Philander Prescott. I found him dead, but Emily was nowhere to be found."

"There's lots of possibilities, Mr. Cates. Hopefully, she's out there somewhere trying to make her way to safety. Good luck to you. If I were you, I'd check the fort first. She might be there, and if not. . ." Marsh hesitated, "if she can, she'll be headed there."

"Thanks, Captain, and one thing . . ."

"Yes?"

"Turn around and go back. Your small force can't stand against them."

"We don't intend to get into a situation where we fight the whole Santee nation. I want to end this without shooting."

Nathan wheeled his pony to the left. As he kicked its sides, he called back, "All the same, Captain. Go back." Then he galloped down the trail.

Marsh ordered his men out of the wagons to march on foot the rest of the way to the ferry. They marched double file, speaking quietly to each other, knowing that the situation was extremely dangerous.

Jimmy Foster gripped his rifle tightly and peered closely into the brush on both sides of the trail. "We're in a real pickle," he worried to John Holmes marching alongside him. "Cap'n thinks he can talk 'em out of all this. We're in so deep now that he better be able to because we ain't gettin' out of here otherwise."

"If we don't get back to Ridgely, Jimmy, the fort will fall, too," Holmes replied. "We should've stayed put."

"Cap'n said we hadda try, Johnny. Thing is, he didn't know, none of us knew, how bad it was."

Behind them Eddie Cole spoke up. "Ya, hear those people yell at us on the trail. They kept sayin' we was dead men if we kept goin'. I say turn around and get back."

"Too late for that, Eddie," Foster called back, "there's Faribault Hill just ahead. From there we see a whole sweep of the valley, and we're close to the agency. Cap'n Marsh will push on from here. He wants to talk to the red devils."

If the men of Company B were appalled by what they saw from the trail, the view from the top of the hill sickened them. No building within sight was left unburned. The unmistakable forms of dead bodies glistened whitely in the hot sun and dotted the landscape. Three miles distant on the bluffs of the agency, a smoky haze floated ominously.

Marsh dismounted and paused at the crest of the hill. With his sergeants and interpreter Pete Quinn, he viewed the destruction. Their faces were sober but resolute. Only Bishop spoke. "We going down, Captain?" He knew the answer.

Marsh handed him a locket and a letter. "Maybe you'll have to send these to my wife, Sergeant." Then the captain swung back onto his horse, pulled his sword from its scabbard, pointed down the trail into the valley and shouted, "Forward!"

Down into the desolate valley of the Minnesota River marched the forty-six men from Company B.

༄ 43 ༈

REFUGEES STREAMED INTO FORT RIDGELY all afternoon. Samuel and Elizabeth Hinman were among the first to arrive, getting there shortly after Marsh and his men had left.

John Jones and Jim McGrew stood with Tom Gere as more wagons rumbled into the fort.

"I wish we had walls," Gere said half to himself.

"No time to build 'em now, Lieutenant," Sergeant Jones answered, his tone matter of fact.

"From what I'm ahearing, it sounds a mite bad out there. I'm hoping the captain will be all right." McGrew added.

"Look, sir. We've got some bad stuff coming our way." Jones earnestly looked at Tom as he spoke. "You're in charge, and McGrew and me think you'll do just fine. But we want you to know that you can count on us. Advice, support, anything you need."

"I appreciate that, men. I'll use it. What should we do first?"

"Get some water in here," McGrew said emphatically, "with no infernal well, we can't be caught dry if there's a siege."

"Organize details to do that. I'm going to interview more of the refugees and try to find how widespread this is."

235

"Lieutenant, one more thing." Jones looked him in the eyes. "Appear strong and decisive. These people, the soldiers and the civilians both, need you to lead them. They need to see you strong."

"Thank you, John. I'll do the best I can."

Gere did act decisively. He moved among the refugees, made sure that the injured were sent to Dr. Muller, and talked to them about what had happened. The magnitude of the uprising was certainly greater than he had at first imagined. Reverend Hinman told him that Little Crow himself was involved and that no white person in the valley was safe. But mixed with tales of horror were the inexplicable stories of Indians who had rescued white friends.

Jones and McGrew oversaw the filling of wooden barrels with water from the creek behind the fort. Tom walked by as they were filling their last container. "What concerns me, sergeants," the Lieutenant spoke softly, not wanting to be overheard, "is that the refugees are coming from closer and closer to the fort. The Sioux are moving toward us."

"I'm worried about the captain and the boys out there," McGrew added. "I'm afraid they've gone into a hornet's nest they didn't expect."

"They're good men," Gere said. "Most of them were at Yellow Medicine when the Sioux tried to take the warehouse. They stood up well under stress."

"At least Whipple got here safe. We might need him." McGrew commented on the arrival from the agency of J.C. Whipple, a veteran of the Mexican War and a former artilleryman.

"I wish Sheehan would get here soon." Jones looked to the north anxiously. "Corporal McClain had the best horse on the post, and he left even before Marsh got on his way. It just depends on how hard Company C's been pushing." Gere followed Jones' eyes as he spoke. "John," he added, "how's your wife doing? When's the baby due?"

A worried look flashed over the sergeant's face. "Fine, Lieutenant. She's doing fine, and the baby's due anytime now."

"If you need anything, let me know. Have you talked with the Mullers recently?"

"They know her condition. Right now they've got their hands full . . ."

"Look, Captain! Another one!" McGrew pointed to a rider galloping into the fort.

Nathan Thomas rode swiftly up to the three soldiers. He dismounted from an exhausted and lathered pony and quickly approached Gere. "Tom, has Emily made it here?" he blurted.

"I'm sure not. Have either of you seen Miss West?" he asked the sergeants. Both shook their heads.

"I don't know what to do." Nathan was exasperated, "When it all started, I got a blow to the head. When I came to, it was over, and Emily was gone. I know she went with Prescott. I found him dead, but no sign of her."

"First," Tom told Nathan, "we've got to get your head looked after." The blood above his ear had dried into a thick wad in his hair. "Then rest, and we'll plan some course of action."

"I've got to do something now!" Nathan exclaimed. "This is my fault!"

"It's no one's fault, boy-o," McGrew interrupted. "This just happened. But the lieutenant's right. There's nothing you can do now. All you'll do is get yourself killed riding back and forth out there. Beating the bushes lookin' for Miss West, you'll find a redskin."

"But . . ." Nathan took a step forward and stumbled. Jones grabbed him in his strong arms and held him up. Fatigue and the blow to the head had combined to dizzy and weaken Nathan.

"Help him into Captain Marsh's office. I'll let Dr. Muller know he's got another one to look in on. Rest, Nathan, we'll see to Emily as soon as we can."

As he lay on Marsh's cot, Nathan recalled Little Crow's promise to not make war on women and children. He thought of Emily and what he had caused to happen. Then sleep washed over him like a great ocean wave.

ல 44 ௧

MILY RODE A SPOTTED PONY as she accompanied the small band of Santee riders who had killed Philander. She rode double, sitting behind Traveling Star, the boy she knew as her student Johnny.

After Traveling Star had whacked one of his companions on the head, Emily had tearfully arranged Philander's body before being taken away. While whites might have held a grudge against him, the Santee respected Traveling Star for standing up for his friend and nothing more was said. Emily was now his to protect or kill.

As the young teacher held on around his waist to keep from falling off, Traveling Star spoke to her quietly over his shoulder. "Don't be afraid, Miss West. We are taking you to my village, Little Crow's village. I will put you in my parents' lodge, and you will be safe. My uncle, Lightning Blanket," he pointed to the lead rider, "has declared no harm shall come to you. He joined us after Mr. Prescott was killed. He would have saved him, too."

"Johnny . . . Traveling Star. What about Nathan Cates? Do you know anything?"

"I was not in the agency. The youngest of us held the horses by the river. But I was told that Little Crow put him under his protection and that he got away. Once he left the ferry, I cannot say what happened to him. He killed Younger Fox and took his pony."

It came as some small relief that Nathan was not dead. "Did they have to kill Philander, Johnny?"

"We were told to kill all whites who tried to escape the agency. Some Santee saved whites anyway. But these," he gestured to the men he rode with, "saw blood, and no mercy was in their hearts."

"Thank you, Joh . . . Traveling Star. I owe you my life."

"You were kind to me and the others, Miss West. Little Crow told us not to harm women and children, but many of the young men would not listen. They were bad to the women. It is good I was there."

Emily blushed. They fell silent as the little party rode into the village of the Sioux war chief. Traveling Star placed Emily in a lodge with his mother. All the warriors were gone. Only old men and boys were left to watch over the women and girls.

The young Santee said to Emily, "My mother will be with you. Even if you could, it would not be wise to try to get away. Here you will be safe. Away from here is death."

Emily nodded at Traveling Star, fully believing his words. Then he was out the flap in front of the tepee and gone. She was alone with his mother, a still-young-looking woman with straight black hair and dressed in a stained soft leather dress. The Indian woman looked at Emily with sadness in her eyes.

Emily slumped onto a fur robe on the floor and put her head in her hands. Soft cries built to sobs as thoughts of the horror she had witnessed and her fears for Nathan's safety coursed through her mind. Emily clung to the hope that somehow she and Nathan would survive and find each other.

☙ 45 ❧

IT WAS A LITTLE AFTER MIDDAY when John Marsh ordered his men down Faribault Hill and into the Minnesota River Valley. They marched to the river bottom where a trail ran alongside the river for three miles to the ferry. Tall grass grew on either side of the narrow road. On the left thickets of wild plum and willow also grew. Trees and stumps were interspersed on the right.

They marched at a good pace, anxious to reach the ferry and be away from the cover from which the young soldiers expected gun shots and war whoops with every step they took.

"Look there!" Jimmy Foster called out to his comrades. He pointed across the river where a small band of Indians was chasing two fleeing white men. Their desperate screams of terror drifted faintly across the Minnesota to the soldiers. The Santee rode down the whites and clubbed them from behind, then shot them as they lay on the ground.

Foster and Sutherland raised their rifles to shoot. "Shoulder your weapons!" John Bishop commanded. "They're out of range, and you can't do them any good. Be disciplined and act like soldiers."

About a mile from Redwood, Marsh ordered a halt. He called his sergeants and Quinn together as the men rested. "Gentlemen, this is it. We'll go to the ferry and cross over to the agency. There I hope to find some cooler heads and get this under control."

"I haven't seen any Indians since they was runnin' down those men t'other side of the river," Trescott said. "That worries me."

"Don't worry, Sergeant," Quinn replied, "you can be sure they've seen you."

"How are the men, Sergeant Bishop?" Marsh asked. He looked at the small huddled groups, some sitting on the road. They were talking in low tones, a few chewing hardtack or drinking from canteens.

"Scared, sir, but they'd be fools not to be. They were tested at Yellow Medicine. They'll do fine."

"I think you're right, Sergeant. They're good boys. We'll move out in files of four, that should take away some of our exposure. Make sure the men's rifles are primed. The river turns ahead where a small creek enters it. Watch the willows there, it's especially thick. We'll continue to the ferry house just north of the ferry and reassemble there. Quinn, stay near me. Gentlemen, good luck. God willing, we're going to save a lot of lives today."

As they drew near the ferry, each clump of brush and willow, each high growth of grass or sandbar presented possible concealment for the Santee. However, when they reached the ferry, an open clearing stretched between the buildings and the water. The hot sun beat down on their backs, yet many of the soldiers broke into a cold sweat.

They stopped at the ferry house, and the forty-six men stood at shoulder arms in their ranks while Marsh and Quinn walked down to the riverbank.

"Do you think any of the agency folks are still over there?" Marsh wondered, looking at the smoke that overhung the agency.

"Anyone over there's dead, Captain," the interpreter answered.

They looked across the river to the smouldering buildings and the wooded slope leading up to the village. Marsh walked over to the ferry barge moored on his side of the river.

"Oh, God, look at this! Poor Charlie!" The ferryman was lying next to his boat, his stomach cut open and his skull smashed apart. "Why do they have to do this?" Marsh exclaimed angrily.

"They think you enter the spirit world in the condition you are in immediately after death," Quinn explained. "No one's afraid of being haunted by a crippled spirit."

"They can all go to Hell!" Marsh snapped.

"Look, Captain!" Sergeant Findley hurried to Marsh and pointed to the flats across the Minnesota. A few warriors rode slowly along the riverbank. They seemed to not even notice the soldiers on the other side.

Then a lone Indian appeared standing on a log next to the boat landing on the agency side. He was dressed magnificently in beaded buckskin, eagle feathers adorning his head, bright paint highlighting his face. It was White Dog.

"What do you want, White Dog?" Marsh called out.

"We want a council, not a fight. Come over to the agency, and we will smoke and talk." The Santee stood proudly like an eagle about to soar. He was performing the great deed he had promised weeks before. Little Crow himself had said to White Dog, "I have a task that only you can do. The whites trust you. You worked for the agency. They will listen to you. Do what I say." Now the people would know that his heart was with his tribe.

"I don't like it, Captain," the interpreter told Marsh, "let's leave now."

"Not yet, Quinn," the officer replied. "I don't think they're fool enough to attack a concentrated force. That's not how they fight."

"Captain, forty-six men don't concentrate much."

As Marsh and Quinn conversed with White Dog, Bill Blodgett and Will Hutchinson went to the riverbank to fill canteens. They knelt at the edge of the cool water and dipped their containers. Across the river, in brush, Blodgett saw a flash reflected from the sun.

"Will, looky close over there. Squint your eyes into that brush. It's crawlin' with Indians."

Hutchinson peered intently across the water. "You're right, Billy. They're thick as flies on a dead cow. We better tell the sergeants."

The two privates hurried over to the rest of the company. "Sergeant Trescott," Blodgett cried, "across, over there!" He pointed at the distant brush. "There's Sioux all over the riverbank."

Trescott and Findley looked carefully and then jogged to Marsh.

"Captain," Trescott said, trying to appear calm, "there's a whole lot of Sioux waitin' for us in the brush on either side of the landing."

"I've noticed, Sergeant." Marsh looked over at White Dog, still waiting next to the wharf. "It's natural that they would be there. We're going across. Move the men forward. We're coming in the barge now!" he shouted to the waiting Santee.

Meanwhile, John Bishop gazed into the river from the shore. The water was discolored. Something was stirring up the riverbed upstream. It could only mean that the Dakota were crossing and moving. To a soldier, there could only be one reason for such a manuever: a rear attack.

Bishop hurried to Marsh and pointed to the roily condition of the water. "Cap'n, they're movin' behind us. They gotta be."

White Dog, watching the soldiers and the river, quickly reasoned that the soldiers were becoming alarmed and might not enter the barge. The plan to ambush them as they crossed was falling apart.

The Santee's face became agitated. He looked into the brush where the warriors waited, then back at Marsh. Were the bluecoats moving back? White Dog couldn't tell. He decided to act. The Indian raised his rifle and fired a shot into the air.

Quinn yelled, "Look out!" An instant later a volley ripped from across the river. The interpreter was hurled backward, riddled by a dozen bullets. Several soldiers fell, mortally wounded.

Marsh, standing next to Quinn, was untouched by the volley, only splattered by Quinn's blood. He shouted to his men, "Fall back to the ferry house!"

Their retreat was cut off as Bishop was proved right. The Santee poured in from behind and gained the house first. Private Sutherland reeled around and shot at the onrushing Dakota. A bullet thudded into the Indian's chest, and he fell next to the river.

The screams of the Dakota were deafening. Gunfire and smoke filled the air as Company B tried to make a stand in the open between the ferry buildings and the river. There was no time to form up or fire by company.

Bishop shouted, "Fire at will! Fire at will!" The men knew that they were fighting for their lives. The Indians rushed at the soldiers, and the fight turned hand to hand.

Bishop had fixed the bayonet to his rifle, and he slammed it into a Santee's stomach. He felt the weapon grind against a rib bone as he pulled it out. Another Indian closed in on the sergeant from behind. The Dakota raised a club as Bishop tried to extricate his bayonet. From a few paces away, Trescott fired his revolver. Bishop's attacker grabbed his head and tumbled into the river. Trescott smiled at Bishop, then grabbed his chest. Red streamed between his fingers as the sergeant fell face first into the dirt. He didn't move after that.

The soldiers were fighting as a trained unit. They fought like veterans, not the green troops they were. There simply were not enough of them. Marsh realized they would soon be overwhelmed and looked toward the wooded willow thicket where the creek entered the river.

The air filled with the screams of men and horses. Bullets whizzed as deadly missiles flew through the air, sometimes thumping into soldiers. Officers yelled orders above the chaos as steel bayonets and rifle butts clanged and thudded the Santee.

"Get to the brush! Move to the willows!" Marsh cried. They struggled toward the wooded area, clubbing and shooting as they went. Fifteen of them reached the brush. From there they poured fire back at the Dakota. The Indians raked the thicket with bullets. But now the soldiers fought from cover, and the attackers were held off.

Marsh slid next to Bishop. "John, where's Findley?"

"Dead, sir."

"Damn," Marsh shook his head, "we've only got fifteen men here." The captain raised his pistol and fired. "There aren't thirty laying out there. Where are the rest?"

"In brush, maybe in some of the buildings." Bishop reloaded as bullets snapped leaves and small branches above him. "Blodgett got hit in the opening shots. I know he got to the ferryman's house. I saw a few try to fight down the road we came on."

"We've got one chance, Sergeant." Marsh squeezed off another shot. "We've got to make it to the fort. We'll back down the thicket as long as we've got cover. I just hope they don't cut us off."

The survivors of Company B desperately moved out, retreating slowly and firing as they dodged and scrambled through the thicket in the direction of Fort Ridgely.

Bill Blodgett lay in Martel's house as bullets splatted through the walls and windows. He had been shot through the side, but no major organs were hit. Billy knew that he couldn't stay put. Soon they would rush the house. He ran out across the road and into the barn. Private John Parks was half sitting against the barnwall, propped up, his gun in his lap.

"Let's go, Johnny, I'll help ya," Blodgett cried.

"Too late for me, Billy. Keep goin', I'll try to cover ya."

"No, John, com'on! I'll carry ya."

"Billy, I'm shot in the back. I can't move. Go, Billy! Now!"

Blodgett ran out the door and into the tall grass and brush. Rapid fire to his left attracted Billy to where three soldiers were standing with their backs to a tree, each firing in different directions. He raced to them, intending to take the final quarter of the tree. Before he could reach them, all three fell dead. Billy looked in the direction of the shots and saw a Santee reloading his rifle. Blodgett took quick aim and fired. The Indian folded to the ground.

Billy scurried back into the brush. The sound of pounding feet on the path in front of him dropped the private to his knee, his rifle aimed straight ahead. Luckily he didn't fire, because Eddie Cole was suddenly in his sights.

"Eddie, follow me! Run faster," Blodgett yelled.

"I'm wounded, Billy. My hand."

As he lifted his hand to show his friend the wound, the two reached a fork in the path. Billy went to the right. Somehow lifting his left hand sent Eddie reeling to the left. He kept going, separated from the other private.

Ahead, Blodgett heard a racket. He quickly dropped to his belly and began to crawl off the path into brush. Ezekiel Rose ran over his feet, closely pursued by two Santee.

Billy edged under some wild morning glory vines, reached back and straightened the grass. Then he heard a loud scream and Eddie Cole's voice.

"You beg like an old squaw," an Indian exclaimed. As Billy started to go to Eddie's aid, he heard the sickening blow of a tomahawk crunching into Cole's skull.

The Dakota were only about twelve feet away. They sat down and smoked their pipes next to Eddie's body. The sweet smell of their tobacco slowly drifted to Billy's nostrils. He remained hidden; to fight now would be folly. It was almost two o'clock. The battle had begun at one thirty. Twenty-two soldiers had been killed outright. Some were wounded. Others, like Billy, lay hidden or were attempting to escape. The rest, with Marsh, continued to retreat along the river.

≈ 46 ≈

FOR OVER TWO HOURS MARSH and his fifteen men fought and clawed their way back through the brush and thicket toward the fort. Then they reached a clearing. On the fort road, Santee waited, like predators stalking prey. They were convinced that the soldiers would soon have to leave the brush and come into the open.

Marsh and Bishop looked out from their cover of willows. Both men were bloody and tattered. The sergeant had taken a bullet in his arm. The tangled brush had torn their clothing and ripped their skin.

"Look up on the road, Captain," Bishop gestured with his rifle. "Sioux are everywhere. They'll cut us to pieces before we can reach cover again."

Marsh glanced at the road and then across the Minnesota. "We'll cross to the other side, Sergeant, then move down the south side of the river."

"The water's fast here, and I'll bet over our heads. Can we make it?"

"It's only about fifty yards, Sergeant." Marsh seemed thoughtful. "I'll go first. When I get to the other side, follow."

Using the thicket as a screen, John Marsh waded into the water. The riverbed was uneven, with dips and holes, making depths uncertain. He held his sword and pistol above his head as the water slowly deepened. He was

247

almost two-thirds of the way over when the water reached his chin. Marsh dropped his weapons and began to swim. A current pulled him down, and the captain's fatigued legs cramped.

On the north shore, Bishop and the remaining men heard Marsh's desperate cries for help.

"I need a strong swimmer to go for the captain," Bishop yelled through the brush.

"I'm goin' for 'im," John Brennen announced as he threw off his shoes and sprinted into the river. Jim Dunn and Steve VanBuren followed close behind. Brennen attacked the water and quickly reached Marsh. The river was treacherous and swirling as the athletic private grabbed hold of his captain just as Marsh was sinking for the second time.

Brennan pulled him to the surface, and for a time Captain Marsh was able to hold onto his rescuer's shoulder. But the struggle had weakened him, and the water broke them apart. Marsh slipped out of Brennan's grasp and sank. The strong current dragged him down and away.

The three privates, in despair, pulled themselves back to the north side where Bishop awaited them.

"I had 'im, Sarge." Brennan shook his head and looked in anguish at Bishop. Tears were forming in the young man's eyes. "I had 'im, but he just slipped away."

"You tried, John, it's all you could do," Bishop sympathized. "Now let's the rest of us try to live."

"Sergeant," Levi Carr spoke to Bishop in an excited whisper, "the Sioux, look, they're crossin' over to the south."

"They saw Marsh goin' and thought we all must have," Bishop reasoned. "We'll just stay on this side while they wait for us over there." He looked over the terrain, then called out to Corporal Hawley. "Charlie, there's a low hill just off the road to the north. If we can get behind it without them seein' us, we maybe can make it. It's not more than a few miles to Ridgely."

Hawley looked at the rise in the land. "Not much. But it might be the only chance we got. Oh, Svendson can't walk no more. He's shot up too bad. We gotta carry 'im."

"Assign two pairs of men to switch off carryin' him, Charlie. Then let's move." Bishop, about the same age as the men he now led, was decisive.

In minutes, what was left of Company B ran directly north of the thicket, using it as a screen. Then they curved around the base of the hill, putting it between them and the Sioux waiting in ambush on the other side of the river.

John Bishop led the fourteen survivors as they pressed on to the fort. They were straggling and desperate but resolute that they must reach Fort Ridgely. It was their only hope for sanctuary.

෨ 47 ෬

NATHAN THOMAS AWOKE NEAR TWILIGHT. His head still throbbed and he was terribly thirsty, but he felt better. Then he thought of Emily and hurried unsteadily out the door. Tom Gere and Dr. Muller were standing on the porch.

"Tom," Nathan cried, "what's going on? Has Emily made it here?"

"No sign of her, Nathan," Gere answered. "Dr. Muller and I are waiting for word of Captain Marsh. Not hearing anything is getting pretty nervewracking."

"How are you feeling?" Muller inquired of Nathan. "I looked in on you while you were sleeping."

"I'm fine, just a little headache. Tom, I've got to find Emily."

"No one is to leave this post, Nathan." Gere looked sympathetically at him. "It's my order. No one could get far out there now anyway. You wouldn't be helping yourself or Emily with your hair on some Sioux's lodge-pole. I know it's hard, but wait. We should know something more soon. Hopefully, both Marsh and Sheehan will be here any time."

Another wagon full of refugees trundled into the fort. Gere called to Arlington Ellis, "Sergeant, we're getting overloaded in the wooden buildings. Tell them all to move to the stone barracks."

"How many have come here today?" Nathan asked.

"Two hundred fifty, maybe three hundred," Gere answered.

"What's your garrison strength?"

"Our effective force, Nathan, is twenty-four men. Scary, isn't it? One more thing. The government finally saw fit to deliver the annuity money. Four men delivered $71,000 in gold here this afternoon."

Nathan shook his head in disbelief. "The timing of this is a cruel joke, Tom."

"And not a very funny one," Muller added.

It was near dark now. Suddenly a cry came from the pickets outside the fort. "Men comin' to the fort!" Gere ran to meet the two shadowy figures that wearily walked toward the headquarters.

"Dunn, Hutchinson!" Gere was shocked at their ragged, ghastly appearance. The men's clothes were ripped, their faces and hands streaked with dried blood. "What's happened? Where's the company?"

"'Bout half are dead, Lieutenant. They hit us at the ferry. Sergeant Bishop, he's got what's left of us 'bout half a mile away. We were . . ." Dunn choked with emotion and couldn't continue.

Hutchinson picked up where his friend left off. "We got sent ahead to make sure that you was still here."

"Where's Marsh, Trescott, Findley?" Gere tried to keep his voice under control.

"Dead, all of them." Hutchinson couldn't meet Gere's eyes as he told him.

Gere and Muller stood in numbed silence. Then the young lieutenant regained his composure. "Sergeant Ellis, send men out to bring Bishop and the others in. How many are there?" He turned to Dunn as he asked.

"Altogether, there's fifteen of us left."

"Fifteen!" Again Gere was shocked. "Dr. Muller, prepare the hospital. I'm sure they'll need your attention. Corporal Good, get me Willie Sturgis. Send him to the headquarters. I'll be there."

When Sturgis entered the office, Gere was busily scratching out a letter at Marsh's desk. "Corporal, I've had the best horse left in the post sad-

251

dled for you. Take this," he quickly handed an envelope to Willie, "and deliver it to the commandant at Fort Snelling. And see that this letter," he gave Sturgis another, "gets to Governor Ramsey. We must have reinforcements at once. Galbraith and Culver should be at St. Peter with the Rangers. Tell them what's happened and that we desperately need them here."

Sturgis, realizing the faith being placed in him for this critical mission, gave his best military salute. "You can count on me, Lieutenant Gere. I'll get them dispatches delivered."

"Good luck, Willie." As Tom watched him leave, he knew that the future of the garrison and the lives of all within it lay in the young corporal's hands.

Willie Sturgis galloped wildly into the darkness. He didn't really like the dark. It had scared him when he was a child. But tonight the blackness folded over him like a down comforter. This night the dark hid him from harm and brought saftety, not fear.

Willie rode through the valley and out onto the highlands. After twelve miles of frantic riding, the horse was spent. Fortunately, Sturgis overtook a peddler in a wagon fleeing to Henderson. For ten miles they traveled together until the road forked. The peddler went his way, while Willie continued toward St. Peter.

Where the road divided, a settler's cabin stood. The corporal pounded on the door until a sleepy-eyed man opened the door. "What in thunder do you want at this hour!" the man exclaimed.

"I wanna save some people's lives, mebbe yers," Willie blurted. "The Sioux, they've massacred the agency, they killed Captain Marsh and half the company. I need to get to St. Peter to get help or the whole fort'll be wiped out. They're comin' this way, mister."

The settler was immediately wide-awake. "Help me hitch the team, soldier. I'll getcha to St. Peter!"

Through the blackness of the night, over roads that bumped, dipped, and twisted, the horses pulled the rumbling wagon at breakneck speed along the river. At three in the morning, August 19, just as a faint glow of pink showed in the east, Sturgis rushed into St. Peter.

Rumors had spread down the river valley and several were anxiously awaiting word from the northwest. Culver, Galbraith, and Lieutenant James Gorman of the Rangers quickly gathered around the exhausted corporal.

"Major Galbraith," Willie addressed the agent, "Lieutenant Gere sent me. We need you back at the fort."

"What's happened, Willie?" Culver asked.

Sturgis quickly summed up the tragic events of the day and his mission to St. Paul. The men stood in shocked disbelief.

Galbraith wrung his hands together. "I don't believe it. It just can't be."

"You can believe it, Major," Willie said emphatically, " and now they need help at Ridgely."

"Yes, yes of course, Lieutenant Culver. Gorman, see to the men. We'll leave immediately." Galbraith stared at his feet, slowly shaking his head as the lieutenants roused the Renville Rangers.

News of the attacks raced like a swollen stream through St. Peter, and panic gripped the town. The Rangers had marched off from Fort Ridgely without weapons. They had expected to be armed at Fort Snelling.

The townspeople of St. Peter hastily rounded up enough muskets and three rounds of ammunition for every man in the Rangers.

Willie Sturgis had difficulty getting horses until an appeal to the town sheriff yielded the lawman's own team. Willie then pounded down the road toward St. Paul. Part of his mission was accomplished. The Rangers, including Louis Bordeau, were on their way to Fort Ridgely. Now he had to get to St. Paul.

❧ 48 ❧

ABOUT THE TIME DUNN AND HUTCHINSON were telling Tom Gere about the attack at the ferry, Billy Blodgett pulled his stiffened body to his feet. Since two in the afternoon he had lain in the tall grass near the ferry. He had endured the screams of agony from suffering comrades as they were tortured and killed. For at least an hour, the Santee had roamed the battlefield, mutilating and scalping.

Billy covered his ears to blot out their cries for help. There was nothing he could do for them. As blood seeped from his side and abdomen, Blodgett doubted if he himself would be alive much longer. The sun beat fiercely on the dead and the living. Billy stayed concealed all day as Santee at times came within ten feet of him. He had no food or water, and the heat combined with his wound made him intensely thirsty. His tongue felt like a scaly dead lizard in his mouth.

The tempting cool water of the river flowed nearby but Billy, nearly crazed with desire for the refreshing liquid, didn't dare leave his hiding place. Between nine and ten that night, he noticed fires blazing across the river atop the agency bluffs. Beating drums, whoops, and high-pitched screams echoed down onto the bottoms. The Santee were celebrating a day of victory. Indian guards still moved among the dead, but the revelry up in the

254

agency distracted them, and several stood at the riverside and looked up at the precipice.

Billy seized this opportunity to make his move. At first he was so stiff that he was hardly able to force his body ahead. The pain from his wound was nearly unbearable. He might be dying, Billy thought to himself, and they might catch him, but staying put was certain death. He made his way to the river, downstream from the Santee, and submerged his head in the life-restoring water. Then he made his way down the river through the thicket that Marsh had followed earlier.

The vines and branches pulled and ripped at the soldier as he fumbled through the blackness of the night. There was no moon, and he felt like a blind man falling into an abyss. He closed his eyes to protect them from being scratched, and with each step he felt his wound stretch and open. For several hours, he pushed through the night until finally he could go no farther. Billy had made about three miles before he collapsed into a fitful sleep.

At daylight, Blodgett again started moving along the river. He found grape vines and ate a couple bunches of the fruit. It was his first food of any kind in over twenty-four hours. Using the cover of trees and brush by the Minnesota, he mustered six miles. But his efforts took a toll. His strength was sapped from battling with the tangled vegetation. He knew he couldn't last another day struggling as he had.

Billy looked in the evening haze to the north. He must cross the river bottom, climb the hill and gain the fort road across the prairie to Ridgely. It was now a race to see if his will could drive him to safety before his body gave out.

After an hour he reached the road and started slowly upward. Finding a deserted cabin alongside the pathway about three miles from the fort, Billy entered and searched for food and drink. A voice from outside startled and alarmed him.

"If there are any whites in there, let them come out and go to the fort. I just passed an Indian camp in the valley, only a short distance away."

The voice might belong to a treacherous half-breed trying to lure him to his death.

However, the pain in his gut and side left Billy feeling he had little to lose. He shouted, "I'm a soldier from Fort Ridgely!" and walked out into the darkness.

A white man stood in front of the cabin. "It's good to see another living white person," he said, both men feeling relieved. "I'm John Fanska, from New Ulm. I was on business at the agency when the attack came. I took an arrow in the back." He turned to reveal the bloody stub of an arrow shaft protruding from inside his right shoulderblade.

"Name's Billy Blodgett," the soldier replied. "I was at the ferry. Far as I know, they killed most of the company."

Fanska grabbed the obviously exhausted young man under his arm and said softly, "Let's the two of us see if we can get each other to Fort Ridgely."

On Wednesday morning, August 20, at two in the morning, Billy and the German from New Ulm staggered into the beleaguered garrison. It was thirty-six hours since the young soldier had been hit in the opening volley at the ferry. His last memory of the day was collapsing into the arms of Dr. Muller.

ೱ 49 ೲ

LITTLE CROW DISGUSTEDLY WATCHED the revelry of the young men at the agency. They must act now, he thought. The victory at the ferry must be followed up with an attack on the fort in the morning. Mah-ka-tah and the Soldier's Lodge opposed his plan. New Ulm and other smaller settlements on the river looked like easier conquests to them. They didn't understand. In the morning, Little Crow hoped, he could make them.

The Santee chief left the burning agency and rode the couple miles to his village. He had been told that One Arm's woman was there, and he wanted to talk with her before journeying to the fort.

When he reached the village, he went directly to Traveling Star's tepee. The fire was burning low in the center of the lodge. Near it, on buffalo skins, lay Emily West. Her eyes grew wide with fright as Little Crow slid through the opening.

"Don't fear me, Miss West," he tried to sound reassuring. "No harm will come to you here. It is my word that protects you."

"What about Nathan. Tell me, has anything happened to him?" Emily beseeched.

"He was not killed in the attack. I saw to that. We put him to sleep for a time, though. Now he is gone. I think he left for the fort. If he made it,

257

I don't know. There were many warriors between him and the fort. I think he did mke it though, for he is a most determined man."

Emily let go a deep sigh of hopeful relief. "Thank you for helping him."

"Listen to me, teacher. I don't have much time here. Stay with Traveling Star and his mother. This will help you to be safe. I said you are not to be harmed, but the young men do not always listen to what I say. There are other chiefs, and we are not an army like the whites have. My soldiers do what they wish sometimes.

"Tell One Arm that this was going to happen if he came here or not. The two of us talked, Miss West, and I promised him that war would only be on soldiers. It was what I wanted, but the young braves became crazed with blood and killed all whites they found. This is war the way the Santee fight it, and we could not change. Tell One Arm it is just the way things were meant to be and he shouldn't blame anyone, not himself, not even me."

"I don't understand," Emily seemed confused.

"Just tell him. He will tell you more if he wants." With those words, the war leader disappeared through the tent flap. As Emily listened to the dull thud of horse hooves disappearing into the night, she pondered the words of Little Crow.

ഇ 50 ര

HEN NIGHT FELL ON FORT RIDGELY, the sky was as black as the depths of an ominous cavern. It matched the despair of the desperate people gathered there. On the parade ground, groups of refugees huddled near campfires. Most were farmers, many of them German immigrants. Some had laid blankets on the ground. Generally they had only the tattered clothes they wore. Some women and children whimpered or sobbed, quietly grieving for lost loved ones. Little knots of men conversed in low tones. Sleep came hard to the frightened.

Lamps and lanterns cast glimmering yellow glows through the windows of the headquarters building. Tom Gere had called for a meeting of what amounted to his advisers. It couldn't be an officers' meeting, for he was the only officer left.

Sergeants Ellis, Bishop, Jones, and McGrew, the sutler Ben Randall, and Nathan Thomas joined the lieutenant. They all stood in front of Marsh's desk. "Men," Gere began in what he hoped was a calm voice, "in light of what's happened this afternoon, we've got some preparations to make." Eyes turned somberly to John Bishop as Gere issued instructions.

"Sergeant Jones, form a detail of men from the company and any able-bodied civilians willing to help, and barricade the gaps between the buildings. Use tipped-over wagons, furniture, barrels, whatever you can find. Mr. McGrew, see to the cannons. I think you'll have the opportunity to do more than practice with them.

"Nathan, I appreciate your help. Please go to the hospital and tell Dr. and Mrs. Muller to move their patients inside the compound. The hospital is very vulnerable to attack.

"Mr. Randall, enlist more civilians to help us. I want to know how many are capable of adding to our effective force here. We need as many fighting men as we can get. Replenish our water supply from the creek with anything that holds water." Even though tension gripped the garrison like a vise, Tom Gere appeared confident and efficient. He hoped no one detected the doubts and fears that fought within him.

"Sergeant Ellis, why haven't the civilians moved into the stone barracks?" Gere wondered.

"They feel safe where they are. Some moved. Many don't want to," the sergeant answered. "A bunch of 'em are in the wooden barracks, but a lot of 'em are just out in the open."

"See that they all move. The women and children especially will be much safer behind stone," Tom replied crisply. Then, looking at Bishop, he directed, "John, get some rest. We'll need all of you soon to man your posts, and I don't know for how long."

"I'm ready now, sir." Bishop's eyes blazed determination.

"If you must do something now, help Sergeant Jones, but . . ."

At that instant, a gunshot cracked through the stillness outside the fort complex, followed by the cry, "Indians, Indians!" from one of the pickets.

The men rushed out of Marsh's office to find other sentries running into the fort, while civilians poured from the wooden dwellings and their parade ground encampments toward the stone barracks.

Fear had accomplished what Ellis had not been able to do. The refugees now looked at the barracks as a safe haven from attack. They jammed into the two doorways and bounced back like accordians. Men began to smash windows and dive in through the openings. After several moments of cries and pandemonium, the refugees all found their way into the stone barracks.

The soldiers waited tensely, rifles cocked and ready for an assault. All was deathly quiet around the fort. For what seemed an eternity, though actually was only minutes, they waited. Nothing happened, no sound, no glimpse of movement anywhere, just quiet.

Tom Gere called out, "What picket called the alarm?"

Oscar Wall hesitantly called back, "Me . . . sir."

"What did you see, Private?" Tom demanded.

"Well, sir. Something moved. I thought . . ."

"Did you actually see an Indian, Oscar?" Gere insisted.

"No, sir, not really. I just thought . . ."

"It's okay, Private," Gere took the edge from his voice. "I think you cried out a false alarm. The clouds are so thick there's no moonlight for you to see by. But at least you managed to get the civilians into the barracks. Sergeant Bishop, detail the pickets and lookouts. The rest of you," he raised his voice," carry out your orders as I gave them."

The sergeants, along with Nathan and Randall, went to their tasks. The log hospital was a small building behind the stables outside the fort proper. Nathan walked in to find Alfred and Eliza Muller tending to Ole Svendson.

The post surgeon wore a blood-spattered white coat over his uniform; his wife's white apron was likewise stained. The light from several lanterns danced and flickered on the walls. Cots lined the length of both sides of the single room. Billy Blodgett, fresh from abdominal surgery, and John Fanska, his shoulder bandaged, lay upon two of them apparently sleeping.

The cots were primitive wooden frames with rope springs. Mattresses were large sacks stuffed with straw. The ropes tended to sag and had to be tightened periodically. The straw tended to pick up little six-legged critters. Hence the saying, "Sleep tight and don't let the bed bugs bite."

But bed bugs were the least of the worries in the overcrowded room. Once the cots were filled, patients, refugees and soldiers, lay upon straw beds on the floor whereever space allowed.

Muller glanced up at Nathan with tired, bloodshot eyes. He reached into a field medicine kit resting upon a nearby table. His hand passed over a handsaw fastened in the kit's lid. No need to amputate this time. Svendson's legs were shot up, both by bullets and arrows. But no bones appeared to be broken. Neat fractures could be set; compound fractures of a limb almost always required amputation. Ole was lucky, no bones had been hit.

"Give him more whiskey, Eliza," he called. "I'm going to go in deep to get out the lead and arrowheads." As his wife-nurse poured the amber brown liquid down the man's throat, Dr. Muller took a long, slender instrument from his kit and gently probed in the wounds. Svendson screamed in pain. "This one's not that deep, Eliza. I can get it. Give me the narrow forceps and bring a lamp closer."

Eliza handed her husband the instrument, and Muller dug into the jagged, bloody wound as Eliza held a quivering light over his right shoulder. A moment later Muller produced a round lead ball. Ole Svendson's body, held rigid with pain, collapsed like a wet rag with relief.

"Rest a moment, Ole," Muller advised gently as he wiped the bloody forceps on his white coat, "but you've got three more, and I've got to get them all out."

"What's all the excitement out there, Nathan?" Eliza wearily asked.

"False alarm, ma'am, nothing to worry about yet. But to be safe, the lieutenant has suggested that you move to a safer area. The headquarters building would be good. You're stuck out here where it could be difficult to protect you if there's an attack."

"We have badly injured men here. Tell the lieutenant that we could put their lives in peril if we moved them." Dr. Muller turned back to Svendson as if he didn't want to be bothered.

"Doctor, you really must go. You'll need some help, and I'll see that you get it. But you must move." Nathan turned and left the hospital. He felt like a soldier again.

The fort was a beehive of activity as midnight approached. The gaps between the buildings were filling up with barricades. Water buckets were being passed. Soldiers and civilians were on the move.

Shortly before one, Gere and his small group of advisors met again around the flagpole. "I'd like a report from each of you," Gere said. Though he tried to appear calm, tension was evident in his young face. "Sergeant Jones."

"We filled up holes as best we could, Lieutenant. It's not like rock, but it'll give us something to use for cover."

"Sergeant McGrew, what about the cannons?"

"Well, sir, Mr. Whipple, Sergeant Jones, and me, we figgur that if the red divils come, it's gotta be from the ravines. We got the big guns set and ready to fire in those directions. Gun crews are three men a cannon. That's bare bones."

Gere continued. "Sergeant Ellis, with the help of Oscar Wall, got the refugees all moved to the barracks." Slight smiles cracked the apprehensive faces of the men.

"Mr. Randall, any luck with the civilians?"

"Tom, there's about twenty-five that are fit to fight. Joe Coursolle just got here with his wife and baby. He's a good man. The baby's sick though. Doc Muller's lookin' after 'im. Maybe others could fight, but if they don't want to, they'll just be in the way. I think I got the ones who are able to fight anyway."

Tom Gere looked at Nathan. "Maybe some of you don't know that Mr. Cates here was an officer in the First Indiana and was shot at Shiloh. In our present circumstances, a man with his experience is invaluable. He's not in our army, but I'll give him responsibility as I see fit. What about the hospital?"

Nathan shifted on his feet uneasily. He didn't like having attention called to him. "Somewhat reluctantly they moved," he reported. "The Mullers are using Captain Marsh's quarters as their surgery."

They stood in silence for a moment around the flagpole, their faces worried but determined. Tom Gere cleared his throat and spoke once more.

"Thank you, gentlemen, you're doing your jobs well. I don't know what's going to happen tomorrow. The odds against us may be overwhelming, but this fort must be held at all costs. May God be with us."

The night was warm and tense. Twenty-five civilian refugees who formed a thin line of defense when spread around the now-enclosed fort joined twenty-four soldiers. They didn't sleep much that night. The men stayed at their posts, talking in low voices while they waited and watched for an attack that they expected at any moment. Occasionally a flash of what they called heat lightening ripped a jagged edge through the sky, but rain didn't come.

Nathan gazed into the darkness. Crickets and owls chirped and hooted like it was any warm August night in Minnesota. He became lost in his thoughts. Emily was gone, maybe dead. People up and down the valley had been slaughtered. Captain Marsh and much of his command were killed. Now he was trapped in a Union fort with almost 300 people, mostly non-combatants, who were in danger of being overrun.

Nathan felt that he was in a large sense to blame, for he had gone to Little Crow and talked about war. He was intelligent enough to hear a voice deep inside that told him it would have happened anyway. Yet guilt was a stronger emotion and overwhelmed all other feelings.

This was not a war against soldiers. What had begun was a slaughter of all whites in the valley, a massacre in the true sense of the word. He prayed to God that Emily, whom he had sworn to protect, was safe. Many thoughts rattled through his mind, disjointed and without order. Nathan longed for the deep sleep that had dulled his brain in the afternoon and kept him from remembering.

❧ 51 ❧

URING THE NIGHT OF AUGUST 19, Santee began to move in large numbers down to the river bottom near Fort Ridgely. Early the next morning, they held a council on a knoll on the rolling prairie in plain sight of the fort.

Little Crow stood in the middle of his war council's circle. The early morning sun shone vividly on painted faces and lightly clad bodies. They wore breechclouts and leggings. Around their middles many had broad, colorful sashes into which they tucked food and ammunition.

Young and old were there. Wabasha's band had arrived. Mankato's force had been joined by more from his village. Big Eagle knew he must now take a stand. He had been at the agency during the assault but had killed no one. His band had not gone to Redwood the day before. Now they were ready. Lightning Blanket, Mah-ka-tah, and others of the Soldier's Lodge sat together as part of the circle.

Little Crow was adorned with eagle feathers and paint, a blue circle ringed his right eye. Beseeching his warriors, he pointed to the fort. "We must take the soldier's house. Today we must attack."

From Ridgely, Gere watched the proceedings through a telescope. Nathan and John Bishop stood near him. Tom lowered the eyepiece. "There must be close to 300 Sioux out there. They're having some sort of meeting. Little Crow himself is talking to them."

"What are they waitin' for!" Bishop sounded exasperated.

"If Little Crow could just issue an order, they'd be here," Nathan said. "Lucky for us, they've got to talk things out. The delay means they have a difference of opinion."

"Every minute they delay brings Sheehan and the Rangers closer," Gere added as he handed Nathan the telescope.

Little Crow didn't know that Company C had left for Ripley. The war chief pointed his rifle at Ridgely and implored his warriors, "They have over 100 Bluecoats in the fort. All the young men must fight to take it."

"Little Crow," Mah-ka-tah stood to face the war leader, "we talked as we rode from the agency. The soldier's house is still strong, but we can take it later. We should go to the towns of the valley. They are full of food and guns and there are no soldiers to help them. We can take whatever we want easily. They would not even know we are coming."

The war chief of the Santee scowled at the young warriors representing the Soldier's Lodge and angrily responded. "You are Santee warriors. When we fought the Ojibway, we did not fight their women and children. It is the white soldiers we must kill, not the white people of the towns. You gain nothing by that. But if the Bluecoats are driven from the valley, *all* the people from the towns and farms will follow them."

As Little Crow spoke, small groups of young warriors continually broke away from the council and rode off. Soon his force of fighting men had been halved.

Lightning Blanket nodded at the departing braves and told his chief, "The young men are all anxious to go. They listen to Mah-ka-tah. The Germans in the valley have stolen land promised us by treaty. We will make them pay for stealing from us. We will take New Ulm."

Anger and frustration flashed in Little Crow's eyes, but he knew his words were falling on deaf ears. With resignation he responded, "Our warriors must come tomorrow." His voice rose in volume. "We must take the fort. We must get all the men together, and we must attack at noon. To

266

delay is wrong. To make war on women and children is wrong. Chiefs," he looked around the council of his leaders and glared at Mah-ka-tah, "do not delay tomorrow."

The Santee scattered toward the river.

"Where they goin'?" Ellis wondered aloud.

Ben Randall, the storekeeper, drawled in reply, "For easier pickin's, I imagine."

"'Spect they'll be back?"

"Yes, sergeant," Randall peered at the disappearing Indians, "I 'spect they will."

At midmorning, Tim Sheehan and Company C entered the beleaguered garrison. By late afternoon, the Renville Rangers arrived. Loud cheers and huzzahs greeted each arrival.

With the injured and disabled, the fighting force of soldiers at Fort Ridgely now numbered 160 enlisted men and officers. Including twenty-five volunteers from the refugees, the effective number of defenders stood at 185. Counted among them was Louis Bordeau, desperately looking for a way out and a way to help Mah-ka-tah.

❦ 52 ❧

THE SANTEE TRAVELED SEVENTEEN MILES to the southeast to New Ulm. That afternoon they ferociously attacked the river town. New Ulm was a bustling, growing town of nearly 1,000 people, mostly German immigrants who had settled after the 1851 treaties. The Germans were a stubborn, obstinate people, determined to build a better life where their needs were best suited. They chose land that Little Crow insisted was Santee under the treaty.

The Dakota didn't sweep down into an unsuspecting, defenseless village as they expected, however. While several townspeople were killed and the outer ring of houses burned, New Ulm defenders fought back valiantly.

Charles Flandrau lived near St. Peter. After he heard the alarm started by Willie Sturgis, he organized a relief force and traveled to New Ulm. That night he brought 125 men to aid the city in driving off the Dakota. A thunderstorm drenched the town and also discouraged the attackers as they returned to Little Crow's village on the Minnesota.

Willie Sturgis reached Fort Snelling at three in the afternoon of August 19 while New Ulm was under attack. He had traveled 125 miles in eighteen hours and was fortunate to find Governor Ramsey and General Malmos together consulting about Civil War maneuvers and recruits that Minnesota was sending south.

The dispatches from Gere were met with startled disbelief. They compared the missives and reread them.

Then Ramsey asked Malmos, "What troops do you have ready? We need to move immediately."

"We have the Sixth Volunteer Infantry. I'll put Sibley in command," the general replied.

"The Sioux call Sibley the Long Trader," Ramsey considered. "He knows Indians, their country, customs, and language. He's worked as a trader among them for many years. I hear they trust him. But he's tough. Move them out by steamboat. They've got to get there quickly."

By six that afternoon, the Sixth Minnesota was on its way.

THE SANTEE BRAVES TRICKLED BACK in small bands to join Little Crow. Mah-ka-tah rode by Big Eagle, who stood near their war chief's house.

The young brave spoke first. "We fought well, we scared the whites and killed some. But the town was well defended and the storm was bad."

"You were marauders, no more," Big Eagle scolded. "You should have listened to your chief. You did what you wanted without leaders, and you did no good."

"Tomorrow we will all fight at the fort. We will show you how we can be brave men," Mah-ka-tah said defiantly.

Big Eagle stepped into Little Crow's home. The war leaders were there: Medicine Bottle, Mankato, and Little Six. Little Crow outlined the plan to his leaders.

"The northeast corner of the fort is the weak point. We will force the attack there. I will ride on the west side to distract the Bluecoats. Medicine Bottle, when the warriors are ready, fire three shots and the attack will begin on all sides. But it is on the northeast corner where the break should happen. We will use the ravines and woods to hide ourselves before we attack."

As first Lieutenant, Tim Sheehan took command of the garrison from Tom Gere. "You've done well, Tom," he said at an officer's meeting. "The water supply is adequate if we ration. You've closed up the gaps between the buildings. We're as ready as we can be, given the situation.

"Gentlemen," He looked over his lieutenants and sergeants, including Ben Randall, Joe Whipple, and Nathan. "I fully expect an attack tomorrow. From the looks of their movements today, it appears they went south. New Ulm was a likely target.

"I want cannons deployed in the corners of the compound. Sergeant McGrew, you and some boys from Company C have charge of the northwest, the only place where they can't hide in the damn ravines. Lieutenant Gere, the northeast ravine is very close to the log buildings behind the barracks. The attack likely will come from there. Mr. Whipple, when's the last time you fired a cannon?"

"That would be 1848, Mexican War. But don't you worry, Lieutenant, I still know how to shoot. Just give me some boys to help me," Whipple nodded.

"You'll have them. Join Lieutenant Gere in the northeast," Sheehan said. "Sergeant Jones, you're the most experienced man here. Lieutenants Culver and Gorman and their Rangers will join you in the southwest.

"Sergeant Bishop, deploy pickets this morning and man the twelve-pounder at the southeast corner. Nathan, help there, if you will.

"We'll assemble on the parade ground when the Sioux appear and move the men as needed. At all costs, we must not permit the Sioux to make a mass attack. They would most certainly overwhelm us. Most likey they'll come out of the ravines on foot. The cannons must be used to stop such an attack. Any questions?"

"When do you think Fort Snelling will get here, Tim?" Norm Culver asked.

"Soon, I hope, assuming Sturgis got there sometime yesterday. They could be here in a day or two. Let's hope they find us all still here."

As the men filed out, Tim stopped two of them, John Jones and Tom Gere. "How's your wife, John?" he asked the sergeant.

"The baby could come at any time now, sir."

"Keep the Mullers informed, Sergeant, and let me know if I can be of help. Speaking of the Mullers, Tom, you look terrible." He looked with concern at Gere.

The young lieutenant gingerly touched the side of his neck beneath his jaw. He looked liked he had enormous chaws of tobacco in both cheeks. "I saw the doctor earlier today, Tim. I have the mumps."

"The mumps! Aren't you supposed to get them when you're a child?" Sheehan burst out.

"The doctor tells me that would have been preferable," Tom ruefully replied.

"Stick with us. We need you."

"I'll be there, Tim. I think we all will be there when it counts."

ജ 53 ഝ

THROUGHOUT THE MORNING, TENSION built as they awaited the inevitable attack. It was another scorching day. The grass surrounding the fort was high and more brown than green as it showed the effects of days of withering heat.

The ravines on the south, west, and east of the fort were green and cool. There the Dakota would assemble. Shortly before noon, a cry from Bishop's picket line brought Sheehan running. Private Will Hutchinson, supported by two men, was ushered into the fort. He was weak and nearly naked, with blood oozing from bullet holes in his chest and back.

"Good God, Private, we thought you dead!" Sheehan exclaimed.

"Near am, sir," Will croaked. "After I was shot, I crawled to the river and laid in grass. Then I found a leaky old boat and floated down the river 'til I got here."

"Bring him to Dr. Muller, men." Sheehan touched Hutchinson's hand. "Good to have you here, Will."

Louis Bordeau had been busy. Using the inky blackness of the night, he had stuffed rags into the cannon in the southeast corner. Guards at the other big guns prevented him from getting close enough to attempt any sabotage on them.

He knew that an attack would soon take place. He resolved to attempt to help the Santee from within the fort rather than escape. That could come later. He had watched the gun placements. Bordeau had even been in the fort when the men were drilling and practicing.

The powder and shells were kept some distance behind the guns. A Bluecoat would take them to another soldier, who dropped them into the guns. They thought it was safer, Bordeau supposed, to keep the gunpowder away until it was needed.

His plan was to strike the soldier as he waited to carry the shell and then drop a burning taper into the box of powder and shells. Now all he could do was wait, along with everyone else, until the inevitable arrived.

The wait wasn't long. Close to one o'clock on the afternoon of August 20, a lone horseman on a white pony appeared on the prairie clearing northwest of Fort Ridgely. It was Little Crow, dressed magnificently in a beaded leather shirt and breeches. An eagle headress flowed down his shoulders.

Sergeant Bishop recognized him immediately and urged him to dismount and confer with Sheehan.

Little Crow replied, "I will not come into the fort, Bluecoat. But I will talk to the young lieutenants if they come out onto the prairie."

Sheehan ordered his men to form a line on the west side of the parade ground near the south end of the commissary building facing east. Then he went to watch Little Crow as the gun crews raced at the double quick to their cannons.

"He's just sittin' out there waitin' for you, sir," Bishop told his lieutenant.

As Sheehan watched the pony prancing just out of rifle range, shots from the northeast echoed behind him. Mark Greer of Company C dropped in the first volley with a bullet through his chest. Bill Good took a bullet in the forehead but miraculously wasn't killed.

Tim watched men fall and realized the perilous position into which he had put his men. "Every man to your post!" he screamed over the din of gunfire. "Fire at will from buildings and barricades!"

The men scrambled to support the guncrews and fire from cover between the buildings. Some went into the stone barracks and shot from the windows. Whipple and Gere were closest to the point of attack. The civilian gunner trained his howitzer on the ravine and fired shrapnel at close range.

The crew with Bishop at the southeast quickly discovered Bordeau's mischief and began pulling rags from the barrel. While Nathan rushed to his post, he noticed a man in leather breeches and colorful shirt approach the powder holder who stood about fifteen yards behind the cannon. He recognized him as a Renville Ranger.

Nathan watched in amazement as the man clubbed the gun crewman over the head with a wood stave. As the man crumbled to the dusty earth the Ranger reached for a burning stick. Nathan saw the red glow, the smoke from the taper. Instinctively, he knew what was about to happen. The powder! He was going to drop it into the powder!

Nathan raised his pistol and fired. The shot zinged past Bordeau's ear. He turned just as a second bullet buried deep into his chest. As the French-Santee spy tumbled backward, the burning taper flew harmlessly to the ground.

Everyone was engaged in battle. Nathan quickly looked around. As far as he knew, no one had seen him shoot Bordeau. It was better if they hadn't. Bordeau's mission might have helped the Confederate cause, but the "Cause" was fast losing its appeal to Nathan.

McGrew, supported by musket fire from Company C, slammed shot at the woods to the northwest. But the sergeant knew that the critical point of the battle was at the northeast where Gere's marksmen were desperately trying to support Whipple.

Many of the Dakota gained the row of log houses behind the stone barracks and began to shoot from them. They rained bullets into the barracks and hoped that by shooting through the windows they would have some effect.

Marie Coursolle, in a corner of Dr. Muller's hospital, hugged sick little Cistina Joe to her breast and tried to cover his ears as she gently rocked her body. She wished that she, too, could hide from the continuous sounds of smashing glass, rattling bullets and thundering cannon, to say nothing of the cries and moans of the wounded men in the cots around her.

McGrew wheeled his howitzer into the open and swung it around to shoot past the long side of the barracks and into the ravine. "Explosive shot, boys!" The sergeant yelled above the chaos. "We'll blast it over the ditch!" His first shot exploded beyond the crevice. He cursed at Wall and Levi Carr of his gun crew.

"No offense, boy-os, but we got to cut the fuse a little shorter."

Bullets hailed around them as the gunners reloaded and fired again. The second shell exploded in the middle of the attacking Santee and moved them out of their position.

McGrew and Whipple concentrated their fire on the log houses and soon drove the Santee from them to a line by the ravine. By this time, fighting had become general around the perimeter of the fort as Little Crow moved in with his forces from the west and south.

The ravine in the southwest was short. It brought masses of Santee to within easy musket range of the fort. Jones faced murderous fire. He blasted away with his six pounder as the Renville Rangers poured volley upon volley at the screaming Santee, making a charge too hazardous for them to attempt.

The Dakota from the ravine began to rain flaming arrows on the wood shingles of the fort's buildings. On the headquarters building, the fire took hold. Joe Coursolle grabbed a ladder and, with the help of a water bucket brigade, formed by other refugees, they were able to extinguish the blaze.

Nathan led a mixed group of civilians and soldiers at the southeast. With his revolver, he carefully squeezed off shot after shot at the determined attackers. The gunfire was continuous as the soldiers shot from behind bags of grain or piles of logs stacked between the buildings.

"Mr. Cates," Bishop shouted from his cannon, "we're runnin' low on ammunition. There's more in the magazines, we need it!"

"Keep up the fight here, Sergeant. I'll see to the magazines." Nathan darted across the parade ground to the northwest corner. McGrew and his men were still raking shot toward the ravine when Nathan got there.

"Sergeant," he panted, "we need ammunition from the magazines."

McGrew looked at the small sheds two hundred yards away. "We need men to start haulin', boy-o, but we can't take 'em all from here. Weaken us too much. Get three from Gere and come back."

Again Nathan was sprinting, this time a shorter distance to the northeast. "Tom," he called to Gere, "we need three men to carry powder from the magazines."

Gere turned from the twelve-pounder just as Andy Rufredge of Company B dropped hard onto his back. A shell had smashed into his face and cut his lower jaw off near the ears. Caleb Ryks, only seventeen, stared at the ghastly sight. The private's jaw had dropped on his chest. Caleb, numbed by the sight, exposed himself to fire. A volley of shot cut him down.

Eliza Muller, who had been circulating throughout the battle, was quickly at Rufredge's side. With help from two teenaged refugee boys, she carried him on a litter to their makeshift hospital. There was nothing that could be done for Caleb.

Gere, meanwhile, turned his attention to Nathan. His face was black from gunpowder and streaked white by sweat. The horror of Rufredge's injury was in his mind for only a moment. There were more immediate matters to concern him.

"Chase, Foster, Waite," he shouted at three privates, "go with Mr. Cates."

The four men were quickly back with McGrew. "We'll pour shot over the sheds and try to keep 'em back in the woods," the sergeant roared over the gunfire. "They'll have to come into the open to stop us. Then our riflemen can open up on 'em."

Just as the six men started sprinting across the two hundred yards to begin hauling munitions back, Sam Stewart excitedly cried to Nathan and McGrew. "Look, look, there's someone in the end cabin!"

A woman appeared in the window, desperately waving at the soldiers. She didn't see a Santee running between the cabins and enter behind her. "Let's go!" Nathan shouted at George Dagenais, one of the Rangers assigned to Gere. The mixed-blood ran behind Nathan to the cabin. Thomas ripped the door open as the Santee raised his gun to fire. Dagenais' rifle barked from behind Nathan, and the Indian crumpled to the floor. Martha Jones wrapped her arms around Nathan's neck sobbing hysterically. "It happened so fast . . . I couldn't get out."

"It's all right, Mrs. Jones, we'll get you back. Private, help me," he called to Dagenais. The two men assisted the pregnant woman into the fort. Suddenly her legs buckled and pain seared across her face. "Ya hit, Missy?" McGrew asked with concern.

"No, the baby's coming," Martha agonized through clenched teeth.

"We'll get her to the surgery," Nathan yelled at the sergeant.

As the two men helped the woman to the far end of the compound, McGrew's crew kept up the covering fire that enabled the six men to carry munition crates through the blistering heat and gunfire to the stone barracks.

The surgery and headquarters buildings were filled with wounded. Some were lying on the porch outside the doors. Dr. Muller, Eliza and several refugee women were working feverishly to save lives. Their clothing and hands were covered with blood.

"The baby's here," Nathan informed Eliza as she rushed across the room to him.

For a moment Eliza looked bewildered, then turned to the women. "Move him to the porch," she instructed as she gestured to a private holding his arm. "He can recover out there. Clear a spot for Mrs. Jones."

As the women took Martha Jones into their care, Nathan and George Dagenais hurried back into the compound. George returned to McGrew's corner while Nathan ran back to the southern end of the fort.

Sheehan's voice kept ringing out encouragement as he moved from position to position around the defense line. Suddenly a loud boom from the southwest rose above all other sounds. Jones' cannon had blasted at the Dakota, sending them reeling back. Together with the covering fire from the Rangers, the Indians were kept at bay.

The Santee now fell back. They maintained a steady fire and occasionally tried to mount an attack here or there along the line. But Little

Crow knew that they had mounted their best effort and failed to break through the fort's defenses. For over six hours they had battled continuously, and gunfire had never stopped. With night nearing and a rain beginning to fall, the Santee pulled back to the agency. Thick clouds began to descend like a curtain ending a play.

For the first time in many hours, an unearthly quiet hung in the air above Fort Ridgely. The garrison had been wreathed in powder and smoke. Then the skies opened and a steady rain cleansed the fort. After moments of silence, the soldiers and civilians realized that the battle was over and let loose with cheers that echoed down the ravines and into the valley.

❧ 54 ❧

HE SANTEE DAKOTA WERE FRUSTRATED and angry as they rode the dark, soggy trail back to the agency and Little Crow's village. They had tried their best but failed to take the fort. Many a good warrior had died in the face of the big guns.

Once again the leaders gathered in their war chief's house. They were a quiet and sullen lot this time. A blaze burned in the fireplace as the dirty, drenched, bloodstained men sat on the floor and contemplated what to do.

"It was the rotten balls," Mankato said, referring to the cannon shot. "If it were not for them, we would have easily run over the whites."

"The Bluecoats fought bravely, braver than I thought they would." Little Crow poked in the fire as he spoke.

"Let us try again tomorrow. Then we will take them." Mah-ka-tah tried to sound confident, but he wasn't convincing.

"The fort is too strong, I don't think we can take it," Little Crow wearily replied.

Just then howls and whoops broke the stillness of the depressed men. They opened the door and were amazed to find over 400 fresh Santee warriors filling the village.

"We are Wahpetons and Sissetons from Yellow Medicine, and we have come to help our brothers kill the white men," a painted brave on a spotted pony shouted.

Another paint-smeared warrior cried, "We don't need our chiefs to lead us. They are old women. We come anyway!"

For the first time that day, a smile creased Little Crow's face. He turned to his chiefs and told them, "Now we have a chance. We will put almost 800 against them at the fort. They have fewer than 200 to face us. We will attack again, and we will not fail."

For a short time they talked of battle plans. Then the tired leaders went off to sleep. They agreed not to attack until the rain stopped. Little Crow had one stop to make before bed. He walked to the tepee where Emily West was captive and stepped inside.

Traveling Star had been with them at Ridgely. With other boys his age, his responsibility had been to hold horses and bring food to the warriors. His father, once a farmer Indian, had fought bravely alongside Lightning Blanket. Traveling Star, his mother, and father were eating salt pork from the agency stores as their chief entered.

Emily was stitching a tear in her dress when she saw Little Crow standing by the fire in front of her. The soft sound of rain plopping on the canvas and running to the ground was the only sound for a moment. Then the Santee leader said, "I just want to tell you this. One Arm is alive. Today he fought at the Soldier's House with the Bluecoats. He fought bravely." That was all he said. In a moment Little Crow was gone.

Tears filled Emily's eyes and blurred her vision. She put her needle down and lay on a buffalo robe thinking of Nathan and of home.

It RAINED STEADILY THROUGH THE NIGHT in the river valley. It was the type of rain that farmers loved, one that soaked into the soil and quenched the thirst of corn and grain. Fort Ridgely remained tense and vigilant. Most of the refugees remained huddled in the stone barracks. There they exchanged stories of the horrors they had witnessed and of the loved ones lost.

Half the garrison was on duty at a time. The others rested or tried to catch a few minutes of sleep in whatever dry place they could find. It was their fourth night in a row with little or no sleep. Eliza Muller and some other women circulated along the defensive line with hot coffee.

Nathan watched the ravine to the southeast, but the night was so dark it was like staring into an ink well. Rubbing his tired, sore, blood-shot eyes didn't help his vision. He wished he had a rain slicker as the rain soaked into the woolen coat he had been given by Tom Gere. Raindrops streamed off his wide-brimmed hat.

Eliza handed him a cup of coffee in a tin cup. Nathan held it in his hand a moment to warm himself. "How are things in the hospital, Mrs. Muller?"

"Many wounded have come to us. So far we haven't lost anyone. Not even Private Rufredge. His jaw looked absolutely horrid. But Dr. Muller stitched and set it. Without infection he should recover. I'm worried about the little Coursolle baby. He had a fever when he got here, and he's not getting better. He's so tiny," she paused, "and so sick."

"What about Mrs. Jones?" Nathan asked as he stared into the wet blackness of the night.

"She's all right. But the baby was stillborn. Too much happened." Nathan couldn't see the tears that formed in Eliza's eyes. She quickly wiped them.

"You're providing great service, Mrs. Muller," Nathan said softly.

"So many are, Nathan," Eliza replied. "Some of the refugee women, especially Mrs. Reynolds, have done almost as much as I have."

"Mrs. Reynolds? The teacher's wife?" he asked.

"Yes, Joe and she had quite an adventure. His school was ten miles upriver from the agency, you know. They took two wagons, one with several girls who worked at the school. The wagons became separated. No one knows what happened to the girls, but the Reynolds' wagon had to escape several close calls from pursuing Indians before finally crossing the river by the fort. An Indian on a white horse helped them and kept a large band from overtaking them."

"From the stories it seems that there might be about as many helping us as there are fighting. Though it sure didn't seem like it this afternoon."

"No, it didn't. Good-bye for now, Nathan. I'm sure Emily's safe," Eliza said as she moved down the line. "I have a feeling about it."

"I hope you're right, ma'am," Nathan called after her.

Private Andy Williamson was at Nathan's side. He had his own burden. His father was the Reverend Thomas Williamson, the Yellow Medicine missionary.

"Any word from refugees about your father, Andy?" Nathan asked.

"Nothing. I haven't found anyone here from the Upper Agency. I'd like to think that someone there helped him. I've heard many stories from the refugees of lives saved by the Santee themselves. I hope the same was done for my family, but I just don't know."

The younger Williamson wiped rain from his brow as he spoke. His receding hairline indicated that, with age, he would closely resemble his father. "I heard an interesting rumor, though," he added.

"And what's that?" Nathan wondered.

"Some people said they heard Indians talking about a Confederate agent in Little Crow's camp. I don't know if there's any truth to it, but it could have happened. This would be a good time to stir them up."

Nathan was glad no one could see the shock in his face. He recovered his composure to say, "There'll be lots of rumors, Andy. Don't put too much store in them. I'm sure the Confederacy has enough on its hands than to worry about Indians in Minnesota."

Soon Nathan was relieved by another detail of soldiers. He found a dry corner in the commissary building and slept fitfully. He was serving as a soldier again in war for which, in spite of himself, he felt he had some responsibility.

Emily was lost out there somewhere. He hoped Eliza Muller was right and that she was waiting for him. Before he fell asleep, he vowed that he would move heaven and earth to find her.

Wednesday, August 21st, the rain continued out of slate-gray heavens. The Santee stayed huddled in their tepees and waited for it to stop. Then they would move down the river to Ridgely 800 strong.

Tim Sheehan peered into the misty drizzle down the road along which relief from Fort Snelling would come. There had been no word from Sturgis, no word from anyone. No refugee had even entered the fort in nearly twenty-four hours.

Sheehan couldn't know that the Santee had holed up near the agency to wait out the rain or that Sibley, after a quick start, was stuttering and stopping along the way. The army had camped at Henderson and only an order from Ramsey had gotten them moving again.

A frustrated Willie Sturgis had tried to form his own relief regiment. Former Agent Brown, who was in Henderson, had discouraged such an effort as dangerous and doomed. The few who were determined enough to go with Sturgis turned back when they encountered a large band of Santee a few miles from town.

Willie could only fume and wait while Sibley planned and organized for the march to Ridgely. It was he who delivered the order from Ramsey that got the Sixth Minnesota moving again.

Early on the morning of the 21st, Sheehan gathered his officers in the commissary, the headquarters still being used as a hospital. "Gentlemen," the bleary eyed lieutenant looked over his damp, tired men, "you were brave and valiant yesterday. The cannons kept them back, and there were many individual acts of valor. Amazingly, we only lost two men dead.

"Today we've got to be ready. All we can do is expect more of the same and be ready for it. Keep the powder dry. Sergeant Ellis, appoint a guard detail, and let's get more water in here."

"Any sign of the reds today?" Culver asked.

"Nothing so far," Sheehan answered.

"They don't like to fight in rain. That's one thing I've learned by being around here as long as I have," interjected John Jones, red-eyed and haggard.

"I'll second that. At the agency they liked to stay in their tepees on days like this," Whipple supported Jones' comment.

"Either way, we must be ready because they will come again, today, tomorrow, whenever. They'll be back." Sheehan was sure of what he said.

"Perhaps, troops from Snelling will be here before then." Samuel Hinman said, joining the little group.

"I hope so, Reverend." Sheehan turned to face his men again. "I asked the pastor here to offer a prayer."

The men bowed their heads and clasped their hands as Hinman began, "We thank You, Lord, for Your mercy yesterday. Please comfort John and Martha Jones and welcome their baby into your Kingdom. We ask that You give us strength for whatever the future brings. If lives must be lost to save us and further Your glory, so be it. Amen."

It rained the whole day in the valley. At Ridgely the garrison kept watch. The water supply was replenished and the barricades strengthened. The small force was miserable, soaking wet, and tired, but ready to fight.

∞ 55 ∞

THE NEXT MORNING DAWNED with golden sun lighting up a clear sky. The spirits of all in Fort Ridgely soared with the high sky. Surely help would come today. As the morning worn on, however, it wasn't more soldiers they saw approaching, but rather the movements of Santee around the ravines and on the prairie.

All the defenders of Fort Ridgely had been at their posts since dawn. Sheehan moved rapidly around the perimeter, urging his men to be alert and to report anything out of the ordinary to him.

Shortly after noon the Dakota began to crawl through the long grass on all sides of the fort. They had attached grass and prairie flowers to their headbands to camouflage their movements. Mankato and his head soldier, Thief, would help Little Crow lead the warriors that day. After a general attack, if they didn't break through elsewhere, the Indians planned to concentrate on the southwest corner.

Joe Coursolle looked out from his position and decided to check quickly on his wife and Cistina Joe while there was still time. He rushed to the hospital. One look at Marie told him the worst. Clenching his hand and leading him to the corner of the room, Marie rolled a blanket back from a tiny, still form. Cistina Joe was dead.

Joe squeezed Marie's hand and blinked back tears. Then he hurried to the carpentry shop and returned with a small wooden box. Pastor Hinman accompanied the grieving parents to a corner of the post where a small cemetery had been laid out. Joe tenderly wrapped their baby in a blanket and placed him in the box. He gently lowered the little coffin into a shallow grave he had dug.

As Pastor Hinman softly committed the child to God, Joe held Marie close. "There's no time to mourn, Marie," he whispered, "but I swear to you, I'll find our daughters. We'll all be together, and we'll remember little Cistina Joe then."

Suddenly a shot rang out, followed by screams from all around the fort and a thunderous volley of gunfire. The Courselles and Hinman rushed to the hospital, where Joe left Maria in relative safety before he raced to his post.

A seemingly continuous flow of Santee burst from the woods and ravines as Whipple and McGrew once again poured shot into them. Gere's northeast gun crew along with Company C in the northwest squeezed off shot after shot in support.

Then burning arrows arched through the afternoon sky. Their smoky, flaming trails etched the blue before piercing the cedar shakes of the fort's buildings. The rain of the previous day and night, however, left the wood too damp to burn.

McGrew once again wheeled his cannon out from its corner and turned it toward the ravine on the northeast to support Whipple. His men rolled the twelve-pounder close to the crevice and blasted a wide sweeping canister shot into it.

Little Crow began to rally his men to move toward the southwest. As he signaled to Thief, a bullet tore into his shoulder. Mankato rushed to his side.

"I do not think I am badly hurt," the Santee chief told his friend. "I can move my arm. I believe the bullet went through and didn't hit bone. But you must take over and lead the the young men."

"Yes, Ta-oya-te-duta. We will move to the south corner and break through." Mankato left Little Crow to direct the assault.

The Dakota emerged from the northeast ravine and made a wide arc toward the northwest woods. Indians in the southern part of the ravine began moving farther along to Nathan's and John Jones' position.

Meanwhile, pressure built at the southwest corner. The Santee occupied the sutler's store and the long barn to the south. Murderous fire from those structures riddled the back of the headquarters building and began to blow away pieces of Jones' barricade.

Sheehan watched the movements with McGrew. "Sergeant, they're trying to get together for a massed attack on the southwest. We've got to keep them apart."

"We'll do it, Lieutenant darlin', but whatcha say I land a shot or two in the sutler's store first," McGrew winked at Sheehan.

"Do it, Sergeant," Tim ordered.

With his second shot the sutler's store exploded into splinters. The Santee now set the long barn ablaze and moved into the stables, the closest of the fort's outbuildings. McGrew ran down the western defense line to Jones.

"John," he cried above the battle roar, "they're movin' around to mass an attack on you. Sheehan says we got to keep 'em apart. What say we roll out the really big gun."

Jones looked over his shoulder at the twenty-four pounder in the center of the parade. "Get it, Jimmy. Set yerself up at the end of the commissary and blast the hell out of 'em."

The ravines stretched out on the west side of the fort like an index finger and thumb on a left hand, the thumb angling at about forty-five degrees to Jones' corner. The Santee were attempting to advance down the finger from the north to join other warriors massing in the thumb for the attack.

McGrew sighted his big gun at the Santee traversing in the open between the woods and ravine. The blast shook the prairie and reverberated down the valley. He swung his cannon straight west and dropped a shell into the ravine near where the Dakota had hidden women and children. Swinging farther to the left, another shot burst in the chasm between the two converging bodies of warriors. Panic gripped the Santee in the ravines as the thunderous blast shook the ground and sent earth and Indians flying into the air.

Gunfire from the stables was placing Jones' position in peril. He had sent his crew to help McGrew as McGrew's men continued to man the cannon in their position. From his vantagepoint, Jones could not fire at the stables without exposing himself to murderous fire.

"Oscar," Jones yelled to Private Wall, "I've got an idea, help me."

He began to shove his six-pounder back toward the parade ground in front of the headquarters building. Nathan noticed the men struggling to wheel the gun and joined them. As the three men strained to push the heavy 900-pound weapon, Eliza Muller ran out from the surgery and helped them roll it into position in front of the building.

"What are you doing, John?" she cried.

"The stables are directly behind the headquarters building. Open the front and back doors and we'll shoot right down the hallway and through both doors."

"We've got people in there, what if you miss?"

"See no one steps in front of the door. I won't miss, Mrs. Muller."

Less seriously wounded soldiers were on the porch. When they saw the cannon trained in their direction they scattered as best they could.

Eliza rushed to the building and opened both doors. The stables were plainly visible on the other side. With bullets whizzing all around, Jones rammed a pick into the tiny hole at the top rear of the cannon to release the powder. Then he set the little brass prime tube in it. A long string was attached to a friction pin in the narrow tube. Jones gave it a quick jerk and the primer ignited the powder. The cannon lurched back with the blast. An instant later the stable burst apart in splinters and flames.

The sergeant's battle-streaked face lit up in a broad smile. "A writer, a woman, and a one-armed man. Best damn gun crew in the fort!" he exclaimed. Then Jones and several soldiers, who ran to his aid, quickly moved the cannon back into position in the southwest corner.

The Santee gunfire around the fort became broad again as they built up to their final big push to break through the southwest. The voice of

Mankato could plainly be heard booming over the gunshots. The mixed-blood Renville Rangers could understand.

"Lieutenant Gorman," George LaBatte cried out, "he told them to club their guns and charge us. This is it. They're all coming at us!"

"Didja hear that, Sergeant?" Gorman roared.

"Private O'Shea," Jones yelled at his chief assistant, "canister double shot. Fire on my command!"

Then they came, storming out of the thumb of the near ravine, over 100 warriors sprinting toward the almost obiliterated barricade. "Prick and prime!" Jones screamed, "Fire!" A tremendous crash from the cannon spewed shot, fire, and smoke. Nearly twenty Dakota were flattened by the low, screaming missiles.

Then the Rangers followed up with a volley. As the ravaged Santee dropped back to the cover of the ravine, the riflemen yelled at them in Dakota, "Come on! We are ready for you. Come back!"

Sheehan raced up and slapped Jones on the back, "Hot work, Sergeant, hot work. You stopped them!"

"Yeah, Tim, we stopped them," Norm Culver grabbed Sheehan by the arm as he spoke, "but we've only got a few rounds left. We can't stand another attack."

"I know, Norm." Sheehan looked into Culver's excited, powder-blackened face, "I got the blacksmith cutting chunks from rods and Eliza Muller has women making cartridges. We'll have some to you soon."

In minutes the first delivery of three-quarter-inch slugs and powder car-tridges came from Eliza Muller and her workers. The shot whistled through the air when fired and ripped horrendous chunks out of anything it hit.

Nathan had rejoined John Bishop as the fight was carried to the southeast. Once again artillery kept the Santee back. One young Santee somehow avoided the cannon and small-arms fire and reached the log pile that served as cover. He leaped over it, slammed Nathan to the ground, and raised his club for a crushing blow. Thomas fired his pistol point blank into the Indian's chest. Shaken, Nathan regained his feet and stumbled into a fir-ing position behind the logs again.

The fight continued with no break. A great cloud of gunsmoke hung like a clinging fog in the still air over the fort as the din of battle was unstinted. The occasional blasts from the twenty-four pounder crashed over the lesser sounds of musket fire. The effect was one of ceaseless pandemonium and mayhem.

Finally night came, and once more the Dakota withdrew. Again they had failed. Soon they had disappeared, leaving only a howl of rage that rang from the ravines and over the fort.

Sheehan called for another officers' meeting that evening. Each of the key posts reported in. Only three had been killed and sixteen wounded in the two-day battle. Dr. Muller had still not lost a man once they were brought to his care. Sheehan ordered that the men sleep in shifts. No one in the fort believed that the fight was really over. Until support came from Fort Snelling, they would remain on guard and vigilant. Tension still reigned thickly in the garrison.

Before midnight, a voice cried out of the blackness, "Man comin', there's someone comin' in." Between the commissary and one of the officer's buildings, a solitary man rose from his hands and knees and stood straight.

Sheehan and Culver hurried over the parade ground to him. Gere was recovering from his bout with the mumps. The man before them was white, his clothes tattered and torn. His face, unshaven for days, was blood-streaked from scratches.

"I'm Andy Hunter," he said in a raspy voice. "Dr. Williamson is my father-in-law. We've got forty people from the Upper Agency back by the ravines. Can we bring them in? I crawled from there on my hands and knees. We heard the gunfire this afternoon, and we had to make sure you still held on here."

"What happened up there?" Sheehan asked with intense interest.

"Monday afternoon we got word about the Lower Agency. John Otherday got everyone into the Annuity Center and guarded us through the night. They burned some of the outbuildings, but they never got to us."

"When did ya leave?" Culver questioned.

"Tuesday morning. Otherday led us out. Other Sioux helped, too," Hunter was tired and began to speak almost in monotone as if reciting a Sunday School piece. "Chief Little Paul hid Dr. Riggs and other families on an island. Chaska had sent out a warning earlier and led us.

"We all joined up on the prairie a ways from the river and headed here. We saw dead all along the way. They got George Gleason. He was sent off with Sarah Wakefield, the wife of the agency doctor. We didn't find any trace of her. Can we come in?"

Gorman had joined the other two lieutenants. Sheehan, for the first time since he returned to Ridgely, seemed indecisive. He motioned to the two other officers and they spoke in low tones about ten yards from Hunter. "Norm, Jim," Sheehan said wearily, "I'd like nothing better than to invite these people in. But would it be fair to them?"

"What do you mean, Tim?" Gorman asked.

"I mean that if the Santee hit us again, I don't think we can hold them out. If they get by us, everyone in this place will die. That includes the refugees, and with the Upper Agency folk that means about 350, mostly women and children.

"You're right, Tim. This could be a death trap for 'em," Culver added.

Sheehan said, "I just hope they don't run into worse out there."

The young commander of Fort Ridgely walked back to the waiting refugee from Yellow Medicine. "Mr. Hunter, this is the toughest decision I've had to make. It's for your own good that you do not come in here."

A look of hurt surprise moved over the refugee's face. "But we're exhausted, we need a place that's safe."

"That's just it. This place is no longer safe." Sheehan's decisiveness returned. "We're almost out of ammunition. You heard the gunfire this afternoon. We can't sustain another such attack. If we bring you in here and the Sioux attack again, you'll all be killed. I'm terribly sorry, but you may very well be safer by heading downriver to a town. If anyone's injured and in danger of not making it, you can leave them here. For your own good, the rest need to get away from here."

"No one among us is dying, Lieutenant. We'll press on," Hunter said with resignation in his voice. "Before I go, could I see my brother-in-law, Andy Williamson?"

"Certainly," Sheehan answered, "and I'm very sorry it's not safe for you here."

After a brief meeting with Williamson, Hunter disappeared into the darkness. A short while later the Yellow Medicine refugees began the long walk to Henderson and potential safety. Fort Ridgely remained on alert, ever waiting for relief from Snelling.

ᴂ 56 ᴔ

ITTLE CROW AND SOME OF HIS WARRIORS limped disconsolately back to his village near the agency. The chief needed to recover from his wound. Although they were fresh from defeat at Fort Ridgely, many Santee warriors were eager to resume what they thought should be easy plunder at New Ulm seventeen miles distant on the south side of the Minnesota.

On August 19, only about 100 braves had made a half-hearted attempt to take the town. Now nearly 700 would hit it, led by Mankato, Wabasha, and Big Eagle. Charles Flandrau had arrived in New Ulm after sunset on the day of the first attack. He had with him 125 men. For the next few days he had organized defenses in the town. Other volunteers came from neighboring towns until the fighting force numbered almost 300 men.

The day after the second assault on Ridgely, the Santee stormed out of the woods by the river and attacked New Ulm. The defenders fought bravely, but gradually the superior numbers of Santee closed in on the town. Flandrau had ordered buildings burned to deprive the Indians of cover. The Dakota also started buildings on fire near the river. Since the wind was blowing off the river toward the town, the Indians followed the smoke into New Ulm.

293

Nearly 100 warriors charged out of the smokescreen at a barricade of inexperienced soldiers and townspeople. The green defenders fought like veterans and their sustained volley drove back the Santee and saved the city.

The next morning, the Santee fired a few long range shots and left. Flandrau met with his officers and assessed their situation. One hundred ninety buildings were burned; thirty-four defenders were dead and sixty wounded. Many were under the able care of Dr. William W. Mayo, who had traveled to New Ulm from Le Sueur during the battles.

Food and ammunition were in short supply. Mayo warned that an epidemic of disease threatened those hiding in cellars and houses.

A decision was made. On Monday morning New Ulm was abandoned. Two thousand people, some in the 153 wagons, others walking, began the thirty-mile trek downriver to Mankato.

Little Crow also made a decision. Attacking forts and strong cities had resulted in failure. Soon soldiers would come from St. Paul. The Santee chief knew that his people, too, must move. He abandoned his village and moved his Dakota gradually to the north, first to the nearby Rice Creek Village, and then, by August 28, to the Yellow Medicine Agency where the Sisseton and Wahpeton chiefs remained.

They brought the white captives, mostly women and children with them. Guarding the captives was but another in a mounting series of difficulties facing Little Crow. After failing to take Fort Ridgely, some of the Sisseton and Wahpeton soldiers had left his band and returned to the prairies. Farmer Dakota, opposed to the war, formed their own secret societies to help the white captives and end the war.

Amidst the burned-out buildings of the Yellow Medicine Agency, Little Crow once again gathered his chiefs. This time the dissenting Upper Agency leaders joined them, led by Little Paul.

While many of the Yellow Medicine warriors had joined Little Crow, few of their chiefs were involved in the war. Their speaker, Little Paul, vehemently chastised the Mdewakanton leaders in council. "You are fools to make war on the whites settlers. It only makes the soldiers more determined to crush you. Fight soldiers. Give me the captives, and I will see that they are returned to the army. Maybe that will help you. Maybe they will hate you less."

Little Crow silently hung his head. He would not speak, for he agreed with some of the points made by Little Paul, particularly that the war should be conducted against soldiers. He let others raise their voices against the "peace" Indians, knowing that to support Little Paul's words in council would cause his own chiefs to repudiate him.

Cut Nose looked at the Sissetons and Wahpetons with contempt. "If we are to die, these captives shall die with us," he snarled.

"Soon the British in Canada will help us maybe. They hate the Americans, too," Red Middle Voice's tone betrayed his own doubts.

Little Paul looked at the Mdewakantons with disgust. "The Queen's People will not help you. Don't you know that the British dislike everyone who is wicked and disobedient?"

Standing Buffalo echoed Little Paul's concern for the hostages. "Release the captives. If harm comes to any of them, we will know no end to the white man's vengeance."

The meeting ended with both factions frustrated and discouraged. The Mdewakantons would not budge on their determination to hold the captives. The next couple of days were tense as each side accused the other of wrongdoing. Violent squabbles broke out, but, fortunately, the only gunfire was aimed into the air.

On the evening of August 31, the Dakota met again in council, north of the Yellow Medicine River near Reverend Riggs' Hazlewood mission in the Upper Agency. Little Crow and about twenty-five of his chiefs and warriors gathered in a circle on the prairie. Within the circle, a large kettle bubbled with dog stew over a fire. Nearby, strangely out of place, an American flag fluttered in the breeze from a staff planted in the earth by Little Paul.

After smoking, Little Crow rose to his feet, his wounded arm held stiffly at his side. He began to speak. "Chiefs, the fort is too strong. Another attack would be foolish. But this war is not over. We can still drive the whites from the valley. The Dutchmen have left New Ulm."

Big Eagle stood to address the chiefs. "The big guns of the fort have slammed shut the door down the valley, and big towns like New Ulm were too strong. We must find easier places." Having made his point, Big Eagle dipped a ladle of the greasy stew from the pot and ate.

"We must move soon," Mankato cried. "The white man's army is coming from St. Paul. We can't stay in our villages. What are we to do?"

Little Crow had grown stronger. His wound was stiff in his shoulder, but he was ready to lead. "I say again, it is not over. I hear the Long Trader, Sibley, is moving up the river. His army is slow like a turtle, and he is cautious. Mankato, Gray Bird, and Big Eagle must go down the south side of the river toward him. Seize whatever you can. New Ulm now stands empty and burned.

"I will lead more warriors into the Big Woods to the north. There are towns there, like Forest City, that the whites have not abandoned. It has many fewer people than New Ulm and is not as strong. Then we will rejoin you," Little Crow looked at Gray Bird. "We will come behind the Long Trader's army, and our two bands will attack from opposite sides."

"We have little choice," Wabasha said. "We must move and attack. To stay here now is death."

"Yes," Little Crow agreed, "the people must move from this place. Wacouta, I ask you to see to the people and our captives' safety. White Dog speaks the white man's tongue. I will send him and some warriors to help guard as well. See that the whites stay safe."

"I will," was all Wacouta replied.

"We should free the captives," Wabasha asserted.

"Not yet. We may need them later to bargain," Little Crow replied. "See that nothing happens to them, Wacouta."

Traveling Star led Emily West from their tepee. "Miss West, we must strike our village and move. You will travel with the other whites who have been captured. But you are still under my family's protection. If the others are taken away, you will stay with us unless it is safer to go."

"Why not just let me go now?" Emily wondered.

"Too many bad Indians are between here and the fort. You would be harmed. It's best you stay with us."

Emily joined a growing group of women and children, who were herded together like sheep near the center of the village. Forlorn acceptance had replaced fear in their eyes. They did what they were told. One man was with them, Spencer from the agency. Two young girls were huddled together near Emily. "You're Miss West, aren't you?" one of them whispered.

"Yes, I am. How do you know me? Who are you?"

"I'm Mary Schwandt, and this is Mattie Williams. We worked with Joseph Reynolds at his school upriver. We saw you once when we came to the agency school for supplies."

Both girls looked as if they had been through Hell. Their faces were bruised and scratched, their dresses ripped, and their hair was matted, dirty and twisted. Probably a light color, the true shade of their tresses was a mystery to Emily.

"Have you heard anything of Mr. and Mrs. Reynolds?" Mattie asked almost shyly.

"No," Emily answered, "I was taken in the attack at the agency. I don't even know what happened to everyone there."

The young women stood with the others waiting as the village was dismantled. Young warriors watched them for any sign of attempted escape.

"There were two wagons. Last we saw, the Reynolds family got away. Our driver was killed and . . ." Mary's eyes filled with tears and she couldn't continue.

"There was another one of us," Mattie said. "Mary Anderson. She got shot in the stomach. We tried to get away in the slough, but they followed us in and took us. Miss West, they've done horrible things to us, even to Mary."

"Where is Mary?" Emily inquired.

Mattie finished her story. "A good Indian named Wacouta tried to cut out the bullet, but he couldn't get it. She . . . she cut it out herself and then she died." Now tears welled in her eyes also.

A dirt-smudged blonde girl, who looked as if she would be pretty under other circumstances, edged over to them. "Do you mind if I stand with you?" she said carefully.

"As long as we don't call attention to ourselves, I don't think they care how we line up," Emily replied. "You're welcome here. Where are you from? I don't remember you at the agency."

"Meeker County. Monday I was standing alongside a lake by our farm. They came out of nowhere and took me. My name's Jenny, Jenny Olson."

The girls stood together and talked in hushed tones until a large Indian with a big gut came over and made them help the Santee women drag lodgepoles to the ponies to be made into travois and loaded with their necessities. Others were fortunate to have captured wagons and were able to load their goods into them. Soon the entire camp was on the move, captives included.

ॐ 57 ⌘

IT HAD BEEN A LONG, HOT DAY under the prairie sun. Solomon Foot and his neighbor, Andrew Nelson, were cutting hay. The soft *swish, swish* of the sharp, curved scythes slicing into the prairie grass released a pleasing aroma into the air. But the men didn't notice or care much about things like smells or sounds. Those were to be enjoyed during a warm, late summer night or in the dew of an early morning. At five on a Wednesday afternoon, Foot and Nelson were tired, hot and grubby. Foot leaned on his scythe as he wiped his brow and peered into the horizon. In the distance a speck appeared. It quickly moved toward the two men.

"What have we here?" Foot asked. The faint drumming of hooves indicated the rider was in a hurry.

Nelson stopped his cutting and waited with Solomon as the rider came closer. "There'd be smoke if he was comin' to warn us of a grass fire," Nelson offered. "Wonder what he wants?"

Foot absently cut another swath or two with his scythe. "We'll know soon enough."

In minutes the rider reined up in front of the two men. His sweaty, foaming horse blew and snorted heavily as the man breathlessly gave his message.

"The reds are on the warpath. They killed Baker and Jones and some women at Acton, five altogether. Then they cut loose on the reservation at the agency. They're killin' people up and down the Minnesota River."

"Where you from?" Foot asked. "You real sure about this?"

"They sent me out from Forest City. I seen the bodies at Acton. And I believe what I heard about the agency. I got to keep movin', there's more people to tell. Let your neighbors know." With that he slapped his reins onto his tired horse's rump and was off again.

"Well, Nelson, what do you make of that?"

"Seems a mite strange. I can't believe it's a general uprising. Maybe a few dead, but a war? I don't know what to think."

"Just the same, Nelson, we've got families here. We best heed what he says until we hear different. The Acton murders could have happened. Jones sold whiskey. Indians could have gotten into it and started killing."

"We goin' to Green Lake, Solomon?"

"That's the plan. Over the Fourth, some of us agreed to gather at Frank Arnold's place on Green Lake if there's trouble. Go home, Andrew, get your brother and family. We leave tonight. Come by my place. We'll head to Erickson's, get him and his folks and head to Arnold's. Late tonight we'll be there."

"Looks like rain, Solomon," Nelson nodded to the west where rolling black clouds were building on the horizon.

"I know. Let's hope it holds off. Let's move now."

The two men went to their respective homes. They hoped it was another false alarm or just an isolated incident. But dread filled their hearts with the feeling that this was different, that somehow life in the Kandiyohi lakes would never be the same.

Foot tried not to appear excited as he entered his cabin. Adaline was preparing supper. The smell of frying potatoes and venison sausage permeated the main room. She looked up from the hot stove, a light sheen of sweat dampening her face. Brushing a moist curl from her forehead and smiling at Solomon, Ady asked, "Where's Andrew?"

Her husband looked at the rough wooden table. A place setting was provided for Nelson and two of Foot's children. The three older siblings were attending a school near Green Lake, a short distance from brother Silas.

"Andrew won't be here, Ady. There's been a change of plans."

"What's the change?"

"A rider came by while we were cutting hay. News from Acton and the agency. He said that Indians killed five people at Acton, including Robinson Jones, and then attacked the agency. I don't know what's true and what isn't. You know we've had false alarms before. But I expect there's enough truth to this that we'd better take some precautions."

Adaline's face drained of color. In an anguished voice she exclaimed, "Solomon, we've got to leave now! Let's take the children and go into the grove and hide in the brush."

"Ady," Solomons's voice was measured and calm, "there's no immediate danger. We have a plan. Andrew'll be here soon. Then we'll go to Erickson's and on to Arnold's on Green Lake. There will be plenty of time to stop by Silas's and get the other children on the way. But we'll leave tonight. We'll have a quick bite to eat. Then you pack what we need, and I'll harness and hitch the oxen. When Andrew gets here, we'll leave."

As Foot put the wagon in order, Swan Swanson and his family rolled into the yard. New from Sweden, they had reached America in 1856. Two years later they had staked a claim near Solomon.

"Nelson says we should go now." The young Swede's blonde beard shook as he spoke. "He wants to scatter his stock, says he'll catch up to us on the road or at Erickson's. You ready?"

Solomon looked at Swanson and his family, the wife and three children huddled on hides in the back on the open wagon. "Just a few minutes, Swan," he nodded at his neighbor. "I'll get my family and be right out."

Adaline was ready. Clothing, bedding, and a basket of food were packed. Foot put on a wide-brimmed black hat and overcoat. Then from his gun case he took his Colt revolver and slid it into his belt. His rifle was already in the wagon. "Let's go, Ady. Swan's here. Andrew'll catch up to us on the road."

"Isn't it too hot for the coat, Solomon?" Adaline asked.

"It'll cool. Might rain. Besides, it's hard to see black at night. And I've got lots of room for ammunition in these pockets."

Oscar Erickson lived a few miles away between Mud and Eagle lakes. The Foot and Swanson wagons rolled the rough road as silently as they could. But the jingle of the harnesses and blowing and snorting of the sturdy oxen could not be avoided.

About halfway between the cabins, Foot heard a distant cow bell. "Ady, sounds like some scared cattle a ways off. When we get to Erickson's, we best spend the night there. I don't like the looks of the weather."

"Is it just the lightning, Solomon? I know that stock start running when Indians approach."

"I'll just feel all around better if we stay put tonight. We'll get an early start and make Green Lake in good shape tomorrow."

The two wagons continued down the narrow path. The blackness of the night was brightened frequently by flashes of lightning. Distant thunder, like the faint roll of a drum, seemed to come ever closer as the small party hurried to its destination. In spite of the danger, Foot's two small children slept peacefully on soft furs in the back of the wagon. Solomon and Adaline watched each shadow intently and prayed silently that providence would lead them to safety.

Later that night they arrived without incident at the cabin of Oscar Erickson. It was a simple square log structure with split shakes on the roof. The rail fence stretched in front of the cabin with trees and lakeshore beyond that. The young Norwegian farmer and another man, Carl Johann Carlson, came through the darkness into the yard to greet them.

"Foot, Swanson, it's glad I am you're here. We got word of the Indian attacks, too. We're ready to leave. Do you need anything here first?"

"I'm glad you stuck to the plan, Oscar. Swede Charley," Foot always called Carlson by that name, "good to see you're safe. Your wife is with you, I expect?"

Carlson nodded his head, "Lily's in the house with Oscar's wife, Gjertrude and the children."

Foot climbed down from his wagon as did Swanson from his. "Ady," Solomon spoke to his wife as he helped her down, "take Mrs. Swanson and go into the cabin with the other women. I need to talk to the men."

With questioning eyes, the two women went into Erickson's home. Their children were left sleeping under the watchful gaze of the men. Foot looked at the three men, all in their late twenties to early thirties. They were men with families, all having come to Minnesota to build a new life. They wanted to farm on some of the earth's best land. But they never had put much thought into who had owned the land before or how it had been obtained.

Now they looked scared, and indeed they were. Drops of sweat formed on their foreheads. They even smell scared, Solomon thought.

Foot kept his voice low. "Fellows, we can't go any further tonight. It's going to rain for one thing. But more importantly, I believe that Indians are about. If we're traveling on the open prairie, we won't stand a chance if they attack us. Together, here in this cabin, we have a much better chance of defense if we need it."

"Ya real sure they're out there, Solomon?" Swede Charley asked.

"Pretty sure, Charley. Let's get the wagons inside the fence that surrounds the cabin. We'll leave the oxen yoked in the field in front of the house. Oscar, we need plenty of water in the house. Swan, Charley, would you help the children get to their mothers after we've unhooked the oxen? I'll stand watch. If they come, it'll be from the south and west."

"I'll get buckets and fill them at the creek." Erickson turned, then stopped. "Solomon, where's Nelson? I thought he was coming with you."

"He was, and I tell you, I'm a little worried. It's awful late, and he should have caught up with us by now."

The men went about their tasks. Foot, rifle in hand, rested on a fence as he peered hard into the pitch-like blackness of the night. There! In the distance between the flashes of lightning he saw silhouetted objects moving on the trail. They came closer and soon crossed the creek and rode up to the high ground near the cabin. Foot knew immediately they were Dakota, twenty or more.

Solomon strode immediately to the cabin. All were now inside: his wife and children, the Swansons with three children, Ericksons with one child, and Swede Charley with his wife. The cabin was sparsely furnished, a bed in the corner, a table with some chairs, and a trunk rested on the packed earth floor.

"They're here," Foot spoke firmly and tried not to show the anxiety he felt, "put out the light, we don't want them to see into the house. Close and fasten the doors."

"Can't we just leave one lamp on?" Christie Swanson spoke. Her children huddled around her. Fear showed in all their faces.

"No. There can be no light in this house. Listen to me. Your lives may depend on this. The Sioux must not see into this cabin tonight. They have a great advantage if they do, for then they can see us, but we can't see them."

"We must do what Solomon says," Swan spoke up. His naturally ruddy face was flushed red.

"You betcha," Charley Carlson added, "he knows these people. We're lucky to have him here. We must listen to him."

Adaline, her hand quivering, clutched her children to her as she walked across the room to a table in the one-room cabin. She leaned down and blew out the light. A puff of smoke briefly hung in the air above the lamp. For a moment, the women and children seemed transfixed by it. Then they began to cry, not just soft wimpers but loud sobs and moans.

Foot slowly shook his head and removed his overcoat, hanging it over a window. There was no point in trying to speak to the men. Unless he yelled in their ears, they wouldn't be able to hear him above the crying. After several minutes, it subsided to wimpers.

Foot turned to his wife and laid a hand on her arm. "Ady, I want the women and children to go into the loft. Help them up there." He felt her move and knew she would do as he had asked. The loft covered about half the upper area of the cabin. Adaline soon had the children and women scrambling up a ladder.

Solomon Foot walked over to the window and removed the coat that covered it. He opened the window and shouted in the Dakota tongue. "Who are you?"

Forms came closer out of the night. "How, How! We are Dakota. Who are you?"

"I am Solomon Foot. I am here with my friends. We have women and children here. Do not come closer. They have heard of the murders at Acton and they are frightened."

"We know of you, Foot." The form of the speaker was taller than the rest, but Solomon couldn't make out any details. "You have nothing to fear from us. We are hunting. There were murders at Acton. But those were done by bad Indians from the north."

As the Indian continued to speak, Foot noticed a rider with his pony jump the fence near the front of the house. Solomon left the window and went to another. Looking out, he saw that the Indian had dismounted and was kneeling down by the side of the house.

"Get away," Foot shouted.

But the Indian stayed put, a dark form against the cabin. In Dakota, Foot shouted again, "Move away now, or I'll shoot you." With that, the brave sprang upon his pony, jumped the fence and was gone.

As all in Erickson's house settled down, Foot kept watch to the west where several hundred feet away the Dakota had camped. They turned their ponies loose to munch on grass and gathered around a campfire, signs that they intended to spend the night.

It was mostly quiet in the little cabin the rest of the night. Except for Foot, all slept in the loft. Occasional snoring or a fitful, sleepy whimper punctuated the silence. From the Indian camp the stillness was broken by a periodic, "Hiya, ya, hiya."

It started to rain big drops that thumped on the cedar shakes of the roof. Solomon had never been happier to see the skies open up. Flares of lightning continued to brighten the yard and illuminate the lumpy forms lying by the smoldering fire. It rained all night and saturated the cabin.

"Hard to burn it now," Foot muttered to himself. "And Indians won't be attacking in a downpour."

He studied the small dwelling and its occupants. The others had all come from Sweden or Norway looking for a better life. They hoped to prosper and be free of all the levels of authority that tied them to failure in the old country. They were good, solid, hardworking people. They had few extravagances and dressed in simple homespun.

He smiled to himself as he thought of the Scandinavians' battle with the English language. Some were doing pretty well with it. Others spoke no English at all. Sometimes "they" was "dey" and "that" was "dat," and other words were given similar new pronunciations. Often they spoke their native tongue to each other. Out of respect for the Foots, the immigrants spoke English when they were around. They were trying to become Americans. Solomon hoped their future wouldn't end here in this little wooden cabin.

All through the night, Solomon Foot kept vigil while the others slept. Plans of action whirled in his head. Nothing took hold.

"Tomorrow," he thought, "there's nothing to do but wait for morning and let what happens then decide what we'll do."

≈ 58 ≪

DAYBREAK BROUGHT A BRIGHT SUNRISE and mist in the air. The Dakota stirred from their soggy blankets. They were hungry, and a poor night's sleep in pouring rain had done nothing to improve their foul dispositions.

As the Indians tried to start up their fire again, the people in the cabin began to awaken and move around. Solomon was still peering out the window when Swan Swanson, hair tousled from sleep, climbed down from the loft and asked him, "Anything new, Solomon?"

"No, Swan, about twenty of them stayed put all night as near as I can tell. Let's move your trunk over to this west window and put the table on it so its top is flush with the window. That'll leave us some space at the top and a peek hole at one side. We may need the protection. I don't trust our visitors much."

The sun rose higher, warming the wet earth and loosing birds into song. In the nearby lake, buffalo fish jumped above the surface and splashed into the water. Sunbeams burst through openings into the mostly darkened cabin. The young children, distracted from their fears, played in the rays of light.

Foot and the three other men watched intently from the cabin as the Dakota wiped and dried their rifles. Foot stroked the stubble of his beard and turned to his companions. "Last night they told me they were a hunting party. They sure are behaving like one. No one bothered us during the night. I know quite a few of those bucks as agency Indians. Maybe they'll just go on their way."

"Hear dat?" Oscar Erickson turned to the others, his strained face looking relieved. "Solomon tinks dey'll be leavin' soon."

The women looked out with wan smiles. The children clapped their hands.

Foot slowly shook his head. "Let's not get too relaxed. I hope they'll be leaving. We'll have to see."

A short time later, a small group of the Dakota came to the house. Foot went out to the yard to meet them. The Indians stood outside the low wooden fence, and Solomon reached over it to shake hands with each of them.

"Good morning, Foot," the taller one from last night spoke first. The others, except one, nodded their heads, smiled, and mouthed friendly greetings.

"We will be leaving soon to hunt," the tall one spoke again. "Do you have any bread for us? We can't get a fire started, and we are hungry."

"Send one of your band to the house, and we will give you some," Foot answered. His eyes kept being drawn to the Indian in the back who had not greeted him. A hood covered the top half of his face. He looked the others in the eyes and then reached over and raised the hood. The Indian's face was painted with black and red. Hatred filled his eyes. Their gazes locked for an instant and neither spoke.

Then Foot said, "I know you. You were on the Pipe Creek when I was trapping." He received no reply, just a sullen look.

Solomon went back to the house and soon a young brave came to the door. "Bread," he said. Gjertrude Erickson, at Foot's direction, had readied a few loaves and handed them to him.

"What do ya make of it all, Solomon?" Swan asked. "Are dey really going?"

"I hope so. It looks like they are after they eat. All appeared friendly, except one, and maybe he just had a bad night's sleep."

He looked around the room. The women were preparing a cold breakfast of sausage and bread. The younger children, tired of playing with sunbeams, tugged at their mothers' skirts. The older ones huddled together.

"As soon as we've eaten, if the Sioux haven't left, I'd like the women and children to go into the loft until they're gone."

"Do ya really tink dat's needed?" Oscar Erickson asked.

"Just being safe," Solomon answered.

"Anudder's comin'!" Swede Charley exclaimed from the west window where he was peering through the peephole.

An instant later another Dakota was at the door. "Need potatoes, and a kettle to cook in." It wasn't a request but a statement. Adaline brought a kettle over to him.

Swede Charley walked to the entrance. "I'll go over and dig the potatoes for 'em, Solomon. It's better dat you stay with the others."

"I wasn't about to go out there with him, Charley. I've got a fixed principle: let them serve themselves and do their own work."

Charley tugged at his scraggly blond beard, fixed his broad brimmed hat atop his head and said, "If it will help to get dem on der way so we can get going to Green Lake, I'll gladly do some of der work today." He left for the potato patch.

Foot turned back and spoke to his friends in the cabin. "Maybe Charley's right. Get some food in their bellies, and they'll leave. But I don't like helping the reds." Solomon didn't see two Dakota round the corner of the cabin with Carlson as he went to the garden. Adaline and the others saw through the still open door.

From the south in front of the house, a Dakota shouted, "Foot, come here, we wish to talk with you."

"What did he say?" Adaline asked.

"He wants to talk to me, Ady."

Fear and perhaps a forboding flashed across her face. "No, Solomon, stay here. They mean to kill us all. I know it."

"Now, Ady," Solomon reached down and stroked her hair. "It'll be all right. I talked to them before. They could have shot me then if they wanted to."

"Maybe they've just been trying to find out how many we are and what guns we've got."

His wife's comment made Foot pause briefly in the doorway. He watched the tall Indian who, with words and signs, was attempting to communicate with him from behind the fence. "I've got to go, Ady."

Adaline wrapped her arms around her husband and silently held tight, then released him as he walked out the door, closing it behind him. From peepholes in the cabin the others watched.

The Indian, a damp blanket draped over his shoulders, apparently didn't have a gun. He stood smiling behind the fence as Foot approached. It was now nearing midmorning. The sun was bright, and the day would be hot. All was green and lush as the creek gurgled nearby. Other Dakota seemed to be going about their business. To Foot it looked like a nature scene from one of those magazines back east.

When Solomon was about twenty-five feet from the fence the Indian's smile vanished, and Foot looked him in the eye. He had seen rage and wild anger in the eyes of animals he had hunted and trapped. The same look was on the face of the man before him. Foot immediately realized the danger he was in. A gunshot muffled from around the house. Instinctively he knew that Swede Charley was shot.

Foot turned as the tall one took a rifle from beneath his blanket. He faced the cabin, but the painted-face brave who appeared from behind obstructed his path. Painted-face fired. Solomon felt a burning pain in his side between his hip and shoulder. Other Dakota picked up rifles that had been covered on the ground and began to fire. Solomon fell as the tall one shot and missed him.

Foot was on the ground only for a moment. Several shots had pierced his body, and now the Dakota were reloading their single-shot weapons. He struggled to his hands and knees in the grass. Blood ran down his left arm, splotches of red appeared on his side and shoulder. Solomon scrambled to his feet and ran toward the cabin's entrance.

Painted-face finished reloading and started to raise his rifle just as Foot was upon him. Solomon wrenched the rifle upward with his still powerful right arm, and the gun fired into the air. Foot released the gun barrel and brought a crashing blow onto the top of the Indian's head as he stumbled to the doorway. The door opened, and Ady grabbed her husband's hand and pulled him inside.

Solomon stood on wobbly legs inside the cabin. "Ady," he gasped, "pay no attention to me. They're coming for the house. Get guns and shoot." He then crumbled to the floor unconscious.

His wife propped him against a wall, turned to her companions and shouted, "You heard Solomon. Women and children stay upstairs. Oscar, Swan, we've got shooting to do!"

At first Ady loaded guns as Erickson fired. When she realized that Swan's gun wasn't being reloaded, she noticed him backed into a corner. Fear and cold sweat were pasted on his face.

"What's wrong, Swan?" she asked. "Shoot!"

"I can't. I just can't," he sobbed.

With a look of sympathy and disgust, she took his gun from his hands and fired through one of the peepholes. The gun pulled hard. Maybe Swan thought there was something wrong with it, she thought. Ady and Oscar continued to fire from the door and windows. Glass was shattered by Indian fire. Balls ripped through weak chinks in the wall and smacked into the opposite side.

In agony, Solomon Foot came to. He crawled on his hands and knees to the water bucket to quench his burning thirst. A big gulp revived him, but he felt shot to pieces with terrible pain, like he had swallowed hot coals. Gathering strength, the frontiersman watched with pride as his wife aided Erickson in their defense. He struggled to his feet against a wall and croaked, "Ady, I can shoot. Come here and reload for me."

Adaline hurried to her husband and silently handed him his rifle. Foot punched some of the chinking and clay from between two logs and looked out. Not fifty feet away stood a Dakota. Foot aimed through the hole and fired at his face and head. The Indian's mouth flew open in surprise. He grabbed his head and fell to the ground.

Ady snatched the rifle from her husband's hand and handed him another. Foot moved to the west wall of the cabin to get a different view. What

311

he saw shocked him. "Oscar, Ady, they're just standing there looking at me like they don't know what to do. Looks like no one's shot any of 'em before. Let's see what they do now." Foot aimed again at a nearby Indian's chest. One shot brought him to the ground. In his excitement and elation, Solomon exclaimed, "Thank God, there goes another of the red devils to Hell!"

"Solomon, don't use such language," Adaline rebuked him sharply.

Even with our lives on the line, she's concerned about what I say around the children, Solomon thought. With a tight-lipped smile, he muttered, "Sorry," and exchanged his rifle for a loaded weapon.

Sheer will and the excitement of the moment, enabled Solomon to ignore the pain and continue the fight. He moved from lookout to lookout around the cabin shooting at the Indians. Ady followed continually, keeping him loaded.

Foot neared Swan Swanson, still huddled in the corner. He reached into his belt, took out his revolver, and handed it to him. "Shoot them, Swan." He said it lowly and evenly as he would to a child. Swanson took it and began to fire through a hole near the south window.

Solomon crouched down by the west window and looked out the end by the trunk. Ahead by the side of an oak tree he saw an Indian's shoulder. He took careful aim and fired. The form disappeared. An instant later a ball smashed through the small gap between the window and trunk and tore into Foot's right breast near his shoulder. He collapsed onto the floor. Ady rushed to him and dragged him across the room to the bed in the corner. She succeeded in getting him into a half-sitting position.

"Can't move my arm, Ady." Suddenly he wrenched forward and vomited blood. "I think the bullet went clean through and took a rib or two with it. Water . . ."

Ady quickly brought a ladle and bucket of water. Solomon, burning with thirst, took a swallow and then vomited again. Ady held him by the shoulders. Blood showed on either side of his right one. The ball had gone through.

Foot, still sensible, steeled his will again. "I can't help you anymore. But you've got to keep shooting. Swan, Oscar, Ady, keep low, keep moving around the cabin, and keep shooting."

He nearly fainted again but managed to revive by splashing a ladle of water in his face. Bullets continued to crash through windows and holes in the walls. Glass, wood splinters, and rifle shot spun about the lower floor of the cabin.

"Stay low. Stay low," Foot urged again as loud as his weak voice would carry. Secretly he prayed that one of the flying missiles would hit him and put him out of his terrible misery.

Erickson stood by the trunk and fired out the window. Then he fell backward screaming in pain. Moments later Ady rocked back. A bullet had grazed her right breast and arm, leaving a crimson crease on her chest. The other women hurried down from the loft.

Swan, after emptying Foot's revolver, had taken the blade from a hay scythe and was holding it like a primitive sword, poised and ready for whatever should come through the door. The women, Ady included, gathered around Oscar. Erickson's screams and groans caused the children in the loft to cover their ears and wail.

Foot rose up to a half-sitting position. "Stop him from screaming. Stop it all of you," he half shouted and then began to cough blood. "Listen to me, we can't let them know that someone's been hit. They have to believe we can all still shoot. Somehow quiet him."

"He's been shot through the groin, Solomon," Ady replied.

"Help him up. Try to get him to the loft." Foot gestured up with his eyes.

Erickson, crazed with pain, stumbled to his feet, then grabbed an axe from near the fireplace and began to beat it against his head. Fortunately the back of the axe hit him and not the blade. With effort, pulling and pushing him up the ladder, they succeeded in getting him into the loft and onto a bed directly above Foot.

The screaming stopped. "Listen," Foot croaked.

"To what? It's quiet." Ady was at his side again.

"That's what I mean. There's no more shooting."

"Look, the front door!" Lily Carlson from her perch in the loft could see an Indian approaching boldly to the front of the house.

Ady went to the door and fired a shot. An answering shot blasted by her and lodged in the wall behind her.

Then Foot sensed what he had feared since the night before. He sniffed the air. "Ady there's fire in the house!"

From between logs on one side of the cabin, smoke was oozing into the room. Ady Foot grabbed a teakettle full of water from the stove and carefully poured it through the cracks. Miraculously the fire went out.

The shooting had stopped. Ady moved from wall to wall checking. There were no Indians to be seen, only their ponies. "I can't see any Indians, Solomon, just their animals. Shall I shoot them?"

"No, don't shoot them. We want the Sioux to leave on them. Besides, they are just innocent animals who aren't to blame for what's happened."

"They're leaving!" Gjertrude Erickson shouted from the loft.

"Which way are they going?" Foot cried.

"North, I'm sure it's north."

They waited to be sure the Indians were gone. Ady opened the front door. The sun was directly overhead. It burned hotly and wilted the grass of the battleground. Dead and injured Dakota had been taken away. But reminders were left: Charley Carlson lay dead in the potato patch, the cabin was riddled with bullet holes, and two men were gravely wounded inside.

Swan Swanson dropped his scythe to the floor. Trembling like a wind-blown aspen leaf, he looked to his wife and children.

"We've got to leave this house, Swan," Christie Swanson pleaded.

Swan wiped his brow and looked at Foot. "I'm takin' my family and goin' to da brush. Mebbe we can hide on one of da islands in da lake. It's not safe here. They'll be back sure. We never shoulda got cornered here in da first place."

"Would you rather have faced them in the open, Swan?" Solomon asked. "But you may be right. I don't think it's safe here, either."

Swan began to pick up his belongings.

"Might I come with you?" Lily Carlson, red-eyed and worn, cried from the loft.

"Get your things together. We go now."

In minutes the Swansons, their children, and Lily Carlson left.

Solomon urged, as they were about to leave, "Get to Green Lake, then to Forest City. It'll be safe there."

"See you there, Solomon," Christie Swanson said hopefully.

Foot looked at her grimly, "Maybe, maybe not, Christie. I'm hurt bad."

With that, they left.

During the afternoon, Solomon's pain became more than he could bear. "Bring me a razor, Ady, if I cut a vein and bleed my left arm, maybe it'll relieve the pain on my right."

Ady brought the razor. Foot, however, had darker intentions than just to let some blood. A deep cut into a vein would end his pain permanently. Solomon fully expected to die anyway and didn't want to endure the agony any longer. Erickson's moans dropped down from the loft where his wife ministered to him.

"Solomon, you'll do yourself more harm than good," Ady said as she reluctantly handed him the razor.

"Gotta try something, Ady."

Foot bared his left arm and tried to slice deep into the main artery. But his right hand and arm were simply too weak to make a deep cut. Yet blood flowed freely and Solomon felt immediate relief. He lapsed into a deep sleep.

Remaining in the cabin were the two wounded men, their wives and three children. Throughout the day and long night, the two women calmed their children and ministered to the wounds of their husbands. Solomon had been hit five times, Erickson just once but more grievously. The ball had entered his groin from the front and passed out his body. The next morning, Friday, Ady alternately watched over her sleeping husband and, gun in hand, kept an eye out for a return of the Dakota.

About noon she saw Indians coming out of the north driving cattle. They also had wagons and oxen. Ady walked to her sleeping husband and gently shook him.

"Solomon, they're back, what should I do?"

"How far?"

"Just out of rifle range. They're staying off the road past the cabin."

"Cowards. They're afraid of us. They think the cabin is bad medicine."

The Dakota rode around behind the house, a haystack and a stable hiding them from any shots from the cabin. Then they fired at the north end of the building. The balls thudded weakly into the wall but didn't enter the cabin. Afraid to come nearer, the band rode away.

"Why didn't you fire?" Solomon asked his wife.

"I only have two rounds left, Solomon."

"Poor Ady, you thought we were done for. I've got a whole pocketful of ammunition in my coat. I'll bet Swan thought we were out of ammunition, too. That's why he was using that fool scythe."

Foot felt the need to stretch out on the floor instead of lying on the cramped cot. Lying on his back, he felt free from pain. His mind raced with questions: what of his other children with Silas at Green Lake? Had the other settlers met at Arnold's? Were they coming to his assistance? What of his neighbors to the north? When would the Sioux return and find that the cabin was protected by but two women?

He called his wife to his side. "Ady, I feel better. I'm weak, and I still can't keep anything in my stomach, but I want to live, and I'll fight. I can't travel. But you must. Take Gjertrude and the children and head for Green Lake. Follow between the lakes and stay off the high ground."

"No, Solomon, my place is with you. You need me."

"The children need you. If you leave and get help, we all have a chance. Stay here, and we all may die."

Tears stained Ady's cheeks, making white streaks down her gun powder-blackened face. Silently she nodded assent to her husband's wish.

Ady and Gjertrude each tried to make their men as comfortable as possible, leaving food, water and guns within reach. Oscar remained in the loft, Solomon below. After tender embraces, they took the children and left.

"See you in Forest City," Solomon called. But in his heart, he didn't believe it.

316

꙾ 59 ꙮ

S SOLOMON FOOT AND OSCAR ERICKSON lay in agony, they had no idea what had transpired the night before at the Endreson homestead.

Several miles to the west of the Erickson cabin, on the north shore of Solomon Lake, Lars Endreson and Endre had been working the fields near their small cabin on a tranquil Thursday evening.

On three sides, fields and tall grass surrounded a clearing in which the log structure rested. In front of the cabin, across an open space, a grove of trees hid the placid waters of the lake.

It was a beautiful August twilight. The early morning rain had settled dust and left the prairie fresh. The sun balanced just above the flat horizon like an orange ball on a rope.

The Endresons had no idea that only a few miles away their daughter's family, Solomon, and the others had put up a desperate fight for their lives and driven off the Dakota.

Lars, Endre, and Ole were cutting lush green hay west of the cabin. Guri, with her little daughter, Anna, had walked into the tall fragrant grass east of their home to a root cellar. Lars wanted fresh potatoes for supper, and a good portion of their recent harvest lay in the cellar.

The girls, Britta and Guri, were working a small garden close by. Dirty fingernails and smudged faces were prices they willingly paid for good vegetables. Britta was munching a raw carrot she had just pulled up when her eyes grew wide in surprise and fear.

Young Guri looked into her sister's eyes and spun around. Just to the east of the cabin there must have been twenty Indians following an ox-drawn wagon through the long prairie vegetation. The wagon parted the grass like the prow of a ship. The Santee following in its wake.

"Papa!" sixteen-year-old Guri cried. Lars had already spied the Indians. "Stay here, boys," he said evenly to Endre and Ole. "It's probably just a hunting party. I'll see what they want."

Brown Wing was the first to step into the clearing of the homestead. Lars, mindful of Solomon's words not to show fear, walked boldly toward him. "What do you want here?" Lars demanded as he intercepted the Santee near the front of his cabin.

The Indian smiled amiably, putting the Norwegian off guard. Then he smashed his tomahawk alongside Lar's head, crumpling him. Endre grabbed his scythe and started to rush through the fresh cut hay to his father.

A volley of shots from the Santee braves cut him down. Britta and Guri screamed and raced toward the cabin. Ole sprinted toward the high grass behind the house. A musket ball smashed into his shoulder, and he tumbled face first onto the hard ground.

Two Indians reached the cabin door before the girls and wrestled their arms behind them. Britta and Guri screamed and kicked until Brown Wing held a knife to Britta's throat.

He looked meanacingly at her older sister and shouted above their screams, "You and the little one will quiet now, or I will kill this one."

Almost instantly the girls managed to reduce their anguish to a whimper. "Take them with us," Brown Wing ordered another warrior. It all had happened in less than a minute. A peaceful farm scene had become bloody mayhem in an instant. Then all was quiet again. The Santee searched the cabin for anything useful to them and then began to leave, dragging the two girls with them.

"Wait!" a young brave near Brown Wing shouted. "I think the boy moved." The Indian hurried to Ole and turned him onto his back. He studied him a moment and pronounced, "No, he is dead."

With that the Dakota disappeared into the tall grass.

Through it all Guri Endreson, her hand over little Anna's mouth, had remained helpless and terrified, huddled against a stone wall in the root cellar. The mother kept both their heads hidden from the first shot. But she couldn't hide from the screams that wouldn't let go. Even when all was quiet, the screams still echoed in Guri's head. When she was sure the Indians were gone, Guri scrambled from the little hole in the ground. Holding Anna close, she felt her world slipping away.

"Are they sleeping, Mommy?" Anna whimpered.

"No, baby, they have gone to Jesus," Guri answered. She wiped the tears that were beginning to stream down her cheeks with her long sleeves.

Guri went into the cabin and came back with pillows and blankets. She gently placed a cushion under Lars', Endre's, and Ole's heads and covered them with blankets.

Then she knelt by her husband's body, little Anna beside her, and silently bowed her head in prayer.

Guri rose to her feet and placed her hand on Anna's head. "We go to Eagle Lake. We must be strong. Maybe we can find Gjertrude and Oscar."

The Santee had driven off the stock, so the woman and her daughter began to walk to the east, staying in long grass for concealment. But despair led to confusion during the night. The girl and the woman took a wrong trail and, in the morning, found themselves back at their own cabin.

Bitter tears of frustration stung Guri's eyes as she realized that her hours of flight through the praire grass had meant nothing. They were back where they started, still in great danger. Then for the first time since the killings, sad joy reflected in the woman's face.

"Look, Mommy," Anna squealed with delight. "It's Ole!" Her mother's eyes had already focused on the boy she presumed dead. Ole was squatting on the ground in front of the cabin frying a slice of thick bacon over an open campfire.

The mother rushed to her son and wrapped her strong arms around him. Ole winced in pain in spite of his joy in the reunion. His shoulder was bloody and torn. "You're not dead! Ole, you're alive. How?" Ole's blond hair was dirty and bloody. His left arm hung limply to his side. Tears streaked his dirty face.

"I was running, and they shot me. When they were leaving, it hurt so much I moved just a little. One of them came back. I held my breath and pretended I was dead. Then I must have fainted. When I woke up the pillow was under my head, and I had a blanket on me. I thought you and Anna were dead, too. I was going to Uncle Martin's in Wisconsin. Where are Britta and Guri?"

"They took them, Ole." Guri leaned over and kissed her son gently on his forehead. "It's not safe for us here. We must go."

They found a sled that the Dakota had left and managed to round up two oxen. One was their own that had run off when the Indians attacked. It had returned to the cabin site. The other was from a neighboring farm and had wandered to Endreson's.

Both oxen were young and unaccustomed to the yoke. With difficulty—Ole able to provide little help—Guri managed to hitch the animals to the sled. They set off on Friday afternoon for Oscar and Gjertrude's cabin hoping to find a wagon.

About half a mile from the Erickson site, Ole left Guri, Anna, and the oxen and went on ahead. All was quiet and desolate at his sister's place. A wagon stood in front of the cabin, but it wasn't Oscar's. A burned haystack smoldered in a nearby field. In the distance a dog barked.

Ole crept toward the wagon door as softly as he could. He placed his ear on the door and listened. Groans. He distinctly heard groans. The Indians must be in the cabin, he concluded. As silently as possible he slunk into the prairie where his mother and sister waited.

"They're either all dead or gone, Mother," he reported. "I heard sounds coming from the cabin. I think they might be Indians. I didn't dare to go in. Oscar's wagon's gone. They maybe took it and got away."

"You did right, Ole," his mother agreed. "I hope you're right that Gjertrude and Oscar left for safety."

"What do we do now?" Ole asked.

"First we try to find help. Soon, I think, we must go to Forest City. People are there, I'm sure."

The rest of Friday afternoon the little band of survivors traveled to homesteads between the Endreson and Erickson cabins. All were deserted. Some were burned. No stock remained. In some instances they found the dead and mutilated bodies of their friends and neighbors.

Weary and unsure of what the next day might bring, Guri directed that they return to their own cabin to spend the night. Lars and Endre lay undisturbed, covered by blankets. Guri and her children went back into their own cabin. Once a home full of life and joy, the place now brought memories of broken dreams and tragedy.

The lamps were still on tables, but they didn't dare light them. Guri washed Ole's wound in the darkness before he crawled up the ladder to his bed in the loft. She tenderly placed Anna in her own little bed. Within moments the girl was asleep. Guri's brown muslin dress was bloody, dirty and ripped. She didn't care as she collapsed onto her own bed. Lying there, on the mattress she had long shared with Lars, the events of the past two days finally overwhelmed her.

Lars and Endre were dead, Guri and Britta carried off to a fate perhaps worse than death. What had happened to Oscar and Gjertrude? What would happen to her and her remaining children? It was all too much. Guri's shoulders shook as she was wracked by sobs and the bitter tears streamed freely down her cheeks.

When she was cried out, reason once again claimed the Norwegian woman. She must be strong. She knew it clearly now. If she weren't strong, Ole and Anna would likely die on the prairie of exposure or at the hands of Indians.

Tomorrow, she silently resolved, they would go back to the Erickson cabin. Maybe the sounds Ole heard hadn't been Indians. After they knew for certain, they would leave for Forest City.

❦ 60 ❧

I T WAS EARLY FRIDAY AFTERNOON when their wives and children left Solomon and Oscar. The cabin was shut up and quiet. The sun beat down on it, rendering it hot and stuffy inside. The silence beat in Solomon's ears. Each sound of nature, or the creaking of a board as Erickson shifted his weight, snapped Foot's mind to attention. Any moment he expected the Sioux to return. He reached out and touched his loaded rifle. He'd make them pay if they crashed through the door.

The long afternoon stretched into a long night. Foot had placed the mattress on the floor and had stayed there. Blood oozed from his wounds, and he still had difficulty eating or drinking; he grew weaker. Oscar Erickson was still alive, as occasional groans signaled. Oscar's legs were useless to him, and he hadn't left the loft since the women had put him there.

Saturday morning dawned bright. The day would be another scorcher. Solomon awoke to the sound of a mourning dove's cooing. In the distance, a loon's call, a lonely forlorn sound, echoed over the lake. Steady but ragged breathing from the loft told Solomon that Oscar was sleeping. Taking a small sip of water, Foot was gratified that he was able to keep it down.

Although the cabin was shut, flies came in through various openings. They gathered on Foot and his blood-soaked clothing. At first he swatted them away, but it proved fruitless, and he grew weak with the effort. He studied his shoulder. To his disgust and horror, maggots were crawling around the wound. Then, looking down at his body, Solomon imagined his clothes were moving. Closer inspection revealed maggots all over his body. The flies had obviously been at him since he was first incapacitated. As the sun rose higher, the cabin grew hotter. Foot began to smell the pus from his wounds and the stench from his clothing.

Steps. He distinctly heard the sound of footsteps outside the cabin. His left hand tightened on the rifle at his side. But an Indian wouldn't be so careless as to give himself away so easily. Could it be a neighbor? Solomon prayed. He struggled to raise his head so that he could see the door easier.

His eyes locked on the hole in the door. A face, he saw a face and the eyes were blue. It was not an Indian!

"Who's there?" Foot cried with all the energy he possessed. The face disappeared. "Oscar! Oscar! Wake up, there's someone here!" Solomon shouted to the loft. "Call to him in Norwegian! I don't know if he understood me!"

"*Hvem er det?*" Oscar called weakly.

"Ole Endreson," A young voice said. "Oscar, is that you?"

"Yes, Ole, it's me and Solomon Foot. We're hurt bad. Come in through the outside cellar door and up the trap door."

Several minutes passed. Then the trap door moved. Young Ole climbed up into the dimly lit room, fear and anguish in his eyes. His left arm, bandaged, hung limp at his side. Immediately he unbolted and opened the front door. Bright light washed into the room as if sent to cleanse it.

Foot shaded his eyes. By squinting, he made out a form in the doorway, the sun behind it. It was a woman, wide and solidly built. She spoke loudly, "Oscar, vere are you? Vere are Gjertrude and the children?"

Guri Endreson strode into the cabin. Her dress was ripped and filthy. Scratches from tangled brush marked her strong hands and her round face with blood-dried streaks. Her wide-set eyes narrowed as they adjusted from the day's brightness to the dim light within.

"Guri," Oscar moaned to his mother-in-law, "I'm up here.

"Ole, see to Solomon, ask if he needs anything," Guri said as she hastily struggled up the ladder to the loft.

Foot merely held up his hand to Ole and slowly shook his head. He would need Guri's help soon. Now he wanted to hear what she had to say, even though they spoke mostly Norwegian to each other.

Oscar spoke first. "They attacked us Thursday morning. Charley Carlson is dead. Gjertrude and Ady Foot have taken the children and gone to Green Lake. They left Friday afternoon. What day is it now?"

"It's Saturday, Oscar."

"Then they should be safe in Forest City by now. What of Lars and your family?"

Her voice lowered. "They came Thursday toward evening. They murdered Lars in the yard. Endre was in the field cutting hay when they fell upon him. They shot Ole and left him for dead. I was by the fruit cellar when they came. I had little Anna with me, and we hid in the cellar. They didn't find us. Oh, Oscar!" For the first time her voice trembled, but only for a moment. "They carried off Brita and Guri. I don't know what's happened to them."

"Why didn't you go to Green Lake?"

"I tried, Oscar. I thought Ole was dead. Me and Anna started right away. But I got lost, and we went in a big circle and wound up at our cabin again. Imagine when I saw Ole sitting up trying to make his breakfast!

"Ole came here yesterday. He saw the wagon near the house and knew it wasn't yours. All was so quiet. He thought Indians were still about when he heard groans coming from your cabin. We were about to leave again for Forest City when I thought maybe it wasn't Indians Ole heard here."

Oscar slumped back. The conversation and the horror of Guri's message had fatigued him.

Guri straightened herself, looked over Oscar and down at Solomon. "Now I take care of you and Solomon. You have wounds that must be tended."

Because of his many injuries, Guri turned to Solomon first. Congealed blood glued him to the mattress, which had to be peeled from his body. She washed and cleaned his wounds and then bound them with clean cloth. At Solomon's insistence she gave a brief summary in English of what she had told Oscar.

Little Anna sat in a corner while Guri, with help from Ole, finished with Foot and then did the same for Oscar. From Oscar's trunk they obtained clean clothing and dressed them.

"We must leave here," she told the two men, "I have yoked two oxen from my place. They are young and unbroken and must have escaped the savages. We will hitch them to the wagon in front of the house and bring you away from here."

Ole and Guri packed the wagon with blankets, bedding and needed supplies. Then Guri went into the loft where she lifted and carried Oscar down the ladder and into the wagon. Ole, with a bullet still in his shoulder, was useless in lifting and couldn't help. She came back into the cabin and carried Solomon through the door as a husband would his bride the first time across the threshold.

Guri was a large and strong woman, but Foot was amazed at her power and determination. "How can you do this, Guri?" he mumbled.

"Because I must," was her brief reply.

The men were propped on blankets into a half-sitting position. Guri placed Foot's gun by his side and started down the trail. Solomon didn't know where they were going, only that they were getting away. His efforts to help Guri get himself into the wagon exhausted him, and he fell into deep slumber.

It was early evening when Foot awoke. They had reached the Diamond Lake settlement. Several log cabins rimmed the lake. Some were burned; all the buildings were deserted. Guri shouted some "haloos," but no one answered. They drove on until nightfall, when they stopped beyond the lake and rested the oxen. Guri again tenderly bathed and dressed their wounds, then watched over the men as they slept that night. Solomon's gun rested in her lap.

Sunday morning marked one week since the killings at Acton. About noon, the little band reached an empty farmhouse. Guri gathered eggs from a chicken and found a ripe tomato. Solomon broke an egg and downed it raw. Then he bit into the tomato. It was the first food he had eaten since Thursday morning.

Without incident, they reached Forest City late that afternoon. Just before they crossed the Crow River, a man rose like a phantom out of tall grass and offered escort into the village. When they crossed over, the populace rushed to meet them.

Ady Foot raced to the wagon and grasped Solomon's hand. Tears of joy filled her eyes. Solomon looked at her with questioning eyes.

"All is well," she blurted out. "Our children, your brother, Silas, everyone is here. The Swansons and Lily Carlson are here too. Even Andrew Nelson made it. But he had a narrow escape."

"Thank God in heaven!" Guri shouted. She pulled the oxen to a halt and jumped down from the wagon into the waiting arms of her daughters Brita and Guri. "What happened to you," she exclaimed, "how did you get away?"

"The stupid savages carried us off. Then they lost some ponies and told us to stay put while they looked for them," young Guri answered.

"We didn't stay put long," Brita added, "we ran off. Mr. Piper and Mr. Ferguson found us and brought us here."

George Whitcomb stepped out from the little crowd and said, "Bring them to my house. The doctor is on the way there. These men need help."

Guri walked over to Whitcomb. "Oh, give me something to do, some work. Give me work or I will die. I can only think of my loss. I must have work to think of and use my mind."

Whitcomb clasped her hands. "Woman, you have already done more than most humans would attempt. But I understand your need to get your mind off what happened. There'll be plenty here for you to do. Soon we'll start building a stockade. We may be in danger of attack."

As Solomon recovered from surgery in Whitman's house, Ady waited by his side. He looked over at her. "Ady, I'm glad that so many of our friends made it here."

Ady gazed at him with sadness in her eyes. "Yes, Solomon, but so many didn't get here. Carl Peter Jonason, Lorentson, Backlund, others I don't know. And at West Lake, the Broberg and Lundborg families. They were at church last Wednesday. The Indians came and killed thirteen of them. Thirteen, Solomon! They nearly wiped out the whole Broberg family."

Sobbing, Ady softly placed her head on Solomon's chest as she knelt at his bedside. His eyes wide in disbelief, he gently patted his grieving wife's hair. And, in the eyes of the veteran frontiersman, tears formed and slowly trailed onto his pillow.

⁊ 61 ⱥ

As Sibley edged toward Fort Ridgely, the Santee continued to raid small settlements and homesteaders on both sides of the river. Within the fort a few refugees straggled in and were accepted.

The wounded and Gere recovered. No one who was brought to the care of Alfred and Eliza Muller died. Stories and rumors dominated the discussion of soldiers and refugees alike in Fort Ridgely. By August 27, five days following the attack, the post was still on alert. Randall, Sheehan, and Nathan gathered on the headquarters porch.

"If only we knew what was happening in the valley," Ben Randall grumbled. "There's no word of anything. Where are the men from Snelling, or anywhere for that matter?"

"Maybe Sturgis didn't even get through," Nathan speculated.

Sheehan gazed down the dusty road leading toward St. Paul. "I'd bet my very last dollar Willie made it," the lieutenant said emphatically.

"Tim," Nathan looked Sheehan in the eye, "I've got to go after Emily. I'll risk having to outrun Indians. I have to find her. I can't wait anymore."

"I know how you must feel," Sheehan was sympathetic, "but it would be pointless and extremely dangerous. If they have her, she's surrounded by hundreds of Sioux, but she could be already . . ."

"Yes, Tim," Nathan said forcefully, interrupting him, "but I've got to do something."

"Nathan," Sheehan squinted down the road again, "when reinforcements get here, patrols will be sent out. They'll have burying to do besides looking for the Sioux. I'll see that you go with them. It's the best way to look for Emily."

Nathan was frustrated. "But when will that be?"

Sheehan shaded his eyes with his left hand and looked into the eastern sun. A distant long thin line had appeared on the road. "From the looks of things, Nathan, not very much longer at all. Our reinforcements have arrived. Our little nightmare here is over."

One hundred fifty calvary under Colonel Samuel McPhail, an advance unit from Sibley's command, rode into Fort Ridgely led by Willie Sturgis. The next day, August 28, the Long Trader himself, with over 1,200 men of the Sixth Minnesota, entered the garrison.

Two armies of Dakota were also on the move. Little Crow was making a wide swing to the north, toward the settlements on the edge of the Big Woods, with about 110 warriors. His plan was to continue plundering and then to attack and disrupt Sibley's supply wagons from the rear. Gray Bird, Little Crow's chief warrior, along with 350 men, including Big Eagle, Mankato, and Wabasha, were moving down the south bank of the Minnesota toward New Ulm. Some hoped to try to take the town again, then cross the river and approach Ridgely from behind. They decided to let whatever happened guide their movements. If they were lucky, the two Indian forces would trap the white army between them.

Wacouta kept a small band of warriors and the captives on the move as well. But he was trying to avoid soldiers and not fight them. It was a duty well-suited to Wacouta's sentiments. The Dakota sub-chief did not enter into this war with enthusiasm and was glad to accept the role of protector. It concerned him that there were Santee who wanted to kill the prisoners. They were women and children and didn't deserve to die. He only wished that White Dog had not been sent with him. Having White Dog watch the captives was like assigning a fox to guard chickens.

The captives moved slowly across the trackless prairie. Occasionally they spoke quietly to one another, but mostly they were lost in their own thoughts. Jenny Olson longed for the cool waters of Lake Ripley and her parents' farm. She could visualize her parents, their table filled with a bounty of Scandinavian foods. She thought of the young soldier who had talked with her on the banks of the lake and pondered what had happened to him. Mary Schwandt and Mattie Williams wondered about the fate of the Reynolds family and grieved for Mary Anderson.

Emily West's mind turned back to her parents' store in Minneapolis and the bustling town she had left. But more often she thought of Nathan. She knew he was out there, alive, and that he would find a way to come for her. He had promised, and she knew that somehow, somewhere he would find a way to keep his word, to rescue her. Those hopes kept her moving.

Their captors were civil towards them. Only White Dog bothered Emily. He kept his distance, but something about the way he watched her, the look in his eyes, left her feeling resented and hated.

ᛤ 62 ᛰ

ENRY HASTINGS SIBLEY—THE LONG TRADER, as the Dakota called him—was the first governor of Minnesota. For seventeen years he had worked for the American Fur Company. When the first annuity was paid to the Dakota, he was at the pay table and claimed nearly one-fourth of the money for his employers. Sibley, himself, had become a wealthy man through his service to the American Fur Company.

Now fifty-one years old, he was slender and kept his thinning dark hair and mustache neatly trimmed. Sibley was more suited to politics than soldiering. Compromise and smooth dealing were more his style than decisive action. However, he had a commanding presence and men followed him. He knew he looked good in his blue uniform and resented the dust of the trail.

Sibley had taken over Marsh's office as the Mullers moved back to the log hospital. The long barracks was now filled to overflowing as soldiers and refugees occupied every available space. Company B camped in tents out on the prairie.

Officer's call now required more than just a small room. The addition of the Sixth Minnesota led to a meeting of officers in the commissary. A couple dozen assorted majors, captains, and lieutenants sat on low, wooden benches in the fieldstone building as Sibley stood before them. He spoke smoothly in a commanding voice.

"Men," the colonel began, "we still await equipment from St. Paul, and our troops must be further trained. However, relatives and friends of murdered settlers have reminded me that it's been nearly two weeks since most of the dead were killed. They must be buried. I will send a detachment of Company A under Captain Grant and some cavalry, the Cullen Guards, with Captain Anderson. Major Brown will be overall commander of the mission. Take whatever wagons you need and follow the ferry road to the agency. If there is anyone in need of help, you will aid them. Bury all corpses at the ferry and the agency and, if possible, locate the body of Captain Marsh. Also, if you can, try to find out where the Indians have gone and what they're up to. The Lower Agency has continued to be a rendezvous point for them. Be cautious and watch where you camp. Don't bivouac near mounds or ravines."

"What if we encounter the Sioux?" Brown asked.

"A relief column'll sent out immediately. I don't think they'll risk another pitched battle, however," Sibley said confidently. "For now, the rest of the command will maintain a presence in and around the fort and aid refugees. And we will drill, as you know this army is frightfully inexperienced and undersupplied. Last night I even walked the picket lines making sure they were awake."

After a discussion of post responsibilities, the officers moved out of the commissary. Tim Sheehan waited and approached Sibley.

"Beg your pardon, sir. I have a request to make."

"Yes, Lieutenant." Sibley glanced up from papers he was reviewing.

"There's a civilian here, a former officer with an Indiana regiment until he was injured, name's Nathan Cates. He's been a trader at Redwood. He's fought bravely and I promised him that when the company was sent out of the fort on a mission like you've outlined, that he could go with it."

"Why does he want to accompany the regiment?" Sibley looked full at Sheehan.

"A woman was taken from the agency. He wants to find her, sir."

Sibley walked over to the door of the stone building and looked out on the sun-splashed parade ground. "You say he was a soldier? He won't get in the way?"

"Not this man, Colonel." Sheehan was definite.

"All right, tell him he's attached to Brown, it seems like I heard his name mentioned around Snelling for some reason." Sibley scratched his cheek thoughfully, and then shook his head. "No matter, there are some other civilians going, about twenty, Agent Galbraith, trader Nate Myrick, Dr. Daniels among them. By the way, Lieutenant, if there's trouble I want you on the relief column."

"Yes, sir, and thank you." Sheehan's reply was crisp as he saluted and did an aboutface out the door.

On Sunday morning, August 31st, Joe Anderson and fifty cavalrymen, the "Cullen Guards"; Hiram Grant with 100 infantry; and seventeen wagons left Fort Ridgely bound upriver. Joe Coursolle rode with the cavalry, his daughters much on his mind.

Major Joseph Brown, former trader and agent of the Sioux Agency, trotted at the head of the column with Nathan Thomas. Brown also had a particular interest in the mission beyond what he had been ordered to do. His wife and children lived near the Upper Agency and were now captives.

The columns buried about twenty victims that first day and camped that night on the Minnesota River bottoms near Birch Coulee Creek. The next morning Brown divided his forces. He crossed the river to the agency, along with Captain Anderson and the Cullen Guard cavalry. Most of the civilians, including Galbraith, Myrick and Nathan, also crossed.

Grant and the infantry continued their march along the north side of the river. At the ferry, they buried Quinn and twenty soldiers. Then they proceeded about five miles up the valley toward Beaver Creek.

Nathan walked into the desolation of Redwood Agency looking for Emily, yet hoping he wouldn't find her among the rotting, bloated bodies that lay scattered throughout the village. Shaken, Galbraith viewed the burned-out ruins of his agency. Hardly a building had been left standing. In defense of Ridgely, he had performed bravely, but now the agent was hit with the realization that he could have been at the site that fateful Monday and would certainly have been a main target.

Nate Myrick had been equally fortunate. His brother had sent him to pick up supplies in St. Paul. When they came upon Andrew's body, mouth still stuffed with grass, no one needed to explain its meaning.

The two columns went into camp together that night after the cavalry crossed back to the north side of the Minnesota. Pickets were posted, and no signs were visible of the Santee. Nate Myrick and about a dozen other civilians left the next morning for Fort Ridgely. They had seen enough. Nathan Thomas was determined to stay with the company as long as they were on patrol.

In the morning, September 1, the command was divided again. Nathan, with Anderson and the Cullen Guard cavalry, remounted and crossed the river once more, then rode up to Little Crow's camp. Not much remained of the Santee. They saw some firepits, garbage, and items left hastily behind. In the deserted camp, Brown and Anderson conferred with Galbraith and veteran trader Alexander Faribault.

"They've been gone from here three, four days," Faribault said after examining tracks and dead fires.

Brown sifted ashes through his fingers and looked northeast. "They must be runnin', probably up the Yellow Medicine or beyond. I don't think we have much to worry about from them here."

"Shall we continue riding upriver, Major?" Captain Anderson asked.

Anderson nodded. "We'll scout ahead some, although I don't think we'll find much besides more dead settlers."

From a distant hill, Big Eagle watched the movements of Anderson and Brown's men.

Captain Grant and his infantry advanced north toward Beaver Creek. They made frequent stops along the way to bury men, women, and children. About mid-morning Grant stood upright in his saddle, his tall, slender body taut as he saw what looked to be an Indian drop into the grass ahead.

"Lieutenant Baldwin," he ordered, "take twenty men and surround that spot ahead by the knoll. Someone's in there. If it's a white, capture 'im. If it's an Indian, kill 'im."

Baldwin and his men rushed into position and closed a circle slowly toward the quivering grass. To their amazement, a naked woman suddenly jumped to her feet. She was terribly wounded. A long, blood-encrusted gash snaked across her stomach and her back was riddled with perhaps a dozen bloody holes from buckshot. She was so dirty it was impossible to tell if she was Indian or not. Her hair was wild and matted.

"Don't shoot!" she yelled. "I'm Justina Krieger, a white woman!"

Grant rode forward and wrapped her in a soldier's blanket. Then she was carried to a wagon. Dr. Daniels examined her and reported to Grant.

"Quite a story, Captain. It seems that the Sioux happened on a band of refugees she was with. They pretended to be friendly, said it was Chippewas causing the trouble and urged them to turn around and go home. The folks did. When they got near their settlement, the Sioux killed some twenty-five to thirty of them. Mrs. Krieger saw her husband killed and several of her children. She knows some got away. She took seventeen shots in the back while attempting to rescue her baby. Then, thinking her dead, they cut off her clothes and sliced her stomach. She's been wandering around out here for thirteen days, half crazy, eatin' roots and drinking from creeks."

"Amazing," Grant slowly shook his head. "I wonder how many stories there are like hers? Will she be all right?"

"With rest, she'll recover, physically anyway. We've made a bed for her in the wagon. She can stay there."

"Good, Doctor," Grant brushed back his sandy hair. "Let's move on to Beaver Creek."

At the creek, Grant's detachment found thirty bodies and buried them. Then they continued another three miles, left the valley and climbed hills to a trail that led them back to Birch Coulee.

Grant and a scout rode ahead to the coulee and selected a campsite for the night. He chose a slightly depressed area with woods about 200 yards to the south and a ravine about the same distance to the east. The seventeen wagons were placed in a circle with ropes tied wagon to wagon to act as a picket line for horses. It became a corral less than one hundred yards across with tents in the middle.

About sundown, Captain Anderson's company rode in. Joe Anderson dismounted. He was worn, dusty and sweaty, as were his men.

"Hiram," he informed Grant, "we must'a rode dang near forty miles today. Crossed the river a coupla times. There ain't no Indians to be seen."

"What about Little Crow's village, Joe?" Grant asked.

"Faribault and Galbraith said it looks like they've been gone at least a few days." Anderson dumped the remaining contents of a canteen on his head and shook the water from his long brown hair. "I don't think there's a Sioux within twenty-five miles."

"Pitch your tents on the south side of the wagon circle. My men have the north," Grant instructed. "We'll head back to Ridgely in the morning. 'Bout sixteen miles, I think."

Nathan and Alexander Faribault walked around the camp as the sun slowly changed to a reddish-orange ball on the horizon.

"Don't like this spot," the old trader grumbled. "Grant picked and Brown went along with it. What they thinkin'? We're in a low spot. Not much for hills, but the ground rises all around us. A man can't see what's happ'nin' behind the rise on two sides. Woods and coulee nearby for cover.

"Only clear vision we got is the prairie to the north, and there the Sioux would have six-foot-high grass to hide in. Didn't they learn nothin' from Ridgely?" Faribault spat disgustedly. He was near sixty, gray haired with a scraggly gray beard. His body was still strong and wiry. Faribault had traded with the Dakota and lived on the frontier for over twenty years.

"Apparently," Nathan followed the old man's eyes, "they're very sure that no Indians are nearby."

"They might be very surprised." Faribault squinted at the setting sun. "I hope they're right. But it don't feel good. At least they got pickets posted all 'round the camp." He stretched, sighed, and looked back at Nathan. "Find anything of your woman?"

"Nothing, I suppose that's both good and bad."

"Looks to me like they got her, son," Faribault replied. "I heard they got a passel of captives they's haulin' around. Just pray for the best."

❧ 63 ☙

ARLY THE NEXT MORNING, the soldiers' world exploded. Private Bill Hart was on picket duty, posted about thirty yards out from the camp. The sun was just beginning to glow over the horizon. Hart saw grass moving between himself and the camp. Thinking it a wolf, he fired.

Then all hell came crashing down on the soldiers at Birch Coulee. During the night over 200 Santee warriors under Big Eagle and Mankato had encircled the camp, using the raised ground for cover. When the shot rang out, they leaped from the grass within a hundred feet of the camp and loosed a deadly rifle volley.

The Bluecoats rushed from their tents and formed a line to return fire. As his men fell like grain sliced by a scythe, Grant shouted, "Break right! Break left! Get behind the wagons and keep firing!"

Instinctively his officers sprang to action.

Lieutenant Gillham yelled, "Follow, boys!" and led thirty men to the east side of the camp. Another thirty raced with Baldwin to the northeast part of the camp. Joe Anderson defended the south with his men while Captain Grant spread the rest along the western perimeter.

Nathan had slept in a tent with Faribault. Hearing the gunshots, he crawled from his tent and helped to tip a wagon, from which he returned fire.

337

Faribault at his side yelled in his ear, "I told ya, boy. I didn't like this spot. Told 'em so, too. No Sioux around, they said. Bull!"

"Keep your head down, Alex," Nathan cautioned. He carefully squeezed off a shot. "It's going to be a long day."

Horses screamed as they were hit by shot. Smoke and the sound of drums and warwhoops filled the air in addition to the never-ceasing roar of gunfire. The soldiers tipped the wagons on their sides for cover; only the one containing Justina Krieger was left upright. The Dakota had the high ground and were able to rain shot like hail into the soldiers.

After one hour, the Indians had been driven back but were still within rifle range. The Sixth Minnesota had lost half of its force killed or wounded. Eighty-five of the eight-seven horses were dead.

Grant yelled, "We've got to get lower, there's not enough cover. Dig, dig trenches with whatever you've got—knives, bayonets, hands. Dig!"

The men dug. Bullets passed right through the wagons. Teams of men piled up dead horses and dead men for more barricades as others dug.

"I think they be diggin' their own graves." Faribault whispered in Nathan's ear.

After a period of intermittent fire, the Santee began to rain shot from all sides. The soldiers hugged the earth of their little trenches and shot back at Indians they could see or at movements in the long grass that hid the attackers.

The sun scorched the backs of the Sixth Minnesota as the day wore on. They had no water, no food and no relief from the shot and heat. Their tongues began to thicken and swell.

Baldwin crawled on his belly to Grant. "Captain, we're runnin' low on ammo. I ordered more out of the ordnance wagon. But, blast it! The fort sent sixty-two caliber bullets for fifty-eight caliber rifles."

"Damn!" Grant slammed a fist into the dirt. "What else can go wrong? Have the men shave down bullets. It's all we can do."

Nathan and Faribault were near Justina Krieger's wagon. During the course of the fight, she moaned incessantly for water. Many of the wounded and active fighters were parched and desperate to drink.

Faribault tried to spit. His lips made a dry *pfft* sound. "Feels like I got a mouth full of cotton," he croaked.

Nathan's own tongue was becoming thick and dry. "Alex," he mumbled through cracked lips, "help me gather up some canteens. I'm going to the creek in the coulee. Maybe I can bring back enough to help some of the wounded."

"I'll go with ya," Faribault offered.

"No, Alex," Nathan stared intently into the tall, brown-green grass between them and the creek. "Maybe one man can crawl through without attracting too much attention. Two, and they'll follow the grass movement easier."

"But, son," the old man tried to be gentle, "you only got one arm."

"Alex, I can do it." There was no doubt in his voice.

Around his neck, belt, and shoulder, Nathan managed to attach eight canteens. Then he began to slither snakelike slowly through the vegetation. It was about seventy-five yards to the creek. Santee were scattered in the grass. Nathan had to be very cautious to avoid contact with them.

Then he heard a voice shout in Dakota. Instantly Indians rose up in the grass and fired another withering salvo at the soldiers. One was five feet directly in front of Nathan. After firing, the warrior looked down and saw Nathan on the ground before him. He lowered his rifle to shoot, but Nathan deftly snapped a shot with his revolver, and the Indian slumped into the grass.

➳ 64 ᘐ

WHEN THE FIRST SHOTS SHATTERED the morning air at Birch Coulee, Company B was sleeping in tents outside Fort Ridgely. Oscar Wall lay on the ground. When he rolled onto his side, his ear to the ground, he heard the unmistakable sound of gunfire rumbling through the earth. Soon Oscar and many other soldiers were stumbling out of tents shouting for Lieutenant Gere.

"I hear it, too, boys!" Gere shouted as he sprinted to the fort. "Grant and Anderson must be having a hot time of it."

Sibley immediately dispatched a relief column. While Nathan lay in the grass crawling toward the creek, 150 soldiers under Colonel Sam McPhail, with a mountain howitzer in tow, neared Birch Coulee.

Thomas crawled past the body of the Santee and soon was dipping canteens into the refreshing coolness of Birch Coulee Creek. He plunged his head into the stream and gulped thirstily. The relief it brought was quickly forgotten, for as Nathan emerged from the water, he was looking up the barrel of a rifle.

He froze, and his eyes followed the black steel tube to the face beyond. The Indian was painted red, a lightning bolt across his cheek. The hammer was already cocked on the gun. The man's thumb went to it and slowly released the hammer as the gun was lowered.

"We are even, One Arm," the Santee said.

Nathan let out his caught breath, water dripping into his eyes. Then he smiled with recognition. "Johnny, is it you?" he whispered hoarsely.

"I am Traveling Star, no longer Johnny. You helped me. I have helped you."

Horses tethered nearby began to neigh and whinney at the intruder. Traveling Star glanced at them. "I am to watch the horses. Warriors come back here during the battle to eat and drink. Soon someone may come. You must leave or go back to the soldiers."

"I'm going back, Traveling Star. Let me fill a couple more canteens." Submerging the open containers, he spoke to the young brave. "Thank you. Have you seen Miss West . . . Emily?"

"She is safe, One Arm. My family protects her. Now she travels with the other captives toward the Yellow Medicine. Wocouta and Standing Buffalo are with the band, but so is White Dog, and because of that there may be danger. He still hates both of you for what happened. He thinks the agency fired him because of it. Now you must leave. Do not go to the soldiers. They will all die soon."

"I can't run, Traveling Star," Nathan attached the last filled canteen to his belt, "this water is for a sick woman and wounded men. I'm going to them." As Nathan disappeared into the grass, the Santee boy soothed the horses to quiet them.

Moments later, a boom reverberated over the prairie. The sound of hoarse cheers echoed from the soldiers' camp. Help had come from Ridgely.

Red Eagle raced to the coulee east of camp. "Red Legs," he cried to a subchief, "move east of the coulee and fire at the soldiers, make a big show but don't get too close."

McPhail was two miles distant. The Santee made a massed show on a rise of ground and fired long-range shots at the soldiers.

"Sheehan," the colonel called for his lieutenant. "I'm not going to head on in like Marsh did. We'll camp here. Ride back to Ridgely and tell Sibley to send more men. I think they outnumber us, and I'm not about to ride into the coulee to count them to make sure."

341

As Sheehan rode back to the fort, Nathan emerged from the grass and was heartily welcomed by the circle of soldiers. Alex Faribault slapped him on the back and helped with the canteens.

"Get the doctor to help us," Nathan suggested.

"He's dead," Private Jack Frazier replied. "I saw him go down in one of the first volleys. We'll help with the water. You go to the woman."

"How many wounded do you think there are?" Nathan asked.

"From the looks of things, fifty . . . sixty, maybe. It's hard ta say," Faribault said. "Frazier, about a swallow a man is all we can give 'em. Not much, but it's somethin'."

"Best I could do, and I had to look up a gun barrel to get it, Alex." Nathan crawled away toward Mrs. Krieger's wagon. "I'll tell you about it later," he called back to the questioning old frontiersman.

Alex poured a gulp of water down a gutshot man's throat just as a bullet skipped up dirt in front of him. Indignant, he yelled, "You do wrong to fire on us! We're not here to fight, just to bury the white people you killed!"

Nathan slipped into the canvas-covered wagon. Light streamed in from dozens of bullet holes, but other than a graze on her arm, Justina Krieger had not been physically harmed further. Still, she was dazed and nearly delirious when he raised her head to drink and washed her face.

Grant watched in dismay as the relief column pitched a camp. Occasionally the howitzer belched a shot, but no massed force was coming to help them.

"What's goin' on, Captain?" Corporal Jim Auge asked.

"They don't dare come down here," Grant said thoughtfully. "Afraid there's too many of 'em, I suppose. Unless I miss my guess, they'll have sent for more men. We gotta hold through the night."

Twilight slowly enveloped the prairie and the coulee. The fighting fell off to occasional shots and ramdom volleys. Then as the darkness became complete, the prairie went silent, except for the wounded. The soldiers stayed dug into their little trenches, enduring the pitiful cries of the agonized sufferers.

Nathan explained his encounter with Traveling Star at the creek.

"Ya got lucky, young man." Faribault tried to spit but couldn't. "At least now ya got a place to start lookin' for Emily. That is, if we get outta here alive."

"I have to," Nathan reminded his friend. "I made a promise."

"And dead men don't keep promises," Alex finished with a sage nod.

ஸ 65 ஐ

SEPTEMBER THIRD DAWNED WITH a beautiful sunrise, promising another day of blistering heat. Riding out on the prairie was a lone Indian on a white horse. It was Gray Bird. Corporal Jim Auge, an interpreter, was of white and Santee blood. Grant, with Brown standing nearby, had sent him out to talk with the Indian.

In minutes, Auge reported to Grant and Brown. "He says they got reinforced during the night, that there're as many of them as there are leaves on the tree. Then he said that they'll charge us and take no prisoners. But," he paused, "if the half-breeds and anyone with Indian blood comes out now, they'll be spared and protected."

About ten half-breeds, or mixed-bloods, gathered about Auge and his captain. Auge explained to them what Gray Bird had said.

"What are you going to do, Corporal?" asked Grant.

Auge hesitated. He studied the men huddling around, then looked at the captain and major. Joe Coursolle looked at him and spat in the direction of the mounted Indian. "We're going to stay with you, Captain," Auge said.

"Then tell him this, Corporal." After a few words from Grant, Auge turned back to the waiting Indian. "You do not have enough to take our camp. We have two rifles ready per man and 200 men. Come if you want to die."

With a snort of disgust, Gray Bird rode away into the coulee.

"A slight exaggeration of our strength, Captain. How many effective men do we have?" Brown wondered.

"Maybe sixty-five, Major," Grant answered. "Our casualty count is twenty-five dead and sixty-five wounded."

Gilliam suddenly yelled an alert. "Captain, Major, they're on the move!"

On the prairie side of the camp, large numbers of Santee were encircling. The Dakota were preparing for one more massed attack. Then, just as quickly as they had appeared, they were gone. In the distance a trumpet sounded. A long column was joining McPhail's camp. Sibley and 1,000 men had arrived. The Dakota vanished like mist into the long grass of the Minnesota prairie.

Sibley was aghast when he viewed the camp. Men were lying dead and black from the scorching sun. Many were badly wounded and begging for water. The stench of dead men and horses was gagging the soldiers. Tents hung as rags from their poles, they were so riddled by shot. The wagons were shot to pieces. Amazingly, Justina Krieger lived, although over 200 shots had splintered her wagon.

By eight o'clock that night the survivors had reached the sanctuary of Fort Ridgely.

ഔ **66** ഌ

NEARLY 250 REFUGEES HAD FLOCKED to Forest City. The small village, located on a bend of the slow-moving, muddy Crow River on the edge of the Big Woods in Meeker County, was the largest settlement in Meeker County, having almost 150 citizens.

Trees lined the river, but Forest City was built on the open prairie, a collection of houses and cabins clumped together in no particular order. The largest structure was the hotel of J.D. Atkinson. Solomon Foot's Kandiyohi lakes region lay about forty miles to the southwest.

Since the first attack at Acton and the murder of the Jones family, there had been little Dakota movement in the area. A Company of the Ninth Minnesota Infantry under Captain Richard Strout had been sent to Forest City and had moved around Meeker County to provide a presence to discourage Indian plunder.

On September 2nd, Little Crow's band was sighted north of Acton by a patrol led by Captain Whitcomb. This heightened concern for safety in Forest City. The decision was made to build a stockade for protection.

Solomon Foot was now in the tenth day of recovery from his wounds. They had healed and, fortunately, no bones had been broken. Still stiff and sore, each day he improved.

In the home of A.C. Smith, plans were being made for the defense of the village. Postmaster James Atkinson, Whitcomb, Jesse Branham, Ole Ness, and Solomon Foot sat at a round table in Smith's dining room. In spite of everything Mrs. Smith kept a neat house. A framed picture of Lincoln hung on the wall. Several oil lamps lit the room and cast a shadowy, yellow sheen on the men's faces.

"First off," Smith said, "we've got to let Strout know there are Sioux in his area. He's making a swing down by Acton now."

"I'll ride out there and warn him soon's we finish here," Branham offered.

"Good, Jesse," Smith nodded at Branham. "Take Sperry and Holmes with you and see you get good horses."

"You all heard I saw a passel of them this afternoon out Acton way," Whitcomb added. "We've got to be ready for them here."

"Anyone here ever build a stockade?" Smith asked.

A small man with a large nose, bushy mustache, and a widow's peak hairline slowly raised his hand. "I have," responded Ole Halverson Ness, one of the county's first settlers.

"I thought you were just a farmer from Norway, Ole. You got some surprises for us." Smith smiled at the little Norwegian.

Ness stood up to his full height and proudly stated, "For six years I vas in da Norvegian Army, I vas. My fadder fought vit Napoleon. My son Martin vas in da army, too. I can build your stockade."

"Good," Smith said. "We didn't know all your background. I think you should be in charge of erecting it."

"My hotel is in the open, away from the trees," Atkinson suggested. "Let's build the fort around it. There's a stack of logs already cut for a new church. We can use them."

"It's wise to keep in the open, away from the river." Solomon winced slightly as he shifted in his chair. "Don't give the reds any cover."

"Den tomorrow ve build it right dere," Ness said confidently.

"And then we wait," Smith concluded.

As they filed out of the room, a fiftyish, graying, slender man approached Solomon Foot.

"Mr. Foot," he said deferentially, "I'm Olav Olson from up by Lake Ripley. My daughter, Jenny . . . they took her." His voice choked up. Swallowing hard, he composed himself. "The Indians, they took my Jenny on the 18th of August. I know you were hurt, so I waited. But . . . could you, could you help find her?"

"Mr. Olson," Solomon began, "there's an army out looking for captives. I'm barely recovered from being shot. I'd advise you to wait."

In the shadows behind Olson, Foot heard the sobs of a woman crying. Olav stepped aside, and the light from the nearby house fell on the face of a blonde, middle-aged woman. Her eyes were red and swollen, and tears ran in rivulets down her cheeks. "This is my wife, Pauline, Mr. Foot."

Pauline Olson dropped to her knees before Solomon and grabbed his hand. "Please," she begged in anguish. "Please find my Jenny."

Olav implored him, "They tell us you're the best there is around here. The 'Daniel Boone of the Lakes,' they call you."

Solomon looked helplessly and wearily at the two. With resignation he answered, "After this thing here is done. The fort built, the immediate crisis over. I'll go look for Jenny. That is, if my wounds will permit it."

"Thank you, thank you, Mr. Foot." Pauline slipped a small daguerreotype photograph of a pretty, blonde girl into his hand.

"I'll do what I can, when I can." Foot already regretted being influenced by a mother's tears.

Early the next morning the stockade started going up. It would be 120 feet square with a double row of ten-foot-high logs. Ole Ness went about his job of supervision quickly and efficiently. The men of Forest City and the refugees from the surrounding area were organized into teams of responsibility, some cutting logs, some digging them in. The construction progressed with surprising speed.

Foot watched the activity, not willing to risk ripping open his wounds with heavy lifting. An attractive, black-haired woman walked by. Noticing Solomon, she stopped to talk.

"You're Solomon Foot, aren't you? Isn't the fort going to be just wonderful? It'll be the best fort around."

"It's coming right along," Foot replied. "Two rows of upright logs should keep arrows and bullets out. Who are you?"

"I'm Daisy Ness Dahl. That's my father, Ole, in charge of the building."

"He's doing a fine job, Mrs. Dahl," Solomon nodded appreciatively.

"He's a Ness," Daisy smiled proudly. "You'd be surprised what great people the Nesses are. Why, the first school in the area was in our granary."

"I'm sure they are, ma'am." Solomon couldn't help smiling. "Where's your husband?"

"He's a painter." She grew serious. "He got a job painting at the agency. That's the last we heard. I hope he's all right. Our oldest boy, Jerome, is taking care of things now. He's such a wonderful boy, smartest in the county."

Men heaved a log into place.

"Oh, lookey, lookey!" she cried, "Watch those logs go up!"

Solomon watched as men and oxen placed the ends of the logs in the ground and pulled them perpendicular. Daisy Dahl scurried off to get a closer look.

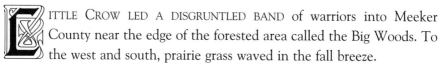 ಚಿ 67 ಲ

LITTLE CROW LED A DISGRUNTLED BAND of warriors into Meeker County near the edge of the forested area called the Big Woods. To the west and south, prairie grass waved in the fall breeze.

Since the fight at the ferry, there had been no major victories for the warriors. They had been frustrated in their failure to take New Ulm and Fort Ridgely. However, the Santee had succeeded at ravaging small settlements and individual homesteads, and many wanted to continue that type of warfare. Since most of Little Crow's warriors had divided into two bands, there had been no contact with each other. Little Crow didn't know that Gray Bird had fought a big battle at Birch Coulee.

The tired leaders of the raiders gathered under the shade of an old oak tree near a long, narrow lake. A finger of land stuck into the lake and over 100 warriors camped in the open on it while their leaders conferred.

Walker Among Sacred Stones, a veteran warrior, spoke for the braves who wished to continue raiding small villages and farms. "Little Crow, let us do what has worked. We can kill the settlers, burn their homes and drive them from the valley."

Little Crow felt as if he were speaking to a child. He had grown weary of explaining his brand of war to his people. "Walker Among Sacred

Stones, you must understand. As long as the soldiers are here, the whites will come. If we drive the soldiers away, the valley will be closed to them. Besides, warriors fight warriors, not the defenseless, not women and children."

"You speak well, Little Crow," the dissident warrior acknowledged, "but we have smoked and talked about this. Most of the young braves want to raid the farms, not attack soldiers and towns."

"I am your war chief," Little Crow narrowed his eyes as he reminded all within hearing.

"Then lead those who wish to follow you in *your* kind of war." Walker Among Sacred Stones turned to the band and shouted, "Those who wish to fight as we did in the valley, those who want to raid the farms and settlers, not the soldiers, follow me, and I will lead you."

To the sullen dismay of Little Crow, seventy-five left him. Only thirty-five men remained. Little Crow was so disgusted that he refused to lead what was left of his command. He turned his followers over to his brother, White Spider. Little Crow would be just a soldier.

LATE AT NIGHT ON SEPTEMBER 2, Jesse Branham, Tom Holmes, and Albert Sperry rode the twenty miles from Forest City southwest to Acton by a circuitous route. As they approached Strout's camp, they were amazed to find no pickets. They trotted directly into a sleeping camp on the yard of Robinson Jones. The cabins of the settlement were unburned and stood as empty monuments to the bloodshed. No soldier slept in them.

"Where's the captain?" Branham shouted.

"I'm Strout," replied a middle-aged officer with heavy arms and a belly that flopped over his belt. He wore a red cotton shirt and sky-blue soldier pants held up by suspenders. "What do you want?" he asked.

"Do you know that Sioux bands were sighted near here this afternoon?" Branham inquired.

"We haven't seen any. You sure about this?" Strout sounded unconvinced.

"Captain Whitcomb reported it. I was with him." Branham tried to hide the edge in his voice.

"Set out pickets," Strout, reluctantly persuaded, ordered his sergeant. "Lieutenant Clark, there may be action in the morning. Have the men see to their weapons."

Within minutes Clark approached Strout with urgency. "Sir, we just opened the ammunition crates and there's a problem! Most of our bullets are too big for the muskets! Four out of five don't fit. Blasted quartermaster!"

Strout frowned heavenward as if seeking divine intervention. Taking a bullet from Clark, he slowly shook his head while examining it. Frustration was evident as the captain barked his reply. "Have the men carve them down and pound them to fit! There's nothing else we can do!"

Then Strout turned to Branham. "We'll break camp at first light. I want you to lead the mounted detail out front tomorrow. There's just five of you: the three that came from Forest City, my chief scout Al DeLong, and Marshall. Follow the trail you took last night and lead us back. Stay a few hundred yards ahead. We fixed a couple of crossings over low ground, one just east of the Baker cabin and the other at the south end of the lake. They should hold up for the wagons. Let me know at the first sign of trouble."

"They're out there," Branham replied, "I could feel it comin' in. Keep 'em all marchin' close. How many ya got?"

"Sixty-three infantry, and with the teamsters and your men, seventy-five."

"Watch 'em, Captain. We might be in for a long day."

At daylight, the Ninth Minnesota left the deserted Jones farmstead and marched due east. They passed out of the Acton woods near the Baker cabin and onto the prairie. Strout's soldiers marched both in front and to the rear of a line of eight teamster-driven wagons.

In a show of false bravado, the soldiers in back struck up a song they had made up on the march from St. Paul:

> *Brave Captain Strout and Company B,*
> *They will make the Redskins flee*
> *And drive them west into the sea*
> *And stop the war whoop forever.*

The Union forever, hurrah boys, hurrah
Kill every Indian papoose and squaw
The Indians must be slain, or driven to the plain
And silence the war whoop forever.

"What in the name of God are they doing back there!" Strout exclaimed from the front ranks. "Lieutenant Kinney, ride back there and shut those fools up. This isn't a picnic. We might be riding to a battle!"

Kinney wheeled his mount to the rear and galloped back.

Far in front, Branham and his men rode east through the swale, aided by the new log reinforcements in the marsh. Then the trail curved to the south and up a rise onto rolling prairie. In front some 150 yards away was a wheat field and on their left, to the east, Long Lake.

DeLong, who had been slightly ahead of the other four, hurried back to Branham.

"Hey, Jesse," the scout said and pointed ahead, "lookey there, in the wheat field . . . the sun is shinin' on somethin'. I'd swear it's reflectin' off a gun barrel."

"Al," Branham said, squinting into the wheat field, "there's more than one in there. I think there's big trouble ahead. You better ride back and tell the captain."

At that instant a shot ripped from the distant wheat field and clipped through nearby prairie grass. The scouts had stumbled upon Little Crow's camp. Branham and his men returned fire as DeLong alerted Strout.

The infantry of the Ninth rushed to the front at the double quick. As Branham briefed Strout, the captain quickly sized up the situation. He turned to First Lieutenant Clark.

"Form the men into an open line between the road and the lake. Look ahead. They're in the wheat field, inside the fence lines. But I think we outnumber them. We'll fire a volley and then advance. That should push 'em out of there."

As the soldiers moved into position, the Santee lay in the wheat field. Little Crow and White Spider watched from beside a wooden fence.

353

"Little Crow, we are too few," White Spider assessed. "Walker Among Sacred Stones must be near. I will climb to the top of the fence and signal him." The Santee began to rise to his feet. Little Crow placed his hand on his brother's shoulder and held him down.

"No, you must lead today. I will signal." Little Crow clutched a red blanket and climbed to the second rail of the fence. Balancing there, he waved the blanket over his head.

"Look at that fool redskin," Clark cried.

"We're primed and ready, sir," a sergeant informed.

"Then FIRE!" Clark screamed.

A ragged volley cut loose at Little Crow. The Santee leader, unscathed, coolly stepped off the fence. He made a graceful bow and then waved his hand high at the soldiers. "I gave them something to remember," he murmured to White Spider.

A rousing cheer erupted from the soldiers. Strout, in spite of himself, turned to Branham and proclaimed, "By God, that's about the bravest thing I've ever seen a man do!"

The cheers were cut short. Walker Among Sacred Stones had seen and heeded Little Crow's signal. From the brush and grass to the north and across the road to the west, shots exploded at the soldiers.

"Kinney," Strout ordered, "they're mounted behind us. Take some men and try to hold 'em back."

But, buoyed by reinforcements, White Spider and Little Crow were able to hold Kinney at bay and close in on three sides. As the soldiers were pushed off the road toward Long Lake, the teamsters panicked and galloped their teams south down the trail.

Strout was quick to grasp their state of peril. "Clark, we're being pushed toward the lake. We can't let them get between us and the water. Form up into four squads, fix bayonets and, God help us, we'll charge through 'em back to the road!"

Through a mayhem of screams, shots, and falling men, the Ninth Minnesota fought with guns, fists, and bayonets back to the trail. Heading south, they caught up to the wagons and reached the base of a bluff at the southwest end of the lake. There, the men gathered around Strout and returned fire as the captain engaged in a frantic council of war. His officers and scouts gathered close to him. "Men, we have two choices. We can stand and fight on this spot, or we run like the devil!"

"Much as I hate to say it, Captain, we gotta run," Branham rasped. He held a hand tightly over his chest, crimson blood trickling between his fingers. "Got me in the lung," Jesse choked and coughed. "We stay here and fight and they'll just pick us off. They've got better rifles. I seen Springfields."

As if on cue, Private Stone grabbed his chest and crumbled dead at their feet.

Strout considered his scout's words. "Thank the Lord we took time to fix that crossing yesterday." He pointed down the trail to a marsh where corduroy logs formed a passage. "But we better head to Hutchinson. We'll never make Forest City."

"Captain," Branham interrupted, "one more thing. We got wagons filled with all kindsa stuff—food, sugar, flour, blankets. Get as many men on the wagons as we can and throw the stuff off. If I know the reds, they'll stop to pick up whatever they think they need. It'll buy us time."

"See to it, Clark," Strout snapped. "Let's get ready and go!"

In minutes the men of the Ninth Minnesota began to race past the west side of Long and Hope lakes. Strout was prophetic. Had the crossing not been repaired, many soldiers would have been stalled there and killed.

The Santee chased, stopping periodically as Branham predicted, to search through discarded parcels hurled from the rumbling wagons. It took eight hours of a running, sometimes frantic, fight before the soldiers reached Hutchinson and the safety of a stockade. Eighteen soldiers were wounded. They left behind three dead at Long Lake.

The two Dakota bands reunited and were reinforced by another twenty from the Upper Agency. Then they broke into two groups again; Walker Among Sacred Stones led one group to attack Forest City, while Little Crow moved on Hutchinson.

ॐ 68 ॐ

AS THE TWO DAKOTA FORCES FOUGHT at Birch Coulee and Acton, Wocouta's band advanced across the prairie farther up the Minnesota River past the burned-out buildings of the Yellow Medicine Agency.

Jenny Olson stayed as close to Emily as possible, with Mary Schwandt and Mattie Williams usually nearby. It was well known among the hundred-some white captives that Emily was under the protection of Lightning Blanket's nephew and that Little Crow had an interest in her as well.

By staying close to her, the three girls hoped to fend off any mistreatment by their captors. More and more "friendly" Indians were moving close to the camp. The Wahpeton and Sisseton were still officially neutral, even though many of their young men were fighting with the Lower Dakota. In fact, a band under the Sisseton leader, Sweet Corn, had begun a siege at Fort Abercrombie on September 3rd.

Now they grew closer to the villages of such chiefs as Little Paul, Akepa, and Red Iron, men who were not involved in the war. Nearly 200 mixed-bloods were also captive. They spread word to the white prisoners that the farther they were from Little Crow, the safer they would be. The Upper Dakota leaders would protect them.

Emily knew that as long as White Dog continued to guard them, they were still in great peril. Occasionally she would notice him unabashedly staring at her. His eyes gleamed with something between lust and hatred.

"That skinny, ugly one," Jenny gestured at White Dog with a slow nod of her head, "do you know him? He keeps looking at you."

"He worked for the government at the agency." Emily stared straight ahead and made no notice of the Santee. "I kicked him once. Nathan had disputes with him. He hates us. I'm told he thinks he lost his job because of us."

"Will he leave us alone?" Mary whispered.

"For now, yes. As long as he fears our protector's retribution. If ever he feels out of their reach, then . . ."

"Have you heard anything?" Mattie was almost pleading for hope.

Emily looked at the tattered, dirty girls who were only slightly younger than she. They were scratched, usually hungry, and disheveled. The look in their eyes told of the desperation they felt and the horrors they had endured.

Emily realized she must look like them. She, too, wanted hope. "I've only heard bits and pieces that things didn't go well for the Indians at Fort Ridgely. They've split into two bands, but I don't know where they went. Just that White Dog was ordered to watch us."

They slept that night huddled together on the warm prairie. Emily awoke with a strange sensation. She looked into a form silhouetted by the moon and heard White Dog's voice.

"White woman. I hope One Arm comes to try to save you. Then I will kill you both."

The form disappeared. Emily hoped it had been a dream, but she knew in her heart that it wasn't.

↘ 69 ↙

T HE SANTEE BAND OF WALKER AMONG SACRED STONES reached Forest City early on the morning of September 4th. To their astonishment, a stockade had been erected in little over one day. Some 240 refugees and a few soldiers under Captain Whitcomb were waiting for them.

A narrow catwalk had been constructed at the top of the stockade. A couple dozen defenders silently peered into the early morning light. Ole Ness proudly stood on the walkway above the front gate and looked at the fort. "Vell, Mr. Smith," he said to the town lawyer, "vat do ya tink of it."

"Ole," Smith shook the Norwegian's hand, "you've done a fine job. It's amazing we got it up so fast. If they'd hit us before we were finished . . . well, we don't have many fighting men the way it is."

"She'll hold good. Double row of logs," Ness smiled with satisfaction.

Smith walked away. "Good, Ole, keep an eye out."

Solomon Foot looked out over a sidewall. His wounds were healing well. He was feeling stronger, strong enough to stand a stint of guard duty. His Colt revolver was tucked into his belt; nearby, his loaded rifle barrel rested against the wall. George Whitcomb walked over to him. "Solomon, I've got a bunch of inexperienced volunteer soldiers. I'd appreciate any help you can give us."

"I've been attacked once already in a cabin. I feel a lot better here, Captain, if they're fool enough to attack." Foot motioned over the wall. "They've got a whole lot of prairie to cross and little cover to get here. The Crow River is almost a mile away. This is a good spot and a solid fort."

"Do ya really think it's safe?" Sam Schultzel was almost trembling as he stood near them.

Olav Olson looked closely at the constable of Forest City, a fat, bald, mustached man who'd been given the job because no one qualified would take it. "Are ya cold, Schultzel?" he asked.

"Ya," was all the lawman said.

Olson walked past Schultzel to where Whitcomb and Foot stood. A dewy, warm morning was breaking, and the shadows of the night were fading quickly. Olav's sharp eye caught a movement from behind a clump of brush. Instinctively he pushed Solomon to the side. An arrow whizzed harmlessly by Foot's head. Solomon nodded his thanks to Olson.

Schultzel was not so lucky. A Dakota missile struck him in the throat and protruded out the back of his neck. A brief look of stunned surprise flashed over his face. Then he folded to the floor of the walkway.

Foot quickly recovered and sighted movement behind the bush. He took careful aim and squeezed off a shot. A scream and a body on the ground were the result. Then the air was filled with whoops and shots. But the Dakota couldn't gather for a mass attack like at Ridgely. As Foot had predicted, there wasn't enough cover.

Walker Among Sacred Stones had expected to overrun a small unprotected settlement. The stockade left him with no choice but to fire long range and finally, late in the afternoon, after burning most buildings in the village, to withdraw toward Hutchinson. Little Crow had had similar unsuccessful results while attacking the stockade there. Both bands satisfied themselves by raiding farmers who had not had the good sense to seek shelter in the forts.

The next day, no Dakota were seen near the Forest City stockade. Whitcomb led another scouting party out and could find no Indians in the area. That night, Solomon Foot made up his mind. He walked with his wife amidst the little city of tents and rough shelters that refugees had construct-ed within the fort compound. "Ady," Solomon said to his wife, "Olav Olson's daughter Jenny was taken by the Sioux near Lake Ripley. He and Mrs. Olson have asked me to go out looking for her."

"You're still hurt!" Ady's voice filled with alarm. "You can't do it!"

"Ady," Solomon said gently, "Olav saved my life yesterday. I can do it. Actually, I'm pretty well healed as long as I avoid heavy lifting."

His wife's eyes reddened as she began to sob softly. "You won't go alone, will you?"

"I won't ask anyone else to risk this. Besides, I'd rather be alone. Too many folks attract too much attention."

"How will you manage to free her alone? That's crazy, Solomon."

"Ady, trust me. I'll know what to do. I talked to Whitcomb. He said reports are that the Sioux are back in the valley. I'll head to Fort Ridgely first and try to find out if they know anything there."

Ady was not convinced. As tears rolled down her cheeks, she held her husband in her arms and whispered, "This is insane, Solomon. But you are the bravest insane man I've ever known, and I love you. Come back to me."

"You know I will, Ady. That's a promise."

Early the next morning Solomon Foot bid good-bye to his family and rode toward the gate on a horse borrowed from A.C. Smith. He wore dark woolen pants and a blue muslin shirt with a brown vest, all obtained from Forest City people.

Foot faced a fifty-mile ride south to Ridgely. As he rode out of the stockade, Daisy Dahl caught up to him. "When you get to Fort Ridgely, if you see my husband, Slim—he's a big man, a painter—please tell him his family is here waiting for him. We've heard nothing of him since the agency was attacked."

Foot smiled at her as he tipped his broad-brimmed hat. "I will, Mrs. Dahl." Then he kicked his horse in the sides with his heels and headed south.

❧ 70 ❧

THE RAGGED REMNANTS OF THE BIRCH COULEE company limped back to Fort Ridgely along with Sibley's relief column. The morning after their return, Forest City was under attack but no one in Ridgely knew it.

That afternoon, Sibley called his officers together in the commissary. The thick stone walls of the building provided welcome relief from the stifling heat outside. The colonel, in spite of the weather and near disaster at Birch Coulee, looked cool and unruffled. He was well groomed, with a clean blue uniform and his mustache newly trimmed.

"There will be no more expeditions outside of this fort for the next two weeks," Sibley began. "We will train, and we will wait to be resupplied. Much of our cavalry has left due to expired enlistments. Our men are good, but our equipment is poor and our transportation is inadequate. We lost ninety horses at Birch Coulee. We can't launch a foray against the Sioux without horses."

Stacks of newspapers lay on a table in front of a stone wall. Sibley walked over and picked up some, then dropped them with a loud plop. "Perhaps some of you have seen how our efforts are being reported in the papers. I'm being called a snail and the 'State Undertaker.' I'd like to see our newspaper editors come out here and fight Indians. I won't be stampeded into moving until I have the soldiers, horses, and supplies necessary to conduct a successful campaign."

Norm Culver raised his hand and cleared his throat. "Sir, what about reinforcements from the regular army?"

"Lieutenant," Sibley replied, "Governor Ramsey has made repeated requests of President Lincoln and Secretary of War Stanton. The best they've given us so far is to suspend our quota of troops for the Civil War. The war is going badly for the Union, and they are reluctant to send troops here. Ramsey has asked surrounding states for help and will continue to ask Lincoln."

"What about the refugees?" Tom Gere asked.

"For the next few days, no one will leave this fort. It isn't safe. After the fight at the coulee we know the Sioux are near. I would hope that soon we will be able to start moving the refugees to St. Paul or other cities along the way, but not just yet.

"Pickets must be told not only to watch for Sioux, but also to keep people from leaving the fort. I also am concerned about the captives held by the Sioux. To march before we're ready could endanger them further."

Sheehan leaned over and whispered to Gere, "I know one refugee that won't want to hang around here for a few more days."

"Nathan will have to. It'll be tough getting by all the pickets Sibley's putting out there."

After Sibley detailed the training schedule for the next days, the officers walked back to their men and duties. Nathan was waiting for them under the flagpole on the parade ground.

"Tom, Tim," he said, "I want to head out this afternoon. Emily's up near the Yellow Medicine Agency. I've got to find her."

"Not for the next few days, Nathan. Sibley's orders," Sheehan replied.

"I'm a civilian. His orders don't apply to me," Nathan retorted angrily.

Tom Gere tried to be sympathetic. "Listen, Governor Ramsey has given Colonel Sibley broad powers. He does have authority over civilians in this region. In a few days you'll be able to leave. Frankly, those days probably won't make much difference to Emily. The army won't be moving for a least two weeks, so the Indians likely won't be moving much either."

"Tom's right," Tim Sheehan continued. "At least the Sioux shouldn't feel compelled to run. There won't be anyone chasing them."

"What about the people out there?" Nathan persisted.

"The valley's empty of people who aren't in larger towns or in this fort," Sheehan explained. "When this army moves, it will be to put down the uprising once and for all. But it won't be for a couple of weeks."

At that moment, Sibley himself walked up. "Any problem here, gentlemen?" he inquired.

"No, sir," Gere answered. "Our friend here would like to leave as soon as he can."

Sibley looked at Nathan. "I've heard about you. Heard that you acquitted yourself well at the coulee. I've also been made aware of Miss West's situation. In two weeks we'll move to conquer the Sioux and rescue the captives. You would do best to wait for us. You can ride along if you wish. But the danger's too great today, and my army's not ready."

"I just want to leave alone, now, Colonel," Nathan insisted.

Sibley straightened his shoulders and spoke in his official voice. "No one will leave this fort for at least three days, and then only if I deem it worth the risk. Anyone attempting to leave will be arrested and placed in the guardhouse for two weeks or until we leave. Carry on, men." Sibley walked back to the headquarters building with long strides.

Nathan followed him with fuming eyes. The next few days would be hell for him. He considered simply leaving, but two weeks in the guardhouse wouldn't be worth the risk compared to a three-day wait.

SOLOMON FOOT KEPT UP A GOOD PACE through another sunny August day. The country through which he passed was completely devoid of people, red or white. He saw occasional signs of Indian depredations, burned-out cabins, sun-bloated bodies, and dead animals.

Foot rode through the yard of Robinson Jones' homestead and recalled his visit there the past spring. The cabin was now a burned out shell. Raiders had passed by after Strout left.

Solomon remembered happier days, the smell of bubbling stew, the warmth of the cabin, and talking to friends on a cold spring day. It was all gone now. Foot rode slowly by the tree that had been used for target practice before the shooting. He noticed the lead-filled holes in the bark.

Foot dismounted and stretched. Although he was sore, he felt good. He munched some beef jerky given him by A.C. Smith, then took a swig from his canteen before mounting again. He couldn't help but think of his dead friends as he continued on his way. He knew he was lucky. No one in his family had been killed. But the horror of the last couple of weeks swept over him as he rode, turning Solomon very melancholy.

It was almost a straight shot south of Acton to Fort Ridgely. The only streams to cross were narrow and easily forded. The land was flat with clumps of oak trees breaking up the prairie like islands in an ocean. Fields of grain were waiting to be harvested, but this year only birds and animals would tend to the abandoned crops.

Occasionally Foot removed the photograph from his vest pocket and looked at the blonde, bright-eyed girl whose image it captured. She had a pleasant, intelligent face. She looked like many of the Scandinavian girls in the area. If she were alive, he hoped he could distinguish her from others.

He thought it safer to keep moving, taking only occasional breaks to rest his horse. As night began to set in, Solomon decided not to camp. He was drawing near Fort Ridgely and thought it better to push on through. Although he had seen no Sioux the entire day, he knew that they were closer to the river. He didn't want to be set upon in the middle of the night as he slept.

It was after midnight when he rode down the fort road and saw Ridgely in the distant moonlight. As he drew close, two sentries stepped forward with ready rifles. "Who are you and what's your business," one demanded.

"Solomon Foot from the Kandiyohi Lakes. I need to inquire about someone at the fort. Then I'll be moving on."

"Pass on." The guard lowered his weapon. Foot entered the fort.

A guard near the parade ground told Solomon to stable his horse for the night and allowed that he might as well sleep in the hay himself. It was a short night's sleep for Foot. He was up with the regiment just after dawn.

Willie Sturgis walked into the stable as Foot was saddling his horse. "Mornin', sir!" Willie's lopsided smile made Solomon feel welcome. "Sergeant of the guard reported that we had a visitor last night. Colonel Sibley wants to see you."

"Fine, son," Foot finished with his horse and turned to Sturgis. "Where do I go?"

The corporal led the man from Kandiyohi to the headquarters building and into Sibley's office. The colonel was gingerly drinking a steaming hot cup of coffee from a tin cup. The eastern sun shone through a window, but the room remained dim and a lantern was still burning on the colonel's desk. Sibley walked to Foot and extended his hand. "I'm Sibley, you are . . . ?"

"Solomon Foot, from the lakes northwest of here."

"You just rode here from there?" Sibley was surprised and concerned.

"Actually, Colonel, I came here from Forest City," Foot answered.

"Tell me," Sibley asked intently, "what of the Sioux in that region? What is the situation in your area?"

Foot went on to detail what he knew of the war in west central Minnesota, how Strout had fought near Acton, as reported by Branham, and the attack on the stockade at Forest City. He told of his own experiences in Kandiyohi County and of the families killed at West Lake, and of how raids had emptied that part of the state of people.

"You've had some amazing adventures, Mr. Foot," Sibley seemed genuinely impressed. "What brought you to us in the middle of the night?"

"A girl was captured by Lake Ripley, about eight miles south of Forest City. Her parents want me to look for her, and I agreed."

Sibley turned around and clasped his hands behind his back. "We know now that Little Crow divided his force and sent one branch down the river toward us and the other into your area. Both branches entered into conflict with soldiers and were frustrated but not beaten. I'm very interested in their current movements. You didn't see any on your way, and we've had no sign here for a couple of days. I have a proposition for you. You can go look for the girl, but I want you to also serve as an unofficial scout for me. Report back whatever you find of the Sioux and their movements."

"Sounds fair, Colonel," Foot mused. "I don't have a problem letting you know what's out there. People are getting impatient, though. When's the army moving out?"

"The plan now is for September 18th," Sibley said, then paused. "One more thing, there's another man in this fort that I think you would find useful. He wishes to undertake a similar mission. His name's Nathan Cates. Sturgis will take you to him. God be with you, Mr. Foot." Sibley shook Solomon's hand again before Willie escorted him to the long barracks where Nathan was quartered.

"Mr. Cates," Sturgis announced, "this here's Solomon Foot from up northwest a ways. He's lookin' for a woman the Sioux got, too."

The two men shook hands. Their eyes locked for an instant as each measured the other's strong grip, one nearing forty, broad shouldered and muscular, hair graying slightly and receding, the other not much over twenty with the build of an athlete. Foot noticed the empty left sleeve, but he also noticed a glint in the younger man's eye that indicated a steely resolution.

Solomon nodded at Nathan and said, "Sibley thinks you and me should team up. Seems like we've got the same goal. We each are looking for a young woman. I expect if they're both alive, that they're near each other."

Nathan liked what he saw in the older man. There was a confident strength about him that he had felt with some of his superiors in the Confederate Army. "I was told by an Indian at Birch Coulee that most of the captives are being moved up the Yellow Medicine River past the Upper Agency."

"Then let's not waste any time and get going," Foot responded.

"Is the ban lifted?" Nathan turned to Willie Sturgis.

"Nathan," Foot replied, "you and me are also Sibley's scouts to the west on this mission. We have his personal permission to leave."

"Thank God for that," Nathan retorted.

The two men walked onto the sunbright parade ground and began to gather supplies. They were given two extra horses to use as pack animals and later, they hoped, as mounts for the rescued captives.

Gere and Sheehan came by the stables to bid them good-bye. "Good luck," Sheehan said. "You have a tough job ahead of you."

"At least Nathan knows the person he's looking for," Solomon replied. "All I have to go on is a picture."

"Let me see it," Gere asked. He looked at the offered photograph and commented, "pretty girl," before handing it to Sheehan.

Tim Sheehan studied the image for a moment and then exclaimed, "I met this girl by Lake Ripley. Her name's . . . Jenny!"

"That's right," Foot agreed, "she's from Meeker County."

"She seemed like a nice girl." Sheehan slowly shook his head as he looked at the picture. "I hope you find her."

"Hope we find both of them," Foot said as he swung onto the back of his black mare. Nathan mounted a brown-and-white-spotted animal, and they began to ride down the road out of Ridgely.

"Wait a second." Solomon abruptly reined in his horse and looked onto the parade ground. A big man was tossing a wound leather ball underhand to some children. He wore cotton overalls and a shirt with big drops of white paint on them. His voice boomed with laughter.

Foot slowly rode over to the little group. "You're Slim Dahl, aren't you?"

The big man looked up at Solomon, his bright, blue eyes dancing merrily. "That's me," he answered. "How did you know?"

"Your wife, Daisy, told me to look for you here. She's at Forest City and wanted me to tell you that everyone's all right, and they're waiting for you."

"Thank you." Slim's smile showed he was genuinely thankful for the news. "I'll get back as soon as Sibley says the coast is clear. They sure don't need painters at the agency anymore."

Foot straightened in his saddle and prepared to leave. "You should be able to leave pretty soon, Slim."

As he turned, the painter called, "Mister, did she tell ya that the Nesses are the greatest people around?"

Foot smiled and nodded.

"That figgurs," Slim laughed, "she tells that to purtneer ever'body."

NATHAN AND SOLOMON CROSSED THE RIVER at a ferry near the fort and continued up the south side of the Minnesota. Ruins and decaying bodies still blotted the countryside. "Can't they bury these people?" Solomon sounded disgusted.

"They tried," Nathan replied. "That's what we were doing when the Dakota attacked us at Birch Coulee. The other side of the river, more graves were dug."

As they continued up the brown ribbon of water, through the tall green-yellow grass, Solomon did most of the talking. He described his home and his hopes for a new life for his family on the frontier. When prompted by Nathan, he told the story of the attack on the Erickson cabin. For his part, Nathan revealed little, just the lie given him by Jefferson Davis.

Both discovered some common ground that stood them apart. The Indians were not devils to them. They realized that the Dakota had been mistreated by the government and that the war was caused by much more than four young braves killing some people at Acton.

"In a war like this, there's more than enough blame to spread around," Nathan told Solomon. "Working as a trader and around the government here, I've seen a lot of ignorance in action and very little compassion. This did not need to happen."

"I know the reds were cheated," Foot continued Nathan's thought, "but it's their tactics that grind me. They're making war on the innocent. This isn't a war of soldier against soldier."

Nathan shifted uneasily in his saddle. "Sometimes even wars aren't fought according to plans," he said. "Their ideas are different from ours. They represent a totally different outlook on life. We're trying to change that, trying to put them into a white man's box. It doesn't work."

"That don't make it right, son," Foot added.

"No, it doesn't," Nathan concluded.

By mid-morning they were at the Redwood Agency. Nathan explained to Solomon that he had recently been there and that nothing about the girls could be learned by searching through the burned out buildings. Seeing no one alive, they kept up a steady pace toward Yellow Medicine.

ॐ 71 ॐ

THE SANTEE PUSHED FARTHER UP the Minnesota to where it was entered by the Chippewa River. They were frustrated and confused. Bitter divisions between the Upper and Lower bands were becoming wider. The safety of the captives was at the heart of their dispute.

Little Crow continued to lead the majority of the braves, but many were listening to those who had opposed the war and wanted it to end. On a cloudy afternoon on September 7th, they met in council again. Leaders from Yellow Medicine and Redwood both sat in the sacred circle to smoke and talk. The captives were held nearby.

Little Crow, looking older and more haggard than he had a mere few weeks earlier, spoke first. "Long Trader left a message for me at Birch Coulee. I have received it and replied. I told him why this war happened. How the government and the traders have mistreated us. Long Trader is concerned about the prisoners. He won't talk unless they are returned, but we cannot return them. They are all that we have to make sure we are treated fairly."

Little Paul shouted from across the circle, "Give me all the white captives! I will deliver them to their friends. Stop fighting. No one who fights with the white people ever becomes rich or remains two days in one place, but is always fleeing and starving."

"Yes," Standing Buffalo agreed, "they must be freed. Red Iron will not let us cross to Big Stone Lake as long as we bring hostages. They formed a Friendly Soldier's Lodge to stand against us. We are making war on women. Little Crow, you are bringing about the end of our people. We cannot win this war, and it should never have happened. Return the white captives."

Murmurs of agreement came from many of the Sissetons and Wahpetons. Indignant, Little Crow spat words like bullets back at them. "Maybe if more of the Upper bands had helped, we would be winning. Many of you are old women. Sweet Corn now leads young men at Abercrombie. Why are you not with him?"

Little Paul answered, "If you could not take Ridgely, Fort Abercrombie will not fall to us, either. They waste their time in siege up there."

Cut Nose loudly snorted his disapproval. "It is where we all should be."

Little Paul's face burned with passion as he instantly shot back, "You have been threatening us and trying to get us to join you in what you have done. The Sissetons and Whapetons want no part of this war. Our chiefs will form a lodge to show that we stand apart from you!"

Rda-in-yan-ka, Wabasha's son-in-law, rose to answer Little Paul and Standing Buffalo. "I am for continuing the war. I am opposed to the delivery of the prisoners. I have no confidence that the whites will stand by any agreement they make if we give them up. Ever since we treated with them, their agents and traders have robbed and cheated us. Some of our people have been shot. Some have been hanged. Others were placed upon floating ice and drowned. Many have been starved in their prisons. It was not the intention of the nation to kill any of the whites until after the four young men returned from Acton and told what they had done.

"When they did this, all the young men became excited, and commenced the massacre. The older ones would have prevented it if they could, but since the treaties they have lost all their influence. We may regret what has happened, but the matter has gone too far to be remedied. In the mind of the whites, we have got to die. Let us, then, kill as many of the whites as possible, and let the prisoners die with us."

Little Crow walked inside the large circle. The tired look on his face disappeared as he raised himself up to challenge them. He looked to the heavens and spread his arms out from his shoulders with upraised palms. "Hear me, great chiefs, those who are here and those who have gone before. One more big fight will come. Let it be at a place of our choosing and at a time of our choosing. We will fight for the way of life of our people. That our children may grow to be men and warriors as in the old days. Let them be able to learn the ways of the old ones and not how to plow. We are all Santee, we must fight as one and not divide ourselves as the white man wishes us to."

Again the war chief looked skyward and shouted at the clouds, "Let those who are afraid leave us. I will fight until they kill me. I know that I will never be taken alive. Now the braves must join and prepare for the last great fight with the whites!"

The majority of the Santee leaders and those young men within hearing shouted approval of Little Crow's words. However, most of the Upper Santee leaders were not convinced. They met the chief's words with stoney silence.

As the council broke up, Little Crow called to White Dog. "Soon many of the warriors with me must leave to fight. The power of the peace Indians grows in the camp. I fear that they will take the captives from those who guard them and give them back to the whites."

"I will kill any who try to take those I guard," White Dog said vehemently.

"No," Little Crow replied, "that is not what I want. Take some of the white women and leave the village. If we lose the other prisoners, we will still have some. To the whites, a few captive women is the same as dozens. They will serve the purpose. Take the teacher and her friends. She has value because she was a government worker."

White Dog's slender lips curled into a smile. Little Crow recognized the thoughts behind it and added, "There will be no mistreatment of these women. We may need them. You will not harm them in any way. Leave Brown Wing and your other braves to guard the captives here and take five braves with you. Go west toward Abercrombie. I will send for you when I need you."

White Dog nodded his assent. "It will be as you say, Tao-oya-te-duta."

That night as the captives slept, six Santee awakened Emily, Jenny, Mattie, and Mary. They held knives to the girls' throats and tied their hands before putting them on horses and heading west. Wide-eyed with fright, the girls struggled to prevent sobs from escaping their lips. They knew that to cry out meant instant death, although they considered that that certainty might be better than what lay before them.

Solomon and Nathan reached the Yellow Medicine River the morning after White Dog had taken the girls away. They had encountered a large force of Dakota traveling down the river and had lain in concealment as they passed. Once reaching the village, they spent the day intently watching from a distance for any sign of Emily or Jenny. The sun was starting to set and shadows stretched to the east.

They were hidden in a stand of oak and brush nearly 100 yards from the camp. "We could be looking right at them and not even know it," Nathan commented to Solomon. Especially the way most of those women look. It's hard to tell if they're even white, let alone distinguish hair color or features."

Foot squinted hard. "Well, Nathan, we've either got to get a closer look or ask someone who might know something."

"Anyone in mind, Solomon?"

"How about that fella riding this way." Foot nodded toward a lone rider heading across the prairie toward the oak trees.

"Should we jump him?" Nathan asked.

Solomon pondered the question for a moment, then looked at Nathan. "We make a fine pair. I'm too beat up to go flying into him, and—no offense—but with only one arm, it's not going to be easy for you, either."

Nathan looked back at the approaching rider. "We need to take him alive. We've got to talk to him, maybe he can tell us about the girls?"

"When he gets close," Solomon said, "I'll distract him. At that moment, jump him. Between the two of us, maybe we can take him."

Little Turtle, a young brave of Red Middle Voice's band, was riding out to look for some kindling for his campfire. Solomon and Nathan separated and remained hidden in brush as the Santee slowly rode into the oasis of timber on the prairie and then dismounted. Foot stood and pulled back the hammer of his rifle. The snap clicked loudly in the quiet of the little woodpatch.

Little Turtle jerked his head toward the sound and dropped the sticks in his arms. He looked to his horse, where his rifle hung in a scabbard. Then he pulled a knife from his belt and began to rush Solomon. From other brush, Nathan blindsided the Indian and slammed him hard on his back to the ground.

Instantly, Foot leaped out of the brush and pointed the barrel of his rifle in the Santee's face. Little Turtle's eyes grew wide with hate and fear. "Drop the knife," Foot commanded. "Now! Drop it!"

Nathan cocked his pistol and covered the Indian as well. Little Turtle looked from one gun barrel to the other and, still lying on the ground, obeyed Foot's orders.

Solomon looked questioningly at his young friend, "Know 'em?" he inquired.

"He's Little Turtle," Nathan answered. "Used to come by the trading post. He speaks passable English."

Foot kept the rifle aimed squarely at the Indian's head and stared into Little Turtle's eyes. "Listen carefully to what I say. We don't care one bit about you, and we mean no harm to your village. But you have two women we want. One's Emily West, the teacher from the agency, the other is a young blonde. Look," Foot held Jenny Olson's picture in front of Little Turtle's face. "Are they in the camp? Do you know where they are? Answer truthfully and no harm will come to you."

The young Santee snarled defiantly, "You are too late. They were taken away by White Dog."

"When? Where?" Nathan asked urgently.

"Last night, I don't know where. But only two can't take them. White Dog has braves with him. You have lost them."

Solomon looked to his young companion. "West. They must have gone farther west. It's the only thing that makes sense if they want to keep the hostages. Let's hogtie this fella and try to find their trail."

They gagged Little Turtle and tied his feet and hands. "Sorry," Nathan said to their captive, "but we need a head start, you'll either free yourself or your friends will come for you. Let's go, Solomon," he called to Foot.

The two men rode west, taking a wide circle around the camp. They needn't have feared being chased by the Santee in the village. Standing Buffalo, Wacouta, and others who favored releasing the hostages were more and more in control. Little Crow and his warriors were headed downriver. While they didn't dare defy their war chief and free hostages, they weren't about to hunt down two men trying to take the girls away from White Dog. In fact, Standing Buffalo was incensed that the four girls had been spirited away from the village in the first place.

Near dark the path taken by Solomon and Nathan intersected multiple sets of hoof prints heading west. Foot dismounted and carefully examined the path, "Seems like this is what we're looking for, Nathan, about ten-twelve horses I'd say."

"This isn't going to be easy, Solomon," Thomas commented.

"You never thought it was going to be easy, did you?" Foot smiled up at Nathan. "We'll continue on as long as we can see the tracks. Then we'll camp until first light. I don't want to risk losing the trail in the dark."

Miles ahead, Emily West pulled her feet beneath herself as she lay on the hard ground near a campfire. The night was warm, but still she felt chilly because of lack of any covering besides her ripped and worn dress. Mosquitoes had also descended, and she prayed thanks each time a breeze sent smoke blowing over her, giving momentary relief from the blood-sucking insects. Strange, she thought, that she would be offering thanks to God for something so simple.

However, she had learned to be grateful for many things that she had taken for granted before. Now the fact she was still alive seemed to be the greatest gift of all. The Dakota braves were not in a great hurry to reach

Abercrombie, but they kept up a decent pace from sunrise to sunset, stopping only a few times a day to rest themselves and their horses. They seemed indifferent to their hostages and paid them only essential attention.

The Indians, however, were becoming annoyed with Mattie Schwandt, who had begun to sob incessantly. The other three girls tried to comfort and console her without success. Mattie was refusing to eat and was growing weak.

At one stop by a stream on the prairie, White Dog spoke to Emily. "Teacher, quiet the dark-haired one or we will."

"Perhaps if you freed us, she would be quiet," Emily retorted.

"Little Crow wants you held, but three will do just as well as four," the Santee added menacingly as he walked away.

Emily went straight away to the three girls who were huddled together. "Mattie," she said soothingly, "you've got to get a hold of youself."

"I can't." A sob wracked her slender body. "I just can't stop."

"If you don't," Emily's voice was stern, "all of us are in even greater danger." The distraught girl looked at her with reddened, swollen eyes and began to cry again. The young teacher regarded the other girls and said resignedly, "We've got to do what we can for her."

Soon they were riding west again, toward the border with Dakota Territory and Fort Abercrombie. Emily was glad Jennie and Mary were holding up relatively well, but Mattie, hunched over her horse's neck, wetting its mane with her tears, gave her a sense of foreboding.

ᔓ 72 ᕉ

SOLOMON AND NATHAN BEGAN THEIR PURSUIT a full day behind White Dog's party. Now after three days of hard riding, they were but a few miles behind them. The next day the Indians would reach Sweet Corn and the siege at Abercrombie. Then it might be too difficult to rescue the girls.

As the descending sun cast lengthening shadows, White Dog called a halt to their day's journey. They stopped at an oak cluster near a small creek. Dry sticks were gathered. Next, a thunderstone, a rock with a smooth hole bored partway through, was used to hold a stick as a leather string was rubbed over it. The friction caused a spark to ignite wood shavings beneath it. After a warrior gently blew on the kindling, they had a fire.

Bright Shadow, the youngest of the braves, handed small amounts of pemmican, a mixture of ground berries and dried meat, to the girls. All but Mattie ate it hungrily. For a short time the Santee talked among themselves around the campfire. Then they rolled into their blankets and drifted to sleep. The girls tried to do the same.

Foot and Thomas pushed on after dark. "I know they must be heading toward Abercrombie," Solomon told Nathan. "Sibley was afraid there would be an attack there. I'm not worried about losing the trail, they'll be ahead of us on the way to the area around the fort."

The moon was three-quarters full and cast a silvery glow as the two white men continued their quest. Then Nathan whispered sharply to Foot, "Solomon, look. Dead ahead. Do you see what I see?" Flickering in the distance, like a warning from a Lake Erie lighthouse in Solomon's youth, was the unmistakable glow of a campfire. As sure as a beacon, it guided them toward the sleeping camp.

"I see it, Nathan," he answered. "We'll ride a little farther and then go in on foot. I don't want them to hear us or have their horses start talking to our horses."

The last hundred yards they slowly, silently crawled into position. The camp was on the prairie, away from the stand of timber and mosquitoes. The two white men used the woods as a screen to get close. Then they waited. "What's that?" Nathan asked.

"Sounds like a woman crying," Solomon replied.

"Should we do something?"

"Just wait, Nathan," Foot answered.

Mattie's sobs awakened the Santee braves. White Dog angrily strode over to her. "White woman, you have troubled us for the last time!" With those words, he raised his hatchet and prepared to strike. Emily instantly grabbed the end of a burning log from the fire and hurled it at the Indian's back. It struck with a thump and sent red-hot ashes searing onto White Dog's bare back.

The Santee slapped the burning embers away and turned to face Emily with pain and hate in his eyes. "Kill the crying one," he commanded one of the braves, all of whom were gathered around. "Now, teacher, it is time for you to die as well." He reached out and grabbed her shoulder. Emily twisted, and the flimsy dress ripped in the Indian's hand.

Another brave drew his knife and reached for Mary and Jennie. Then the night was shattered as black powder blazed out of the shadows by the woods. Two Santee immediately collapsed to the hard prairie earth.

The confused Indians ran for their rifles by the fire. Another was cut down before he reached it. Nathan and Solomon rushed into the circle of the fire light with Colts in hand. Bright Shadow leaped at Foot with his knife flashing in a downward arc. The man from the Kandiyohi lakes fired twice and rolled out of the way. The Santee smashed face first, dead into the dirt. One brave reached his rifle and cracked off a shot as he twisted to the ground. Nathan fired again, and the Indian lay still.

It had all happened in little more than a heartbeat. Only White Dog was left. He held Emily in front of him with his arm under her neck, illuminated by quivering firelight. Nathan raised his pistol to shoot. "Shoot, One Arm," he snarled. "I will slit your woman's neck before you can kill me. I know your secret. Does she?"

Emily West looked at Nathan through wide, terrified eyes. She stood petrified, feeling the strong arm of White Dog holding her tight, smelling the smoke, sweat, and fear that clung to his body.

Nathan ignored Emily's face and focused on White Dog. He held his revolver at arm's length with the Indian in his sights. He didn't say a word. Neither did Solomon. Only the gentle whimpering of Mattie Schwandt and the tense, uneven breathing of the other girls broke the silence.

Then Nathan slowly squeezed the trigger, and his pistol exploded in his hand. White Dog's head snapped backward, and his hands flew into the air. He hurled onto the ground without a sound. He was dead, a bullet through his brain.

Emily nearly collapsed but regained her balance and rushed to Nathan. He held her close and whispered in her ear, "I told you I'd protect you. I just couldn't get here until now. Emily, I love you. I'm so sorry for all this."

She looked up at him, her face dirty and splattered with White Dog's blood, one shoulder exposed where White Dog had ripped her dress, "I always knew you'd come," she gasped. Then she pulled his head down and kissed him.

Solomon pounded Nathan on the back, "That was some shot!" he exclaimed. "What if you missed?"

"Mr. Foot," he replied evenly, "there was never a chance I would miss. I just couldn't."

Foot smiled at Nathan and then reached to his own left shoulder. A splotch of red trickled through his fingers. Solomon's face grew pale. His smile weakened and he grimaced, "Looks like I took one."

Emily and Nathan rushed to Foot's side and helped him into a reclining position. The woman studied the wounded man's face. "I know you from somewhere . . . You're the man from the steamboat last spring, aren't you?"

"Yes, ma'am, I am," Foot croaked.

The other girls tentatively gathered around. Jenny held a canteen of water to his lips.

"You're Jenny, aren't you?" Solomon asked.

"Yes. How do you know me?" Jenny said in surprise.

"Your parents sent me for you. They're safe in Forest City."

A relieved smile quickly passed over the girl's face. "Thank you," she whispered as she leaned down and kissed Foot's forehead.

The camp became still with the quiet of the night. Three of the young girls huddled together near Solomon and slept fitfully. Fears of suddenly resurrecting Indians ravaged their dreams. Nathan and Emily walked hand in hand a short distance away and embraced. They talked softly to each other about what had happened and of what might lie ahead.

"What did White Dog mean when he said he knew your secret, Nathan?" Emily asked.

Nathan tightened his grip and held her closer. "Trust me," he whispered. "There's something I need to tell you. But later, please later."

"Secrets can wait," Emily soothed as she rested her head upon Nathan's chest.

Solomon Foot slept through the night. The next morning, September 12, Emily bathed his wound and cut out the bullet. The girls and Nathan buried the six dead Santee in shallow graves. Mattie had stopped crying and was beginning to regain control of herself.

Then, reluctantly, Nathan handed Solomon's pistol to Emily. "I've got to scout ahead. We're near the Red River and Fort Abercrombie. If it's safe, we'll head for the fort. If I had a choice we'd head straight back to Ridgely, but Solomon needs to rest and regain his strength before he can make the ride back. I shouldn't be gone long."

Emily embraced him firmly. "I know you've got to go, but I don't want to be away from you. Not after we finally got together again."

"Don't worry, I'll be right back," Nathan assured her. "Fire the pistol if there's any sign of trouble. I should be able to hear it."

Nathan rode several miles to the northwest. From a hilltop he saw Fort Abercrombie in the distance, across the Red River. It was a fort like Ridgely: no walls, just a collection of wooden log buildings. A thin line of Indians was visible around the fort. Sporadic gunfire crackled like popping corn as they fired at the fort. A road led down to the Red River across from Abercrombie, where the river was shallow and could be forded. Seeing what he needed to know, Nathan returned to the camp where Emily, Solomon, and the girls waited.

Foot's face was flushed. He had developed a fever. "Do you have a short, hard ride left in you?" Nathan asked.

"As long as it's short, I do," Solomon replied hoarsely.

"Ladies, here's what we're going to do." Nathan turned toward the women. "If we stay here, we'll surely be discovered soon by the Santee. The Indians are spread out in small groups around the fort. We can gallop hard, ford the river and ride through a gap in their lines to Abercrombie. Can you do it?"

"We can all ride," Jenny offered.

"You sure you're up to it, Solomon?" Nathan asked.

Foot wiped the beads of sweat from his forehead and looked over the rolling plain of sun-drenched yellow-green grass. "I am, but I'm getting weaker. We better move while I still can."

The four young women and two men mounted horses and briskly set off to the northwest. After a few miles they reached the hills overlooking the Red River, which marked the boundary between Minnesota and the Dakota Territory. Across the river lay Fort Abercrombie.

They used hills to screen their approach until they neared the river. Then, at Nathan's order, they galloped down the trail and into the river. The ford was shallow, and the horses made it across without swimming. They scrambled up the muddy bank and bounded toward the fort.

The route chosen by Nathan led between two widely spaced groups of surprised Santee. The Indians fired wildly and ineffectively at the small group of whites as they raced through them and into the fort.

A young officer wearing a short, brown beard and mustache ran to them. "What a ride!" he exclaimed. "That was amazing, brave and amazing!"

Nathan leaped from his horse and helped the slumping Solomon to the ground.

"Dr. Cariveau," the officer shouted, "we need you!"

As a stocky man in a white coat hurried over and began to tend to Foot, the soldier turned his attention to his other new arrivals. "Smith," he called to the post quartermaster, "see that these women get whatever they need."

Then he turned to Nathan. "I'm Captain John Vander Horck. To what do we owe the honor of your visit?"

As the women hurried away with Smith and Dr. Cariveau brought Foot toward the post hospital, Nathan answered the Captain. "I'm Nathan Cates. The gentleman there," he nodded in Solomon's direction, "and I came from Fort Ridgely to rescue some captives taken by the Sioux. We did that, and when Solomon was wounded, we came here to get him some help."

"And you're welcome here," Vander Horck added, "but I can't guarantee your safety."

"We also are to report back to Sibley," Nathan continued. "What are the conditions here?"

"We've been under attack, more or less, since the third of September. They hit us hard on the 6th. I've only got about eighty men here and around 100 civilian refugees. The Sioux have at least double our numbers. We used cannon and concentrated fire to drive them off. Now we just hold on. To tell the truth, and my interpreter says he heard 'em talking about it, I think they've lost the stomach for another attack. They just stay out there in scattered groups and shoot at us every now and then. They try to pick us off when we go to the river for water."

"Not another fort without a well?" Nathan asked in astonishment, looking heavenward.

"Afraid so. We just never expected to be attacked," Vander Horck replied. "We've sent messengers to St. Paul for help, but so far, nothing. It is 225 miles, but you'd think someone'd be here by now."

"Sibley isn't much over 100 miles from here, but he's not moving anywhere until the eigthteenth of the month," Nathan explained. "Lack of cavalry, supplies, and green troops. He says he'll end it all when he starts the march."

"I just hope we're all still here when that happens," Vander Horck responded. "But enough standing out here in the sun. Come into the shade of the commissary, and I'll offer you a small glass of water."

ᔥ 73 ᔥ

T HE GIRLS WASHED WITH DAMPENED RAGS, were given spare clothes by refugee women, and then slept until late afternoon. Nathan visited the hospital later that morning after the doctor had finished with Solomon. Foot lay asleep on a cot, breathing easily. Cariveau shushed Nathan to remain quiet and ushered him back out the door.

"I cleaned up his shoulder some more, and he's resting peacefully now. The wound was already inflamed, but he should recover nicely. He's been through a lot recently, hasn't he? I found several newly healed bullet wounds."

"A lesser man than he would be dead," Nathan answered.

"Without him, I never could have got to those girls."

"Let him rest today, son," the doctor replied. "He'll be better tomorrow."

Late that afternoon, Emily joined Nathan as he looked over breastworks toward the river. "Keep low," he cautioned her, "every now and then someone takes a potshot at the fort. You've been a brave woman. Be a careful one.

"There have been so many brave ones, Nathan. Among the captives there's Mrs. Brown, the former agent's wife. They lived below the Upper

384

Agency. She was guiding twenty-some people down the river when Cut Nose and his band attacked. Mrs. Brown—her husband was away—stood up to them and told Cut Nose that her Sisseton relatives would seek revenge if they harmed anyone. The Indians let the white men go but brought the women and children, including Mrs. Brown, to Little Crow. They're still with the captives."

She placed her hand in his. "I always knew you'd come, Nathan. It kept me going. I think it kept the other girls hanging on as well."

"I wish it hadn't happened at all. I should have done things differently." Nathan seemed lost in thought as he looked over the horizon.

"Why do you talk like that?" Emily rejoined. "There was nothing you could do. That reminds me, Little Crow had a message for you."

Nathan looked down into her blue eyes. "What did he say?"

"It was strange, he said you weren't to be blamed. This was going to happen no matter what. What did he mean, Nathan?"

The young man from Virginia sighed, "Soon I'll tell you everything, but not now, not tonight. I just want to hold you." With that he wrapped his right arm around Emily and held her tight. Silently he resolved never to let her go again. He prayed that when she knew the truth about him, she would understand. He had already come to believe what Little Crow had told her. The war was inevitable. He had just been placed in the midst of it.

For much of the next week, each day was like the one before. Solomon slowly grew stronger. The Santee remained outside the fort in varying numbers. Occasionally they would concentrate fire, but mostly they shot randomly.

September 18th was cloudy and rainy. Foot walked out of the hospital with Nathan. "If things are going according to plan, Sibley's leaving Ridgely today, Nathan," Solomon said. "My arm's sore, but I can ride. The Sioux won't expect us to move in the rain. What do you say we head down the river?"

Nathan went to the barracks where Emily and the other women were staying. "Solomon and I are going to make a break to get back to Sibley. You'll be safe here."

"No, Nathan," Emily urged, "You know I can ride, I'm going with you."

"Emily, it's not safe," Nathan insisted.

"And you think it's safe here with eighty soldiers guarding 100 people and a few hundred Dakota outside? I'm going with you."

Solomon and Nathan met with Vander Horck later in the morning. "Captain, we thank you for your hospitality here," Foot said, "but its time we moved back down the river. Sibley wants a report, and we'll include any dispatches you have as well."

"Can you get through?" Vander Horck asked.

"They're still spread out," Nathan answered. "Part of the day they disappeared completely. They're not very anxious to fight in the rain. We'll wait for the right time and head out. Emily West is coming with us. We'd appreciate you watching over the other three women."

"Of course," the captain agreed, "but do you think it's wise to bring Miss West?"

"If you knew Miss West," Nathan replied, "you'd know we don't have much choice in the matter."

Jenny, Mattie, and Mary joined the three as they watched and waited. They wore yellow rain slickers given them by Vander Horck. Nathan, Solomon, and Emily held saddled horses ready for the right moment to make a run for it. After tearful thanks and hugs from the girls, Nathan looked at Emily and Solomon. "They've left the river side. We're not going to get a better chance."

"Let's go," Foot agreed.

Jenny Olson called to Solomon as he mounted his horse, "Tell my parents I'll get home as soon as it's safe. Tell them I miss them."

"Sure I will, Jenny." Foot touched the brim of his hat and slapped his horse's rump with his reins. Nathan and Emily followed, galloping, through drizzling skies, down the road to the river ford and then across.

ஐ 74 ௸

NATHAN, SOLOMON, AND EMILY BROKE through the surprised Dakota lines. They rode low in their saddles as little lead missiles whizzed by them. As they began their journey to the southeast, other events were transpiring in Minnesota and Virginia. Colonel Sibley was finally ready to begin his march from Fort Ridgely. He had planned to start out on the eighteenth but, because of the rain, he had decided to wait until the next day.

He sat alone in Captain Marsh's old office at Fort Ridgely and watched through a window as rain puddled on the parade ground. He clasped his hands behind his back and became introspective as his thoughts turned to the last few weeks and his duty.

Supplies had come. His men had been drilled, and drilled some more, particularly in the art of skirmishing. Two hundred seventy battle-hardened Civil War veterans of the Third Minnesota had arrived on the 13th and 14th of September. On the nineteenth they would move, as Sibley said, to put down the uprising once and for all.

The colonel had 1,600 men and was heartened by news of division in the Dakota ranks. Wabasha had sent a message to him, asking for protection and expressing a desire for the war to end. He said he was a friend of the "good white people." Wabasha didn't mention that he had fought the soldiers at New Ulm and Fort Ridgely. Sibley had replied that all true friends of the whites would be protected and that they should gather under a truce flag and deliver prisoners.

Little Crow would not give up his hostages, however. Sibley had tried to make it clear in dispatches to the Santee war chief that he would not negotiate with him until the captives were freed.

Newspaper reports from St. Paul were an irritant to the colonel. He chaffed at being referred to as the "state undertaker." Ramsey, himself, was growing impatient and had urged Sibley to move. *But they're not here*, the Long Trader reasoned. They didn't know how unprepared his army had been or how ill supplied. Now they were ready, and they would be successful; he vowed it.

News of the invasion into Maryland by Lee and of the Indian attacks shared the headlines in the *St. Paul Pioneer Press*. If Lee were successful, Washington itself would be in danger. Then no one would give a tinker's damn what was happening in Minnesota. The war in Minnesota had to be concluded quickly.

Farther upriver, Santee scouts told Little Crow that Long Trader was on the move. After the last message he received from Sibley, the Santee chief knew that he had only two choices—complete surrender or beat Sibley in one big fight. The army was pushing up the south side of the Minnesota. Little Crow resolved to stop them before they reached the Yellow Medicine.

John Otherday led the army column up the river. They were still short of cavalry. Lack of horses and expired enlistments left them with only twenty-five mounted men. Burial details still went about their grisly task whenever the then partially decomposed bodies were found.

Leading the line of march was the Third Minnesota. Sibley hoped the Civil War veterans would provide an example to the rest of his men. They had been surrendered by their commander at Murfreesborough in Tennessee and had recently been paroled from a Confederate prison. The Third deeply resented what they felt was a betrayal by their commander and were itching to redeem their honor.

The ground was soggy from two days' of hard rain. This kind of march left shoes muddy and stockings soaked. The sun shone brightly, turning the air unusually muggy for September. The first night out, they camped near the Lower Agency. The nearby burned-out buildings stood as lonely sentinels and stark reminders of what had happened.

By late afternoon on the 22nd, they reached the eastern shore of a small lake only miles from the Upper Agency. Sibley ordered camp made on high ground overlooking the surrounding prairie. To the east ran the Minnesota River. North of the encampment, less than half a mile away, an outlet sprang from the lake. It was just a small stream that formed a ravine. The Third Minnesota bivouaced near the ravine on the northwest end of the camp. The Sixth and Seventh regiments camped nearby.

The 275 Civil War veterans of the Third gathered around campfires, drank coffee and chewed on saltpork and hardtack. Rollin Olin, lieutenant, was the only officer who had served with them in Tennessee; the rest were still in southern prisons. Major Arnold Welch had been transferred from the First Minnesota to command.

Songs drifted to the Third from the soldiers camped to the south. Private Billy McGee poked a stick in his campfire and muttered to two companions, "Don't they sound like a happy lot, them that hardly know what war is. Most of 'em barely out of diapers."

"Some of them do," Ezra Champlain reminded Billy. "The Renville Rangers are here, though. They fought hard at the Ridgely attack."

"That's only fifty men," Degrove Kimball said.

"I sure hope they can fight." Ezra stirred a stick in the fire and looked to the south.

"I just hope we got some officers that can lead us," Billy McGee said bitterly. "We never shudda been turned over to them rebs in Tennessee. Our officers was just plain yella. If I ever see Colonel Lester again, I think I'll shoot 'im."

Kimball glanced over at the major's tent where Olin and Welch were conferring. "At least they's all where they belong. Still in prison. All 'cept Olin, and he's one of the only good ones we had."

"Dang!" Billy exclaimed. "I'm tired of hardtack and saltpork. The stuff's so hard I nearly chipped a tooth. How 'bout in the mornin' we head up toward the agency. I bet they got some gardens there and some taters about ready to be dug."

"We don't have orders for that," Ezra cautioned.

"Ta hell with orders," Degrove growled. "Officers' orders didn't do us no good at Murfreesborough."

"I'm with ya, Degrove," Billy offered, "but let's spread word around the company. Might be best to go out there with more'en just a few of us."

That night the men of Company G bedded down with visions of fresh fried potatoes and vegetables dancing before them. In spite of themselves, some began to softly hum the songs heard in the distance.

Late that night Nathan, Emily, and Solomon rode into the camp. They were immediately escorted to Henry Sibley.

The Long Trader smiled broadly, as he stepped from his large white canvas tent, to greet them. His eyes rested upon a scraggly, dirty, disheveled trio. The three had dark-circled eyes, but those eyes glowed brightly with joy and pride

"It's wonderful to see you again," Sibley nodded at the men. "I must admit that I wasn't at all sure if I'd ever lay eyes on you two." He looked beyond the two men to where Emily stood behind them. "You must be Emily West. I'm honored," he bowed slightly, "and gratified that your ordeal is over. Wasn't there another girl you were seeking?"

"As it turned out," Solomon injected, "there were three other girls we managed to free from the Sioux. They're all at Abercrombie now."

"Yes, yes, and how are things at the fort? What have you to report?" Sibley asked.

"The fort was under attack when we got there, Colonel," Nathan interjected, "but the firing was sporadic. Their big fight was on the 6th, and it's been off and on since then. Mostly the Indians are hanging around looking for advantages. Captain Vander Horck needs men and supplies, though.

He doesn't dare venture out far with only eighty men. The Indians are sure to attack then."

"A relief column has been sent and should reach there soon. Maybe by tomorrow," Sibley informed them. "Did you see any other evidence of the Sioux?"

"The captives were held not much more than ten miles from here. We've seen large numbers of warriors headed downriver, but we don't know where," Solomon elaborated.

"Miss West," Sibley looked at the now too-slender blonde, her hair twisted and dirty, her relatively clean dress from Abercrombie incongruous with the rest of her appearance, "what of the captives?"

Emily stepped closer and answered, "They're tired, dirty, and hungry. Some have been horribly abused by the Dakota men. They do have four white men, but all the rest are women and children. Wacouta, Standing Buffalo, Little Paul, Red Iron, and others who favor freeing the hostages seem to be gaining more and more control over the fate of the captives. Little Crow, from what I've heard, thinks he needs them as insurance. But he's gone much of the time. Still, I fear greatly for them if they're not freed soon."

"They will be, Miss, I promise you that," Sibley vowed. "Now, I'm sure you want to rest. We'll have tents set up for you. I'm afraid you're the only woman in camp, Miss West.

"Tomorrow we'll do some serious looking for Indians," he said to Nathan and Solomon. "Otherday thinks the hostiles are real close, and I agree with him. Now you get some rest. Tomorrow might be a long day. Good night."

Then, just as Sibley turned to his tent, he paused and looked back at Nathan. He pointed to the tent opening, "Mr. Cates, if you will, please come in. I'd like to talk with you."

Nathan stepped through the tent flap, followed by Sibley. The tent was a yellowish white, made more yellow by the quivering glow of a single lamp resting upon a make-shift desk made from a crate. Two camp stools sat in the round sturcture. The tent was just tall enough that the ceiling brushed Nathan's hair.

Sibley gestured for his guest to sit. The colonel remained standing. "You're a most interesting young man," he began. "But there seem to be more questions than answers about you. The Myricks certainly had doubts about your loyalties. They brought concerns about you to Fort Snelling. When I first met you, I couldn't remember. Then Myrick's questions came to me.

"We did a little investigating. There was a Nathan Cates in the First Indiana. He was wounded and the description I received matches you. Then, another odd thing happened. A man that apparently you had dealings with in your trading business, a Mr. Meeds, was found to be a Confederate operative. Some people started to make connections between the two of you, even though Meeds insists you only had a business relationship." Sibley looked down intently at Nathan, boring into him with his eyes.

Slowly, he softened. "Then out of the blue, I get a letter from one of our few heros in the war, General George Thomas. The general vouches for your character and requests that I aid you if you need help. That letter, coupled with numerous stories of your valiantry and heroism at Ridgely, Birch Coulee, and Abercrombie lead me to discount others' suspicions about you."

As Sibley extended his hand, Nathan rose and clasped it. "Good night, Mr. Cates. Look to the future, leave the mysteries of the past buried."

"Thank you, sir," was all Nathan managed to say. Sibley expected nothing more. He had intended to make a statement, not conduct an interview.

Nathan left as Sibley sat down at his field desk and began to scribble out his plans for the next day. Uncle George's letter puzzled Nathan as he stepped into the night. "What did his uncle really know?" he wondered.

The ever-present Willie Sturgis, along with Emily and Solomon were waiting for him when he emerged from the tent. Willie escorted the three to newly erected tents. Solomon was bone tired and quickly fell asleep. Emily and Nathan, now safe and secure, were left to thoughts of each other.

ᔑ 75 ᓀ

ONLY A FEW MILES AWAY, LITTLE CROW gathered his war chiefs for another council. They sat in the sacred circle and puffed pipes. "Let them rise and spread out and bring our prayers to the Great Spirit," Little Crow intoned. "Let him hear the pleas of his children for this last big fight."

After he blew a long stream of smoke that tendrilled into the air, the war chief gazed slowly around the circle. Mankato, Big Eagle, Red Middle Voice, Little Six, Gray Bird—they were all there. The chiefs looked tired. Many bore marks from bullet wounds. Most of the leaders of the young men were present and sat with them in the circle. Wabasha was conspicuous by his absence. He had been present at the big fights but had refused to fight personally. Yet, this was not the time to worry about who wasn't there, Little Crow knew. He must fight with those he had.

His people were more divided than ever. As they moved up the Minnesota toward the mouth of the Chippewa River, Red Iron of the Wahpetons and Standing Buffalo of the Sissetons threatened to fight Little Crow's band if they crossed into their territory with the hostages. Now the two bands were camped about half a mile apart near the Chippewa. Little Crow could not be concerned with Red Iron and the other Santee friendly with the whites now. Sibley was too near.

"Tomorrow we will fight Long Trader," he said. "They have twice as many men as we do. But Santee warriors are better fighters. If we fight them like Big Eagle and Gray Bird did at Birch Coulee, we will win."

"Where are the whites camped?" Mankato inquired.

"Close," Little Crow answered. "There is a small, shallow lake near Wood Lake. They are there. In the morning, they will move out toward the Upper Agency. They will be strung out on the road. Our warriors will lie in the long grass on either side of the trail. Before they reach the Yellow Medicine, we will attack from both sides. Many soldiers will die before they can organize. They will have no cover, and we will rub them out."

"It is a good plan, Tao-ya-te-duta," Big Eagle assented.

"I will lead the young men into the grass and kill the whites!" Mah-ka-tah spoke confidently.

Little Crow looked solemnly at his chiefs. "It is our last plan. It is your last chance, Mah-ka-tah. If we fail, we must scatter like the buffalo across the prairie, for the whites will not rest until they have killed or taken us all. Now see to your braves. Tonight they must take position in the tall grass along the road."

Shortly after seven o'clock the next morning, several company wagons of the Third Minnesota, each containing a few men, began to roll the three miles to the ruined agency. Hopes were high for the bounty of the deserted gardens.

Nathan stepped out of his tent and stretched as he watched them rumble down the road. He heard a voice call from behind, "Well, you sure are a sight for sore eyes. I thought I'd ne'er see ya again." Nathan turned to see Alex Faribault grinning happily.

"Good to see you, Alex," he greeted the old trader. "Where do you suppose those fellows are headed this morning?" He waved at the Third's wagons.

"Heard somebody talking that they's hungry and wanted some garden grub. They're headed to the Upper Agency."

"I didn't think Sibley would allow foraging with the Santee so close," Nathan commented.

"He don't know about it." Alex scratched his head and peered to the north. "These fellas are a testy lot. Still smartin' from havin' to serve time in a reb prison. They figgur they seen the elephant and nobody else has. They know Sibley needs 'em. So they do what they want. By the way, speakin' of rebs. I saw a paper Sibley had. Looks like Gen'rl Lee's movin' for a big battle in Maryland. They got Washington awful excited, anyway."

"When?" Nathan asked Alex, trying to mask excitement.

"'Course the paper was a few days old, but, from the sound of things, it could be happ'ning right now."

"Let me know when you see another paper," Nathan requested. Both men continued to watch the departing wagons.

Company G's wagon led the way. Sergeant Bowler was driving. Degrove Kimball sat beside him with Billy McGee behind in the box.

"Hey, Sarge," Billy called, "let's take a shortcut through the grass. This road winds all over creation like a snake on hot bricks."

The sergeant considered the terrain and replied, "After we cross the lake outlet up ahead, we'll be on high ground. I'll turn off the road there."

Following a bumpy ride over the shallow stream and up a low embankment, the wagons reached a gentle hill about half a mile from camp. There Bowler turned his team onto the prairie for a more direct route to the agency.

The Santee lay in concealment awaiting the main body of Sibley's army. The wagons were now rolling amongst them. When a wheel nearly ran over Brown Wing, he could hold still no longer. He sprang to his feet and fired. Degrove Kimball slumped to the side and tumbled from his wagon seat.

Dozens of other Santee opened fire on the approaching wagons. Billy McGee vaulted from his wagon and returned fire. The men in the rear wagons rushed forward and emptied their rifles at the Santee warriors. A thick cloud of smoke from the rifles hung in the air above them.

Mah-ka-tah leaped from the grass near the wagon and swung a club at McGee. Billy ducked as the heavy object *whooshed* above him. He fell onto his back and waited in terror as the Santee warrior brought the club over his head for a final smashing blow.

It never came. Mah-ka-tah was driven hard back onto the long grass, his body riddled with bullets from riflemen in the wagon. The leader of the Soldier's Lodge held his hands, stained with blood, before his eyes a moment. A tear ran down his cheek. He cried for his people as he died on the prairie grass.

Back in the camp, Major Welch burst from his tent. He looked onto the prairie and quickly assessed the situation. "All who want to fight, fall in," he shouted.

Two hundred men of the Third Minnesota raced double quick to the site of the battle. Welch ordered his lieutenant, Olin, "Keep half the men back in reserve. I'll take the others to meet the Sioux. Aid us when you think it's needed or when you hear from me."

The retreating foraging detail met the advancing force under Welch. Together they turned to face the growing Indian mass. The Santee formed a semi-circle and tried to flank the soldiers. They screamed wildly as they poured a steady volley into the Bluecoats.

Welsh ordered his sergeants, "Form a skirmish line. Fire at will, and drive them back."

Ezra Champlain and the other privates of the Third fired rapidly and pushed forward. Slowly, the Dakota were being driven back toward the bluffs and the Minnesota River.

Suddenly, Tom Gere, sent by Sibley, galloped onto the battlefield. "Where's Welch?" he shouted. Then he spotted the major and wheeled his horse to face him. "Sibley says get back to camp the best way you can!" With that order he raced back to the colonel's encampment. He would have rather stayed to fight, but orders were orders.

"Why in tarnation did they order a retreat!" Ezra exclaimed to Billy McGee.

"Because they got as much sense as the officers we had at Murfrees-borough. We're winning. Now there'll be hell to pay tryin' to get back," Billy grumbled.

As the Third retreated toward camp, the battle disintegrated into every man for himself. Little Crow ordered a steady volley in a ploy to cut off their path of retreat. The soldiers reached the outlet stream and scrambled down the bank, through the shallow water and up the other side.

The Santee flanked them on both sides and charged at the Third from the rear. When they reached high ground between the stream and the camp, Welch raised his sword and shouted, "Make a stand, men. The Rangers are comin'! We'll make a stand here!"

The Renville Rangers, led by Lieutenant Gorman, rushed into the fray. Nathan had joined them as they hurriedly left the camp.

"Form up," Welch yelled to Gorman. Then the youthful major grabbed his leg and moaned as he slumped to the ground. Ezra Champlain was instantly at his side.

"I'm shot. Take me in!" Welch cried.

Nathan reached the stricken officer at about the same time. "I'll help you," he shouted at Ezra above the battle's roar. A gangly, blond young lieutenant joined them, pistol in hand.

"I'll cover your backs," he yelled. "Let's move."

In the distance they could hear Sergeant Bowler screaming, "Remember Murfreesborough! Fight, boys! Remember Murfreesborough!"

As Nathan and Ezra supported Major Welch the remaining quarter mile back to the camp, three men ran past them trying to escape the battle. Welch yelled at them, "Go back and fight, you white-livered cowards. Go back and fight, or I'll shoot you."

The wounded major fired a shot from his pistol just over the head of the middle soldier. The three stopped and turned, their faces white with fright, panic in their eyes. Welch pulled back the hammer of his pistol again, and pointed it in their direction, "I said get back there, boys, and I mean it!"

The three returned to face the Dakota.

After they delivered Welch to camp, Ezra said, "We'll leave you here behind the wagons. You'll be safe there."

"No," Welch replied, "there's a little hill here. Leave me on it. I'll watch the battle."

Solomon, Emily, and Alex Faribault watched the distant struggle from the edge of the camp. "Why did Nathan have to run off into this?"

Emily cried. "He didn't even say anything to me. He was just gone. He's not a soldier. He didn't have to go. Nathan's done enough."

"Nathan is a soldier, Emily," Solomon said gently. "He did what he felt he had to do. I would have myself if I were healed up enough."

Alex watched the gathering smoke, thickening in the ravine and spreading. "It's like he figgurs he's got to prove something to somebody."

"Well, he doesn't have to prove anything to me," Emily answered.

"Me, neither," Solomon added.

Nathan Thomas and Ezra Champlain raced back to the battle, along with Jesse Buchanen, the blond officer who had covered their rescue of Welch. "Look there," Nathan pointed across the small lake, "the Indians are moving around to attack the camp."

"Yeah," Ezra replied, "but the Sixth is heading to meet them." As he spoke, a column of soldiers came into view through the trees of the lakeshore. They charged into the mass of Santee and began to drive them back.

Lieutenant Olin, now in command, realized a critical moment was being reached. The Indians continued to mass in his front and on the sides. Olin ordered a charge into the middle of the Santee line directly in front of him. Nathan and Ezra joined about fifty other soldiers in a desperate assault.

The Dakota were taken by surprise during the sudden turn of events. They bravely tried to hold their ground, and the fighting became hand-to-hand. Nathan dodged a charging brave and fired his revolver. To his left he saw Harry Pettibone, his face covered with blood, swing his rifle like a club and knock a warrior to the prairie sod. Then the private raised his rifle for a bayonet plunge into the stunned Indian.

Nathan shouted, "No!" and roughly shoved Pettibone to the side before he could strike. The private looked at Thomas with surprised bewilderment.

"He's just a boy," Nathan shouted, "I know him." With bullets whizzing by, he knelt next to Traveling Star. "Just lie here. It's not safe for you to try to move. I'll try to help you when it's over."

Back in the camp, Sibley paced with anxiety and exasperation. Colonel William Marshall of the Seventh and artillery officer Mark

Hendricks stood near him. "I ordered the fools back twice!" Sibley exclaimed. "Why won't they get back here? They'll get flanked and cut off yet."

"Look, Colonel," Marshall pointed, "Sioux are gathering in the ravine to the right."

"Okay." For the first time in a battle that had been taking its own course without direction from the commander, Sibley was decisive. "Marshall, take the Seventh to the right and move down the ravine to support the charge now taking place in the center. Hendricks, drop some shot into the ravine and soften them up while Marshall gets into position. Move now and quickly!"

The cannons moved into position and began to boom from a quarter-mile away. On a hillside near the ravine, several Santee leaders had gathered to direct their warriors. Mankato lay on the ground watching intently. "Our men are too spread out along the road. We can't get all of them into position," he murmured to himself as much to anyone.

Lightning Blanket, next to the chief, turned to the sky and saw a cannon ball slowly arching toward them. "Move!" he yelled excitedly, "Look, a ball comes!"

Mankato looked over his shoulder at the descending sphere. "It is spent," he said. "I will not move for such a thing." An instant later it plunked onto his back, and the brave Santee chief was dead.

As Olin drove into the center of the Indian lines, Marshall's men drove down the ravine to the right. The Santee broke and fell back before the trained soldiers. The battle was over.

Nathan watched the fleeing Indians and walked back through the battlefield toward the camp. First, however, he must find Traveling Star. Ezra Champlain strode with him. The ground was littered with dead and wounded as they reached the plateau where Nathan had last seen the Indian boy.

A soldier ahead was kneeling on the ground, knife in hand, next to the body of a Santee. He had a handful of the Indian's hair in one hand and a knife in the other. To his horror, Nathan realized that the soldier was about to scalp the Indian. "Hold!" he shouted and fired a shot into the air.

The soldier glanced over his shoulder at Nathan and snarled surily, "What's it to you what happens to dead Indians? They do it to us."

"Private, we are a civilized people in an uncivilized place, and you will not mutilate that body. My next shot won't be in the air."

In disgust the soldier spat onto the Indian, glared at Nathan and stalked away. Ezra went to the Santee and rolled him over. It was Traveling Star. The two white men knelt by the young Indian and sprinkled water from a canteen onto his face. A large knot had swelled from the side of his head.

"He's still stunned," Ezra said. "You ever been hit on the head hard? I was once. I just fell over and thought if those people would just leave me alone, all I wanted ta do was sleep right there. I guess that's what it means to get knocked unconscious."

"I've been unconscious," Nathan remembered.

Traveling Star opened his eyes. They became wide with fright until he recognized Nathan.

"Take it easy, boy," the white man told him, "soldiers are all over here, and they'll shoot any Indian that moves. Ezra, here, and I'll take you to camp. You'll be under our protection. Miss West is there. It's the only safe thing to do." They wrapped Traveling Star in a blanket for concealment and Nathan carried him over his shoulder like a sack of potatoes.

Back in the encampment, Sibley gathered his officers for a report. Olin and Welch, his leg heavily bandaged, joined them.

"What were you doing?" the commander asked accusingly. "You had no orders to make an assault. I ordered you to return, and you didn't. Why did you continue to fight?"

"Well, Colonel," Olin answered laconically, "we were pushing 'em back, and it just seemed like to keep fighting was the thing to do. We won, didn't we?"

"Lucky for you, we did." Sibley couldn't mask his irritation even in the aftermath of his greatest victory. "Casualties?" he asked Marshall.

"Mostly the Third was engaged, with some help from the Rangers, Sixth, and Seventh. It looks like about forty casualties with seven dead. The Sioux suffered heavy losses."

"It's Little Crow's Waterloo," Sibley replied. "He'll never be able to come back from this. Our task now is to mop up, free the hostages, and pursue the remaining bands as ordered."

"Do you think Pope will send us to the Dakotas?" Tim Sheehan was referring to General John Pope, recently named by Lincoln to command the Military Department of the Northwest, headquartered in St. Paul. It was Pope's reward for losing the Second Battle of Bull Run.

"Quite possibly, Lieutenant," Sibley answered. "My last order from him was to push on and exterminate all warriors involved in the outbreak."

"Will we move out today?" Tom Gere inquired.

Sibley paused and considered for a moment. "No, I think not. We'll care for the wounded and work on a plan of action. If we had adequate cavalry, we'd try to run them down now. But we still don't have that luxury. We move in two days. See to your men, gentlemen. Dismissed."

As the officers dispersed, Nathan Thomas and Ezra Champlain walked into camp now supporting an unsteady Traveling Star. They went directly to Nathan's tent, where Emily and Solomon waited.

"Good to see ya, boy," Solomon said, resisting the urge to hug Nathan.

Emily felt no need to resist and clung to him with both arms around his neck. "Please be more careful," she said, her voice choked with emotion.

Alex Fairbault, also nearby, shook a finger at his friend. "One of these times you ain't gonna git away with doin' such foolhardy things. It might be brave, but runnin' headlong into a battle, chasin' into a passel of Sioux warriors to rescue a woman, or crawling through Indians to get water are sure ways to git kilt."

"I'll think about that next time," Nathan smiled at Alex.

"Who's the boy?" Solomon motioned at the young Indian.

"Well," he looked at Emily, "if you scrape the paint and blood off him you'll find your friend Johnny, Traveling Star."

Emily placed her hands on either side of the Indian's face and looked into his eyes. "I have much to thank you for," she said.

"Thank him more later." Solomon put an arm around his shoulder. "I'll put him in my tent. He needs to rest and be out of sight for a while. I'll watch over him."

"Thanks, Solomon," Nathan nodded at him and Alex. "I'd like to talk with Emily for a while."

They walked hand in hand to the edge of the camp near the lakeshore. Then Nathan stopped and gazed into Emily's blue eyes. It was nearing noon, and the sun shone brightly on the silvery lake.

"Emily," he began earnestly, "I haven't been honest with you. I need to tell you some things about myself."

"There is nothing more about you I need to know," Emily replied. "I know the kind of man you are."

"There's something I must tell you, or it'll hang over us forever. At least in my mind."

"Your secret, Nathan?"

"My name's Captain Nathan Thomas, Confederate States Army, on special assignment from President Davis."

Emily couldn't help the look of surprise that flashed across her face. "You're a rebel?" she said hardly above a whisper. "Why did they send you here?"

Nathan swallowed. This was the hard part. "To enlist the Dakota in a war on the frontier against forces of the Union."

Emily shook her head in wonderment. "To start this war?"

"Yes," Nathan answered, "but think back to what Little Crow told you. In the end, I didn't matter. The war would have happened anyway. In fact, it wasn't supposed to start when it did. Davis's plan was for fighting to begin just as Lee invaded Maryland. The Dakota were to make war only on soldiers. I felt terrible when it started, but I couldn't stop what happened."

Emily stood silent. Her first impulse was anger and even disgust. She turned her back. For a long moment, she tried to sort out thoughts and emotions. She remembered what Little Crow had said about Nathan. "Don't blame him," the Dakota chief had cautioned. Her mind replayed images of his bravery and courage in rescuing her and the others. Finally she turned to face him.

"There was a reason you were sent here, Nathan, but it wasn't what you thought. Powers greater than Jefferson Davis determined that you'd help end this war, not start it. The Confederacy tried to use you, but in the end you did just as you were supposed to do."

"I believe that," Nathan agreed. "It took me awhile to realize it. I'm sending a letter resigning my commission. Even with just one arm, I've proven I could fight and command, but I'm not going back."

"Are you in danger?" Emily wondered. "Who knows about this?"

"Only a few, some might suspect. There are only two living people that I know of who know. One's Little Crow, but I don't expect him to sit down and talk about this any time soon. There's a man in Minneapolis whom I had dealings with. He's in prison. He hasn't talked."

"What will you do?" Emily asked.

"I'm not sure I can fight for either side. I can't raise my sword against Virginia, and I won't fight for Jefferson Davis's government, either." He thought of his aunts, of Professor Jackson, even of his Uncle George. "I guess I've let some people down," he said sadly.

Emily stepped closer to Nathan and looked into his eyes. She reached up and brushed his dark hair from his forehead. "You are a man of honor. Whatever you do, it'll be for the right reasons as you see them."

He held her tightly with his arm and kissed her. Then he gently whispered into her ear. "After all this, you still think so?"

"I want to be with you, Nathan," Emily answered.

"Where will we go? What will we do?"

Emily considered his questions. Then her face brightened. "West. We could go farther west. The Dakota will need help when they're resettled. There'll be a reservation, and teachers will be needed. We can work together like the Robertsons did."

"I'm a soldier, Emily," Nathan replied.

"With no war to fight and no army to join?" Emily retorted. "We'll go for now, until the war back East is over. It can't be that long a time."

He kissed her again. "My destiny is where you are, Emily."

ॐ 76 ॐ

HE BEATEN SANTEE WARRIORS RETURNED to their village. The sub-chiefs and other leaders hurriedly gathered around Little Crow. This night they would smoke and council one last time. Fearing the soldiers would come soon, they sent scouts out to warn of the approach. Several of the chiefs had already gathered their belongings and families and were ready to leave.

They sat in the open before their tattered tepees. Little Crow gathered himself up and spoke. "There is nothing for us here. You must scatter like the wind on the prairie. Soon the whites will come. If they catch you, if you remain here or surrender to them, it will be bad for you."

"What of those who did not fight the white man? Many remained neutral," Big Eagle asked.

Wabasha answered, "Mixed-bloods have told me that our leaders who surrender and did not kill white women and children will be held prisoner only a short time. I have encouraged my son-in-law, Rda-in-yan-ka, to give himself up. You should as well, Big Eagle."

"The whites will not care," Little Crow countered. "All will be judged guilty by them. Leave, run to Canada or join the Yankton in the Dakotas."

Red Middle Voice grimaced, his arm hanging at his side from a battle wound. "We should have won the fight. Why did we fail, Ta-oya-te-duta?"

"You are right," Little Crow said solemnly, "the day should have been ours. Eight hundred Santee warriors should beat twice as many as our number. But the plan was ruined when the wagons left the camp early. Our braves were strung along the road. All couldn't get into the battle in time."

Medicine Bottle stopped them as the council began to break up. "Let us remember the spirit of Mankato. I was near him. He died bravely. He refused to move when the cannon ball came."

"Bravely, yes, but also foolishly," Little Six replied.

The next morning many were preparing to leave the camp. Some had captured wagons and were loading them. As Little Crow dropped a sack into his wagon, many warriors and chiefs crowded around him one last time.

The tired chief, feeling beaten, bitter, and older than his sixty years, climbed into the rig's bed and made his final speech.

"I am ashamed to call myself a Dakota. Hundreds of our best warriors were beaten yesterday by the whites. Now we had better all run away and scatter out over the plains like the buffalo and wolves. To be sure, the whites had wagon-guns and better arms than we, and there were many more of them. But that is no reason why we should not have whipped them, for we are brave Dakota, and they are cowardly women. I cannot account for our disgraceful defeat. It must have been the work of traitors in our midst."

For a moment they lingered, once proud leaders of their people, now beaten and ready to run. Finally Little Crow raised his voice. "Go now. The Long Trader will show no mercy."

Little Six and Medicine Bottle joined Little Crow in filling wagons with their belongings. Soon the three chiefs were rolling to the west.

As they left, Cut Nose asked his chief, "What about the captives?"

"Do what you will," Little Crow said. Then he snapped the reins on his horse's rump and rumbled away.

Cut Nose and many of his warriors traveled the short distance upriver to where the captives were held. They found that Wabasha had moved his village next to the hostages and now had extended his protection to them. Killing them would not be simple.

Approaching the village, Cut Nose was met by Wabasha and Little Paul. "Stand aside," he told the Santee chief.

"Little Crow is gone, and I will protect these people." Wabasha stared with determination at Cut Nose, whose one nostril flared in anger.

"You have never been with us, and now you stand with the white man. I am ashamed that you are of my people," Cut Nose said, the words burning his mouth like bitter gall.

Wabasha's warriors were massing behind him as he confronted Little Crow's lieutenant. "I never killed a woman or child," Wabasha said. "You made this a war not of soldier against solder, but of warrior against innocent people, and that is not the way of a Dakota brave. But now I am prepared to fight, warrior against warrior, for these people."

Cut Nose looked beyond to the assembling mass of Santee. Then, with only a snort of disgust, he turned on his heels and led his people away. Soon they were moving across the prairie as Wabasha awaited Sibley.

The Long Trader was in no hurry to reach the Yellow Medicine and the camp holding the captives. He spent the day after the battle known as Wood Lake resting his men and seeing that the wounded were cared for. Then, on September 25th, Sibley marched his army to the Indian camp beyond the mouth of the Yellow Medicine River.

Henry Hastings Sibley rode into the Santee village at the head of nearly 2,000 men. He sat proud and erect on the saddle of a prancing black horse. It was his greatest moment.

Wabasha and Little Paul, as instructed by Sibley himself, stood beneath a white flag of truce. The Long Trader wasted little time in formalities. "I want the captives delivered into my care at once," he commanded. "How many are there?"

Wabasha tried to maintain the air of a chieftain. "Their camp, which I have watched over for you and kept from harm, contains 107 whites and 162 mixed-bloods. They are all there." He pointed to the nearby cluster of tents.

Sibley dismounted. "We will council," he instructed. "Gather your leaders."

Shortly thereafter, soldiers and Santee gathered. Sibley walked before the Santee. There was no circle. He didn't bother to go through the formality of smoking with them. The colonel stroked his thin mustache and opened in his most authoritative voice.

"Consider yourselves all prisoners until I can determine which of you are guilty of war crimes. Those of you who have committed depredations against innocent people will be hanged." Bluecoats with rifles and bayonets ready closed in from behind.

Little Paul asserted that he had remained neutral and friendly. "I have grown up like a child of yours. With what is yours, you have caused me to grow, and now I take your hand as a child takes the hand of his father. I have regarded all white people as my friends, and from them I understand this blessing has come."

Sibley met Little Paul's protests with a cold, stony stare. He turned to Tim Sheehan. "Lieutenant, I want this camp encircled by a heavy guard. No one is to leave.

"Gorman," he looked to the leader of the Rangers, "send out some of your half-breeds. I want them to spread the word up and down the river that all Santee in the Minnesota Valley must come to this place. I'll call it Camp Release. Those who refuse to report will be hunted down until they are killed or captured."

Solomon, Nathan, and Emily had ridden at the rear of Sibley's column of soldiers. Traveling Star rode with them. His hair had been cut short, and he wore white man's clothes. They called him Johnny. No soldier had bothered them about him. They knew the young boy was with Nathan and Emily.

All hoped that Jenny Olson with Mattie and Mary would soon be delivered to them from Fort Abercrombie. Emily was also anxious to learn the condition of the hostages whom she had come to know while she was held in the camp.

The captives were assembled on a rise in the ground near the river. As they awaited Sibley's inspection, a photographer took their picture.

407

Mostly they sat on the ground staring vacantly at the camera or off at some distant object. There were no smiles. George Spencer was there, as were Mrs. Brown and her children. Sibley walked among them and promised that they would be returned to civilization as soon as they were processed and he could spare a detail to escort them.

Joe Coursolle also moved through the camp crying out for Elizabeth and Minnie. Then two skinny, ragged, grimy little girls appeared before him. Elizabeth wrapped her arms around her father as Joe reached out to enfold them both in his embrace. "They didn't hurt us," the older girl sobbed, "but we were hungry and missed you and mama and Cistina Joe."

"We're together now," Joe said gently. "Soon you'll be with your mother at Fort Ridgely."

Sibley appointed a military commission to try "war criminals" as they were identified. There were no defense lawyers. The Santee had no rights.

∞ 77 ∞

TWO DAYS LATER A DETAIL from the relief column sent to Fort Abercrombie delivered the three former hostages to Camp Release. The siege at the fort had been lifted and the Indians driven away. Emily, Jenny, Mattie, and Mary embraced in hugs of joy and relief. Their long ordeal was nearly over.

Solomon Foot had waited for news from Abercrombie. Now it was time to escort Jenny back to Forest City. He saddled up his horse and another for Jenny. Nathan and Emily stood nearby.

"Nathan," Solomon said, "we've known each other for only a few weeks, but we've been through a lifetime together."

Nathan warmly clasped Foot's hand. "We made a good team, old man."

Emily wrapped her arms around Solomon's neck and kissed his cheek. "Thank you," she said in a voice choking with emotion. "I owe you my life."

"I guess I helped some, but we'll never know how things would have turned out. Still, it was my pleasure, Emily."

Jenny embraced Nathan and Emily and then mounted her horse. As Solomon swung his long legs into his saddle, his animal skittered.

"Dang horse," he muttered. "I hate horses. Maybe someday someone will come up with a better way for people to get around." He smiled down at his two friends, snapped a salute from his broad-billed hat at Nathan, wheeled his steed, and lightly swatted it with his reins.

As Jenny's and Solomon's horses started trotting out of camp, Mary Schwandt and Mattie Williams ran alongside. Foot reined in, then reached down to clasp their hands gently for a moment. Then, after Jenny offered a tearful good-bye, they disappeared down the trail to the river.

Gere and Sheehan reached Nathan and Emily as they watched Solomon and Jenny riding away.

"Solomon's gone?" Gere asked with obvious disappointment. "I wanted to see him off."

"He's quite a man," Sheehan added.

"We'll see him again," Nathan replied, "Kandiyohi lakes aren't that far away."

"What about you, Nathan?" Tom Gere asked. "What are you going to do?"

Emily looked at him and waited expectantly for his answer.

"Emily and I are going to be married," Nathan said, gazing down at Emily and for a moment forgetting Gere and Sheehan. "Then, for a while, we hope to work with the Dakota wherever we're needed."

The two lieutenants slapped the young man on the back and grinned broadly. Sheehan, after a brief, "May I?" leaned down and kissed Emily on the cheek. After more expressions of congratulations, the officers started back for a meeting with Sibley.

Then Gere turned back to Nathan. "Oh, by the way, I just saw a newspaper. It's almost a week old, but I thought you'd be interested. Lee lost a battle at a place called Antietam in Maryland. They kicked him back into Virginia."

So, Nathan thought, the war will drag on longer, and there will be no fight on the frontier to act as a diversion. He pulled Emily close. Today she was all that mattered.

ᔆ 78 ᔆ

PASTOR HINMAN HAD THE PLEASURE of joining Emily and Nathan in marriage before they went to the prison camp on the Minnesota River below Fort Snelling where nearly 2,000 were interred. The missionaries Williamson and Riggs, along with Pastor Hinman, had decided to turn the prison into one great school, and they were glad to have help. Emily and Nathan were welcomed.

A law was passed that all Sioux were to be removed from Minnesota to unoccupied land suited for agricultural purposes. The next spring they were moved out. Eventually, most wound up on a reservation called Crow Creek, in Dakota Territory. It was a desolate area, and the ground soon was dotted with graves of the Santee.

Many missionaries were sickened to hear that the military commission had ultimately sentenced 307 Santee to death. Sibley turned the verdict over to General Pope in his St. Paul headquarters. Even Pope felt that the execution of so many was beyond him.

Although both Sibley and Pope felt all sentences were justified, the final order for execution was passed on to President Lincoln. After Bishop Henry Whipple appealed to the president, Lincoln commuted the sentences of all but thirty-nine.

On December 26th, 1862, after one last-minute reprieve, on a cold, frosty Minnesota morning, thirty-eight Santee were hanged simultaneously at Mankato. Among them was Rdainyanka, Wabasha's son-in-law, who had spoken eloquently for continuing the war and had been encouraged by his father-in-law to surrender. He wrote a bitter letter to Wabasha in which he complained that he had been deceived into turning himself in. He asserted that he had killed no one, had not plundered and yet would die while many guilty remained in prison. Cut Nose followed him up the large square gallows.

Chaska went into battle with his people. But when Hapa, his companion, killed George Gleason, Chaska prevented the murder of Sarah Wakefield and put her under his protection. There was no proof that he killed anyone.

However, the words of Mrs. Wakefield were not enough to save Chaska. Despite her impassioned pleas, the Santee leader was hanged with the others in Mankato. Later, an apology was sent to Sarah, informing her they had confused Chaska with another Indian with a like-sounding name.

Red Middle Voice and his family never made it to Canada. They were slaughtered on the northwestern prairie by a wayward band of Chippewa.

Little Six and Medicine Bottle escaped to Canada. There they were kidnapped by Minnesotans and brought back to Fort Snelling to be executed on November 11, 1865. They were hanged on Pilot Knob Hill overlooking the Minnesota River Valley.

Legend has it that as Little Six mounted the stairs to the gallows, a low whistle echoed up from the valley floor. It was the first locomotive steam engine in Minnesota. Little Six gestured toward the sound and shouted, "As the white man comes in, the Indian goes out!"

Wabasha, Big Eagle, and the Upper Sioux leaders were imprisoned and eventually driven from the state to Dakota reservations. Later, some Santee began to move in small groups back to Minnesota. They returned to their former homes, where some farmed and tried to live in the white culture. Big Eagle died at Granite Falls near Yellow Medicine in 1906.

Little Crow spent the winter of 1862-1863 at Devil's Lake in North Dakota. In the spring he went to an area near Winnipeg, Canada, to try to gain the intervention of Canadian government officials in freeing Santee held in prisons. They refused to help. The next summer, he accompanied a small band back to Minnesota to hunt and perhaps steal horses.

While Little Crow was picking berries with his son in Meeker County, near Hutchinson, a farmer and his son happened by. They shot and killed the Santee leader and brought his body to the nearby town where the Fourth of July 1863 had recently been celebrated. No one knew it was Little Crow. Firecrackers were put into his ears and mouth and set off. His body was thrown into a pit filled with cattle entrails. Nearly a month later, after rumors of Little Crow's death reached Hutchinson, the body was removed from the pit and identified.

Nathan Lampson, the man who fired the fatal shot at Little Crow, was given a reward of five hundred dollars by the state of Minnesota. Little Crow's skull was kept as the property of the Minnesota Historical Society until his bones were returned to the Santee people in the 1970s.

Samuel Meeds became the only Minnesotan hanged for espionage in the Civil War. He never talked about Nathan or any of his other clandestine dealings.

Guri Endreson returned to her cabin on Solomon Lake, where she died June 30, 1881, at the age of seventy-four.

John Otherday, the Santee who had rescued Upper Agency people and scouted for Sibley, was rewarded with several thousand dollars.

Henry Hastings Sibley became a hero because of the victory at Wood Lake. The victory in which he was more bystander than tactician made him a general. In 1863 he led a punitive expedition into the Dakota Territory to punish Indians involved in the Minnesota Uprising.

Tom Gere got his wish and went south with the Fifth Minnesota. He fought bravely at the Battle of Nashville, capturing a rebel battle flag.

Solomon Foot went back to the Kandiyohi lakes, where he farmed for several years before moving to North Dakota. Later he returned to Minnesota and operated a post office.

413

∞ 79 ∞

FOR NEARLY THREE YEARS, Nathan and Emily remained with the Santee, first in Minnesota and later accompanying them on steamboats to various posts, finally reaching the Crow Creek Reservation on the Missouri River. Traveling Star's uncle and father had been killed in the war, and his mother had died in the first winter at the Fort Snelling prison camp. He often called on his white teacher friends.

Crow Creek was dry, and the scarce water was alkaline. Traveling Star asked Nathan, "Why do they ask us to farm here? My father farmed, but he would not be able to make anything grow here. They want us to farm and give us land where nothing grows. What do they expect us to do?"

"They expect you all to become like white men. That's why they call you Johnny and Christianize you and send you to school."

The young Indian looked determinedly at Nathan. "The old ways are better. Many will not give them up. Sitting Bull has come to talk to our leaders."

"You're right in some ways," Nathan replied. "They've given you deplorable conditions and asked you to do the impossible. But there are good people here who want to help you. Reverend Williamson means well, as does Pastor Riggs. You may be right about the old ways, but the future will hold

414

a different life for you. But, I'm afraid that, before all is done, a lot more blood will be shed."

"Will you stay on the reservation?" Traveling Star wondered.

"I don't know what my future holds. I just received a letter from my uncle, which I haven't even opened yet. I'm going to do so with my wife. It may hold some insight into what becomes of Nathan Thomas."

Nathan tramped across the hot, dusty compound to where he and Emily shared a small, crude cabin. It was late August of 1865, nearly three years to the day since the uprising. The Civil War had ended that April.

Richmond was in ruins, and he had no desire to go back there. George Thomas had become a hero of the Union army; his efforts at the Battle of Chickamauga had helped to save the federal army from rout and had earned him the sobriquet, "Rock of Chickamauga." Wondering how his uncle had found him, Nathan was growing ever more anxious to open the letter.

Emily was reading at their wooden table. He settled beside her and ripped the communication open. "It's a letter from Uncle George," he told her. Then he began to read aloud:

Dear Nephew,

I imagine your first impulse is to wonder how I located you. Let me explain. I heard from captured Confederates that you lost your arm at Shiloh and were given some "special" assignment.

Colonel Sibley mentioned a brave one-armed young man in his dispatches to General Pope. Pope is a friend of mine and knew of you from my conversations with him. His description of you, the name "Nathan" Cates and other items were too much to be just coincidence.

I don't know why you were using the name Cates, but when I heard from Pope that there might be some suspicions about you, I decided a letter to Sibley might be timely. Accounts of your role in battles on the frontier convinced me that any allegations were unfounded. I know the kind of person you are.

I have been given command of the Department of the West on the Pacific coast. I need a young adjutant officer to serve under me. I know, of course, of your sentiments at the start of the late war between our states. I don't know, nor do I care what brought you to Minnesota, only that you served the United States Army, unofficially, in a valuable and heroic manner.

I am prepared to offer you a captaincy in the United States Army and a position under me in the West. Please consider and respond.

Your Uncle,
George Thomas
General, USA

P.S. I understand you now have a wife. Congratulations. She is, of course, welcome to come with you."

Nathan stared at the letter and thought silently. Then he looked at Emily. Tears had begun to well up in his wife's eyes.

"I'm so happy for you," she said. "It's a second chance for you, for us. I know the army was your life."

"The West has always given second chances," Nathan replied. "Are you sure you want to go, Emily? It's a long way from Minnesota."

"I just want to be where you are, Nathan. I want to be where I know you'll be happy and needed. I can teach there as well as here."

Nathan rose, then brought his wife to her feet. They locked into a tender embrace. The beauty and the destruction of the Minnesota Valley were behind them, as was the desolation of the Dakota reservation. Nathan and Emily Thomas would face the West and live out the dreams of their future together.

❧ Sources ❧

A Guide to the Upper and Lower Sioux Agencies, prepared by the Upper Sioux Agency and Lower Sioux Agency staff, Minnesota Historical Society, 1981.

Historic Fort Ridgely: A Study Guide, prepared by the staff of Fort Ridgely, Minnesota Historical Society, 1981, 1987.

Recollections of the Sioux Massacre, Oscar Garrett Wall, The Home Printery, Lake City, Minnesota, 1909.

Over the Earth I Come: The Great Sioux Uprising of 1862 (references to Joe Coursolle), Duane Schultz, St. Martin's Press, New York, 1992.

The Sioux Uprising of 1862, Kenneth Carley, Minnesota Historical Society Press, St. Paul, Minnesota, 1976.

Indian Outbreaks, Daniel Buck, The Pioneer Press, Mankato, Minnesota, 1904.

1908 History of Kandiyohi County, edited by Victor Lawson.

About the Author

Dean Urdahl taught American History for thirty-five years at New London-Spicer Middle School in New London, Minnesota. He also coached cross-country running there for twenty-six years. In 2002, he was elected as a member of the Minnesota State House of Representatives.

Dean resides with his wife and editor, Karen, on a hobby farm near Grove City, Minnesota, just miles from Acton, the site of the killings that started the Dakota Conflict of 1862. His great-great-grandfather was the superintendent of the construction of the Forest City stockade.

Dean and Karen have three grown sons, Chad, Brent, and Troy; a daughter-in-law, Rebecca; and three grandchildren.

Other published works by Urdahl include *Touching Bases with Our Memories* and *Lives Lived Large*.